Miller, Evie Yoder
Eyes at the window

DATE DUE

NO 14 0	JY 3 - '08	
NO 24 0	SE 2 - '08	
DE 1 '07		
JA 31 '08		
FE 19 '08		
MR 5 '08		
MR 29 '08		
AP 14 '08		
JY 30 08		
AG 31 08		
SE 1 - '08		
FE 11 '08		

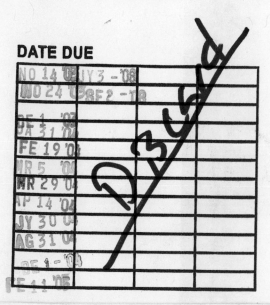

C
FIC
MIL

EYES at the
WINDOW

EYES at the WINDOW

A NOVEL BY

EVIE YODER MILLER

Good Books

Intercourse, PA 17534
800/762-7171
www.goodbks.com

Acknowledgments
Over the past years of research and writing, many people have supplied pertinent information and responded to early segments and drafts of the story that follows. I'm grateful to many readers for their support, questions, and advice. Enough years of work have passed that I may have forgotten, unfortunately, the contributions that some people made; I apologize for my lapses in memory. I know that the list rightfully includes: Marilyn Annucci, JoAnn Borntrager, Lois Yoder Brubacher, Joan Connor, Louise Davis, Joyce Delhi, Gwen Ebert, Dianne Ferris, Firman Gingerich, Emily Grizzard Cutler, Jerry Hardt, Alta Keiser, Lucille Kreider, J.D. Miller, Andrea Musher, Charlotte Nolan, Dorothy Yoder Nyce, Ann Schertz, Ada Schrock, Andrea Wallpe, Bessie Yoder, Cynthia Yoder, Diane Yoder, Frank Yoder, Ida Yoder, Paton Yoder.

To my daughers, Alice Christine Schermerhorn and Sarah Miller-Piper, I offer thanks for your acceptance of this novel as another sibling in need of attention. And to my editor and publisher, Phyllis Pellman Good and Merle Good, I express much gratitude for your belief in this book.

Cover design and artwork by Wendell Minor
Design by Dawn J. Ranck

EYES AT THE WINDOW
Copyright © 2003 by Good Books, Intercourse, PA 17534
International Standard Book Number: 1-56148-405-9
Library of Congress Catalog Card Number: 2003054173

Library of Congress Cataloging-in-Publication Data
Miller, Evie Yoder.
  Eyes at the window : a novel / by Evie Yoder Miller.
      p. cm.
  ISBN 1-56148-405-9
  1. Amish--Fiction. 2. Frontier and pioneer life--Fiction. I. Title.
PS3625.O34E94 2003
813'.6--dc21   2003054173

In memory of my aunt Ida Yoder and her friend Lucille Kreider, who first told me about this story, introduced me to the pleasures of cemetery visits (including the burial sites of "Reuben" and "Jonas"), and encouraged me with the persistent question, "How's the book coming?"

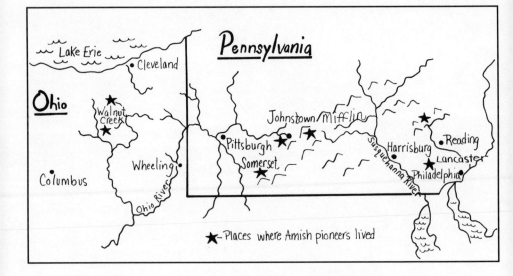

TABLE OF CONTENTS

Really, universally, relations stop nowhere, and the exquisite problem of the artist is eternally but to draw by a geometry of his own, the circle within which they shall happily appear to do so.

— Henry James

Hast thou perceived the breadth of the earth? declare if thou knowest it all. Where is the way *where* light dwelleth? and *as for* darkness, where is the place thereof . . . . Who hath put wisdom in the inward parts? or who hath given understanding to the heart?

— Job 38: 18, 19, 36 (KJV)

PART I

March 1810 — June 1810

1.

J O N A S

March 1810

Jonas Zug is my name, just like my father. I am his third son, born May 30, 1787, but it fell to me to be the one to carry the full weight. I long to ask Father for the portion of goods that is my due, but I fear I will end up living with the hogs. Mother spits grass from her teeth and says that if anyone can put a bridle crosswise on a horse, I am the one. I do not seem able to make the right headway. I trip on a rock hiding in the weeds; I lurch when I should stand upright. Now I may have bumbled away my chance at a girl.

There are six of us children; two more have already passed to their reward. My baby sister, Veronica, is given our mother's name, but we call her Franey. Just last week she marked her sixth birthday. I am thankful I was not born a girl. Once when Mother was ill, Father set me to peeling potatoes. I was clumsy with the knife and later, when Mother spied my thick peelings, she wondered that there had been any potato left to cook. I am not a girl, so how does she think that I might have the hands for potatoes? I may not be as strong as my brothers gone from home, but at least I am a man and can do outside work.

If I could just be on my own and have my woman . . . my own softness by my side. If I could but have opportunity. I have watched Father farm long enough; I have been part of every cycle, year after year after year. I know to keep enough grain back to feed my horses through the winter, so I am not caught buying from another, come spring. Where this worry comes from, that I might not be able to manage, that I am not a manager, I do not know. Well, yes, of course, it comes from the one spitting green. But I fear that if I ask too much, I will end up with nothing. If given my own farm, I might end up in the ditch. I do not mean to be greedy. I but want what other men have.

I like to hear Father tell the stories that his father told of our family's first years in the new country. How the wilderness fairly howled for want of taming; how my people, a godly people, wanted little more than safety from all that might molest: coons in the corn, evil hands interfering with the crop. My people came all the way from Germany, fearing God every step. Here in southern Pennsylvania, Father says we are a long way, two hundred miles, from where Grandfather settled in Berks County. I wonder that he never entertained doubts along the way. If only I could be as bold. If only the wind would stop its howl.

Father tells of other great ones who forded the Casselman fifty years ago, General Braddock and George Washington. Only a few miles south of here, across the border into Maryland, that is where our president named a spot, Little Crossings. That is the place where my father allowed me, on occasion as a lad, to ride with him to the gristmill, run by a Mr. Tomlinson. Father says it was little more than ten years after Washington passed through these parts that my people moved to this very Casselman River, to this very region, not far above the Mason-Dixon Line. How did these men know they could manage on their own, this Braddock and this Washington? Even my grandfather? How was it possible for them, when I know little for certain? Perhaps they did not have the green teeth spitting in their direction.

My father smiles the broad smile at what I have learned in school. I do not like it when he opens his mouth and there is only a cave. He likes to tell how his three sons can read the German. I have not gone to school now for several years because I have learned all that our schoolmaster, Abraham Saylor, a Mennonite, knows to teach. But when I was a scholar, Father asked me each night to show him the ciphering I had learned that day. I found ways to show him without looking into his empty mouth. Father pays a portion of Saylor's living expenses so he can send David these winter months. Franey has asked to go too, but she will have to wait until she is at least nine. I will be much surprised if Father lets her go then, for schooling is not for those with braids. Let her stick to potatoes. Rachel comes between David and me in age, but she has never had the interest in books. She will make someone a blessing of a wife though. I have wished that she were not my sister.

I think often of Grandfather, moving away from the main settlement and surviving. Why can I not admit to this same beckoning that courses in my blood? I have heard tales of explorations on West; as the days warm into summer, I may want to have a look myself. If I can get beyond the wind. Yet I know Father has need of me in the fields; my trampings must wait, perhaps until fall. That is what I do the best. Wait. With John and Abraham both on their own, that leaves but David and me to help Father.

David is a mere fifteen, yet I can see it in his eyes. He intends to outstretch me. I always know what he is thinking. His feet already go beyond mine in the bed, but he may be slipping down from the pillow to appear longer. I not only have my father's name, I am built like him, slight and off to the side. The new boots Father cobbled last fall were a boost to my frame, for they made me feel taller than I am. Aside from the pinch in my toes, I like the way they make me feel, but perhaps it is not right to wear something I am not. Soon it will be warm enough to shed our shoes for the summer, and then we will come and go as nature intended.

I am already in my twenty-second year, so it should not come as a surprise to Mother that I am looking to settle. It is not that I want to take my share of the goods and run. Here is what I think: I am of the age to marry. (I will not look in David's direction when he holds his hand to cover his mouth and thinks that I am gone beyond.) I must find a suitable girl. But with girls it has been worse for me than with potatoes. With girls I have the ten thumbs. Yet a girl is my way out, my pasture. As long as I am at home I must work for Father. But if I could strike out on my own, I could earn money and be about the business of establishing myself. I do not mean to sound resentful—Father has given me much more than a name—but the time has come when it is good and seemly to be my own authority.

John and Abraham left home at eighteen and nineteen, so why am I so tardy? Mother says I was born with one hand over my face. As a child I stood at the back of her skirts peeking. When I was instructed to wait with the other boys before church began, my older brothers had to drag me from my mother's skirts. When I was six years, and again at ten, my mother lost a baby to yellow fever. Each time I knew it was I who had been the strain. I do not speak of this to anyone, for that would be a sign of weakness.

What I have been slow in coming to say is this. There it is again: I lurk behind every tree before I come to the clearing.

I have found a girl to my liking. She is Polly Berkey from the Glades region right here in Somerset County. Some call her home area the Brothers Valley settlement. The name does not matter, but she has come this winter to our Elk Lick Township to be of assistance to her sister with three little ones.

I must confess to a bit of a stumble: I am not certain Polly returns my interest. I first noticed her at a corn shucking frolic for the young folks last fall. The night was almost gone before I ventured to introduce myself. Now I cannot even say how or where I first presented myself, but we have talked on other occasions since. Sometimes I wonder if we actually talked or if I merely wished it so and made up the conversation. My thoughts bring her to me again and again. We have never been close but in my head. I believe she is softer than Rachel. I know this dreaming is wrong and comes from the devil, but I cannot will her to depart.

She has a roundness about her that beckons me. I wonder what it would be like to touch her. Her fingers, with their dimples at the knuckles, look like bread dough that has the rise in it. I stay my hand though, for she might bristle at the feel of my rough nicks and scars from chopping. Sometime, I will reach to touch. I will. Perhaps in the dark. Perhaps then I can bring myself to do that much. If she withdraws her hand, I will pretend I did not do it. That is what I tell myself, but it may not be that simple. How can I ever make headway?

Soon after this new year began, we young ones gathered for a singing, and Polly and I were in each other's company the entire evening. My desire may have overreached itself, but it seemed the other young folks gave their approval. Even Rachel smiled at me when I brought the horse to ride home. I remember Polly saying, "Such ease on the high notes." I am almost certain she said it to me. I whisper it now, over and over; that night it gave me great confidence, and I sang as if Father had cobbled new heels for my voice.

I was enraptured, too much so, and spoke of these events with Levi. We have been as brothers for twenty years and were notching logs for Henry Bitsche's new house. Levi volunteered that things seemed to be steaming with Polly and me. That is the word he used; I am sure of it. It makes a sweat come again to think on it. "Steaming." "Such ease on the high notes." I showed too much haste in speaking with Levi; I rushed where I should have used caution. I have not spoken with anyone in my family; Rachel would giggle or be a nuisance. Now I am especially glad I said no more, for at the last church meeting Polly seemed more at a distance. If I think on it too long, it seems she sought to avoid me as the young people mingled after services. I cannot understand it. I will not think on it further. If this coolness be true, I doubt that I can bear it. Where would I turn for consolation? Where would there be another girl? I cannot bear to think. Even Levi might be amused or look on my fumbling with pity.

I wonder if the fault lies at the door of Eliza and Yost. Could Polly's sister turn her against me? Why? What have I done? They may know I brought Polly home on two different occasions. Perhaps my horse made too much noise, or perhaps they thought the hour too late. They might not like her being courted in their cabin. Yost often visits with us older boys, but not so at the last church meeting. I can see now; he also may have sought to avoid me. If it is Polly's choice to say "yes" or "no," that I will take my chances on. But if someone else is giving thoughts in her direction, that I cannot stomach half so well. My insides fairly heave to think she might be taken from me. I should not have allowed myself to hold so much hope with regards to her.

The last time we spoke at any length, Polly made comment about us being in the same relation. I did not make much of it at the time, for it is not uncommon for cousins to form a union. There is little other way in these new settlements unless we marry outside the faith, which puts us outside the church. And, of course, no one wants that. None of our kind will mingle anymore with Henry and Barbara's Samuel who married that Clodfelty girl from Salisbury. The only other way to avoid cousins is to move to a different settlement where there are more girls to choose from. That is what Levi speaks of doing; he says he wants to find work in Mifflin County where he has an uncle.

As for this change in direction from Polly, I wonder if my lack of height troubles her. She may be an inch, barely two, taller than I, even when I have my new shoes on. Or perhaps someone from Brothers Valley sent word of a renewed interest. I have heard of horses that get lonesome for home; perhaps the same disease muddles her thinking. I will not think on it further, for my mind sweats to seek out the cause of her changed behavior, and I end up feeling a dizzy wrenching in my innards with no plan to bring a remedy. I will try once more: test the breezes with Polly this Sunday at meeting.

I hardly know if it is right to pray for winds that bring a warming in this regard. Yet I hope for a flowing of sweetness like unto that of the sugar maples we will soon tap. If I can refrain from foolish comment and steady my hands, I will yet win this Polly.

2.

ELIZA

March 1810

I am Eliza, faithful wife of Yost Hershberger and blessed mother of three baby girls. In twenty-nine years I have known little but wilderness. A forest in front of me, a forest behind, panthers and wolves on every side. I do not mean to complain, but from what I hear, it would not be this way in the Old Country. Momma still receives greetings on occasion from her sister, Aunt Maggie, the one who lives yet in the Rhineland. She writes that some of our number who stayed behind have become quite wealthy. Yes, of course there was persecution in the Old Country; our fathers and their fathers before them longed for freedom to live at peace, freedom to not join the German soldiers. That is why they had to cross the ocean.

But what have we done? Run from wars in one country to wars in another? Here we flee the Indian and those who would harm the Indian. Momma says herself that Berks County was paradise until the massacre of three of our own. Then there was a difference. Then Momma's family feared for safety and left Berks for Mifflin. Yes, I know the Indian looks fierce with his paint, but sometimes Yost has the look of a panther when his hair gets awry and his eyes pierce through me in the night.

I tell him to smooth his rooster tails so as not to frighten the little ones, but he makes no effort. He says, "If you love the Indian so much, go live with him." Then he laughs his big laugh. Well, that is not what I want, and he knows it full well. I do not think he would let another man tell *him* when to move on.

Yost says these mountains of Somerset County, a good ride south from Mifflin, are where we are to be. He does not see the eyes that I see. I do not mean to complain. I only said something once to Yost, and he replied sharply, "Woman, get thee behind me." It came to me later that he might also have doubts that we have landed in this much ruggedness. That is not likely however. I was the one who spoke up when it was my duty to be silent. I chose to leave my father and mother and their log house and cleave to this man. That is what my mother did and her mother before her. The place of habitation matters little; life moves on from one dark forest to the next. But if these Alleghenies remind the old ones of the Black Forest and the Alps, what have we gained?

Yost is good to me, I will say that, even though there is a roughness about him. He works hard and wants to make life easier for us all. Some day when we have enough income from crops, he says we will have a frame house instead of these logs. If only he would pay the little ones more heed. But after clearing trees and tilling ground with the wooden plow that often breaks, he wants little more than his fill of buckwheat cakes and a night of sleep.

I had to rouse him when I thought baby Marie would not wait till morning for her birthing. It was fetch the neighbor woman or fetch the baby himself, so he rode with haste to get help. Then when we waited all the next day until evening for Marie's time to come, he could not help but make comment on the lost sleep. Too often I am a botheration.

I think it would go better for Yost if he had a son. With each baby he takes less interest. Marie was scarcely dried when he looked on her face and said, "No help in the fields." I was ashamed that anyone else heard. Yost may have felt shame too, for he looked away and went out shortly to tend the animals. He gives all his tenderness to his horses, the cow, and sheep. He has built a larger pen to keep and fatten pigs this summer. He says we will do better by pigs.

As for me, my three babies are my life—my babies and my faith. Each little *bobbel* is a soul fit for heaven. Oh, that they might each one grow up in the fear and admonition of the Lord. It is a grave responsibility to prepare these tender souls to face their Maker. Yost thinks I know nothing of soil, but already I have spoken of eternity with Lizzie. She is but four tender years. I tell her we must be ready when Death comes. She looks at me with her dark eyes and nods to show she understands. I do not tell her that there are eyes in the forest.

Our own Minister of the Book, Isaac Joder, does well to warn of the dangers of lukewarmness. "God giveth the increase," he says. "Trust in God." We have barely settled in the wagon after church and Yost mutters, "It takes muscle to clear brush." That is what he thinks because that is what he does. He does not mean to contest with the minister. Clear more land, raise more crops, buy more animals, clear more land, raise more crops. I no longer remind him that in Germany the land is already cleared.

Polly has been a help this winter. Some days she seems little more than a child herself, but she has taken up easily with the spinning. Momma must have known Polly was her last, for she did not work her as she should have but treated her more as a pastime. If only Polly could keep her hair in place. It hangs in long, fine strands at her ears. I do not mean for her to hang her head, but sometimes I must tell her that she looks as if she is at loose ends.

She is backward with chores about the cabin. She leaves a pile of dirt at the door where Yost scatters it when he tromps in. And she has no head for remembering names. But the little ones love her rhymes and games. Susanna has attached herself to Polly like a burr on a stocking. I worry that Polly might make a wrong step with this Jonas boy while she lives with us. Yost reports that he is on the clumsy side and rather given to emotion like a woman. He nearly beat his father's horse to death once when it would not pull their wagon out of deep mud.

I wish I had more of a peace about this place. There is such a loneliness here, and some days I do not feel strong. I think I have lost pounds this winter. Momma would say that I had little to spare. I have always been the tall, thin one of us girls. Poppa called me his fine stem of wheat with the ripe head. It is a blessing to rock the girls in the middle of the day because it gives me a rest. And I do not have to bend over the spinning. Last summer when Momma visited, she guessed at my downward spirit. "Eliza," she said before she left. She grabbed my arm hard as if she wanted me to mind. "Eliza, be of good cheer. Your green eyes have gone gray. You have your man and your babies. Be not so restless. All that happens comes from the Lord."

I know the words and the truth whereof she speaks, but I have not found rest. I should be happy in my Yost and my babies, but the work is hard. There is always water to carry and socks to knit, food to grow, coals to keep burning. So many worrisome animals lurking. I did not tell Momma that I have seen grizzlies trampling the brush. I said nothing of the foxes with their eyes at night. Death lurks everywhere. These same eyes give Yost the needed push, but I do not find it so. I have not found rest.

3.

$\mathcal{P}$ OLLY

March 1810

$\mathcal{M}$y name is Polly Berkey from up the Brothers Valley settlement. I have lived here with my relations all this winter, spinning flax and tending the little ones for my sister. Susanna is the dearest one of the three girls. She is my little lap baby, pulling at my skirts. "Olly-ap, olly-ap."

At first I did not like this house. A cabin says it better. I wonder if Eliza is not discontent as well, but she will not say a complaint. It is dark here all the time. Yost built this cabin with the start of mountains at the back and in front a large stand of sugar maples. He says they protect like a fortress. When Poppa and I rode in on horseback one late September day a week after baby Marie was born, I could not see an end to this woods. All along to our left huge trunks of chestnut and oak lined the path, ending in this stretch of sugar camp. The branches overhang the path like large fingers reaching around us on all sides.

Although the ride of some forty miles along the Little Youghiogheni was rough and tiresome, I would have gladly returned with Poppa the next day to my own sweet home. There we have a room upstairs for us girls to sleep and we have more of an openness. The sun is there and the sky. Even there it is nothing like the lovely Kishacoquillas Valley where I lived my first five years and where there was air and light and the flax bloomed like the sky was turned upside down.

The plan was for me to stay the winter here at Yost's cabin along with Badiah, my horse—a good riding horse for Yost on these winter trails. Yost makes little jokes about having two extra horses to feed, but I think I have earned my keep. When we get a new set of sheets spun and blankets woven, Eliza will have new clothes ready for everyone and linens enough for another year. It may be yet this month that Poppa will return, and we will ride back to my beloved house and to my momma. I wonder how she fares this winter. We have been much surrounded by snow, but Yost says—when he has gone to Meyersdale for more flour—that they report a milder winter to the north. It is like this cabin sits in a little pouch that all the storms fly to.

Oh, how the wind has howled! I have learned to spot the tracks of deer outside our door. At dusk we sometimes see them moving along the base of the mountain. They are a beauty to watch. Lately we have also noticed bear droppings where the pine trees edge up the mountain. Yost is concerned for the farm animals, and I will not let the little ones out of the house except when we all bundle our way to church on the wagon.

Eliza does not seem to worry at all. At least she does not give her fears a voice. One of the first nights I was here there came a dreadful rain, so hard it came in under the door and around the back window. The thunder and cracks of light seemed to split the night, the way something tries to break into my head at times. I did not want to rise from my pallet for fear to wake Susanna and Lizzie—they turned restless in their bed—and for fear to step in water that lapped on the puncheon floor.

Finally I called but softly, "Eliza? . . . Liza?"

I heard a stirring in the bed along the far wall, heavy silence, and then Yost's snoring began again, deep and trailing along like wagon wheels on uneven stone. The wagon stopped, started again, stopped.

Eliza answered, low and soothing, "It will be all right, Polly Anna. Go back to sleep."

Polly Anna, that is what she calls me whenever my fear leaps from my mouth. I do not know how she knew it would be all right. She is not my momma. I lay awake until the storm spent itself. Jagged shapes made ugly faces on the roof beams whenever the lightning cracked. I thought to turn my face into the pillow. But if something dreadful was going to happen, I wanted to know it, not be caught unawares.

We never spoke on it, but I believe Eliza did not follow her own advice that night. It is something of a bewitching thing when two people lie awake on their beds, pretending to sleep and not wanting to move to show they are awake. But the stillness of their bodies stretched tight speaks with a loudness back and forth.

The only subject Eliza and I speak of at length is the children. They are each a little drop of molasses in this cold winter. Lizzie's big brown eyes make me think of Yost; Eliza says there is in Susanna a strong likeness to my own roundness as a baby. Momma's sisters always said about me that I was just like Momma through the cheeks. The littlest baby, Marie, is as sweet as her sisters. She sleeps the night through already now several months. What a blessedness it must be for Eliza to look on these children as her own. I would be afraid that I might cause harm if they were mine.

And now since Christmas there is Jonas Zug for me to think on. He has been showing attention and has twice brought me home from the young folks' gathering. Eliza says not to give him encouragement. Yost thinks there may be sad problems among our people some day if too many cousins marry. I do not know how he could know a thing like that. I wonder if he makes things up. Yost says that in the Christian Joder relation there are now four of the seven children not quite right. Then he adds, rather on the sly, that there is some question about the other three, before Eliza can hush him up. Now in that instance, Christian and Mattie are first cousins. Whereas with Jonas and me, it is not so close.

Let me think to say this right. Jonas and I are cousins on my father's side. When Poppa's mother died, his father, Henry, married again, this time to a Speicher from Ben's Creek. They had but two children. The youngest of them, Veronica, is the mother of Jonas. So he and I have the same grandfather, but the grandmother is different.

For myself, I wish Jonas had been given more looks. He is not bad to look upon, for he has the broad shoulders. But his green eyes have too much of the cat in them. I wonder if he might decide to pounce of a sudden. He walks too fast, with his hands half out of his pockets, and stands like an awkward scholar on one foot and then the other. He should watch the deer and see how they move. Eliza says that his looks are of no consequence. But the babies being right in the head, that is a serious matter. Of course she is right. Still, it is something of a compliment to have someone paying interest. Jonas has a strong, clear voice and will one day be the *Vorsinger* at church. I am almost for certain.

• • •

Eliza says she will make a pie baker of me yet. She watches me, giving instruction when I err. Her fingers are light and quick. She says, "Do it so," and before I have set my eyes, the thing is done. Her fingers are a blur. I am able to roll out the crust with fair success and fit it in the clay dish. The middle is not a problem either, the apple or cherry, but when I try to lift the top crust, I get it but halfway on. Then when I press the top edge to the bottom, it does not want to stay and falls apart. My fingers have too much of the fat in them. I wonder that Eliza has not given up on me.

The little ones love to play after supper. That is my favorite time. The room has a draft, but with our new woolen stockings and undergarments we forget the chill. Eliza looks to the baby, nursing and caring. I will sorely miss Eliza's precious ones when I journey back to the Brothers Valley. But that is all I will miss. Lizzie loves the rhymes and songs and Susanna tries to join in. Sometimes Yost objects to what he calls nonsense. That is when we have gone on too long or when Susanna's laugh gains too much shrillness. Then Yost frowns with his eyes closed. "Enough," he says. I bundle the girls in their sleep gowns and make preparation for the night's rest. Sometimes Lizzie cannot stop so easily and we whisper together yet one more time:

> *Es kisselt und kasselt*
> *Und du der stadt hier.*
> *Vas bringen sie mit?*
> *Ein haus voll kinder*
> *Ein stahl voll rinder*
> *Ein eissiger buck*
> *Ein bixie geladen*
> *Ein drumme geschlagen.*
> *Beduss, beduss, beduss.*

• • •

Our life has taken a dreadsome turn. Baby Marie has gone on ahead. Oh, can it be true? A little child was not meant to lead in this way. I try to think on a better world but cannot train myself in any one direction. This awful passing! One event piled on another. It takes my breath to think on it. Momma came this night and is much broken. We are all broken. Eliza cannot stop her wailing.

I tried to tell Momma what happened. Yesterday morning was not a Sunday for church services. We went instead to visit Yost's brother Daniel and his wife, Sadie. They live over near to Turkey Foot. The time for Sadie is very near. We took an extra blanket. Marie, yes, our beloved Marie, had outgrown it. Oh, how my heart weeps when I think on it. How little we knew.

We young folks had a singing that evening, but it was some distance at the Peter Gnaegy farm. Yost did not offer to take me. Instead, we returned to this cabin. I wanted to go, but I feared to ask since Eliza had cautioned me about Jonas. Yost was all taken up with the approach of sugaring. If only we had but waited until daylight. All of this might have been spared.

There had been a gradual warming for most of a week. The snow was all gone. Last Thursday, I believe. Yost announced that if the weather held, we would be able to commence collecting sap after the Sabbath. Yes, it is true. We should have waited until daylight. Eliza will not say a word on it. When we returned from Daniel's yesterday, Yost stopped the wagon beside the sugar camp. He made us all shush to listen. He insisted that he could hear an occasional plunk, plunk of sap on wooden pail. For myself, I was fully chilled even with Susanna and all the blankets pulled tight. All I could think was whether the fire would still have its coals when we got inside. Now it seems a trifle to fret of being cold. Nothing knows of cold as long as the blood flows. I could not bring myself to touch Marie's cold body.

Yost waited until the big clock said midnight. I am sure of it. Then, right away, when Sunday was past he put on his work coat and said he would be ready for us soon. And not to make him wait. If we had gone out as soon as darkness descended, not waiting for the new day and thinking that no one would see, then I could understand this dread occurrence. A necessary punishment. But Yost waited till the Sabbath was over. I am sure of it. Still, it is true. We should have waited for daylight.

Eliza and I checked the children. She added a log to the fire and made sure the lamp was safe. Then we tucked the children once more. We did all of this in readiness for being gone but a short while.

When we reached the sugar camp, Yost had the horses hitched to the large sleigh. It was very cold. I do not like to be outside working when I can see my breath. We went with diligence from tree to tree, carrying each bucket, undoing each lid. Then we emptied the contents into the large wooden keg on the sleigh. It was a sorely tiresome task. My fingers could scarce move. The buckskin mittens kept getting in the way and my woolen scarf kept slipping off. Some buckets on the outer edge of the camp had a thin layer on the bottom. Others on the inner parts of the camp had but a drop or two. We went to each tree. We were very diligent. Eliza held the lantern while I carried the pail. Then I held the lantern while Eliza did the walking back and forth. I never once thought of trouble. Only of the cold. Yost worked all by himself, doing full as much as the two of us together. An owl shrieked mightily. I wonder if that was the exact moment.

When the sap had been collected, Yost bade the horses pull the sleigh closer to the house. Last fall he used rough stones to build a little furnace. He reminded us that we would not have far to fetch water from the creek for boiling the sap. Oh, we should have waited. The night is too full of the Evil One.

Yost's plan was to finish the tapping, then cook the sap later in the light of day. Who can bear to think of something sweet in the mouth? The night gives off such a bitter taste.

Yost took the horses to the stable. Eliza and I quickened our steps so we could warm ourselves inside the cabin. My legs felt wooden. The cold had stiffened every part of me. Inside, the fire had kept itself well. Our lamp still flickered. I stood huddled in my coat when I heard a sharp cry from Eliza. I heard her shoving furniture around and saying, "My baby! Where is my little one?"

My fingers stuck in the ties of my hood. In my haste I could not undo the knot. "What is it? What is it?" I cried, running to Eliza, still tugging at my *bels kapp.*

"Marie! Marie is missing. I cannot find Marie," she said. She rushed past me to the door and out to call Yost. I will not forget Eliza's voice shrieking, "Yost, *schnell, bitte! Schnell!* Yost!" She had joined the owl's cry. The panther was in her eyes.

I saw the empty cradle. I dropped to my knees to look underneath. I crawled to feel under the beds, looking everywhere at once, kicking at my pallet. Eliza and Yost came in. No, that is not right. Eliza came first and lifted the lid of the woodbox. "Fetch me the lamp, Polly!" Then Yost came in, stomping and wondering what it was about.

I stepped onto the chair and dripped oil from the Betty lamp as I whirled toward Eliza. The box held nothing but wood. "Marie! My baby, my sweet one. I cannot find her," Eliza wailed.

Now Lizzie and Susanna stirred. I went to their bed and tried to soothe. Nothing came from my lips. I reached for Susanna's shoulder but pulled back sharply. I might have wakened her more.

Yost stood on a chair everywhere to look up high. How she would have climbed, I do not know. Then I heard a terrible, full-throated sobbing from Eliza. She was the one who thought to look between the upper and lower beds. Their very own bedstead. Yost came to her quickly, looking with the lamp. I heard him say again and again, "My love, my love." Then more tenderly, "Oh, my beautiful one." I had never heard a word of endearment from Yost before. If sweetness only comes from him in such a time as this, I do not ever wish to hear it again.

Next he was asking—it was more of a bark—"Where are the candles? Get a candle, Girl." I did not know why he needed a candle yet too. We only have the one. I hurried to light it in the fireplace. I thrust the candle's flame toward him and saw for myself. The baby had turned to a blueness. Oh, where had this night come from?

By then Susanna's whimpers and all our bustling and noisome cries had wakened Lizzie as well. She sat up on her bed, staring at the backs of her mother and father as they knelt in grief at their bed. I rushed to Lizzie. I wanted to shield her from the sight. I sat on her bed and said, "Too much evil, there is too much evil." I said this again and again. "*Übel, Übel, Übel.*"

I could hear Eliza's terrible wail, "I do not understand; I cannot understand."

Lizzie echoed like a chirp, "What? What? Is it? What?"

Yost pulled Eliza to her feet and dragged her to a chair. She put her head on the table and moaned and swayed. With Lizzie in my arms I tried to pat my sister. I did not know how. There were too many people to comfort, and I could not be sure of my own feet. I looked toward the window and gasped. A face peered at me. It was a face like to the shadow I had seen there before. Early yesterday evening—when I pined for the singing—I had seen something at the window. The same eyes. But they disappeared, and I passed it off as but my imagination.

My body heaved against the table and Lizzie cried out in my grasp. I righted myself and looked again. The face—I am sure I had seen it—was gone. I dragged a chair near to Eliza, not knowing how tightly I squeezed Lizzie's arms. She cried and tried to wiggle free.

"I cannot understand. Cannot. Too much evil," Eliza kept saying. I did not know what to say. I repeated her words. I do not know how we made it through the night. I sought to help Eliza by looking to the little ones. Susanna was full awake, and I had both my babies in my arms. The three of us sank onto the girls' bed.

When Yost came in with a wooden crate, I shielded the little ones' faces in my bosom. Over their buried heads I saw him take the straw bag from the cradle and make a bed in the crate. He placed the dead babe in the crate and covered it with a cloth. I have seen him carry a dead lamb from its mother's stall in much the same manner. Then he lifted the crate and slowly turned, looking around the room. Finally, he placed the crate on the center of his own bed. No one slept that night in that chamber of death.

4.

YOST

March 1810

ather of a murdered child . . . does that say who I am? What does that make me? Someone to gawk at? A fool? We do not ask for extra names or labels in this life. Nor do we ask for trouble. Sometimes all come at once, even when we yell to high heaven.

A murdered child? My child, murdered? I cannot believe it. I know it is true, but I will not believe it. Let me find the devilish fiend who did it. I do not feel pain, but my blood is thicker than any spring tonic of sassafras root could purify. My hands tighten into fists all the day. Eliza says my anger will consume me. I say, "Then let me be set afire." That only makes her wail at a higher pitch. The doer of this deed deserves years of torment—unless he confesses, and that right quickly. Yesterday might have been soon enough. Trouble happens. Of course. That is to be expected. But no human makes trouble for a Hershberger. No one makes me look like a fool who cannot protect his borders. God gave us Hershbergers a mighty build for good reason.

Yes, my baptized name is Joseph Hershberger, but everyone knows me as Yost. There were already too many Josephs among the Hershbergers, which prompted someone to suggest Yost as a substitute, and that has stuck. I know what trouble looks like: a fox in the chicken pen, a hailstorm that strips two acres of corn. Everyone is visited with trouble now and then— Eliza would say every now and now. I remind her, this is the frontier. She cannot seem to forget the homeland, where fancy ladies sip tea with their little fingers curled. Troubles have been like flies that come, then leave, and return to buzz at the head before finding another party.

But this last trouble—I am at a loss. I do not say that to Eliza, but she sees my fists. Trouble is not the right word. This is far more than an annoyance. This is far beyond a patch of yellow jackets over which a fool dances with a fever until he finds a way to strip himself of his pants. This is Evil, done in a matter of minutes, leaving a yoke at the neck. A yoke that cannot be lifted. But I will smash the breath out of the Devil who did it.

I do not want to relive the events of Sunday night, but they run through my head against my will. Two babies crying, two women wailing. It was a relief to go for help. I turned to my father even though he is getting on in years. His white hair steadies me. He returned with me at once and sent my brothers on their way to spread the word to other families.

When morning was fully broken, the two of us rode to the home of Shephat Campbell, a Justice of the Peace in Somerset County, apprised him of the situation, and requested his presence at the scene. Later that morning he arrived at my farm, as had many relatives and friends. His white horse pranced like a foreigner. A dandy. I saw his pistol with its shiny handle in his belt. Many times since Sunday I have touched my shotgun above my hearth.

Campbell commenced to carry out his inquest duties with dispatch. All I could say was that I had gone to my sugar camp, seventy to eighty yards from my house, about one hour after midnight. My wife and the sister joined me within a half hour to tap the sugar maples. By two we had finished our work. That is when we returned to the house and found the baby taken from the cradle. Found the breath pressed from her. That is what I will do with this Evil One. Father frowns at me when I say that.

For the inquest my father found eleven other good men among those already assembled. All solemnly affirmed these events, adding that it was not known who had done the deed, nor whom to suspect. No other person is known to have been about the house that night. Unless this Polly can be believed. What a *dumbkopf*. These twelve men—my father, my uncle Jake, my brother Daniel, and such—all substantial freeholders of land in Somerset County, set their hands and seals on this testimony, the fifth day of March. "In the year of our Lord, 1810." Believe me, this deed cannot be any part of the Lord's year.

That was Monday. The next morning proceeded with the funeral and burial. Yet that first night, Polly had delivered her jolt. I have to look twice to make sure she has a head on her. Most of the crowd had cleared out that Monday evening—all the people who came to gawk at me in my spectacle. The father of a murdered child. A Hershberger. People from a distance found neighbors to stay with for the night so they would not need to travel home and then return again in the morning. Eliza's parents maintained their vigil by the corpse. Moses took over responsibility for the fire and ice. In the interests of preservation he made certain no one tried to build a hot fire. They kept Marie's body at the farthest corner from the fire, surrounded by blocks of ice to keep more of a coolness. My hands could have done the same work as that ice.

While Eliza pretended to rest with Lizzie and Susanna that evening, Polly and I huddled at the fireplace. Neither of us had slept the night before—who would want to lie on that bed?—although Polly may have napped a time or two with the children during the day. I had trimmed my fingernails with my pocketknife and had come close to dozing when I heard Polly say softly, "I think I saw someone. At the window last night." I thought I was dreaming.

I straightened in my chair and then stood above her. I placed both hands on my knees and bent toward her. "What did you say?" I did not yell because she is as skittish as a colt. My neck had a severe ache from having laid off to the side.

Polly mumbled more quietly, "I saw someone outside. Outside the window last night. Eyes. Before we went to the sugar camp. After we came back and found Marie's body."

"Why in every name under the heavens did you not speak of this before?" Now I thundered. I did not care if she had the itch to bolt. "Before or after?" Eliza quickly moved behind Polly, placing her hands on her shoulders and patting her. That is the problem with Polly. Someone has always been patting her.

"She did speak of it," Eliza said, "but with all the women-folk coming and going, there was no privacy. I thought she babbled as in a dream."

"Privacy?" I could not believe these women. "You both knew this? And neither of you said ought because of a house-ful of sniveling women?"

"I was afraid to speak more," Polly said. "When I first saw the face, I thought I imagined it. It disappeared in an instant. When I saw a shadow again—after all the life was snuffed—I thought the fearsome night had made me see things. I was chilled and could not think straight. With people in and out ever since, I could not stay my thoughts. What if a grizzly prowls?"

"You think a grizzly unlatched the hook and walked . . . ."

Eliza interrupted me, patting Polly, rubbing her neck and shoulders with both her hands, "Are you sure you saw a face? Polly Anna, are you for certain?"

At this, Polly commenced crying like a muskrat with its nose in a trap. It took both her sister and mother to free her. I could not stand to hear these endless carryings on and went outside. I had married one Berkey but not the whole family. I walked the length of the trees—Daniel and some of the other men had emptied the sap that evening—daring a grizzly to attack me. My mind leaped.

Who could have done such a thing? And why? For what reason? Had the Red Man returned? I have tried to warn Eliza to be on the alert, but she can be soft in the head. She thinks animals intent on harm must all be four-footed. I do not consider myself a man who has enemies. I live peaceably with all men; I am more than generous in my dealings of grain and animals. That is the way we Hershbergers do things.

When I had given the women time enough to collect themselves, I returned to the cabin, only to be met by Eliza with the hush-hush look, saying that Polly was now abed and was not to be bothered.

"Not to be bothered? What can you mean, Woman? She has bothered me aplenty with her silence. We cannot fight Evil with hush-hush." I stalked to the pallet where Polly lay; the floor boards shook. I demanded that she say more. If her parents thought me rough, that is their assessment. I did not touch the girl. She has had too much of the baby in her for too long. I needed to know what she had seen. We men had conducted an inquest, and she had not been in any way forthcoming.

Polly staggered from her bed and lurched to the fireplace, pulling a blanket raggedly about her shoulders. She looked like she had found my store of jugs. It is miraculous how she can sit in front of a fire and be cold. She sat with her head down, shivering and shaking. I stood there in front of her, determined to wait her out. I have outwaited coons and watched them walk into a trap. I was not going to let Polly escape without giving some answers.

"Speak up, Girl; we should have been told this morning what you know. Better to speak now than never." I tried to soften my voice and leaned down to her, my hands on both my knees again, my face even with her face. She covered her eyes with both her hands, as if she were afraid to look at me. "Do you mean to keep this a secret all your life? Do you mean to crawl around on all fours? Shall we put you off in a cave with the bears that you are fond of imagining?"

At this Eliza came between us again, "Yost, have patience. The girl is trying to draw herself together. Be a little less push and a little more pause."

I straightened my body and stared down at Eliza. What a fool of a woman, smoothing and fiddling with Polly's hair, as if I were the one in error. Whose side was this foolish woman on? Were all the Berkeys protecting this goose of a girl? I did not want to look at Moses. Did Polly intend to keep us waiting another day? Did she even know what she had seen?

I walked to the hearth and ran my cold fingers along the smoothness of my shotgun. Then I reached for the inner pocket of my hunting jacket. I needed something for my hands to do. I had not smoked my pipe since I was married; Eliza would not hear of it. Her parents did not know I had such. I wondered idly how it happened that a week earlier I had had a hankering to buy a pouch of tobacco while trading for flour.

Polly must have sensed Eliza's anxiety at my rummaging, for she raised her head and began to speak. "It was a man. With large eyes. Like yours." She stopped again as I turned and stared at her, foregoing my search for tobacco.

"Large eyes, like yours," Polly had said. Understanding crashed through my wild thoughts. The same idea had come sneaking at me several times that day, but I had pushed it aside as an old habit, lacking solid foundation. Now the idea took shape in my mind, as visible as a stripped field of wheat. I would have to be the one to name the culprit.

I hitched my pants on the side that had no suspender and said to Polly, "Reuben. Was it Reuben?" And then more roughly, "Was it my brother Reuben?" I would shake it out of her.

She nodded solemnly as she looked down, "I think it was. It looked like him." She seemed calmer, even relieved as she spoke more quickly. "I saw a man late last night. After Marie—. When you went to get Badiah to ride for help. When Eliza made me walk part way to the barn with the lantern. I saw a man with a brownish-black hunting jacket prowling around the sugar camp. I returned with haste to the cabin and bolted fast the door. I had seen a face at the window earlier. Twice. The second time I covered my mouth with my hand to stifle my shriek because of the little ones." Polly went on, repeating the same things. I did not need to hear more.

Eliza and I looked at each other. She shook her head, trembling. "Not in the family."

I nodded grimly, my thumb hooked in my suspender. "Yes. In the family." Then I said to Polly, more gently, "Are you for certain it was Reuben? He does have a brownish-black hunting jacket. But are you for certain?"

Polly nodded, "Yes, it was a jacket like Reuben's." She braced her clenched fists on her knees, her chin dropped to her chest and her feet stretched tight in front of her.

Eliza came to me and reached her arms around my body. I drew her to me and settled my beard on the top of her head. "To think that it is in the family," she said. Her grief gave way again to much sobbing.

I could not cry, for dark feelings raged within. When Reuben's evil nature had come to me in flashes during the day, I had shaken it off. I do not see how his anger could have grown to such proportions. I do not desire revenge, but Reuben will pay mightily. I do not know what that payment will be, but he will not escape. I know how to set traps for very large animals.

Then another thought came. I lowered my voice, "Eliza, did you also see this face?"

"No," came her muffled answer as her forehead pushed into my chest.

"To think that he came here today," I said, "with the face of a mourner. He will pay. He will need to hide that blank face."

No words had been exchanged that day between Reuben and me. That was not unusual because we have not been on good terms for several months, ever since he tried to cure my Lizzie of livergrown. Since that time we have not spoken, other than the absolute civilities that Father might expect. Reuben knew better than to utter condolences today. But he showed up to ensure that his absence would not draw suspicion. The Devil's Auger-maker!

Moses interrupted my thoughts as he added a piece of hickory that hissed and sparked in the fire. Eliza and I parted; I do not know how long we had clung together thus. I had forgotten how a woman can be a comfort. Then I set myself to the task of bringing my brother to justice. There was no rest in me that night; I rode to talk with my brother Daniel, who I knew would keep everything in confidence. The year of our Lord, indeed. I will make these matters right.

5.

$\mathcal{R}$ EUBEN

March 1810

$\mathcal{I}$ am Reuben Hershberger. I have not been this world's most noble saint, but I did not know until today that I was so full of the Evil One.

Yes, it is true that Yost points the finger at me. Again. But never before with such a serious charge. I cannot understand how he convinced the others with such speed. I should have defended myself more quickly, but I did not want to believe he hated me this much. Anna knows full well I was at home all of Sunday night; she has said that to all who ask. But whenever something has gone wrong for Yost, he has always blamed me—last year's wheat crop, two dead horses when we were lads. Now this.

How can it be that someone would enter a cabin and kill a baby? This wilderness is a fearsome place, but how could something like this happen? How can they blame me? There have been no Indians in these parts for thirty some years. Perhaps a tramp or vagrant of some sort wandered through. Yost may have refused him supper. Later, the tramp came back to settle the score. All is speculation.

Yesterday morning when we first heard of the murder, Anna

and I and the children readied ourselves to go at once to Yost's house. All of my family was there, as well as most of the Berkeys. There was much wailing inside the house, especially from the child's grandmother, Mary Berkey, for whom the child was named. She says that the variation, Marie, was too modern. There is no way to justify such carryings on. Yes, of course, it is a sad time, but the child will know no suffering in this world of toil and trouble. My own Bevy and Jacobli seem much subdued by it all, as well they should. Anna reports that Yost's Lizzie will not say a word to anyone but her mother. Their Susanna, again the baby, cries at nothing, on and off, on and off. Theirs is a cabin full of wailing sirens.

I stayed outside the cabin most of the day, until it was time to come home to tend my animals. Yost would not say a word to me, and I did not try to reach across that wall he has put up between himself and me. It looked to be made of hard wood. I should have made the first move, but I did not. I could have put a hand on his shoulder, but I did not even reach to shake. I did not want him to turn his back on me in front of all that crowd. I did not know then that his venom had already tainted me. I did not believe my brother would do this to me.

Our county's Justice of the Peace, a Mr. Campbell, was called for an inquest. He wore a long, black cloak and a cocked hat and looked as out of place as I felt. All twelve men assembled on the jury—including my father, my brother Daniel, and my uncle Jake—all of them signed their names that they did not know who to suspect of having committed this awful deed. Why did Father not choose me to serve?

As best I can get the story from Daniel—he was tight at the lips—Yost had waited till the Sabbath was over, then went out to his sugar camp shortly after midnight. Eliza and her sister went to the camp also about a half hour later. Both of them solemnly say that when they left the house, all three children were sleeping and Marie was in the cradle with a feather cover over her. Furthermore, Anna reports that the women had knotted together strips of cloth and bound this like a string across the cradle so that if Marie stirred in her sleep, she could not fall out. Daniel says that after gathering sap, they all three came back to the house about two in the morning. Everything was as they had left it; except Marie was not in the cradle, the cover was turned to one side, the strips of cloth were torn. They searched the house feverishly and found the baby's body pressed down tight between the feather bed and straw bag of Yost and Eliza's rope bed. There was no life.

When I said to Daniel that we must find out who did this, for some of the rest of our children may be at danger, he looked at me with strange eyes. I did not make much of it at first, but after the questions I recalled the look, a cold stare, as if he knew something. I cannot believe my brothers would turn against me. There have been differences, yes, but I did not know there was this kind of animosity. Yost is three years my senior and has always been my biggest thorn. I have never known where his dislike came from, if dislike is the word. Hatred sounds too harsh for brothers. I will call it dislike, while something gnaws at me that it is worse. I see Daniel's eyes, and I know that he did not take me at my word.

For some time Yost and I have not been on good terms. Whether it goes back to the land Father gave us—did the creek run through his side of the property or mine?—or much farther back to when as a boy he thought he was always stuck with the heavier work clearing land, while I was allowed to put my nose in a book at night, I am not for certain. For me to suffer at Yost's hands is nothing new. I have endured his taunting for years, always when Father's ears were out of reach. "Reuben, Reuben, gully gully Geuben." Then when I complained, he made me look in the wrong.

I have always been bigger than Yost. Well, of course not always; he was born before me. But when it became a matter of importance to us as young boys, I was already bigger. He is strong for his frame—there is no question—but I am built like an ox with two legs instead of four. Only once before did he manage to scare me. We had jumped in the river without the encumbrance of clothes, one hot summer evening as lads. He put his hand on my head and, taking me by surprise, held me under water with great force. Even when I thrashed and kicked, his hand stayed on my head like a giant tick sucking blood. After that I was careful never to turn my back to him. Now, this.

Wherever his dislike comes from, he made no attempt to conceal it last fall when I tried to cure his Lizzie of livergrown. Yost's oldest came two weeks before my own firstborn, Bevy, now nearly four. This business with Lizzie, the *brauching*, was worth a try, for the child had cried day and night. Now I know I should not have interfered, but then I only sought to bring relief. I instructed her to crawl forward three times around the table leg and then three times back. Yost was enraged, so enraged when he came on the scene that he yelled at me, "Never, never, *touch* or say anything to my Lizzie again. Never. Ever." I can still hear the way he said the word, "*touch*." It came somewhere between a cry and a croak, the way a bull's bellow can make me jump when I am unawares. When we were boys, Father did not allow us to yell. Now we are grown men. I suppose Yost told Father about the *brauching* with Lizzie. I am certain he told the story as he wanted. Now Yost points at me again.

I took my family back to Yost's for the funeral today. Nearly all in the settlement were there, having got word by nightfall on Monday. Everyone is drawn thin and tight-lipped from worry. The ministers speak of rest and hope in a better world, but there is little of either for any of us now. I fear my own situation can only get worse. I will not sleep at all tonight if I let myself think where this could lead. The thoughts come nibbling, first at the toe like a crab, then grabbing the entire heel. It is like a bad dream that gets a worse supplement each night. I tell myself that since we are brothers, Yost will slow his rage. Surely. But I have never known him to begin a quarrel and then abandon it. He always thinks he must win.

Yes, I was slow of foot to join the church. Is that where the rub comes? I was not against the church as such, but it was not important to me as a young man. My family had been Amish for well over a hundred years. I joined because it was the way to get my Anna. She has brown eyes like me, but they are not as dark. They are more mellow, drawing me to her. I was nineteen and of a mind to marry; Anna was five years older than me, of a more patient temperament, and lived five farms over. It was not a bad ride by horse for Sunday night courting. There were few young girls in Elk Lick Township back then besides the Berkey family. And Yost had already skimmed the cream off that crock. If I had married another Berkey, that would only have made matters worse. Anna and I were hitched, and that has been my good fortune. The Livengoods are as their name: good stock of Swiss background. They came over to the New World, just as my family had, with but few belongings, an old shirt wrapped around a small bundle, surviving the ocean that had no end. I cannot let Yost ruin Anna's family reputation.

Growing up, there was little time for us boys to play. We toiled from the light of morning till darkness took over. But the few books in German from the Old Country ever beckoned me. Father was not unpleasant to work for, as long as we persevered. I could heft a pitchfork better than most, so I was safe from his rebuke. But there was little time for more than clearing fields and laying up brush for fences. That is all Father thought about. When we went out to work in the morning he reminded us, "Idle hands lead to idle thoughts." After our break for dinner that Mother brought to the fields, Father added, lest memory failed us, "Idle minds lead to idle deeds. We are clearing land. That is but the start. We are clearing a living."

Of course he was right; to survive we had to work. But I do not want Jacobli to think that work is all. Now I could be drowned in this cesspool of Yost's making. What all has he told Father? My feet may need to kick as never before to escape Yost's hand clamped on my head. He dislikes me because of Jacobli. Is that what I must be punished for: my son? Or is it my attraction to books? When Aunt Barbli died, she left me her book of *Egyptian Mysteries*. Aunt Barbli, now there is a spot of softness in my family. She taught me what I need to know. She gave me my special strength even if Yost does not want to hear of it. Aunt Barbli would come to my aid if she were with us now. She would know how and in what manner to answer these questions.

As a lad, Sunday was our only day to rest. The good Lord must have known there would be men like Father. On the Sabbath we were allowed to do only the minimum of tending animals. We were to think about holy things and especially think on the Bible. As a boy, this was sorely troublesome. After we drove to church by wagon, sat through three hours of meeting, ate our dinner, and drove home again, there was not much time left. So it happened that as I got older, I took to staying at home on some Sundays. As I look back, I wonder that my father allowed this. I recall the looks of reproach as the rest of my family went off to church, yet Father did not insist that I go every time.

When Anna's family moved here from Mifflin County, some distance to the west of Berks, she was scarcely shy of her twentieth year. It took but a few years for the natural progression. Anna was quite for certain that her father would not allow us to marry if I had not joined the church. I obliged and we married in 1804. That will be six years come fall. She gives me all I can want, every night that I am not too tired. She is a beauty. Now her parents have moved north again to the Brothers Valley settlement where their married sons live.

I cannot bear to think that Yost might cause pain for Anna. And for our little ones. Surely it will not come to that. I am not a dreamer or a strangely sort as Yost wants others to believe. I do not claim to know much of the ways of God, but I believe He will stay the hands of those who seek to blow the trumpet. Surely. I want to believe the good, not fear the bad. How could Yost have swayed Father's thinking? If I had been quicker to sense Yost's intent, perhaps I could have headed off this trouble.

Daniel came posing questions today after the burial and funeral. I have been too slow to comprehend; I did not know I was simple-minded. I did not say enough. Or I did not speak the right words. I do not know what I should have done. What I should have said. Perhaps things were already too far advanced. Not until Marie's body was in the ground did I fully realize that attention was being directed at me. There I stood, wrapped about with my little brood in the family plot where the Hershbergers are buried, thinking about the treasure of my upbringing. The flat stone that marks the bones of my grandfather, John Jacob Hershberger, lay a few steps away. He came to this country unmarried and ate at his father's table in Berks County. He did his share of work, I am certain. He lived in this New World but twenty years, yet had ample time to marry and bear children. Father always liked to say, "Forty-eight. That is all your grandfather was given. Forty-eight earth years and an eternity in heaven. Watch and pray. None of us knows the years appointed unto us."

There stood my father in the cemetery—I believe he is fifty-six—the dirt of a granddaughter's grave piled in front of him, his own wife's grave of ten years to the side. My two youngest brothers stood on either side of him, green limbs on the end of the branch. Father leaned on his good leg, his head bowed, his white hair beaten to the side by his hat and the March wind. A few steps behind him stood my oldest sister, Catherine, and her family. She did her duty, taking in Father and the boys when Mother died. That is the way it should be with families, coming to each other's aid. Why do I not fit in? Why does Yost want to cast me out?

Later, Daniel and I stood at the stable looking at Yost's new team of work horses. He rests his old plug and says he is all set for the summer. Daniel asked what all I had done the past Sunday. The way he said "Sunday, the Lord's Day," as if I should turn crimson or some other unnatural shade at the very words, made me turn to him and stare. He is the smallest of us brothers, but I was not noticing his size. He blinked first but looked only a little sheepish. "I answered you that question yesterday," I said. "Would my answer change today? Is my word not worth anything?"

He put down more hay for the horses and said, "The word of a Hershberger would mean something in normal times, but with all this mumble-jumble you have said in the past few years, words are not the same when they come from you."

I looked at Daniel as if he were Mr. Campbell with a pistol in his pocket. I was not staring at the scar above his right eye. This was Daniel, two years my younger. We shared a bed growing up. I feared he would bleed to death when he tripped and fell on the upturned ax. I helped him get set up on the Dorley farm when he married.

Then Daniel said, as if to slap me on the other cheek, "Polly says the man at the window on Sunday night had on a hunting jacket. Like yours."

My eyes fell to my Sunday coat. I pictured my brown, leather-like shirt in its place. I could not believe what I was hearing. I was far from the only one with just such a shirt. "She says the man at the window had on a *brown* shirt? How could she make out the color, out the window, in the dark of the night?"

Thinking back, I realize this was another grave mistake. First, I did not say enough; I stood as one dumb. Then I leaped to defend myself. That has not worked in my family with my extra reading. That has not worked in church with my *brauch- ing* gift from Aunt Barbli. Arguing did not help my cause today. Once I realized Daniel's charges were serious, I professed my innocence, I defended my integrity. Every word I pushed out toward Daniel shoved me back two paces. Hershbergers do not think you should need to defend yourself. I heard a voice inside me telling me to be still, to not say what was rushing out my head. I could not pay heed.

My Anna told me yesterday that it was said among the wom- enfolk that Polly had seen a face at the window two different times before they went out to the sugar camp on Sunday night. Or was it one sighting before going out and then again once more when back in the house? Stories swirl everywhere. But this tale from Daniel was the first I heard about a hunting shirt. Like mine.

"Do you believe this girl, this foolish girl?" I wanted to plow a knee into the horse next to me, but I was afraid to raise a ruckus. "Will you and Yost take the suspicion of this half-asleep girl looking through a cloudy glass? Take this over the truthful- ness of my Anna? She knows I was at home on Sunday evening, that I never left the house, that I was by her side all the night."

As I say, I should not have argued. But I did not have time to ponder what would work one way or what another. Daniel of- fered to go get Yost and I assented. I stood, looking from the sta- ble toward the bare fields. Then Yost was there. My father came too. Our father, I thought; we are all brothers. Yost would not look at me. He stood cradling his elbows in the cups of his hands and occasionally made marks in the dirt with the toe of his boot.

When it was clear that he was accepting Polly's story and that I was the object of serious blame, I turned away and pounded a support beam with my fist—something my father would never allow when we were boys. I was being sold by my brothers into Egypt.

I pleaded. I begged. "You are making a liar of my wife. Does that not trouble you? You have no evidence. Only a strange face at the window and a hunting jacket like half the men in Somerset County wear."

I would not say that I yelled these things. But I did not whisper them either. For a Hershberger, yes, I yelled them. Finally a desperate thought came to me for how I could prove my innocence.

I turned to Yost. "Dig up the child's body," I said. "I do not mean to make you suffer more by seeing Marie's face again, but I must be allowed to show I am not guilty. In the presence of you and whatever witnesses you call, in the presence of all these honest people, I will touch the child's body. You and I both know that if I am the murderer and touch the body, there will be a sign of blood or some other clear manifestation of my part in the crime." I lowered my voice, "Please, Yost, by all that makes us brothers, allow me to prove my innocence."

After a moment Yost lifted his head, and I thought I had broken through. But before he could speak my father said, "No, the body will not be molested. The body shall not be exhumed."

That was the end of that. That is the way things stood.

6.

ELIZA

March 1810

"Out of the depths have I cried to thee, O Lord." What a help in time of trouble. Oh, the precious words. And what a balm for the soul, these songs of the saints who went before. Their fiery trials, whippings, burnings, torture, all for the sake of the cross. What a cloud of witnesses we have. I try to latch on and hold tight.

The last two nights I have been torn about. I never thought such grief possible. Even this morning as the dirt was piled high, and then higher still, on baby Marie's grave, my heart felt crushed and sunken with each shovelful. I was so encumbered with sorrow that I needed help on both sides as I climbed the hill to the gravesite. My tears have been my meat and drink; I still go about with a wet cloth to my eyes.

As the funeral made its way through the hymns of the faithful and the words of all the ministers—Bishop Benedict Blauch came all the way from the Brothers Valley—I felt the Savior's arms slip around me and His great love enfold me.

> O Christ, help Thou Thy little flock,
> Who faithful follow Thee, their Rock . . . .

Oh, to stay safely thus. I must look to my soul lest bitterness seeps in like a silent poison. If only Yost could give me comfort. I have not known his touch all day. His mind is elsewhere.

Bishop Blauch held high our *Ausbund* and pointed to the words of our brave Michael Sattler:

> If one ill treat you for My sake,
> And daily you to shame awake,

Yes, that is the part that brings such a stream.

> Be joyful your reward is nigh.
> Prepared for you in Heav'n on high.

How am I to be joyful? How can there be reward when my Marie has been ripped away?

> Of such a man fear not the will
> The body only he can kill;
> A faithful God the rather fear,
> Who can condemn to darkness drear.

Oh, there is much, much more. How often I have sung those verses when others had met with grief. I never thought they would one day be mine. We are such a poor, poor flock. So much we do not understand. Of a sudden, an arm ripped out of the socket.

To think how heavy that person must feel, wandering alone and cursed, condemned to darkness drear. I cannot bear to think there may be one among us with soul so dark. Or that he could be in the family. Oh, that he might know forgiveness, that his deeds might be blotted out. How could any human do such a thing? To one so helpless? Yost says a four-footed beast would have left tracks.

I know Marie has gone on to a far better place. But I need to give suck. My fullness leaks, and I cannot find a way to stop the flow. I try to cling to the blessedness that Marie never need fear animal, storm, or darkness. Nor the wickedness of man, ever again. She will never see the wild eyes in the forest. How I wish I could join her on those heavenly shores. I see her in her cradle reaching up with her tiny hands to me. Then I remember: she is high and lifted up. I am the one far below.

Bishop Blauch reminds us that we do not choose our time of departure, that those of us left behind must persevere. We know not what hardships lurk before us; we can only trust in the merciful kindness of our Lord. At least Lizzie and Susanna were spared. For their sakes I must not lose heart. I do not know what stayed the enemy's hand, but I could not bear to have lost all three. I draw my babies close whenever I can; I do not care that they are too big to be babies. Even with Lizzie I find myself patting and rocking as if she needs to burp. If only Yost would hold me.

Lizzie asks, "Will the bad man come again? Will he, Momma?" I wonder if she saw something that night. But when I ask, she buries her head in my bosom. I gently move her head so that she does not start my milk to flow. I do not want to frighten her worse, so I do not speak further of a man. I do not tell her my wild imaginings: first, one baby taken; then Susanna; then the oldest. All gone. What did I do to deserve this? Why have we come to this wilderness? I should have insisted that Polly stay in the house that night with the girls. But I wanted to get the job done as quickly as possible. I could not keep up with Yost by myself. Yost says we were not enough on our guard. I did not know the Evil One could

strike so quickly, without warning. I cannot say this to anyone, but I fear I did not treasure Marie enough—our third girl
in a row. I fear she knew, even at her tender age, that my mind
was set on getting an early start with the bread that day. Now
I cannot make amends. ". . . daily you to shame awake."

With Susanna I find no success in bringing comfort. She
never could say Marie's name right, and now she shrieks,
"Meee, Meee, Meee!" I try to explain that Marie cannot answer, that she is with Jesus. "O Christ, help Thou Thy little
flock." Polly can do nothing to calm Susanna either, but Polly
sits vacant much too much.

Many dear friends speak encouragement. I wonder if this is
how it went for Job. I have trouble keeping food down. Nothing has appeal. Now I know why the cow bawls when she is
not milked on time. Yet my spirit is fortified by the brethren.
"All things work together for good . . . ." Oh, that I could believe the precious promises! This would never have happened
in the Old Country. I must learn not to complain. Yost turns
and walks out if he comes upon me moaning.

Momma is having a dark time of it. She will not speak evil,
but a drab cloud has settled over her; her cheeks look gray
and her lips droop. When she first got here she could but wail,
"Why not this old, worthless body? Why not take this poor
lump of clay?" Now she sits and stares, rubbing her thin, gray
cheeks and wiping with her hand, first on her brow, then
above her lips. Then back to the cheeks. Always rubbing. I
cannot bear to watch.

Momma and Poppa will return home tomorrow, but Polly
stays yet two more weeks. Poppa has agreed to ride back for
her and Badiah. There is not much work that remains for
Polly. I wonder if it might not be better for her to leave at
once. She faces questions right and left. But she says she
needs more time for her leavetaking, so we will make the best

of it. We have had enough of untimely departures. I only hope she is not lingering for another look at that Jonas. We do not need another mishap.

Yost has become quite set against Reuben. Yet Reuben proclaims his innocence with straightforwardness. Yost insists that is the way Reuben has always been, denying he ate more than his share of the meat, denying he got the best land. This open sore between brothers is an added grief; I cannot see how it will heal.

My heart grieves also for Sadie, Daniel's wife. Her time is near and with this, her first child, I fear the babe may be marked by these sad events. In spite of the jostle to and fro, she came to the funeral, riding sidesaddle. She said she could not stay at home alone; I cannot blame her for that. I thought to offer her Marie's few garments, but I could not bring myself to part with them just yet.

Yost's sister Catherine stitched a white shroud for burial, and Marie's Grandpa Hershberger built a white oak coffin for her final resting place. I cannot say I cared to look on Marie's body; by this morning there was a foulness about her shriveled, dark form. Darker than gray. I try to find rest in this dark woods, but comfort will not come. All I see is this plate of weeping set before me. Oh, that the outstretched hands could reach to me.

7.
JONAS
March 1810

Father has set me to pruning apple trees; he says we will have the best-looking orchard along Elk Lick. Mother says that it is too early, that there will be hard frosts yet. But Father bids me, "Go, do it." I do not mind the work although the blade of the broadaxe is too wide. Father's shaving knife works better. It is a relief being outside in more agreeable weather, doing something with myself. I am no good at the waiting.

How I dislike making choices: which branch to cut, which to leave untouched. I seize a branch but pause to deliberate. Shall it be life or death? What is to keep a runty-looking branch from desiring life? Then I weary at my slowness and commence hacking away with an excess of haste, paying little thought. Whack, whack, whack. I want to decide quickly which branch appears strongest, yet I also know to consider the final, pleasing shape. I learned my lesson last year when I pruned everything in one direction. Father was caught between dismay and a cackle. Dismay was the victor when a spring storm left one tree broken in its entirety and two others bent to the ground on the side where I had left them heavy.

It was the same way sorting potatoes last fall. I despise deciding if this one is large, that one small, another in between. When Mother pestered me about my slowness—she called it dawdling—I gave her the look of storm clouds and commenced throwing potatoes about, paying no heed to their size. She chided me that I was bruising our best crop. I got up and stomped away. I cannot be a manager of potatoes. Why must potatoes be sorted? I am not in the habit of giving backtalk, but I shouted as I walked away, "Do your own woman's work. Or get David to do it." She stood there with a long blade of chaff hanging from her mouth. I thought Father might seek to punish me for the incident, but I overheard him say, "The boy needs more slack in the rope. He needs his own place. If only the Stutzmans with their girls had not moved back to Centre County."

I was relieved to hear my father defend me but surprised he knew of my itchiness to leave home. Whatever it is that gives me loose hands and makes me scratch. He may regret that the Stutzmans moved away, but not I. All those girls have wide mouths with enormous teeth coming out of their fat gums. Many a horse looks better. I may be certain of little, but the Stutzmans will not hear me protest if they stay in Centre County.

What I am looking for, the girl, may be slipping away because of these awful events. I cannot see that the future bodes good for me. I have slipped badly. Father was a juror at the inquest for the murdered baby—a desperate affair—and reports much concern for all in the family. Every time he brings up the subject I want to switch my tail or lift my right foot and stomp in the dirt. Everyone appears anxious, looking behind every tree. Only a few days ago I was consumed with thoughts of my own barn; now I wonder that Father will let me slop his hogs.

Word of the murder came to my brother John's place early that Monday morning. I had gone there after the singing Sunday night; it was closer than riding all the way home. I did this several times last fall and John does not mind. With the weather warming a bit it was satisfactory to make a bed of straw in John's barn. His horses, Boy and Ginger, knew me and were not frightened.

I do not know why Yost did not bring Polly to the Gnaegy farm for the singing. I am almost certain that it had something to do with me. He could have brought her, but he has set himself against me. His eyes make slices even when they pretend to be friendly. Now with events in an upheaval I do not know when I will have opportunity to talk with Polly again. Or if I should even try. I fear she may return soon to her Brothers Valley settlement since there is no more baby to care for at Yost's. I have said it to each apple tree: "Jonas, you will never see her again. Never." If I lose Polly, I will not have courage to try with another. Not that I deserve another chance. *Schmutzig!* Events happened before I scarce could catch my breath, and my feet begged for direction. I cowered with the animals. Dirty.

I wanted to ride to the Hershberger place on Monday in hopes of seeing Polly. But with all the confusion and distractions, I knew my chances were slight. I did not want to risk being rebuffed amidst a pack of smelly women. I also found myself feverish at times that Monday. A chill from sleeping in John's barn. I refused Mother's chamomile tea at first, but later it soothed my stomach. Foul, through and through.

I went to the funeral but rode my own horse, rather than going in the wagon with the family. I did not need to hear Rachel and Franey chatter of this and that. Or cry in their hankies. Yost's yard and driveway were overrun with wagons and horses; I have never seen the like. I knew there would be a crowd, but I was surprised at the number. I thought to turn and go home. Then I found Levi with the rest of the unmarried men, out by the spring along the row of hemlocks. I could not help but look at the sugar maples. Everything about Yost's place is spooky: somber people milling about in black, wearing their stern looks. Black, black, black. I only saw Polly from a distance. I wanted to gawk, but I did not let myself. I do not see how so many could huddle inside for the funeral.

From as far away as the spring we could not hear the words of the ministers, but the singing came through. When my father's voice slowly led out with its wavering, mournful tone, I was overcome. This has happened to me far too often. Tears spring unbidden. I turned away, pinching the corner of my eye with my thumb, adjusting the halter that did not need fixing on my horse. Levi may have noticed, but he never made mention. There are many red-eyed women and old men with watery eyes these days. I do not want to be among them. I must learn to keep better check. I give Mother too much evidence that I am not manly enough.

At last people started to leave, and the commotion of horses and wagons brought more of noise and naturalness. Levi told me he had been on the jury. I jumped when he said that. I had to quickly explain that my surprise was at his youth. He happened to be at the Hershberger farm that Monday when they made the inquest, and since his father has already put livestock in his name, he qualified as a property owner. He was the youngest at twenty-one. Levi said there was no talk about who to blame, but that now suspicion falls on Yost's brother Reuben. He has strange ideas with his powwowing, and he is thought to have been prowling about the premises that night. I did not dare ask questions, but Levi said that Yost is quite near to fully convinced of his brother's guilt even though Reuben denies everything. I do not know what to think. *Schmutzig.*

Later that night as Father and I brushed the horses, I asked more about this powwowing. *"Brauching?* Yes," he said, "a *braucher* is the German word for a powwower. That is an old custom brought from Europe by our ancestors and used as a kind of healing. Some say it is magical. The *braucher* may blow, or rub, or say words on the person in need of healing."

I wanted Father to continue, for I had heard little of this before. I wanted to know more about this Reuben. Levi had made it sound as if powwowing were mixed up with witches or Indians. "Does it work?" I asked. "Do people find cure?"

"That depends," Father said, as he grunted with each stroke of the brush. Whenever he is intent on his work, he grunts. "The most important thing is for the sick person to believe in the power of the *braucher* to heal. It is that simple. If a person believes that *brauching* will heal, he will be healed; if he does not fully believe, he will not likely know healing."

"Do you believe in this *brauching?"* I asked, afraid I would offend with my snooping but too curious to keep still.

"No, *brauching* is not for me. Stay," Father yelled at the chestnut. I could not help but jump at Father's voice. "My grandmother on my father's side seemed to have an unnatural ability to cure a multitude of ailments. But she never called attention to herself. When people claim the power to heal, as I am told this Reuben does, that is not right. That borders on witchcraft and is to be avoided. The church must have nothing to do with that."

I try to imagine my great-grandmother healing my father. Or touching him strangely. I try to picture this Reuben *brauching* an ill woman. Would he say magic words or rub the skin or what? Suppose Mother fell ill. It makes my skin shiver to think of Reuben touching her. I never see Father do so. Perhaps Reuben would seize both her arms and press hard. Or rock her head back and forth. No, that is not possible. I never once touched Polly even though I wanted to find her alone in the dark. I do not like my hands; they have the smell of dirt.

So much makes me uneasy. This Reuben. Polly. Yost. I do not know what to do. Father says everyone is sideways because of the murder. I feel a churning in my pit; my bowels rumble. I remember when Father first explained that a male horse needs a female for there to be a colt. That is the same looseness I feel now. I hunch breathless on the edge of a high ditch where the top ridge seeks to give way. Loose dirt slides all about me. I cannot stay my feet. I want to run, but I cannot think where. I no longer find pleasure in thinking of a girl beside me.

Polly will soon be gone. I know it. I can think of no reason why she would stay longer. I wonder whether to seek her one more time and make my case known. Should I tell all? Whenever I think of entering Yost's cabin, I know I cannot do it. He does not want to see me, and Eliza may be crying for weeks. I have muffed everything. *Schmutzfink*. I see no way to be of use. I tell myself to think more slowly, but I cannot steady myself. My father has no idea of the danger, letting me hold sway with his apple crop.

8.

ISAAC

March 1810

I did not want the Kiss. For six months I have lived with this Kiss on my cheek; I still do not want it. I am ashamed to say that I am one of the Lord's anointed, and I would rather spurn the call. Sarah says I looked unsteady when Bishop Blauch called my name and gave me his right hand to stand. Our beloved patriarch has tottered for years. Perhaps unsteadiness comes with the task.

To be a farmer. That is all I ever cared about. To till the land and tend the sheep. Now I have been given these critters that walk upright and carry stubborn hearts. I do not know how to keep them in line. But here I am, Isaac Joder, a Minister of the Book. Sarah says that sometimes we are given what we do not seek; when the call comes, we must answer. Sarah reminds me, it is a Holy Kiss. Then she kisses me on the lips and flickers her eyebrows.

Another thing I do not want: this roundness about the waist. It makes me look shorter and shorter as I take on this wide girth. Sarah smiles and says there is that much more goodness to spread; then she passes me another cake. I eat because the buckwheat has lasted well. I eat before it gets wormy.

None of that matters. Not the outward appearance. Worse by far than all of my roundness, I do not know how to mend this rift between brothers. I fear it will end in shunning, and I shrink from that as I would from knocking an active hornet's nest to the ground. Someone else has disturbed the nest, and I stand in the midst, surrounded by an angry swarm. I did not make the trouble.

Last October the ordained brethren from all over—Berks and Mifflin, Chester, Lancaster, as well as our own county—agreed that there must be uniformity. Shunning those who err. Placing under the ban those who commit grievous deeds. I agreed with the counsel of the brethren. But I have no desire to drink this cup. I want to wash my hands of the enforcement. Sarah could apply it, but of course she is a woman. Bishop Blauch imparts wisdom from his store of years, but we cannot expect him to come all the way from the Brothers Valley whenever a controversy takes place among rival parties. With eleven families in our River district we easily have need of our own minister. But I did not seek after it.

Sarah says I am more of a stay-at-home, unlike my father and brothers. It is something of a distinction for me to say that the Samuel Joder who is the first white settler in Ohio is my father. At one time I had even thought to follow. Part of me wanted to go. Part of me held back. Now I have one foot nailed to the ground. For that, the Kiss has been for the good. I do not believe I could subject Sarah and my little ones to such unknowns.

Father showed me the deeds for their first exploring party signed by Mr. Thomas Jefferson. That was almost three years ago when Father and some others thought to establish an Amish colony farther west. They traveled all that summer through wilderness, from Pittsburgh down the Ohio River, through more forest, up north again on the Mississippi. Several locations appeared inviting for settlement, but they made no commitment. When they returned by land on the northern route, they ended in that place called Ohio and liked well what they saw.

Only a year later my father and brothers had made up their minds. They headed back to make their stay in Ohio. The next spring Father returned to fetch Mother and the younger ones. And all their belongings. He said nothing of the privations of winter. I know things could not have been easy. He went on at length about huge forests full of oak, springs everywhere, hills that lacked the steepness we have here. He did not tell it all. I know that. If I had not received this call to minister to the flock along the Casselman, I might be out the door, following his glowing report. The Kiss has kept me from that danger. I should thank the Kiss. But I fear that Father neglects his own call to the Book because of this lure of new land. I have never heard of a faithful Shepherd of Those Who Wander.

At the age of eighteen. That is when my first call came. "Isaac, where is my servant?" It came at night as I slept. I answered and joined the church. How easy then to promise to do whatever the church called me to. Had someone ventured that the Kiss would land on my cheek, I would have laughed. That was for other men and old ones.

Then the call came again, later and louder. I was shearing sheep. "Isaac, I am the Lord thy God. Hearken to my voice." I covered my ears, but I could not quench the summons. On that Sunday morning those of us named as candidates were called forward to sit opposite Brother Benedict Blauch. I sat with my hands in front of me, my fingers interlocked. I wanted to bow my head. And cover my ears. I was not accustomed to attention such as that. To be a farmer. That is all I wanted. That is all I want. Even then, sitting at the front, I had no notion. How could it fully register? The changes to come. I have wondered since if our Lord knew that Judas was going to kiss him before it happened. Perhaps he too was caught looking the other way. Knowing only in part. Thinking it could not be.

I was as one struck dumb. Words were said. Stories told from Scripture. Sarah reminds me that when young Timothy was chosen, he was admonished by the apostles. In the same way, I was instructed with regard to the teaching, preaching, and praying that I must do. I was to begin at once. That was a shock. I walked in a farmer; I walked out a preacher. Sealed by the Bishop's Kiss when he found the slip in my Bible. I was told that I would continue as long as I was found blameless. I went to church that day a normal man; I left with a mantle I did not seek.

For nights I slept little. I pined for my father and brothers in their new spot they call Sugarcreek. I could have escaped. I could have joined their adventure. Now I am too late. I worry about how I will farm *and* tend the flock. Whence I will get the wherewithal. Somehow I have managed to put one foot in front of the other. Sarah says the Lord provides. I have had to study the Word with diligence so I may open its truths. Reading the German does not come hard. But I must commit to memory whole passages so that I may hold forth from the heart. Seeking after words. What a burden! When I cut up felled timber I practice reciting aloud what I have studied the night before. Sometimes my voice gives out and I become hoarse from the exercise. Sarah says not to strain or I will only squeak.

These are sorely trying times. Our settlement here in Somerset County demands a heavy price with its stubborn rocks and wild animals. This last attack on our safety, the murder of the Hershberger baby, reminds us that our trials and tribulations will not soon end. I fear that more of our number may depart soon as word spreads of a more tillable land to the west. That leaves those like me who shrink from adventure. The timid ones. Sarah and I are barely making a start at homesteading here; last summer we were thankful for a better yield. We already have our five, and if the Lord wills, we will put more at the table. Sarah knows well how to kindle me.

But this Kiss. How could this Kiss fall to me? I am beset with snares. I cannot escape to the West. Neither do I want to tend the burdens at my door. Sarah says to pray for wisdom. I am not the one. I cannot mend this contention between brothers. I fear I will need Bishop Blauch's help with discernment. Sarah says not to walk with such heavy step. I do not want to choose sides. Yet one of my appointments is to keep the church pure without spot or wrinkle. "Protect and establish what is good; punish and hinder what is evil." That is one thing to hear. It is another thing to know how to do.

If the lines fall in the direction of shunning, the hornet's nest buzzes in my mind again. The intent is for the sinner to seek to be received back into the church as a member in good standing. There is no clearer way for the wayward man to see his error. If you separate a cow from the rest of the herd, she bawls to be let back in. But my inclination is to shrink from difficult tasks. I am no good as a Gatekeeper. It is not only the Hershberger case that buzzes. It is the people, coming and going. All the time. In and out of the settlement. In and out of the church. There is too much movement to keep track of. Yet we ministers all agreed at last fall's conference: all who leave the Amish church and join others are to be regarded as apostate and considered as subjects for the ban. How easy to agree. How hard to enforce. Those words. This practice of the *Meidung*. The ban, as we say today. I can only shake my head. Not that I am opposed. Only that I am not the man. Brother Blauch explains with ease: the *Meidung* is why we have our

Amish church. Our Brother Ammann, Jakob Ammann, discerned the drift from teaching the ban among the Mennonites in Europe years ago. Now we must have courage like unto Ammann's. To do the Lord's bidding and seek to hold the line. Ammann is right. When we adhere to these teachings, we have peace and contentment. But I am not the man. I do not like the feel of the whip in my hand. Let someone else do it.

I have studied the Word. I have read the *Dordrecht Confession of Faith*, dear to Brother Ammann. But let someone else pull the string across the door. I fear that my reproof could lead to a brother's ruin, instead of his amendment. That is why I turn away. I do not want to make an enemy of a brother. Sarah says the Lord will show the way. The erring brother will return to the fold. But I know how weak is this poor servant. If it were hers to do, she might hesitate also.

I keep my thoughts steeped in Scripture. That is the only way to know how to admonish both the fallen and the righteous. When I strike the froe with my sledge, I say the words of our brother Paul: "Now the Lord of peace himself give you peace always by all means. The Lord be with you all." Yes, I have memorized the words, written first to the Thessalonians. Sarah reminds me to include the *h* sound; I am prone to say Tessalonians. Peace always. That is the promise.

9.

$\mathcal{R}$ E U B E N

March 1810

Yes, it is true; the same hand that bites also garners thanks. The same gift of healing that poisons my family relations affords me welcome with my neighbors.

Only Salome, my younger sister, gives me support; she will listen full to my side and show some regard. But the others, all of them, have turned their backs. I would never have expected this. Even Father. I do not see a trail through the woods, only a thicket of brambles. I asked my Anna if she could entertain the idea of turning against our Bevy or Jacobli. She paused in spreading the *rivvels* on the cloth to dry before shaking her head. "That would be to reject my own blood," she said. "I could not sear my flesh." Yet that is what my brothers, my father, and Catherine are doing. I wonder how they sleep at night. I doubt that any of them would admit that a Reuben still exists in the John Jacob Hershberger lineage.

I know where I belong even if the others think my branch has ended with a black tip. I am the fifth in line, born in 1785 in my parents' cabin right here in the middle of these darksome Alleghenies. Father was one of the first white men here. Father had courage back then. William Penn had urged people to migrate to this southwestern part of the state, offering tracts of timberland at five pounds per hundred acres. My father, Jonathan, the one who now condemns me, came with all his belongings a few years after his father's death. I can imagine him thinking, "Go yet, beyond this range. There will be an even finer stand." That is the way he worked us as boys. "Never stop until you have done more than you think possible." Now he turns his back.

There is some consolation that not all reject my gift. Yesterday Levi Speicher came riding for help. He was on Yost's hastily-convened jury, yet he seems to hold nought against me. With his hair parted in the middle he looks more dapper than most Amish boys. But yesterday he was wild in the eyes. His father, Andrew, had been cutting kindling from rotting logs when he uncovered a nest of copperheads. They were sluggish from the winter but disturbed enough at having their home molested that one, maybe several, raised up and struck.

When Levi came, I told Anna of the need and rode at once with him to his father's farm. Andrew had serious swelling from two bites to the leg. His wife had tied bands of cloth tightly above his wounds, but his upper leg gave him much discomfort; his stomach-upset had caused him to vomit twice. Anna asked later, as she soaked the *rivvels* in water to prepare for baking bread, if this call might have been part of a devious plan of my family to entrap me. I had not thought to question Levi's intent. How Anna has been reduced to fear. I thought my summons clear enough, and I am quite for certain that no harm was intended. The Speichers, especially Levi, could not stop saying their gratitude.

Andrew looked relieved to see me although there was a starkness about him. His pulse had stayed strong as he lay on the ground. They had brought him whiskey, put a half-empty sack of feed under his head, and covered him with an array of empty sacks and horse blankets. I took my hunting knife and made two sharp cuts through each wound. His woman and Levi huddled there with me. They both looked away when I made the cuts, but Andrew's body did little more than flinch. His breathing stayed its regular course. His eyes seemed to open wider, staring up, as if he saw a shower of stars in the daytime sky.

Then I took his leg in both my hands, above the wounds, and said in all my strength, "And God created everything that was in heaven and upon earth, and everything was good, except that God cursed the serpent. Cursed shalt thou remain, O serpent." I could feel the power in my hands. "Swelling, I still thee; poison and pain, I kill thee. Draw thy poison, draw thy poison, draw thy poison. Amen, in the name of God the Father, God the Son, and God the Holy Ghost." I stayed clamped to Andrew's thigh, my eyes clenched shut. When I heard Levi's and the woman's fast breathing beside me, I opened my eyes and relaxed my grip. I sank back on my haunches, my hands in fists, my knuckles tight against each other.

Like the sweat that poured out of my body all uninvited, so my father's voice came over the ridges to condemn me. He had not taught me to do this kind of work. I rocked forward onto my knees, hunched over Andrew's leg again. I would allow no doubt as to the source of my strength. The words are in Ezekiel, the sixth verse of chapter sixteen; I had learned them from Aunt Barbli, and I repeated them in quietness and awe. "Andrew . . . Andrew Speicher," I began. "'And when I passed by thee and saw thee polluted in thine own blood, I said unto thee when thou was in thy blood, live. Yea, I said unto thee when thou wast in thy blood, live.' Amen, Andrew Speicher, in the name of the Father, Son, and Holy Ghost."

With that, there could be no doubt. Andrew shut his eyes. One of his hands lay on his chest, fragile, unmoving; the other rested at his side, turned up and slightly cupped. His chest moved up and down. My own body felt weak, as if I had wrestled a beast to the ground. My weight slumped back on my feet again, my shoulders sagged, my hands held the heaviness of my head. I half-dozed and then roused. Levi assured me it had been but minutes. I looked to Andrew and saw the beginning of color returned to his cheeks. He added to my confidence when he said, "The poison . . . has gone out; I feel . . . some better."

Levi was up, fairly dancing and hugging his mother. He shook my hand; then he shook my hand again. Levi hauled his father onto his back like a sack of flour, and then half-walking, half-running, carried Andrew into their log house. The wife and I followed, for she had offered me water and cornbread. I drank and ate my fill, waving aside her protestations that the cakes were left from the morning.

How I needed assurance from the Speichers that my hands work good and not ill. Such a difference from my brothers who brand me a killer. And Catherine, who believes I have recourse with witches. Perhaps I was too enlarged with good feeling from my endeavors with the Speichers, for I went to see Father today, hoping to make headway in pleading my case. Anna begged to go along, but I insisted it was not a woman's place. I wanted one Hershberger speaking to another with no woman to tip the scale. Anna was right. I should have taken her for she keeps me calm. I rode on the shortcut along the Casselman, past Yost's acreage. The trees have no leaves yet, and the path shows no growth along the sides.

Father bristled from the start; one of his eyes seemed stuck, the other jiggled. "I thought you might show yourself," he said as he limped past me to the stone bake oven. "How do you think this makes me look to have one son strike at another son's child? Strike and kill," he added, as he scraped half-burned wood and loose coals with his long stick.

I was not prepared for his wrath, not before I had even spoken. I should have gotten on my horse and made haste. Gone back to my Anna. Father had ruled our family with firmness, even judgment, but because his sparse words had been law, we learned early not to contest what he said. There was no place for argument. One of his favorite sayings had been, "You can always tell a wise man by the smart things he does not say." Now his anger, jagged as his teeth, quite took away the calmness I had resolved to maintain.

"But, Father, you charge me falsely. I did no harm to Yost's Marie."

He would not listen. "I have tried to raise my children knowing right from wrong. But with you, the hay is stacked upside down." He whacked with his stick, watching a hot fire build on the oven floor. "I should never have allowed you to stay at home Sunday mornings. You. Reading those books. I knew, knew in my heart, it would bear no fruit. No good fruit. But I had become an old man." He stood up, staggered on his bad leg. I thought he was going to fall, and I did not reach to catch him. I had never heard so many words from my father at one time. "An old man, long before my years. I did not have the strength. I did not discipline as I ought. I should have listened to Lydia. You have been the grape that falls to the ground and rots." I remembered the pride I felt as a lad when he had said of me that I was not born in the woods to be scared by an owl. Now this.

I picked up twigs lying nearby and aimlessly snapped them into smaller pieces. "What difference did staying at home make?" I asked. "I joined the church as an adult. Reading those books did me no harm. Father," I added. I did not want to sound sullen.

Both his eyes jiggled; his hands shook. "That is what you think. Lydia warned me that Barbli had gone too far with this magic business. At the first signal that you were drawn in the direction of witchcraft, we should have forbidden any further exchange between you and your aunt. Not allowed a foothold. Now I see, but it is too late." He shook his head slowly, one hand planted on his hip, as if to hold himself steady. The other hand shook on the stick that he now held upright like a sheepherder's staff. "There is small consolation, only a very little, that Lydia does not need to see "—he waited so long to finish his sentence that I thought he had forgotten—"what has become of you. Witchcraft." He said the word like it had the taste of poison berries. "We did not apply the proper stick. Why in the devil's name did I not hide those books? Burn them. Perhaps because it was Lydia's sister. I looked the other way."

"It is not witchcraft," I interrupted. "Would you listen? You are wrong! Will you listen? Will you?" I had moved closer to Father, as if my breath on the back of his neck could improve his hearing. He braced himself. I walked away again and then faced him. "Yes, a strange power lies within my hands; I do not deny that. Yes, at times, that is so. But I have always used these hands for good. Ask Andrew Speicher." Father looked at me, startled. "Ask Levi Speicher. Just this morning. For good. Do you hear?" I thrust my hands in front of his face. They are large, thick ones. Solid. "Look! This is what you condemn. These are the hands you gave me. These are the hands my mother fed. I have never sought harm for anyone. No one. No witchcraft. I have never placed a hex on anyone. I only come to someone's aid when they ask, like Levi. Well, but for Lizzie," I added, as I saw Father's bottom lip curl down. His eyes looked red. I saw anger mixed with pain. He is my father and he is old. I stepped back; I tried to quiet my voice. "I admit, I should not have attempted to assist where I was not invited. Not with one of Yost's. But my intention was for Lizzie's good, not for evil. She has outgrown the livergrown anyway; I was but overeager. I wanted, just once, to see Yost tip his hat toward me." I stared fiercely, daring Father to refute that.

"And now you have practiced this overeagerness again," Father mocked. "This *overeagerness* with Lizzie's baby sister. What in the *hill*, Reuben? What, pray tell, did you mean to cure her of?" my father continued. He pounded his stick against the ground. "You must confess your sin. Say what those hands have done. Even though you thought they were tied behind your back. And you meant to do *good*." His words snarled like his bottom lip curled. "Oh, my son, to be so consumed with the Evil One. And know nought of it."

My father's anger had turned to terrible, broken sobs. The back of his hand fumbled at his nose. He turned his back, resting his hands and head on his stick. I could not remember anything I had planned to say. I grabbed another thin branch to break over my thigh. It is one grief to have my brothers and a sister turn against me. But to bear the wrath of a parent turned away is the log that crushes.

"Father, I have nothing to confess. I did not kill Marie Hershberger. Do you hear? Would that I knew who did!"

I had been so caught up in conversation that I had not noticed Catherine join us, carrying six mounds in the dough trough to bake. She must have been listening, for when she brought herself forward into my line of vision, her cheeks were flushed and mottled. She added her own spite. "Such a pity you cannot see yourself as others do. Blind to your own evil. You babble as a sick physician, retching and knowing not of it. You stand on a wagon with legs spread, hands extended to the reins; only, there are no horses." She moved on to the oven. "How can you bring this grief on Father?" she asked over her shoulder.

My father hobbled to the oven also, his stick like a cane. He got down on both knees and shoved the embers to the sides. Then he steadied himself and used the long-handled paddle to place the bread on the hot oven floor. He remained there, staring at the red coals. I do not know what he saw in that fire.

"No one will listen," I said. I sounded like Bevy when she is disagreeable. "You have all made up your minds and shut the door. You have thrown me on the burning coals. Where is the fairness? All I hear is accusation. Aunt Barbli is the only one who would understand. Oh, that I had never seen the light of day, nor sucked at the blueness of my mother's milk."

I halted, too late. Catherine turned and fled into the cabin. My father's tears changed to sobs again. Snot hung from his nose. He blindly rearranged the bread, poking with the paddle, as if the dough had iron sides.

My regret overcame my anger. "What a fool I am!" I said. "I spoke what I ought not. Said words for thoughts I did not know I owned."

"It is time you looked within," Father's voice trembled, "before you lay more victims in your path."

With that he left me standing alone. I watched him stumble and limp to the cabin. I started to follow, to make amends, but changed my mind. I might have made matters worse. I rode back slowly to Anna along the same path, still wary of sluggish snakes. I tried not to think of what had happened, but that is all I could think of.

Only late at night I repeated some of the conversation that had transpired, begging Anna to forgive my overwrought words. The part about the sucking. She says I do not have the words right. I am not certain anymore what I said. "Let that day be darkness," she says is part of it. "The breasts that gave me suck," or some such. She is doubtless correct, as is usual in things pertaining to the Bible. Someone in authority will likely repeat my words back to me, and I will hear them more often than I care to.

Anna does not scold, but she must be close to exasperation. "Where can there be healing?" I ask, as if she is responsible to know the conclusion.

"With time, only with more time," she says. From now on when I am with my family, I will not speak unless Anna be by my side. Anna cautions me that Father may not allow a next time. Oh, darkest of days! Surely this cannot be true. Surely not. Where is the rascal who can take this curse from me?

10.

$\mathcal{P}$ O L L Y

March 1810

*T*he time of my departure is at hand. I cannot bear to think on how I will miss Susanna and Lizzie. In that regard, Marie's loss has been somewhat of a preparation. Though sorely heavy. Lizzie does not ask much regarding Marie anymore. We do not play our games and riddles. Or laugh. Susanna no longer cries all the time, but neither does she crawl into my lap as she once did. I cannot yank her from her mother. The days get warmer, but our cabin remains dark and sad and cold.

In these two weeks since Momma and Poppa left, Eliza has worked hard to keep me busy. She says it is a burden on the head to think too much. When she spies me sitting for a moment, she says, "Polly Anna, be not so vacant. Fetch more water." Or, "Go, scald more hops so that our *Satz* will do better in the bread tomorrow." One thing, and then another. It is only at night when I am abed that she cannot tell whether my eyes are closed. Then I let my thoughts roam freely.

When I finished spinning all the flax, she put me to making straw baskets. I meant to make small ones for her and Lizzie to gather berries this summer. Perhaps Eliza will not venture into the mountain. The first one did not curve as I intended; it looped into a larger shape. I did not know a basket could make decisions. Now Eliza has a new basket for her bread to rise in, but she will need to use the old, wooden buckets for berries. Why am I so prone to blunder? I offered to make a straw hat for Eliza, but she said there is not enough straw. Well, there is rye straw enough to fill the wood box. Perhaps she guessed that the straw would slip in my hands also, and she did not want a hat down over her eyes. I wish I had not looked that night.

Last week Eliza and I refilled the ticking bag for their bed. I am not for certain, but I believe this was Yost's request. I do not like their bed one bit. Eliza and I dragged the bag out the door and shook out the old straw for the horses. Then we went down to the river and washed the tick, spreading it on bushes. After it was dry we stuffed the bag—such a big round-ness—with new straw and sewed it shut again. The bag was too heavy; Eliza has no strength. Yost had to help us lug it back to the cabin and onto the bed frame. For several nights I heard Yost complain of Eliza rolling onto his side of the bed. Eliza must have learned to grip better so as to stay put, or else the straw became more flattened. I have not heard more of this the past several nights. I do not mean to listen to what is not intended for me, but I do not know how to close my ears to what is in this cabin.

There has been all the work of sugaring since Marie's death. Everything is now "before Marie's death" or "after Marie's death." Yost is not himself. He had looked with much anticipation to this spring's stir-off. But when the neighbors came to help with the boiling, he seemed not to care and gave little direction. We ended up with near to three gallons of syrup. Even with that, he would not release the tightness from his face. I think his eyeballs will pop out from studying. He is the one who stares at things. Most of the syrup we boiled hard to make crumb sugar so that Eliza will have a good amount of sweetening.

When our sugaring neared its end and it was time to make a supply of *schpruce* beer, Yost shook his head and proceeded to give away the settlings and dark sugar. He gave it all away. Every bit. I could almost taste the sweetness that Momma makes. I saw Eliza's disappointment and knew she was not strong enough in herself. My pity made me offer to enter the mountain behind the cabin. I could gather hemlock branches and twigs from birch and spice bushes. I might not have found all that was needed, but I would gladly have pulled off leaves of wintergreen for her. Yost took no interest. A couple shakes of the head and more staring. I did not want him to yell at me.

I fear for Eliza. Great sadness has overtaken her. She has developed a cough that bends her to the floor at times. The children take fright when these attacks come. Sometimes she sounds hollow inside; other times she seems plugged with phlegm. She carries a tin cup with her all the time. I have peeked at the ugly brownish-yellow. I worry that something bad will happen when Yost is out of the house. I will not know what to do. What if Eliza cannot catch her breath at all? I try to think what Momma would do. Nothing comes. This cabin is much too cold. Sometimes Eliza cannot sleep at night. I cannot see in the dark, but I think that lying on her back makes matters worse. She sometimes places a blanket under her head. It makes her breathing higher. But that is not sufficient to stop the wretched coughing. Other times she spends the night in a chair. She scarce can call that sleep.

I hear her caution Yost in his anger against Reuben. One afternoon I was rocking Susanna. My eyes were closed, but I could not help but hear Eliza say, "You do not know for certain. Even if he was about the house that night, as Polly thinks, you do not have proof he was in the house."

"Proof? What proof do you need, Woman? He will never admit to any fault. He would leave the cow pen unlatched and tell Father that a strong wind came."

I do not like to hear my name dragged in. What if I made a mistake? Another blunder. If only Eliza had seen the face as well. I am so alone to be the only one. I wish I had kept my head down. I should learn not to look for trouble. But I do not want to be caught unawares. Yost does not like me, but I believe he would protect me if he had to.

Eliza turned from Yost and quoted softly, "Judge not, that ye be not judged." I opened my eyelids a crack. They had their backs turned. I heard her add, "For with what judgment ye judge, ye shall be judged." Other times, I have heard her say, "With what measure ye mete, it shall be measured to you again."

I want to warn her that Yost may commence yelling again. He says little but often bellows, "Quiet, Woman." He gives her the same look that he gave me when I offered to fetch hemlock and birch. I do not know how to explain it. He is a grizzly bear standing on his hind legs.

This back and forth between Eliza and Yost is not for the best. It does not happen often, but even once a day is far too often. Eliza knows better. It is not for her to question her man. Momma never did ought with Poppa. The Bible is very clear about the woman being silent. Eliza may be safe to utter Bible verses to her man, but I would not want to risk it.

Yost is as possessed with Reuben's punishment as he once was with sugaring. He has spoken with several of the brethren about the need for correction. It will not go well for Reuben if he does not hearken to the admonition. I can tell that the worry aggravates Eliza's breathing. Sometimes she puffs. Or pants with her mouth open. I wonder if Reuben would seek to harm me. I tell myself, no. But I cannot be sure. After what happened to Marie, no one is safe. Eliza may have had the same thought. She said I am always to use the crock under the bed. Not go outside, even in the daylight. She does the same. Yost is good about the emptying. He does not seem to mind that unpleasantness.

Some days I am more sure than others what I saw. When Yost leaned down to me on the eve of Marie's funeral and asked what I knew, I was certain the same likeness had peered through the window. Yet there are times when I wonder if I did right to speak. I get confused at what I saw. And when. Eliza says my story is not always the same. It is a dread distaste to cause another serious trouble. Like unto vomit rising in the throat. But as Yost says, "We cannot shirk from the task." I wonder if Yost ever regrets not waiting until daybreak. Once I even wished that Marie had not been born. What a terrible thought! But it is true. If she had never seen the light of day, I would not have come to this dreadful cabin.

There is one small happiness in this family. Sadie and Daniel have their baby boy, a Simon Peter. I can smell the catnip tea in their cabin, just as when I first walked in here and Marie was newborn. I hope we will pay them a visit before I return home with Poppa. But Yost has not said a word. Eliza has not been to church or anywhere since the burial. One time I ventured to say that she should go about in the sun more. It is still cold, but the sun feels good on the face. Eliza never listens to me. I wonder on Momma, if she has gotten her spirit back.

Another person I had thought to see again is Jonas. It seems unfinished to have no leavetaking with him. Eliza would not let me begin a pie and then discard it. I have said nought to her because I know she and Yost do not approve. I saw Jonas across the benches at church last Sunday, but there was no mingling of the young that day. I do not know what I would say, but he seems a sad figure. His face was pale—I only took quick peeks—and he slumped through the shoulders. It is strange to think that Jonas and I might have gotten hitched. Now I think his looks are not half bad, except for his poor color.

I fear I may end up living my life with Momma and Poppa, pining on what might have been. Wondering what is wrong with me. I do not mean to change my story. I cannot imagine bringing aid to Momma the rest of her life. It is hard enough to know how to be of comfort to Eliza. Momma did not look well when she left, and I am no good with the pies. Poppa would be patient, but he cannot live forever. All is a blunder.

The next time I see Susanna she may not even know me. Lizzie will remember, but she may connect me with these cold, sad days. I wish she would think on the games and rhymes we once loved. I do not know how to make her remember one thing and forget the rest.

11.
JONAS
April 1810

Yesterday was a dreadful day. Everything I touched turned sideways. There was a foul smell at the Hochstetler's homestead, as if all their animals got sick at once. Why Laban chose to spread manure the day before we gathered at his place for church is beyond comprehension. The minutes of the church service passed like hours. "One of you shall betray me." "Lord, is it I?" It was the day of spring Communion for our River gathering. Bishop Blauch rode here Saturday to be in readiness for the services. Our own minister, Isaac Joder, assisted for the first time since his ordination, as did my brother, Abraham, our newly-appointed deacon. He looked as stiff as death.

Spring Communion should be on Easter, but since the bishop cannot be everywhere at once and he chose to be with his Glades congregation for Easter, our River church had to wait a week. Communion Sunday is always long, and I knew this would be no exception. I made the mistake of hoping that our new Minister of the Book might forget some of the Old Testament stories that must be told. I hoped in vain.

My troubles started at home. Mother and Father fasted, as is their custom for Communion, and Mother tried to put the yoke on me. "You are getting to be of an age where you should be more serious about possessing the Christian virtues," she said. I stared at the rolls of fat at her waist. "You will never make anything of yourself. Stop your looking. How do you think John and Abraham have risen to responsibility?"

I did not mean to be at odds on Communion Sunday, but she is the one who started the fuss. "I cannot go on an empty stomach," I said. I watched as she stirred milk and eggs. "David and Franey get mush. It will be of no consequence to make a portion for me."

Before she could say more, I went to help Father finish the choring. I do not know what set off the milk cow. Lucy became Lucifer. Perhaps because we started early on account of the long church day. Perhaps because of my own discontent with my mother. Whatever the case, the milking became a battle. When I grabbed at her back teat, she side-stepped with her rear leg, knocking me backwards. I stood and jabbed at her center section with my knee. I pulled hard with the left hand, hard with the right. I have always liked the cool folds of the cow's teats, the way the skin stretches and wrinkles to my touch. But I was ashamed when Father walked by and I had little milk in the bucket. Perhaps he did not want to express anger on Communion Sunday, for he made no comment.

With Lucy taking longer than usual, I had to rush my breakfast. I ate my fill because I cannot last when the service stretches past noon. Mother kept her mouth shut. For once. Thinking it best not to come up against her again, I rode to church in the wagon with the rest.

I do not know what ails me when we sing in church. As soon as Father lined the first hymn:

Take note with zeal, a heav'nly meal,
To us from God's extended,

I felt my throat get thick, my eyes watery. I stopped singing almost as soon as I started. I lowered my head, but I believe Father half-turned and looked back my way.

Communion has always touched me, even when I was a child and lacked full understanding. On any Sunday there is a reverence in church. But on Communion Sunday it is quieter still; the old men make effort to stifle the hoarseness in their breathing. When I was little, my mother grabbed me one time and stepped outside when I could not stop a coughing fit. "Young man," she said. Her thumbs dug into both my arms so hard, I nearly cried out. "You must stop your coughing. It is bad to disturb others in their solemn assembly with God. Do you understand? Very bad." When we returned to the meeting room that day, I sat again with my mother and the women folks on the left side. I wished I could sit with the men; they would not mind if I coughed. Half of them were asleep. Now that I am grown, I get to sit with the other young men, behind the old ones or in a side room. With time I will work my way to the front, even if I do not pass bread as Abraham does. The *Vorsinger*—that is my aim.

As I say, Communion has always tugged at me. Long before I needed to answer for myself I could repeat the three questions that every member hears: "Do you have peace with God? Do you have peace with your fellowman, so far as possible? Do you desire to participate in the Communion service?" God himself waits for the hushed reply of each member. When I was first baptized I feared I would not find voice to answer. I stood silent until the bishop's long glance made me blurt my yes.

Now this sudden springing of tears is an embarrassment I scarce can hide. I recovered myself by not thinking on the words. I know that is not acceptable, to sing and know not whereof, but it was either that or fail to sing at all. If I cannot be manly enough to carry through with a song, letting neither words nor melody undo me, then I cannot expect Father to turn to me. And Mother will be right: I cannot manage anything.

But it is not for her to say. In church we are not to think more highly of one person than another, so she is wrong to call attention to my brothers and their virtues. I do not want to believe that she is right. With John there is some merit. He has been ordained a minister in the Glades congregation already five years. But Abraham is another story. I do not see how he got to be deacon. How tight at the collar he looked. As Minister to the Poor, it is his duty to receive the alms at Communion and see that money is distributed to anyone in church who has need. He kept clearing his throat, but every time he forced a lump to retreat, another wad stepped up and blocked the passageway. He should have given it up and made do with the discomfort of thickness. But no, not Abraham. Here is the worst part: as deacon he is required to settle differences in the church. Enforce regulations. I vow: he will never regulate me.

He has never been a brother except in name. One time we lost two hogs to the woods. Abraham insisted they left on my account. Well, I did not lose them; they left of their own accord. Abraham was expected to guard against trouble every bit as much as I, and he was the older one. I could not have been more than ten. Father and my brothers were laying up brush from the trees they cut for firewood, making a high fence for our animals that winter. I was instructed by Father, as was Abraham, to watch the hogs that they not wander away before the new enclosure was finished. The horses were tame, the cow lazy, but the hogs gave concern.

As happens with little boys, I grew tired of watching and started throwing stones in the river. With practice I discovered how to twist my arm sideways causing stones to hit the water, pop up, and jump forward. I was engrossed with how far I could make the stone skip in the air, whether I could get it to land twice or even three times and then jump again.

Suddenly Father's voice intervened, "The hogs! Jonas! Where are the hogs?" He sounded like Mother screaming in a high, trembling rage, "The hogs, the hogs!" That was before he lost all his teeth. He does not have the voice for roaring to come out of his depths.

I scrambled up the riverbank. It is true: I had forgotten my assignment. *Schmutzig.* But Abraham was supposed to have kept watch also while cutting limbs from sycamores. The hogs had been right under his nose. I ran into the woods, knowing I was quick and could catch those hogs. My feet crashed through brambles and dry leaves, going first one direction. Then I thought I heard them over there. The hogs were never found. Two hogs.

While I searched, I heard Abraham calling me, "Runt . . . runt. Can you do nothing right? You worthless runt."

That evening I heard my father cry. At first I thought it was Mother. Then I heard her voice giving comfort. Those hogs were intended as our meat for the coming winter. They were gone because I could not watch. Already at an early age I had failed the man whose name I carried. Later that fall John shot a deer, but it could not replace the hogs that Father had so diligently tended.

As usual, I have taken the roundabout path to get to the point. Abraham, as deacon, sent my thoughts roaming. Many words linger from the day: "Let this cup pass." "He is guilty of death." Now I demonstrate yet another problem: I am slow to have my say; then I overlook the accumulation and jump sixty paces. I must learn to be more steady.

Before the church service the ministers gathered, as is their custom, in their *Abrath*. When they remain secluded longer than usual, the rest of us fidget. The delay makes us anxious, wondering what may be occupying their attention. Not that anyone whispers thoughts aloud, but we all hold our breath. What I disliked in particular was the thought of Abraham taking part in those deliberations. I fiddled with my hands, unhooked and hooked my coat at the top. While we waited, Father continued the singing, adding verses I had never heard, on and on for twelve or thirteen rounds. The older members followed him well, which tells me that he was not making up words. Finally Father began the *"Loblied,"* always the second hymn. I do not know how he knew. The ministers emerged, their faces pulled tight. Abraham looked as if he had a severe toothache, but an important one that only he could fix.

Brother Isaac showed he had applied himself, reviewing the entire history of the Old Testament. He stumbled only once— a small point as to the parting of the Red Sea. It was of some interest to hear a different voice recite these events, but my stomach started acting upset. I shifted my position in order to quell the inner rumblings. I tried sitting with my arms crossed tight on my stomach. I thought I had the plug in place. But the growling began again. Then I propped my hands on the bench on either side as if I had no care. Levi noticed my restlessness.

Isaac finally finished his part of the recitation. We ate our meager fare with hushed conversation about readying the fields for planting. After a while Levi stretched his head toward mine and whispered, "Did you notice? Reuben and his family are not here." I did not want to admit that I had been gawking also. I had looked for Polly. Now I turned my eyes to the table of menfolks. There sat Yost and his father, but no sign of Reuben. I shifted back to Levi, wondering what he knew. He shook his head, and I did not know if that meant he knew nothing or if he feared to whisper more. I saw my chance for a second helping of cold venison. I was not hungry, but I wanted to keep eating. Mother would say I have no sense. The meat was tough, like unto chewing leather, and in my haste not to be the last one finished, I did not give my grinders sufficient time. I gulped and rushed where I should never have reached.

We rearranged our benches for the afternoon sermon. This time it was Bishop Blauch's turn to review the life of Christ. I could scarce concentrate. When I had gone out to relieve myself, I had smelled again of the disgusting animal waste. Now inside, I thought I smelled it on me. I tried to peek at the bottoms of my boots, but I could see nothing. Brother Blauch went on about Judas, how he betrayed Jesus for thirty pieces of silver, about the others who deserted or fell asleep. The bishop kept repeating, "Master, is it I?" Many of our number bowed their heads at the telling. I have heard the story at least twice every year.

I burped and tasted venison a second time. The bishop seemed to know the state of my innards. "The spirit is willing, but the flesh is weak," he announced. I swallowed hard to keep down the acid. I was determined not to make a scene. The bishop's emotion built: ". . . all they that take the sword shall perish with the sword." Every time he thumped his Bible on the word *sword*, my insides jumped.

My panic overtook me. What if I waited too long? I did not want to go outside where the foul smell would be worse. But what if I could not make it outside? What if Mother had to wipe up my abomination on the floorboards? I had to interrupt the story for those gathered. I made a dash for the door. At first the latch would not lift, but I rattled and willed it to obey. I stumbled to the side of the barn farthest from the latrine. There I left chunks of my dinner and wished for a cat to cover my stink.

A few minutes later Levi came with water to drink from a ladle. Abraham came also, frowning and offering his hand-kerchief. I refused. I was spitting and weeping, whether for pain or shame. I shook my head, closed my eyes, and propped my back against the barn. *Schmutzig.* If Levi had come by him-self, I might have accepted help. But I did not want Abraham to take any credit. I insisted that I would be all right and begged them to return to the service. Levi seemed doubtful, but at last they left me alone. I curled up in our family's wagon and put an extra horse blanket over my legs.

The rest of the service may have lasted another hour, until all were served the emblems and all had washed feet. Some-times I heard heavy bodies and feet moving inside the house. I knew the men would go first, then the women, all the way back to where Polly should have been. Everyone would claim their unworthiness to eat and drink. Everyone would chew a bite of bread, drink a sip from the common cup.

That night Mother went on at length about how favorably Abraham had conducted himself. How he assisted the bishop, followed with more supply of bread and wine as there was need. I am glad I was not there to see. It is niggardly of me, but anyone can be a deacon. Abraham has done nothing to merit praise. If he had stumbled and spilled wine, then he would have deserved attention.

I felt worn from the day's events and from my mother's endless babble. Father inquired if Mother should fix tea for me, but I declined. I went to bed early, turned my face to the wall, and tasted the sourness in my mouth. My mind was not as ready for rest as my body. I thought with distaste on how my mother had likely concluded that I had received my just reward for eating breakfast. I finished the Bible story in my mind—the parts I had missed—of Pilate taking water, washing his hands, and proclaiming his innocence to all the throng. I came to understand that Polly had returned to her home. There was no reason to dwell on that lost possibility. I resolved to live with my pockets empty. I am a hopeless *schmutzfink*.

I must get away. I feel more confined than ever. I have fallen in a deep well and find myself clutching to pull myself up from these moss-slickened walls. Ohio may be my way out. Or Mifflin. Ohio means a long journey, and there cannot possibly be many girls in such a new settlement. With Polly gone, I want my desire to depart also. But not so. I need a girl. I must speak more with Levi, for he says the county just west of Mifflin, Centre County, has an Amish population. If we could hire ourselves out to someone who needs steady hands, there might be an escape. I must get away from Abraham before I do more *schmutzig* deeds.

Only Father holds me back, even with his empty mouth. Much as I would excuse myself with haste from Mother, I cannot do that without also deserting Father. When I try to imagine telling Father, "I am leaving," a blackness rises in front of me. This foreboding reminds me not to let foolish dreams get in the way of duty. When another harvest has passed, however, I must be serious about a change in location.

I feel stretched thin as an old, ragged shirt. My mind has done more work in a month than in all my days before. I want to know today what I am going to do tomorrow. Where will I be in a week or a year? I want hope for another girl, even if I do not deserve one.

I must slow my mind. Not dwell on what Father meant by this remark or that. I must let each day proceed in its own fashion. When I put too much hurry in my pace, events rush to unhappy conclusions. I must be more mum. Avoid Abraham. Pay no attention to Mother's green spit. Let others take the lead. See where things go. I have been kept safe. In another year I will make my escape. I will slowly begin to prepare Father. I will find another girl.

12.

YOST

April 1810

*O*f all the spring tasks to make ready the land, spreading manure is the most tiresome. My muscles often become flabby in the winter because of less activity. But this year—this awful thing with Marie—has compounded the usual sloth. Neighbors managed my stir-off. Neighbors came back to cut timber. My body creaks from lack of use. Now I must pay for letting others be my strength. I have spent too many hours pining on past events, walking the river when I should have busied myself with the work at hand.

Eliza wonders why I do not grieve for Marie. I do not know what the woman means. She says I only think of Reuben and how to get even. Why can she not see that I am doing something about my grief besides weeping? She does not know that I went to speak with Bishop Blauch on Saturday night. Of course she knows that Benedict came from the Brothers Valley and spent the night before Communion with his sister, married to Tobias Stutzman, over along the Turkey Foot. Eliza may suspect that is where I went, but she does not know. I did not tell her because Benedict was not entirely cooperative. He says he has never seen such hardness as Reuben manifests.

He gave me that much, but that is all. I wonder if Benedict rode to see Reuben yet that night. I do not know, but Reuben was not present yesterday for church. There is some satisfaction in that.

The bishop has a hearing problem which makes conversation difficult. I spoke in a loud voice but did not want to yell with others in the cabin. Sometimes he cupped his left ear. Other times he paid no attention. I do not mean to speak ill of a bishop, but I had to repeat the parts about Reuben showing no sorrow and about his story wearing thin in the settlement. When Benedict cautioned me about my anger, I was certain he had paid no attention. *Himmel!* I am not subject to impulsiveness. I do not plunge without thinking on the consequences.

I told the bishop that my own father has counseled Reuben to confess his sin. Benedict said it like a question, "Reuben shows no remorse?" I had just told him that Reuben sticks with his story of not leaving his house the night of the murder, and that he has convinced Anna to nod her head. Then Benedict asked me again, "He shows no sign of softening?" *Himmel!* It was very exasperating, but I stayed calm because the bishop is old. I emphasized that Reuben has defended himself, that he has argued with Father and brought him to tears many a time.

The light in the cabin was dim, only a flickering firelight, but I believe Benedict's face took on a paleness when I said I would not partake in Communion if Reuben were present. Benedict straightened up, cleared his throat, and tapped with his cane. He seemed to be listening, so I added that Reuben was like a patch of thistles stuck in my faith. The bishop harumphed some more and stood up shakily, as if he wanted me to leave. He is a strange one.

I came home to my wife who has turned deaf also. I have

to use my eyes and ears for everyone's benefit. She says I only find fault with Reuben. I ask her what else there is to find with him. She has never troubled herself with thistles. She thinks that if you smile at a thorn imbedded in the flesh, it will work its way out overnight. All she can do is prop the back of her hand on her forehead and repeat her favorite line: "Remove the beam from your own eyes, Yost Hershberger, before you try to take the mote from another's." I tell her it was never meant for a woman to preach. I have also learned it is better not to say all that comes to mind.

Today I needed a brother and Daniel helped me, much more than with manure. How good it is to give and receive aid. I asked him yesterday at Communion if he would come help with the spreading. My muscles peter out much too quickly; my body is mush. All my neighbors have their own to throw. Daniel knows I will return the favor. Sadie and the baby boy came along and have been busy at talk with Eliza all day. How there can be so much to say about someone who has lived less than a month, I cannot figure. Eliza has been like a mother to Sadie. She likes to have someone else to pet, now that Polly is gone. Eliza moans about how far away Sadie's parents live in Mifflin, as if Daniel purposely seeks to cause Sadie suffering.

Early in the cool morning hours Daniel and I worked at emptying the barn of its contents. The waste that came out of the dark corners, thick and packed together, steamed with its richness. I do not mind dealing in muck; it is what gives life. I hardly noticed the smell. After we stopped for dinner and rested on our backs in the tall grass, our knees in the air and legs spread wide, we hitched Ruth to the loaded wagon and commenced spreading manure on a plot that has been worked only one year. I have in mind to try wheat there this summer.

Daniel mentioned that some of his neighbors do not bother with manure; they sprinkle lime and think that will give enough support. Well, lime is of importance—I will add some later—but there is no excuse for not using the natural products God provides. These neighbors of his are German, but not Amish—not even Mennonite—and do not have the same care for the soil. Father always says, "Build the land; it will feed you." Then he shakes his head, "Rob the land; it will stab you." I make certain I am a proper steward.

My shovel and Daniel's fork found their rhythm. He stood on the wagon and pitched leftover straw and manure onto a pile on the ground. Daniel has always had a smaller frame than either Reuben or I, but even he, atop a wagon of dung, looks like he stands above the whole world. I moved the sweetness to the desired spots, spreading it with the right amount of thickness. Father always called it sweetness; then he would grin. Father never liked that word; he said it was a word the English used. But grin is what he did. How yellow and jagged the edges of his few teeth look when he opens his mouth.

My body ached, but I did not want to show it. "Do you remember when we were lads," I asked Daniel, "how Reuben would argue with Father? About where the sheep should graze, or how long they should stay in one spot, even how long their wool should grow before shearing." I paused and looked full at Daniel's youngish face. There is not a line to be found, only a scar above his right eye. He rested his arms on the end of his pitchfork. "You were too young to remember. But Reuben was three years *younger* than I, telling Father how to do. The sad part is—this is odd—often Reuben was right. I do not know where he got the knack. He would say, 'It will rain on the hay tonight.' Father, of course, had his own timetable and had planned to leave the hay in the field another day. Sure enough, it rained." I shook my head and walked away to spread more refuse.

When I returned to the wagon, I noticed that Daniel's pace had slowed. Perhaps we had eaten too much dinner. I felt sluggish. "It is as if Reuben and I were set at odds from the very beginning, rather like the enmity God placed between Cain and Abel," I said. Without further encouragement, Daniel stopped work entirely. He was red in the face and tried to conceal his panting. "The two of us disagreed over land when Father divided some of his farmstead. Eliza tried to get me to seek land at more of a distance—like you did later—rather than stay here where my farmland touches Reuben's. I needed to be near to Father with Mother gone so young. I took what Father gave. I treasured it."

Perhaps the cherry bounce had slowed us down. Daniel's lack of vigor and my own loss of stamina combined to provide opportunity. I have been waiting to talk with him about Reuben's powwowing. I motioned that we should sit down. Father was not there to see.

I guessed correctly; Daniel had no notion of the extent of Reuben's dabbling. I started with how Reuben sometimes got Father to follow advice such as: "Tie a woolen string around your finger for nosebleed," or "Carry burdock leaves in the crown of your hat so you will not suffer sunstroke." Father always allowed Reuben to have too much sway.

"Those are Reuben's notions?" Daniel asked. He rolled onto his side and propped his head in his hand.

"Without a doubt. Do you know about Reuben's elaborate cure for Aunt Mary's epilepsy?" I asked. Daniel nodded, but I doubted that he had heard it all. "This happened after Aunt Barbli was dead and gone. It was something along the lines . . . . Do you remember Aunt Barbli?" Daniel shook his head. "I thought not. Aunt Mary was to cut off all her nails—hands and feet—and wrap all the nails in a bag. Then she was to put the bag in a hole bored in a cherry tree. Can you see Aunt Mary doing that?" Daniel's body shook with revulsion. "Reuben also insisted that Aunt Mary should drink milk from a young sow that had just had its first litter." At that Daniel turned his head, placed a finger on his nose, and shot snot into the ground.

I sat upright, my stiff legs crossed under me. "Aunt Mary did not want to go along with the nails folderol. I listened to them argue, and I held my breath. Reuben insisted that the plan was from Aunt Barbli and that it would work." I slapped my knees with both hands. "He always knew that. Always said his big ideas would work."

I took off my hat and wiped my forehead with my arm. "Aunt Mary kept her head—for once, a woman showed some sense—and told Reuben, 'Be off with you. Go spend your time at something more worth your while than telling tales to an old woman.'" I fanned myself with my hat and leaned forward. "Now here, listen to this. Reuben's eyes stared hard at Aunt Mary—you know how he does—and his lips squeezed up tight like he wanted to spit. I wanted to laugh outright. Then Reuben walked away." I rocked back on my rear end, my hands on my knees.

"He is a big talker," Daniel said. "Sadie has always been afraid of him."

"I suppose he thinks to this day that he had the last word. Two months later when Aunt Mary lay dead, he walked past her coffin with the rest of us. I know what he was thinking. He might as well have said what was all over his face: 'I told you what to do and you would not listen.'" Daniel smiled at my imitation of Reuben's voice. Reuben's build is large, but his voice is soft and rather ladylike. "That is the way Reuben is, always thinking he knows more than anybody else."

Daniel grunted in agreement. Now it was his turn to sit up, his legs stretched out straight, his hands propped behind him. "What happened that time with Lizzie and her livergrown? I always wanted to know. When we take Simon Peter out, even coming here today, I wonder on it."

I nodded. "Some people say that children get livergrown from riding outside at an early age, but I think it more likely in a child of three or four, not in one so young as your Simon Peter. What happened with Lizzie last summer shows how Reuben works his evil. Eliza, of course, insisted that Lizzie was more peaceful after Reuben touched her. She can justify anything."

I noticed a bank of gray clouds moving in from the west. I knew we were foolish to risk getting rained on. I could hear Father's words, "Work first; talk later." But I might not have another opportunity with Daniel. We would soon be consumed with planting and tending our crops. I drank some more cherry bounce and settled on my back. "This may take a while," I warned.

"I have been wanting to know," Daniel repeated.

"Lizzie developed a fever, could not even take a deep breath. When she drew in her chest of a sudden, she cried out. Said she felt pain, a tightness. That is the best I know how to describe it; with a child it is not always clear what is meant. I paid the matter little heed; it was but a natural part of her growing. Eliza, of course, was overly concerned and chanced to make mention of it one time when Reuben and Anna were visiting. Reuben paid great interest."

"Of course," Daniel said.

"Of course. Reuben put all sorts of questions to both Lizzie and Eliza. I tried to put the matter to rest. I said rather sharply—I will admit—'Eliza, this is nothing but womanly fears. Stifle yourself.' Or some such. A firm reprimand can never hurt. It may not help, but it does not hurt."

Daniel laughed and had another swig. The rain clouds had stalled.

"Eliza would not be quiet. Have you ever tried telling a cow not to moo?" Daniel laughed again. "Reuben's encouragement seemed to feed her fears. She rattled on about how she had heard that if the afflicted child went around a table leg in a certain way, that when the child came out from the table, he would be cured. Of course Reuben nodded gravely at that. As if that were not enough rubbish, she said she had heard of a powwower taking a baby—much younger than Lizzie—taking the baby to each corner of the room and shaking him at each spot, going purposely from east to west. Something about the sun rising and setting." I tossed my hands aimlessly in the air. "She tried to sound as if she knew, and Reuben sat there, nodding his head as if Eliza proclaimed great wisdom. He is a wily one."

Daniel nodded again. "Of course."

I sat up; the back of my shirt felt wet from the earth's dampness. "It made me want to ask her why *she* was not a powwower. But I held my tongue." I scooted closer to Daniel, just as I had done with Eliza, and I repeated the very same words I had said in front of Reuben, "'This is all foolishness.' That is what I said. 'Feeble attempts of an addled mind to meddle with what should be left to God. God gives life and health. Man is but the vessel.' Or some such."

I lowered my voice, for Daniel shrank back slightly. "I tell you, be careful with your Sadie. These womenfolks get ideas—they mean well—and they talk among themselves. First thing you know, they stir each other up and think they have the problem solved. Reuben would make a devout woman!"

"Indeed," Daniel said.

"He sat there that day, agreeing with Eliza's every word. I wanted to puke."

"What happened with the powwowing?" Daniel asked.

"I will get there. I thought I could put an end to Reuben's foolishness. I announced that I was going out to feed the animals. Normally you would expect a brother to give a hand. Is that not right?" I wondered if Daniel thought less of me that we had stopped work for such a long break, but he showed no signs of unease at our extended rest. "No, not Reuben. He chose to stay in the house. When he did not get up to follow me, I shrugged and went about my tasks. I put out more hay for the sheep; I carried water from the spring. The usual. All of a sudden, the realization came to me: my firstborn was being molested."

The cloud above us had turned darker. I would need to hurry through the rest of the story. "I tell you, Daniel, it was as clear as when an animal is in difficulty. I can be abed at night and suddenly sit straight up, knowing that my horse is having trouble with the birth. Perhaps bleeding to death. It came to me with that certainty." I snapped my fingers. "I walked fast, carrying two heavy buckets." I banged my fist into my other hand. Daniel's eyes opened wider. "Just like that; I knew. I quickened my pace, continued fast to the stable, set the buckets down hard." I banged my fist again. "The water slopped over, and I ran to the cabin."

Daniel's eyes had darkened. The scar above his eye looked redder.

"I was right. There lay Lizzie with her garment pulled down. Reuben was pressing and stroking with his thumbs just under her ribs. Eliza and the others were gathered about as though they watched agog at the manger. I yelled as soon as I took in the scene, 'Stop that, Reuben. Get your hands off my child!' I rushed at him and would have torn Lizzie away had he not released her on the table. Can you blame me, Daniel? I was nearly beside myself. The others stood there gaping, as if what Reuben did was perfectly natural."

"You had a right to be upset. It would be bad enough with my Simon Peter, but with Lizzie . . . ." He shuddered.

I drank more from the jug and handed it to Daniel, swirling my last swallow. "Finish it," I said. "Reuben gathered his family and wasted no time in leaving. I will say this much for him; he did not argue. I demanded of Eliza to know how she could stand by and allow such debauchery. Guess what happened." Daniel's eyebrows raised with expectation. "She became overwrought with her squalling. Women lose countless hours when they could just as well be working. When she finally spoke she made claim that it had all happened with such innocence. She was taken aback when she thought on her own involvement. Reuben had instructed Lizzie to move about the table leg in a prescribed manner. Three times forward and three times back, or some such tomfoolery. Then Eliza reported that Reuben suggested this other cure. I had no idea that Lizzie's fussing had become such a burden to Eliza."

I looked overhead and saw that the clouds were breaking up; a few patches of light blue showed through. But I would likely need to finish spreading the dung by myself tomorrow.

"Of course, Eliza had to boohoo all over again before she could explain further. How Reuben had asked her to loosen Lizzie's garment and pull it down to the waist. How she had laid Lizzie on the table and Reuben went with his hands, three times over those tiny ribs, one way, and then another, and still another. That must have been the exact time I returned to the cabin. Who is to say what else Reuben might have done, had I not smelled mischief."

"We must bring punishment," Daniel said, interrupting. "A brother who would do that to an innocent child—." He shook his head.

"Why Lizzie did not scream when Reuben touched her, I cannot figure. Eliza insists that Lizzie remained calm throughout, even seemed soothed. Horse manure!"

Daniel grabbed his fork, as if he had read my thoughts about needing to finish alone. He said again, "We must bring punishment."

I stood and stretched. "I spared no words, reminding Eliza that wolves may appear in sheep's clothing. I warned her: 'Be vigilant.'" Now my muscles ached even more after the long rest. I shook my right leg to loosen it. "She seemed chastened. But with the events of last month, she takes more responsibility for Marie's death than is proper. I remind her, it was I who asked her and Polly to assist me with the tapping. She piles grief much too high on her own shoulders. She sags. Have you noticed?"

Daniel looked as if he did not want to answer. He walked away, carrying a forkful.

"She used to hold her head up," I said, raising my voice so he could hear. "Not as one proud, but tall and erect. I have never laid blame on her for Marie's death. But you know how it is."

"Yes, I know whereof you speak." Daniel returned to the wagon. "Sadie sometimes puts all reason in a basket and sets it outside the door. How can it do her any good out there?" He shook his head and turning, cleared his throat and spat. "This livergrown and Reuben's powwowing make everything clear. Do you suppose Reuben's last action with Marie was the fruit of his anger? At you? His anger simmering? What has it been, eight months? Now he is even more dangerous. Who can know what all he intends!" Daniel had worked himself into a dither, as if he understood fully for the first time.

"You know how Father says: 'The stronger the man, the stronger the anger.' Neither of us can deny the power in Reuben's arms."

"Have you told Father the full truth of this livergrown episode?" Daniel asked.

"No, I wanted to spare Father. He has suffered enough. Much too much. All these years he has seen enough from Reuben to reach his own conclusions without my putting more grief at his door."

"Father is too quick to blame himself. He can worry almost like Sadie. Already with our Simon Peter, she asks, 'What will he become? Will he keep the faith. Or stray in a ditch?' I scold her for fretting too much. We can but plant the seeds and hope they take root."

I nodded in agreement but did not want to encourage Daniel. He gets sidetracked easily with talk of the boy. I gave direction on where to distribute more refuse, sending us to bare spots at opposite points.

We talked little more about Reuben, although Daniel commented on how it is a wonder that Reuben's Bevy and Jacobli appear unscathed. "They live in the shadow of this man and eat the food of his provision, yet they are pleasant and smiling." He shook his head grimly. Then he added with a sternness that reminded me of Father, "I am with you, Yost. We must pursue and bring punishment. It is necessary."

I reached to shake his hand; the scar above his right eye stood out aflame. How well the two of us had worked in harmony.

That night as Eliza and I readied for bed, I made comment on how good it was to have a brother I could trust. I went on at length about my debt to each cow and horse. I described the fresh stand of wheat that was sure to follow. How good it was to toil in God's good earth. Eliza smiled from her gray eyes and said, "How pleasant to hear something agreeable from your lips after this month of vinegar. Is there yet hope for our family?"

I could not hold back a little softness, "Yes, we will be a house of contentment in spite of this black spot. We will not let one spoiled branch destroy the whole tree." I drew Eliza to me, rubbed my chapped hands up and down her long back, felt the dip in her spine, felt her slight roundedness. She nestled into my chest and melted. "But I still need a son," I said. "And then another."

13.
$\mathcal{R}$ EUBEN
April 1810

Yes, it is true, the bishop came to our house Saturday night. Anna and I had put in a hard day's work. Hard in a good way, for the labor was full of satisfaction. Anna works steadily, even at what could be considered a man's work. She is built solid, rather thick at the waist, and is not afraid to bend and grunt. She puts on her dark blue kerchief and shows no fear at what may scurry from underneath a rock. I am more prone to yelp at a snake than she.

There is a patch of my land far from the creek that has yielded more than its share of rockiness. Every spring a fresh crop shows up. I planned that this patch could be an extra plot of corn this year. But before I could push a plow through the ground, I knew we would have to remove the biggest obstacles by hand.

The sun shone on us all day, yet never felt hot. A warbler sang as if announcing new babies, and the black crows called to each other off in the woods. The day manifested the freshness of spring—my favorite time of year—with all of nature waking around us for another growing season. Lavender and white violets bloomed in their dark green clumps and made us forget the questions that have been put at our feet this past month. Jacobli and Bevy ran and bounced, helping remove small stones, exploring rustling sounds in the dry leaves. At the end of the day we looked on our labor, a newly cleared acreage and a supply of large rocks for fence building, and knew that it was good. It is not the Garden of Eden by any measure, but we have brought improvement. Even our supper tasted better, although the venison is getting old and the potatoes look shriveled. The food brought contentment because of the gladness in our tired muscles.

Late at night the questions returned with redoubled fury. We had relaxed too much. Anna had put the children to bed early because of their exhaustion from the fresh air. We had taken extra care to clean ourselves for Communion the next day. I had shortened Anna's toenails with my pocketknife, and she was much relieved. One nail had begun to curl sideways. Tomorrow's footwashing is not for display, but the women are more prone to inspect than the men. Out of this tranquil state we were alarmed to hear noises outside and then a rapping at the door. No one comes late at night unless there is trouble: a fire or serious illness.

With trepidation I lifted the latch and found Bishop Blauch. I knew at once, he came for me. I helped him tie his horse more securely—he stepped slowly with a cane—and then invited him in. We asked about news from the Glades district and told about our day's labor. I wished in vain that he brought word of a death in one of Anna's relations living in the Brothers Valley. Slowly, he arrived at his business. "I suppose you are aware, Reuben, of the suspicion that centers on you with regard to the death of the Hershberger baby."

"It would be hard for me to be unaware," I replied. The visit proceeded as I feared. I was defenseless, but Anna was by my side.

"And you are fully apprised of the gravity of this charge, that you are the one responsible for the death of this child?" The bishop slowly stroked his white beard. I had never noticed before how much he looked like my father. The white hair, the steady gaze, the shakiness.

I tried to match his ponderous tone. "I know that some seek to put the blame on me. But I will tell you in all truthfulness, I had nothing to do with the death of Marie Hershberger. I have said that to all who ask. You can ask my Anna to confirm what I say."

The bishop squinted at Anna, as if she were far away, "What do you have to say on this matter?"

Anna had kept her head bowed while I answered the bishop, but now she lifted her head and spoke more rapidly than is her custom. "Benedict, you are a man of honor among our people. You must also preserve the honor of my husband, a hard-working, honest, God-fearing man." She inched her body to the front of her chair. "I tell you, on that Sunday in question, we did not leave our house except for Reuben tending the animals."

Bevy called out in her sleep. Anna paused and then continued. I doubt that the bishop heard the child. "Our Jacobli was not well that day; he felt feverish and had spots all over his chest and stomach. We did not venture to visit the neighbors, nor did anyone come to our door." She looked to the back bed as Bevy cried out again. "That evening Reuben did the chores while it was yet light and then came into the house for the rest of the night.

"Believe me," she went on, rubbing her thumb and finger up and down the thick folds of her dress. "I am a light sleeper, and I sometimes wake because of stirrings about the house. I have heard claws scratching and teeth gnawing outside on these logs. Even mice running across the floorboards will waken me. If Reuben had roused from our bed and left the house, I would know. I say without hesitation: Reuben did not leave my side that night." She sat back as if she had finished a planned speech. She has had practice enough.

"You are a woman of integrity, and you do well to stand by your husband," the bishop said. He reached a thumb inside his shirt at the neck and scratched. "As others say, however, the evidence points in Reuben's direction."

"Evidence! What evidence?" I said, interrupting. "There is not evidence against me. There is only the blind dislike of some in my family." I stopped, for Anna had pushed her chair closer, scraping on the uneven floor, and had reached for my hand.

The bishop continued, shifting his cane, a stick of hickory smoothed and rounded at the top, to his other hand, "Reuben, I am sorry to say that others convey a different story." He paused as if to recall the counts against me. "It is said that you have a quarrelsome spirit. That you have argued with your father." He pointed his cane at me. "That you have spoken insults on your blessed, deceased mother. This unruly tongue of yours is a sign." Now the cane made a sweeping arc and banged on the floor. "You must allow the Spirit of God to take control so that you may do good rather than evil to your fellow man. Do you not recognize that Satan holds dominion, holds sway over your soul? You must cast out the Evil One."

"No!" I said sharply. Anna squeezed my hand and held it tight. I remembered that I was talking with the bishop. My answers were part of my trial. I lowered my head momentarily as Anna had bowed hers. I reached for a more contrite tone. For the first time I doubted that I could satisfy the bishop. "I am not an evil person. Satan does not have hold of my soul. I do not mean that I am perfect or without sin. I slip, as do most of us who attempt to follow." My mouth felt dry and I licked

my lips, swiping at the hairs in my beard. "I do not mean dis-
respect, but I am no worse a sinner than anyone else in my
family." I knew I should stop, but I added, "I will not let them
dare to pretend otherwise." Anna squeezed harder.

I glanced at her, but her head stayed down and off to the
side. How am I to hear false charges and not seek to set the
record straight? If my neighbor says two horses plus two horses make five horses, I will correct him. Why should he go
through life thinking he has five horses when in truth he has
only four? Yet in this Marie case, some people have a brick,
not a mote, in their eyes. They have blinders pulled halfway
down. They see what they want to see.

The bishop remained silent as if he were waiting for me to
condemn myself further. I considered using the example of
the horses, but Anna held my hand tight. Benedict reached
under his beard and pulled on his Adam's apple. His hand
shook as he stared at the ceiling. Finally he asked if I had anything to confess. I must say in his defense, he never manifested any hatefulness or spite toward me in his questioning. I
said that I had done nothing that warranted confession.

Benedict cleared his throat and, dissatisfied with the result,
stood shakily, then walked to the fire to spit. He turned, leaning on his cane, and said, "It is with great sorrow then, that I
will have to recommend that you not partake of Communion
tomorrow. As the Scripture says, 'Anyone who eateth or drinketh unworthily, eateth and drinketh damnation to himself.'"

My eyes became blurred. Anna's hand began to tremble in
mine. "You believe the words of these others?" I asked. I did not
speak very loudly. I may have mumbled. "You do not believe
what Anna and I have said?" I do not know if the bishop heard.

"Scripture says, 'For if we would judge ourselves, we should
not be judged.'" The bishop spoke softly also, bent over his
cane as if his words were a burden.

"What do you want me to do?" I said more loudly again. "Confess to something I did not do? So I will not be judged by others?"

"It is found already in the Old Testament, '. . . a broken and a contrite heart, O God, thou wilt not despise.'" Now the bishop leaned against the chair for support, his cane idle. "Everyone coming to the Communion table must be properly prepared. We must keep the church pure, for we are the body of Christ."

"Yost has snagged your ear," I said. I will admit to bitterness.

"It does not matter who first reports the offense; an offense must be dealt with. An offense against one becomes an offense against the whole church. We are a brotherhood."

"Brothers," I said. What a bitter taste. Anna did not squeeze my hand. She had put her head in both of her hands. She rocked back and forth.

Bishop Blauch sat down again. I wanted him to leave. His hat lay on the table where he came in. He kept talking. I heard little. "All of us at the ministers' conference last year determined that we must confront laxness among our people. I am sorry that in your case this may seem an unjust strictness that has not been meted in the recent past." My eyes followed the pattern in the floorboards. They looked like steps of an uneven depth leading down, down. "We must not be found wanting in the matter of discipline. It is my prayer." No, there was no pattern. Only random boards that I had leveled as best I could. Over there, the spot where Jacobli often tripped in his hurry. "It is my prayer that you will one day soon understand that this setting back from Communion is a necessary step. That it will help you see the error of your ways."

I looked at the bishop dumbly. There are insects that eat at and destroy wood but are not visible to the eye. I have seen their work in many a felled tree. There are serpents that slither quietly in the grass. The bishop sighed heavily and waited. He cleared his throat. When he saw that nothing more would be forthcoming from me, he took his departure. Anna must have seen him to the door and held the light for him to find his horse; I have no recollection. I did not stir.

Anna sat again beside me, alone with her thoughts. Finally I broke the silence. "We will go to that church as usual tomorrow. No one from outside will tell me what lies within."

"No, Reuben, no, no," Anna said. "We dare not go. We cannot fight fire with fire. That will but fan the blaze."

"If we stay away, that confirms my guilt." I said the words dully. "That says I am not worthy."

We went back and forth. I said, "I will not let any man rob me of my peace with God."

She said, "We are already robbed and left to bleed by the side of the road." She ran her hand over my leather breeches. She gets stronger when we have a dispute. I get weaker. She tried to get me to look directly in her eyes. She said, "We must pray that God will intervene. Pray that people will see the light. That some evidence will come to pass, revealing the true circumstances by which this death has occurred."

"Pray?" I could not keep back my scorn. "Pray to a God who allows this injustice? Pray tell! Why? Tell me why!"

"Oh, Reuben, do not lose heart," Anna pleaded. "Something will surely happen to shed light so that your name may be cleared."

"Surely. Surely. Do you know how often I have said *surely* in the past weeks? It is not just *my* name they seek to drag in the dirt. If they will not believe me, that means they do not believe you. Do you think I will let them besmirch the Livengood name?"

"I know, Reuben." She sat back, subdued. "It is not an easy burden. Perhaps my family has been too full of pride. I would not want word of this to travel to my parents. But I suppose they will hear of it."

"They will hear of it, never fear for that. Living in Bishop Blauch's district? Where Polly Berkey has returned home? Yes, your parents will hear of it."

"I know that Polly first pointed at you, but her word alone would have amounted to a molehill. Yost is the one who built suspicion into this mountain. All because of enmity."

I was surprised that Anna expressed such accusation against Yost. She has always minimized our disputes. "That is true, Anna. But remember, we are a *brotherhood*." I pounced on the word. Spit came from my mouth. I waited for her reprimand. When it did not come, I added, "Yost seeks to bring me low. He uses the church as his scythe." Then later, "My father has deserted me."

We sat a long while, some of the time in silence, some of the time speaking. We went to bed without coming to agreement on what course of action to take the next day. Whichever step we took, we would be at odds with Bishop Blauch and the church. I tossed from my side, to flat on my back, to the other side. In the tossing I know that Anna did not sleep either. I never lie on my stomach, but last night I even tried that. Where is my father? I know where he is, of course. On the other side. I have lost him. I tried for a month not to believe it. Now I know.

Ignoring our sleepless night, the sun rose as usual. I stumbled out to the animals and went through the motions of feeding. When I came to the horses, I made no effort to brush or make ready for travel. They seemed puzzled, stamping the ground, as if they keep track of church meeting Sundays. When I returned to the house, Anna had on her everyday, work dress. She fixed the usual buckwheat cakes. Bevy, who had heard us talk of Communion the day before, asked if we were not going to make ready for church.

"No," I said. "Some people do not want us." I hesitated, thinking whether to add to her nightmares.

Anna said quietly, "Enough, Reuben."

That is all that was said about the matter. The children played more quietly than usual, except for their spats over the wooden blocks. Neither Anna nor I did work other than the necessary meal preparation and care for the animals. Few words were spoken. Such a contrast from the previous day when smiles and laughter and satisfaction prevailed. Now I wonder if I want to plant corn on that newly-cleared plot. Yost may have spread rocks again during the night.

After the children were in bed, I got out the whiskey jug and drank more than my fill, something I had not done since a few occasions in my youth. Anna would not partake at all. "Pray!" she says. "Some evidence will come to pass." I need her positive spirit, but I do not believe her. She makes things up. I fear for the future. I fear for Bevy and Jacobli; they will grow up tainted. I see no good coming for any of us, even though the days wake from their cold grip.

14.

ℰ L I Z A

May 1810

The tea is at last running its course with my body. This past month has left a heaviness, and my body has manifested all manner of thickness and disease. First there was the fullness of milk with no baby to drink thereof. Momma had warned me; still I was not prepared. The swelling presented such pain in those first weeks, I thought I would burst. There came so much fullness that I had to remove some of my own into a cup. I did not want to waste it, so the next morning I put it out for the lambs. Here is a bad secret. On two occasions I encouraged Susanna to suck. But I was tender from disuse and Susanna's teeth had too much of the bite; I pulled away sharply. I worried that Polly and Lizzie might return from fetching water and find us in our unnaturalness. I did not want Susanna to start a second reliance when she has been weaned already most of a year. There was no wisdom in it. Now I am relieved to say the problem has passed and I am more of a normal size. I believe I carry more of the sag though, like that of an older woman. I am only twenty-two years.

The dizziness, a whirling and twirling, came with stomach upset and a persistent pain in the head, as if I had too much blood in me from eating meat all winter. My head would go round and round. I have eaten large amounts of dandelion and watercress mixed with plantain to make my blood thinner. A small taste of tea with each meal also purifies my blood. I asked Yost to find me some roots of sarsaparilla and burdock to go with the sassafras that Sadie had brought. These three boiled together in water over a slow fire give me a measure of my strength back. Yost's answer to thick blood is to put Devil's bit in his whiskey, but that would only make my head go round the more.

The tea has helped my cough as well. It is less bothersome at night, which is a relief to us all. I am ashamed to be wracked by so many maladies. This is the time of year when Yost needs help with planting. But I have been faint under my hat, so much so that I had to come into the house early. I wonder if I may be carrying another one already. At first I thought my nerves had stopped my flow, but now I think otherwise. My weakness still overcomes me at times, and Lizzie asks about my crying. I do not want to make her anxious, but I cannot seem to control when the downpour comes or how long it lasts.

I cannot explain the sadness that surrounds me. My tears sit right under the surface, pushing out of my throat and spilling down from my eyes. It is not only Marie for whom I weep. When Yost found that some corn seed had gotten damp and taken on a moldiness, I sat myself down and cried as if we would have no crops. "Woman, gird yourself," he said. Everything seems heavy: the air in mid-morning, the hair on my head. I cry and cry, but the tears will not take their leave. Yost sought to comfort me with his strong arms about me. I do not want to be a botheration.

Yost has finally come out from his foul humor that followed Marie's death. The creases of his fingers have filled again with soil and grime. Now his steadfastness is bent on pursuing Reuben's punishment. Yost likens his resolve to guiding a team when digging a furrow. He says that he must fix his gaze on the end of the row and dare not look to either side.

When I try to speak with him, he leans his chair back on its hind legs and clasps his hands behind his head. He smiles, but it is not a smile that I like. Then he squints his eyes and says, "That is what you think, is it, Woman?" When I motion to pay heed to the floor, that the chair may slip out from underneath, he but laughs at my worries. I try to caution him that Reuben is still a brother, and we should not rush to judgment. I draw on my courage to remind him that if he loves not his brother whom he *hath* seen, how can he love God whom he hath *not* seen. Yost looks on me as from a great height and says, "It is not a matter of loving; it is a matter of doing what is right. Do you not care that Evil be punished?"

I do not know what to say. Of course, I believe we all face a reckoning day. But I am not as sure as he that we are the ones to balance the scales. What if we are in error? What if Evil manifests a false outward show? Yost and I do not remember those awful March events in the same way. Yet his mind is quite made up as to how everything happened. He resided with his thoughts for a month, and now there is no turning him aside. "Polly heard the sound of knuckles on the window," he says. I am not so sure. I do not know what she heard. Then he says, "Woman, you cannot both cry and remember. Decide which it will be." Yost will not be satisfied that justice is done until Reuben is excommunicated—how I dislike that word—unless, of course, Reuben confesses. I do not expect the latter; two months have passed already. If Reuben were to confess, I have a notion that Yost might be sorely disappointed. That is not fair on my part. Yost but wants to know what happened.

I wish that we had our own bishop here in the River congregation. Isaac Joder does well in bringing the Word, but he is young and still learning how to tend the flock. This grievance between brothers must sit heavily with him.

I think especially of Reuben's Anna. No one says that her hand was in the fire; yet she must stay away from Communion also. Yost shrugs and says, "That is Reuben for you." Even if a righting of wrongs comes from this exile, it is a sad day when we have empty places on the church bench.

If our settlement grows, then we can one day have our own bishop to pay closer heed and give oversight. For Bishop Blauch to travel these miles from his home district is no trifling matter. He is not a young gander anymore, and he cannot be in close contact with any of the aggrieved parties. He does the best he can, but it must be a fearsome burden.

The last time he came, he brought word from my family. They are all well and Polly finds work with a Hochstedler family—Benedict says that these ones seek to maintain the old *d* sound—where they have a new baby. In spite of the old folks passing on to their reward and the young ones being snatched, the Lord still blesses us with new breath. Polly, poor Polly Anna. So young for such a fright. I wonder how it goes with her. And with Momma. I wonder if she still rubs at her face.

I look to my Lizzie and Susanna and pray that their lives will be easier than mine. Now that Yost has come out of his den of silence, the girls are more relaxed and seem more like of old. It is a blessing for which I cannot give too much thanks. Nellie, the old mare, has taken a gentle turn and Yost gives the girls rides after supper if there is still daylight. He claims there is room for me to sit astride too, but I prefer to watch. Lizzie rides in front, holding the reins as if it were all up to her, and Susanna sits in the crook of Yost's arm and raises her tiny hand like a flag.

I long for the summer's heat so that I can turn from my weeping and find a permanent end to this cough. We will all be the better in the bright sun, even with this mountain still at our back.

15.

$\mathcal{J}$ O N A S

May 1810

$\mathcal{J}$f this were not the Lord's Day, I would be sorely tempted to say it is mine. That is too prideful. I will say instead: this day gave me great encouragement out of my very despondency. The last time we had our church meeting I took sick and had to excuse myself from Communion. I was not at all certain that I wanted to go this morning; I could almost taste vomit again. Many a day I have gone through the motions of farm work without spirit. The trees have greened, but I carried winter inside me. In spite of my doldrums, I could not bring myself to stay home from church. Mother would have made comment.

We went to the Tobias Stutzman homestead for our services. Not the Stutzmans who had the girls with the big teeth. This one, the wife is a sister to Bishop Benedict Blauch. Tobias' farm sits on a knoll and looks down on the river. If I ever own my own farmstead, that is the way I want it to be: a farmhouse big enough for church meeting, green grass, shade trees for the cows. Huge rocks surround two corners of Tobias' house; then the land slopes off into a flat acreage. His corn has a better start than Father's.

The day began as any other Sabbath with Father leading the first hymn while the ministers were in their meeting. When they emerged and took their seats among us, Father announced the usual *"Loblied."* Then it was that he half-turned on his bench, looked back past several rows of brethren, and fastened on me. I stared in return, surprised at the attention, and then realized he had nodded. That was the signal I had seen him give to others when they were to lead out in lining the hymn.

My first impulse was to slump at the shoulders and seek a place to hide. But Levi's elbow poked my side. I straightened my back and pulled my outstretched feet from under the bench ahead of me. I looked again to make certain I had not tricked myself. Father's gaze wavered not, focusing on me. My voice seemed to come high from the ceiling beams:

O God, our Father, Thee we praise.

It frightened me to think of others listening to such weak sounds coming from my lips. The entire section of women turned as one long, extended neck with one white covering, looking my way. I felt naked, stripped, as if all my body parts hovered with my voice, trembling for all to see. I locked my fingers at the knuckles while the congregation repeated my words.

I wanted to stop, but I could not. The second line came jiggling from my throat:

And laud Thy gracious blessings.

I had to gulp air before I could sing the word *gracious* and again before *blessings*. No one intervened to give help. The brothers and sisters waited till I was through, then followed.

Later, I tried to recall if there had been snickering, but I had no memory. I continued in my halting manner through the first stanza. The bench stayed put beneath me; the floor did not rise to greet my nose. I continued with the entire eight verses before the hymn reached its conclusion. There was a place in the third stanza where I lost myself for a brief time. I took a hasty turn up two steps, when I should have held the note longer. But Father's voice came through and soon had me back on the path.

I regret my initial trembling and the misstep that all could hear, but overall I was satisfied that I managed as I did. I suppose I always knew that if I were ever asked to be the *Vorsinger*, it would first be with the *"Loblied."* We sing that at every church meeting and everyone knows it. Still, it is a departure for someone who is unmarried to be asked to lead out. Levi slapped me on the back afterwards, and the other young men gathered around. I wished I could think of something clever to say, but I am no good with the jokes. I must be cautious and not expect too much. Father may have chosen me more as a respite for himself rather than as a compliment. There are few he can call on; too many of the men have the drone.

Whatever his motive, Father carried a smile today. I took that to mean he was well-satisfied. Franey begged to sit on my lap as we rode home, and I obliged. She and I sang some of the same hymns again in spite of the wagon's bounces over ruts. Franey has a bright, clear voice for one so little. It is too bad she is not a boy. David had to remind me that he is taller by three inches, but Rachel looked on me with more regard. Mother has not thought to criticize yet. Perhaps I will show her that Abraham and John are not the only ones of worth.

How I want Father to call on me again. I will show him when we milk the cows that the tunes come with ease. I need to pay closer heed to some of the words, especially in the later verses. Already I find myself looking ahead to next month when we will gather for church. Mother might not find that an acceptable reason for desiring to meet, but it gives me a forward look.

• • •

Life has its stumblings, large and small. Whenever I strain with too much eagerness, the unexpected intervenes and throws me off my horse. This has to be a large stumble variety. Mother has passed on. It came with such swiftness that none of us can fully take stock.

There I was at the beginning of the week, dwelling on how I might redeem myself as *Vorsinger*, thinking on how long I had to wait until we had church services again. Six days later our congregation has assembled unexpectedly. Mother is gone. Of all the things I had lain awake over, this was not one of them. I should learn to expect what is beyond possibility. My legs shake again, and I do not know what to say when people offer comfort. I do not care to look at any of them. I feel on display and can see only one advantage. When I am suddenly given to tears, no one can think it strange. The funeral was the hardest.

Mother had not been ill, at least not that any of us knew. Father says that on Tuesday she complained of a dull, dizzy feeling. That is all. No warning. The next morning she had barely been up and about when she collapsed by the fireplace. Rachel heard Mother fall and came running to get us men from the barn. Mother could still talk, but her right arm and leg had gone lame. Father bid me help him carry her—he, grunting at her head and shoulders, I at her feet—placing her on their bed. She is a heavy one. The whole side of her body was paralyzed. Apoplexy, Father called it. He sent David to fetch John. "Quick; tell him to bring nettle."

I stayed home with Father but spent most of my time with Franey, redirecting her attention from what might be transpiring at Mother's bed. Rachel would not stray from Mother's side; she clutched and squeezed Mother's hand as if forcing warmth into her. Franey and I went outside, heading toward the creek where mushrooms sometimes appear. Mother always fixed them with pork. Neither of us could stay away long; we both had our minds within the house.

By the time David and John arrived with the nettle, Mother no longer gave response. John struck with the plants along the right side of her body, but all was still except for an occasional jerking. I thought of mentioning Reuben Hershberger's name to Father, but I decided he did not need my nudge. Mother gave no response for several more hours; before darkness fell her breath was entirely snuffed out.

All that night and the next day we notified family and greeted people as they gathered at our house. Everyone from church paid their respects, some speaking at length about Mother's noble spirit. "She gave no thought to herself" is what many said. I must have been sadly wrong. It brings comfort to have all our kin in flesh and spirit come together, but our house became too crowded. With so many people milling about, Franey seemed to cling to me, even when the aunts—especially two of Mother's sisters—gave attention to her needs. I was as glad for Franey's clutch as she for my sleeve. Franey could not sit still long; we excused ourselves and went outside to see if the buds on the May apples had opened. We wandered to the creek again; the bed shows drought, for we have not had rain.

Everyone in the Hershberger family came as well. I do not know how they managed separate times, but Yost and Eliza came already in the morning, and Reuben with Anna did not appear until late afternoon. Father mentioned—and I thought the same—that Reuben had a wildness about him. His hair seemed helter-skelter; his frock coat was awry in the back. He shook my hand, but his felt limp. He came out of obligation, I suppose. I did not look at him directly. My head was down in sorrow, and I had the notion that his head was off to the side. He seemed a small spirit in a large body, almost a ghost of a man. I do not like to think about him. My insides churn again. Everywhere he goes, people talk. Anna looked dark at the eyes and shrunken. They did not stand around to make conversation but were soon gone.

It was equally unpleasant, earlier in the day, to see Yost walk about with a sneer. He has no right to feel mighty. Yet I cannot criticize. I am torn. I believe Yost would make a worse brother than Abraham, for he pushes his will with too much force. I did not care to look on Eliza either. Everyone wears black clothes, but hers are blacker. Black, black, black. She looked with pity on me. She reminds me of Polly and all that might have been. Already it seems a long time ago that I had that ache. I have not found any replacement.

The funeral was the hardest part; my jaws still hurt from holding with so much tightness. We went back to the Stutzman's farm where I thought all had been beautiful on Sunday. The door hinges kept creaking, letting more people in. I thought I would suffocate. My head sank lower and lower on my chest until I remembered again to straighten. John had a part in the service, reading Scripture and making appropriate comments. "Mother would have wanted it," he said. Abraham declined an active part. That is one thing to be grateful for: I did not have to hear his voice. I believe he feared he might break down. One of the brethren from the Glades' congregation was visiting in our district, so he was the *Vorsinger* in Father's place. On many hymns I could not give voice at all, and I noticed the same for Father.

I wanted to conduct myself in a manner befitting a grown man. Franey's small hand in mine helped build me up; she would not separate herself, except for the church service. As we sat through the short sermon and then the long one, it was hard not to think on how things might have been between Mother and me. I should not have taken offense with her so easily. I should have sought forgiveness when I manifested my selfish spirit. Why could I not see this before? I used to think that since Mother was older, the righting of wrongs fell to her. But now she is gone—David takes her spot at the table—and I am left tending my thoughts.

For her tender age Franey has adjusted well. She sheds her tears but does not mope about the place. Rachel is the one on whom death has descended like an affliction. She sits and stares at nothing, scratches at her food like a chicken. The aunts wanted Franey to go with one of them after the funeral, but she made clear to Father that she wanted to stay here. I find satisfaction in her reliance on me. She does not say much, but then, neither do I. I would not want to go with those aunts who prattle all the time. They seem to think if they do not keep their mouths moving, someone will take them for dead.

"Oh, but Franey," Aunt Martha said, "come live with me a few weeks. I would love to have a sweet girl about the house."

Then Aunt Katie added, her hand clutching at Franey's skinny elbow, "My precious one. You poor, dear soul. Whatever will you do without your momma? Come with me and I will show you how to sew a straight stitch. How will you know to be a woman if you live with all these men and this frail sister?"

At that, Franey looked at Father and then again at each of the aunts and said, "That should not be hard, for I am a girl and Mother said that when my time comes, I will be a woman. I will stay here with Father and Jonas and wait for the woman."

I put the back of my hand to my mouth, pretending to wipe at sweat. I do not know where she gets her gumption, but Franey is not afraid to speak her mind. Father could not part with her right now anyway; he calls her his little daisy. The five of us will do the best we can. Elizabeth and Magdalene offered to stay also, but Father does not want them to leave John and Abraham by themselves. Rachel is sixteen and knows how to do a woman's work, if she can ever stem the storm. And David claims he knows how long to let hominy boil and how hot the fire should be for buckwheat cakes. We will see about that.

Several times I helped Mother knead bread, but I am no good at it. I cannot make the dough smooth. She used to say, "Pat. Pat it. Do not smack." She did not know that my hands carry the stink. If Father wants me to take charge of the field work, that I will gladly do. Whatever Father wishes, I will try to measure up. The aunts may think we will flounder without a grown woman—Abraham voiced thoughts along those lines too—but Rachel cannot cry forever. I am thankful we still have Father. We can muddle through without a woman, but the loss of Father's steadiness would be, by far, the greater.

He surprised me by saying that Mother wanted me to do well. All the time I thought her dissatisfied with me. I could never please her, could never do things right. Now he says, "Mother wanted you to make something of yourself." As if that were not shock enough, Father says that Mother lost five or six babies, lost them before they could be born. I had known of Henry and Rebecca, the two lost to yellow fever, but never knew ought of the rest. I never thought of Mother hav-

ing a secret, but Father said she refused to speak of the un-
borns. She would droop at the mouth when someone made
mention of our small family. I did not know we were small. It
is strange what one learns when another person is gone. Now
I wonder if Father hides things also.

What if Father were to take another wife? Another woman
would mean adjustments. Another woman in the house might
be like one of those aunts whose voice races uphill. She might
ask that I not belch at the table or that I leave my work hat on
a hook outside. That would be quite a note for Father to find
a second wife before I have found my first. I must set aside
my daydreams for a girl. I will work hard enough for two people so that life can go with a smoothness. I must not disap-
point Father.

I do not need to move away; that was all selfish thinking.
Since Mother's passing, Levi has not spoken further of our
plans. I will content myself with what needs to be planted.
Mifflin County and Ohio—those thoughts are ashes at the far
edge of the fire. I will take my chances here in Somerset
County. Stand clear of hollow trees. Stay away from hooded
avengers, their mouths drooling.

Brother Isaac made mention at the funeral of the suddenness of death, how we must always be in a state of prepared-
ness: "None of us knows the hour." The youth in me doubts
my own death could come soon. But I will take extra caution.
Isaac reminds us that eternal damnation lurks. All that
writhing and gnashing of teeth in outer darkness: "A burning
like unto nothing known here on earth." I will stay on the
lookout, settle matters when I am older and can be in charge.
Events have moved with their own wind; I see no reason to
open my mouth now.

●　●　●

We are managing surprisingly well. Not that I expected trouble, but the gloves that seemed tight at first, have taken on a familiar fit. Father and Rachel do most of the cooking. Rachel is slowly coming back from wherever she was; she planted onions yesterday. More and more I think of myself as the man of the house, planting crops as if this were my farm. Father does not explain why he spends more time inside. He grunts at the fireplace just as he did at the hoe, but he does not appear ill. So far David has not balked at following my orders. He takes longer at pulling weeds than I think necessary, but we have not had words over it yet. John and Abraham live near enough to help us plant. We finished twelve more acres of corn last week. Father says, "One day at a time; that is sufficient." I do not look at his mouth.

What I had not anticipated is Franey's continued attachment. Mother might not approve, but I see no harm in it. Magdalena and Abraham do not need to know. At first Franey followed me about while I chored, assisting with throwing out fresh hay or fetching a bucket. She misplaced my rope for the work horse and I wasted time hunting for it, but she did not mean to cause trouble. Her brown braids are not as tight as when Mother made them, but she does not seem to mind. She does not distract me with idle chatter but enjoys watching the hogs root and snort. She says Egbert, the biggest sow, always wallows in the same spot. She covers her mouth to giggle. Sometimes I find her holding a lamb and talking gently.

Twice now when we finished supper, Franey came to me with David's slate and said, "Show me how to make my letters." The first time it happened I looked at Father, but he made no response. I am almost certain he heard the request. I have showed Franey the *a* and *e* thus far, as well as the capital *F* and small *r*. When I explained that I would show her how to write her name, she smiled. She is very steady with her right hand and bends down with her nose almost to the slate. I tell her she can do as well without getting so close. She pays attention to whatever I say. During the day I find myself thinking about what I might teach her next, and I remember tricks that Mr. Saylor taught us: "Make half of a circle for the *e* and then bring the tail down and around without closing the hole." There is not much spare time for lessons, but it is a pastime I enjoy. Father continues to say nothing. And Franey follows every direction I give.

Levi and his father, Andrew, came yesterday to help sow the summer wheat. It is late for wheat, but we will see what happens. With Father and David helping, the work did not take long. Last night a gentle rain came up. So many unexpected kindnesses and good fortune. I do not deserve any of them. But I can ill afford to reject help. I walk more steadily now. Perhaps it is my bare feet that make my steps more sure. I want to make good for Father. Sometimes the thoughts still swirl of where to find a suitable girl, but I put them aside. First, I must prove myself. It is strange how Mother's passing has allowed me to make something of myself.

16.
J S A A C

June 1810

There is a heaviness in the air that only a good rain will clear. Dark clouds rolled through our mountains yesterday, rumbling and thundering. A mighty storm to come. But in the end they brought little precipitation. That is the way it has been for several weeks. The skies appear ready to let loose. Then at the last minute they hold their breath. Our crops look desperate for rain. The corn squats, leaves curled, as if to say, "I cannot proceed without a little encouragement." So it is within. The heaviness of tending mens' souls sits on me like a thick sack. We preach against the sin of killing. Yet I wonder where we are heading in our dealings with Reuben. We shy away from pulling on the yoke, yet pull we must. We are to be a church of peace. Why, then, are we consumed with disharmony? I am not the man. I tell Sarah over and over. I am not the man.

Reuben was asked not to be in attendance last Sunday. I was afraid he would not comply. Ignore my instructions. Not that my authority matters, but the church's. Then when I saw his horse and wagon, a sickness hit my gut. How much easier it would have been if only he had stayed away. No, that is not

true. There is no easy path to brotherly discipline. Reuben sat
far to the back, off to the side with the young men. No one sat
beside him. Part of me felt shame. We began promptly with
our worship, but everyone seemed to hold back. Our singing
sounded more lackluster than usual. I should not think of horses, but the members remind me of a horse that needs breaking. The horse keeps its head up, eyes turned aside, smelling
every move before it comes. The horse braces its feet against
the pull of the rope. Her resistance makes me tug even harder.
Then the horse dances skittishly; I jump to be at a better angle.
I will not say that Reuben is the horse. It may be the church.
It may be me. But the battle has been joined.

Sarah knew that I would have traded places with anyone
that Sunday. Anyone but Reuben. But there I was, authority
vested in me. I have made some progress in accepting the
mantle. Sarah repeats, "It is God's will." My shirt stuck to my
back long before noon. I wiped at the sweat on my face as I
spoke. As soon as I wiped, another layer broke forth. The air
was sodden with humidity. Too many heavy bodies in a small
space.

After our regular time of worship, all the children and non-
members were dismissed. The older children took care of the
younger ones. They knew what to do. For me, I had no pattern to imitate. I have never sat through an admonition of this
sort. I am not the man. I followed as best I could the instructions of Bishop Blauch, endeavoring to bring a right spirit of
love and concern. I did not need to announce our deliberations. Everyone knew. I began by reminding Reuben that attention has focused on his participation in the mysterious
death of his niece, Marie Hershberger. I called attention to his
manifestation of a quarrelsome spirit. Sarah says I repeated
myself. I gave Reuben opportunity, in front of all the brothers
and sisters, to confess his wrongdoing. I thought at first he

would not budge. I thought perhaps he had not heard. He sat quietly, his arms crossed in front, looking at the floor. Then he rose to his feet and quietly maintained that he had done no wrong. He was not belligerent, but he would not admit to any fault either. "I am innocent," he said. He said it as if there were nothing more to say. Then he sat down. I wanted to wash my hands. I wonder if Pilate lost sleep at night.

It was a time of awkwardness; I did not know what to do. I mumbled. I did not dare look at Sarah. Tears came to my eyes. But with all the sweat mixed in, I could wipe everything at once. My hope and prayer had been that Reuben would drop to bended knee and plead for forgiveness. Instead, he would not even come forward but remained stubbornly at the back. I stumbled about, reminding all to be in prayer. I do not remember what I said. If Reuben had argued or lashed out at Yost, I could have warned him about his unbridled tongue. All I could think to say was to remind him not to participate in Communion or other church proceedings until this matter was resolved. Sarah says I repeated myself numerous times.

I am not the man. Storm clouds gather above my head. I wonder when they will dump themselves. Why they hold back. Someone else would know better how to do. I seek to uphold all the principles and beliefs of our church. Then we will be stronger. But it leaves such sorrow to take action against one of our number. Many members shed tears, like unto a funeral. The gravity causes us all to look to ourselves. Night and day I see Reuben's sad, dark eyes when he said, "I am innocent." Poor Eliza could not depart on her own strength but had to be carried to Yost's wagon. Sarah says that Eliza fears Yost has been too much the aggressor. When will there ever be peace?

My hope for a quiet settlement diminishes. I expected an admission of wrongfulness. But no. Soon we will have no recourse but to excommunicate Reuben. Perhaps Anna, as well. It is found in the Book of Matthew. The Master speaks clearly about the need to set aside a quarrelsome brother who refuses to make his wrongs right. Bishop Blauch has mentioned other Scriptures for me to study. I read and reread them. I have too much time. With no rain, the weeds do not grow. The Apostle Paul instructs that Reuben's lack of sorrow, following repeated admonition, is what condemns him. He condemns himself. Yes. His inaction toward repentance. That is what makes shunning necessary. I dread to think on this next step: instructing all in the church not to eat or have relations with Reuben. Poor Anna. If I were the right man, I would not hesitate to carry out God's will.

As if this contention is not heavy enough, there is evidence that others find dissatisfaction. The Bitsche and Mast families have not been in attendance for several months. Word has it that they meet with the Dunkards who are reported to have a more lively manner of worship. I cannot jump and make a show when I preach. I will not condemn myself for avoiding display. Why do some of our own crave the spectacle? I am at a loss. How can other groups steal lambs right out of our pen? I must visit these families and see for myself if these reports are true.

Even these defections trouble me less than other cases among us. The John Millers and Jacob Stutzmans come to mind. These parties have lost all interest in the church. It is a sore disappointment. John and I settled here at the same time; we helped build each other's cabins. I think it cannot be that he has lost interest in the church. Some who have cut ties say they do not have time to keep the Sabbath holy. That they need every day to subdue the earth. Every day. That cannot possibly be right. The Lord will not supply full granaries to those who turn away. Yet John Miller buys more land and appears prosperous on every hand. I am at a loss. The serpent knows every devious tug. We must leave the final outcome to the Lord, but it is a sore discouragement to have our lost brothers faring better than some in the church. I cannot bear the heaviness. Then, there is that inn at Little Crossings. It sits too close on many a Saturday night. Our Scotch and Irish neighbors have not been a good influence on our weaker members.

And here I am, such poor, weak clay, appointed to stem the tide. Sarah tires of hearing my doubts. She feeds me more cakes. She adds corn pone and corn mush and says, "The Lord called you; do not question His leading." She does not understand the burden. She is all of assurance. She flickers her eyebrows as if that is the solution. My failure with Reuben hearkens back to my not wanting the Kiss. I knew all along it was not for me. But how could the Almighty make a mistake?

We have no word this summer from Father and others who have removed to Ohio. Sarah says not to go looking for more trouble. Some who have relatives in Mifflin County say that more Amish will move to Ohio this fall or next spring. There is too much restlessness. Too much seeking after improvement. I long for word of my family's welfare but must rest in the Lord's promise to care for His own.

I do not give myself enough to prayer. That must be why I miss the mark. The Apostle Paul promised the Hebrews that their works would be perfect. Perfect. I only seek some small satisfaction. A faithful church. I say the words often to the flock. Verses 20 and 21 in chapter 13: "Now the God of peace,"—there is that word again—". . . that great shepherd of the sheep . . . make you perfect"—Sarah says I should not pounce so on the p—"perfect in every good work to do his will, working in you that which is well pleasing in his sight, through Jesus Christ; to whom be glory for ever and ever.

Amen." I say the words, but peace does not come to our little flock along the Casselman. I must try harder. That is all I know to do. I must pray.

PART II

April 1811 — August 1824

1.

JONAS

April 1811

*I*t is good to be back at Father's table where Rachel makes the gravy thick. But little else remains the same. Rachel stirs a new kind of bread that she shows me how to dip in brown butter, and David likes to stand beside me and look down. I thought he would have stopped growing by now. I had looked forward to coming home, but now I am less sure. A bad taste comes back in these familiar, dark woods. The mountains surround with such tightness. And the wind seems more fierce than I remember. I did not know that my twitch would return.

I have been absent the five winter months. I had not planned to leave; it seemed to happen of itself. Even as we husked corn last fall, I had no intention of being gone. Suddenly one day Levi told of his plans to find work with his Uncle Jakie who needed two hired men. Father nodded as if he had known all along, and almost overnight, Levi and I packed our bags and made our departure. I had established myself all last summer on this farm, even surprising Abraham with my enterprise. Then of a sudden, I was gone to a foreign land. I do not understand how one day I can be certain of my place in Somerset County, and the next day I can begin a nine-day journey to another. But that is what happened.

At first I did not like Mifflin County at all. The sun came up wrong, in front of the house rather than behind, and the water did not have the right taste. Jakie brought water from the nearby spring through a wooden water pipe to the cellar of his house. I did not like his cellar. Not at all. But the body and mind make their adjustments, so much so that when time came to leave my northern home, I had regrets. Mother would call me fickle. I have not thought on her all these months, but now I notice again her absence.

The big news here is that Abraham left Monday with Magdalena, the baby, and their belongings for that other dark place called Ohio. He spent all winter there building a cabin. He left Somerset soon after Levi and I headed for Mifflin, only a week after his first son was born. I doubt that Father would have let me go if he had known that Abraham was about to leap. Father says little of Abraham's choice, but we will all be relieved to know that they have made it safely. Father says it cannot be the same, traveling with a wife and child, as when Abraham tromped alone. The journey will likely take a month—four families traveling in one wagon—crossing streams, doubtless experiencing breakdowns. It is not for me. But if I were to change my mind, and if Abraham stays in Ohio, I would have a place to lay my head.

I do not mind that Abraham has departed, except that it is another difference that requires adjustment. When he came to get Magdalena this spring, he could not stop talking about this Walnut Creek. He claimed he could reach his arms only halfway around many of the oaks there. Halfway. He did not bat an eye, but I doubt that can be true. That is unheard of for soil to produce that large of a tree. If I go see for myself, I will have to endure more of his talk. With every story he told, there was a point where he spread his fingers wide in front of him and said, "And then . . . ." He took a gulp of air and paused to make sure all of us were listening before he finished. His conclusion never seemed worthy of the pause. He shifted in his chair, brought his fingertips together in a tight circle, and looked like he had a bigger yield per acre than anyone in Pennsylvania. Well, he does not even have a start.

I cannot imagine how he survived on berries and squirrel; he looked thin. I wonder what Magdalena thought. If I were her, I would ask questions. The idea of eating roots of plants sounds as appealing as eating dirt. He said he lived in a hut, but it sounded like little more than a roof against the wind and snow, a lean-to covered by tree branches. Now he has a cabin waiting with a fireplace big enough to cover the whole length on one side. That is what he said. I do not think John was impressed. Abraham said he made entry on two quarter sections of bottom land, 160 acres each. He said he has four years to pay off his claims before he receives the deed for the land. His plan seems solid enough, but he will have to bring his crops to harvest and avoid meeting troublesome Indians. Then we will know better what to think. Abraham tried to convince me to stake claim to land also, if only to settle there later. Me. He said there will always be land in Ohio, but if I wait too long, I may be stuck with a brackish swamp. He is such a talker that, I will admit, he stirred my interest. Unless, of course, the black, black hair becomes more than a dream. Then Ohio cannot entice half so much.

As I understand it, Abraham's land starts about a mile from that of Christian Hershberger, the first of our people who, all by himself, found this Walnut Creek valley. Abraham drew the layout with a sharp stick on the floorboards; I can picture the pieces like parts of a puzzle. Of these other couples wending their way, Henry and Lydia Stutzman intend to locate on the other side of the Walnut Creek from Abraham. If I have it right, Moses Detweiler and his wife, Catherine, will be on a ridge and slightly behind Abraham's land. Then up the creek a short span—Abraham thought perhaps two miles to the east—Joseph and Barbara Joder will settle.

All of these settlements have new names to keep straight: Walnut Creek, Goose Creek, Trail Creek. As I understand it, they are quite some ways to the west from where Samuel Joder settled along the Sugarcreek. That is Isaac Joder's father. Abraham calls that area Tuscarawas County. I know I do not want to live there. I could not live in a place that sounds frightful. I do not know why I feel such a racing within when I think of these travelers. I remind myself, it is only Abraham. Still, there is an excitement to have a relative involved in such daring. What if he never gets to his cabin? It helps that these others who travel are all connected as family in some way. Barbara is Magdalena's sister. And of course, Lydia and Catherine were Joders and are sisters to Joseph. Nevertheless, they must traverse Indian trails, strewn with much unknowing. I feel ashamed, fretting about when I will return to Mifflin, when already last night these others may have encountered grave danger. And we know nought of it. I cannot imagine sleeping in the woods night after night for a month.

What surprised me in Mifflin were the large valleys; they came as a jolt to the eye. Levi had tried to explain how the land would look, but I could not picture the truth until I saw it for myself. There they have such a wideness, as though the mountains were shoved back from each other. The biggest valley I saw, Half Moon Valley to the west of Mifflin, has not been settled yet. How easy the farming would be there, with not nearly the imbalance of standing one foot higher than the other.

We sowed Uncle Jakie's summer wheat before we left Mifflin; of course, Jakie is Levi's uncle. I wonder how that crop fares. The work for Levi and me was far from difficult. In fact, I doubt we earned our keep. We busied ourselves with choring and clearing land, cutting down trees and using the split rails to build fence so that Jakie can pasture more livestock. His two sons have already established their own farmsteads, and Jakie is left with a clattering wife and a pack of young girls. When these womenfolk all speak at once, it is like a family of sparrows stuck in a chimney. During a stretch of three weeks in January, snow fell in huge drifts that would not melt. We tried hunting with bow and arrow and supplied a provision of two deer and numerous rabbits for the family. Levi is a better shot than I, for the two deer were his. I preferred being on the lookout for unwanted bear and wolf.

Uncle Jakie will doubtless walk with a limp the rest of his life; he says it is a daily reminder of his carelessness, a lumbering accident the year before. I do not like the thought of forever carrying my past with me. Jakie's body leans far down to the side when he walks, like his right hand is scooping grain out of the dirt. Jakie invited us to return for harvest—he has strong horses to help with the flailing—and Levi said we would keep it in mind. Now I wish we had been more definite. Jakie may find someone else to hire before we get there. That is how others get ahead while I rub the sleep from my eyes.

I met an Amish minister, a Shem Beiler by name, who has owned land in Half Moon Valley some five years already. I believe Shem liked me. That may be my one advantage. It did not fully sink in at the time, but we shook hands in farewell and he gave a considerable grip. He has been a wanderer also. I realize now, that is not uncommon. Shem lived in Somerset some fifteen years before he moved back to Mifflin. Before that, he lived in Berks. I thought everyone more or less stayed in one location as Father has done, but Shem says, "Better to spread out than pile up." I will not be at all surprised to hear that he has moved to his Half Moon Valley in the next year or two.

I regret that I did not establish a more definite contact with the Beiler family. Why am I always tardy? How many four-leaf clovers have I mashed underfoot? Another man would have already gone to see the deacon about the girl. But no, not me. The lure is Mary, a daughter of Shem's. It takes me a month at home before I know that I should have put forth more daring in speaking with her. She is about my age, perhaps a bit older, and looks to be eligible. I could see no infirmity. I do not like fruit that is too ripe, but she has able hands and, from all appearances, a solid set of teeth. I wonder that she has not been scooped up yet, but she has doubtless been occupied helping her mother with the little ones. There were numerous ones underfoot. I did not like that part. Not at all.

What haunts me is the curliness in her hair. The black, black hair. She pulls it back tight, as is the custom, but some of it quite spills over her forehead and down the sides of her cheeks. Since I am home again, I notice that Rachel's and Franey's hair goes nowhere but in a straight line. That is the way with mine as well, but with Mary there is a springiness. At the singings she kept tucking the curls back; I watched her hand trying to subdue the locks. I did not want her to succeed. Perhaps I stared too much, but I could not help wondering what it would be like to run my fingers therein. Suppose she were combing and had her hair down. Rachel's hair goes almost to her waist. This fascination with hair may be unworthy, the way the thought stays in my head. But I make no attempt to set it aside unless I chance to see a cow about to walk out the gate. Last night I dreamed too much again, and David could not stop laughing at me. I am getting far ahead of myself.

There is another difference since returning home. Franey is not the same. Although she ran out the door to greet me when

Levi and I first returned on horseback, she is much more reserved. I wanted to go looking for flowering arbutus with her, but she declined. I wanted to take her hand in mine and have her cling again, but I cannot bring that time back. I fear she thinks I did not do right to flee to Mifflin and forsake her "school lessons," as she called them.

Rachel says that Franey became quite attached to baby Eli during the winter. Father gave up his bed and slept with David, so that Magdalena and the baby could take up residence here while Abraham was gone. I am glad I did not have to be around a crying baby all winter. Rachel says that Franey often rocked Eli so that Magdalena could assist Rachel with the women's work. Now Franey weeps for want of a baby to hold. I asked her why she cries and she said, "I do not like being rent asunder. All these partings and comings back." I wonder if she means it would be better if I had not returned, but I do not ask. Perhaps Mother's passing has been more of a tumult than we thought. Franey's words, "Rent asunder," go through my mind like a foolish rhyme and stay lodged in my thinking, just as "Worthless runt" and "Such ease on the high notes" once did. I am too much inclined to dwell on the words of others.

I do not know where my home is. Of course this is my home place, and there is comfort in being with Father along the Casselman again. He seems to have weathered the winter. But now there is also Ohio and Mifflin to think about. How could a wilderness ever be home? If Abraham returns to Somerset again, where will his home be? For me, there is no home until I have a woman. The black, black hair. I worry that no one will ever want to sleep with me or put food on my table. I know I do not have merit. My unworthiness suffocates me now that I have returned to this darkest spot of the earth.

What if Mary does not remember me? But Shem said, "Well, Jonas, we will meet again." I nodded and mumbled agreement, unsure what he meant or how he knew. He looked away to the fields—toward his Half Moon Valley—and nothing more was said. I wonder what it would be like to work for him. I managed with Uncle Jakie, but he is old. Shem might think me slow or too jerky; I could be a bungler again. If only I had given more attention to Mary. She might recall my singing voice since I am not so backward there.

In Mifflin I did not think on Polly at all. But here, my twitch is back. The left eye flutters just as it did last summer. It causes no pain, but I cannot make it stop on my own accord. I hold my eye tight shut to give it rest, but when I take my hand away, the flutter returns. I try to pay it no heed, but it is a sore aggravation. The condition ceases for several days and then descends again. I never know when it will begin or stop. No one has commented this time—Franey asked last summer—so perhaps it does not bother anyone else. If I put it from my mind, things will go better. I must work hard this summer to please Father and ensure that Levi and I have time to give aid to Uncle Jakie come fall. For all the rest, Ohio, the girl, I must wait to see what happens.

2.

ELIZA

December 1811

Yost came in, all out of breath. I was sitting at the work table that he made for me, sitting on a stool that makes me higher to reach the pan of water without straining. The apples are small and wormy this year, but I have stewed many a panful over the fire.

"I got the colt," he said. "The one I wanted."

I gave notice that I had heard by nodding my head; the knife in my hand scraped and cut through the core of another apple. The smell of apples cooking gives a warmth to our cabin, a warmth we sorely need. I do not look forward to another winter. I know God gives the seasons so that all His creatures may rest, but I do not have all the apples put by. Yost will be in the cabin more of the time; I will need to think how to keep him busy. I wish he would make a new hickory broom.

"Did you hear?" he asked. "I got the three-year-old. Thirteen hands high already."

I do not know why he made the work table so high. Last week I got a crink in my neck, reaching up from my chair to drop apple quarters in water. He says it is a table meant for *standing* to do work; he had not thought I would want to *sit*. Well, he has never done apples.

"Eliza, listen. The man does not know what he lost." Yost smacked his bare hand repeatedly against his leather breeches. "For $20, it is mine. He asked $30, but I had more patience than he." Without taking my eyes from the apples, I saw his belly shake. Yost is not an old man, but his belly shakes like an oldster when he laughs at another's expense.

"Can you not give any satisfaction, Woman? I made the best deal possible and you cannot even look up."

"Look up and smile that you took advantage?" I quartered and peeled another apple.

"I took no advantage. Grimsby is of a sound mind. He chose to close the deal; I gave no pressure." Yost shook the work table, testing its sturdiness. "But it is a solid deal, to be sure."

"Why do you buy a horse in December when we have no need until spring?"

"Woman, it is a blessing you are not in charge here." Yost slapped both sides of his breeches so hard that they cracked, and the girls stopped their play. They wrap old rags around leftover blocks of wood and pretend they have dolls. "Next spring a horse will cost two times what it does now. Maybe three. I have feed aplenty for my animals all this winter. Come spring, I will be ten leaps ahead."

I continued peeling and craned my neck to look to the fire; the juice of apples, hot and spitting, sizzled from the pot onto coals.

"Is that not so?" he asked. "This is one dandy table. Old man Fike at the mill says everything is dandy. He would like this table."

"You said as much," I answered.

His stomped his boots on the floorboards as he came closer. "What does that mean?" he asked, roughly pounding the table with his fist and causing water to slop from the pan.

I snatched a quick look at Yost and saw the vein on his neck bulging. It is hard to see with the way his beard grows, but I know where to look. Something cantankerous—I wonder if Fike uses that word—made me not want to answer, and I turned away to see Lizzie and Susannah pause in their rolling spools to and fro. The wooden dolls sat listening.

"Where is that fine head of yours that you say your poppa always spoke of?" he asked. He laughed his big laugh and pushed on the table lightly. "This one leg is a wee bit short."

"Lizzie, *schnell,* see if the apples bubble," I said. Of course, I knew that they did, but I needed a diversion for her.

Yost turned and tracked back to the door. "It is the prettiest colt you will ever see. Of course, you may choose *not* to see. I would not want to trouble you, what with all the seriousness of apples."

"Look to Joseph," I said to Lizzie. "Does he sleep yet?" Of course, I had heard him stir, but I wanted her to think on something other than the hard slam Yost gave to the door.

We would eat freshly cooked apples on our cornbread that evening. Food calms us all. I put the boiling apples into another crock to cool and set the last batch over the fire, adding a little water. We will have apple butter enough for all winter.

Then my conscience got the better of me. "Come to the door and holler if Joseph cries," I said to Lizzie. I put a kerchief on my head and wrapped my old shawl about my shoulders as I went to the barn.

Yost was patting and brushing the new horse and speaking soothing words as the colt whinnied at my approach. It has a broad, white streak running aslant between its eyes. "It is the little woman," Yost said. "Easy there. Show some respect. No need to jib. Show your legs there, those beautiful legs that will pull my wagon full of grain." Yost turned to me as he grabbed the bridle and pulled the horse's head to look my way. "Much obliged, Good Woman; so kind of you to step inside our humble abode. Meet Sir Prince. Prince, I say now, lift a paw there to the lady."

One dark eye of the horse turned to me, taking me in fully with his stare. In one glance he knew everything there was to know about me. I shivered and pulled my shawl tighter.

"What is this?" Yost continued. "You came with such hurry that you had not time to grab a coat? Perhaps you have not time to tarry over his wide nostrils, to notice that this is no puddin' foot. Watch this." Yost whistled low and solemn. The horse turned his head to his new master and swished his tail, as if he knew already to expect more hay.

I do not like Yost's voice when he says things he does not mean. He thinks he teases when he speaks in a high voice that is unnatural. If I ask why he mocks, he says that he only jests and I should not be so serious all the time. Well, he has time to dicker over the price of a horse but not time enough to go to Polly Anna's wedding. We have not been to the Brothers Valley settlement, not once, since we moved to the Casselman district. But haggling over a horse is not a burden; that does not require too much time.

Yost was right, though, that I had no intention of staying long in the barn. I would pay the colt some heed but not spend the night. "It is a pretty one, and strong," I said, staying well back from the hind legs, my arms crossed and pulled tight in front of me. I do not like horses; I have never seen a pretty one. But Yost had one arm slung over the horse's back while the other hand patted and rubbed at the horse's flank. I wish he would bestow such tenderness on me.

I had wanted to travel to Momma and Poppa's for Polly's wedding the week before last. We had gotten word through

Bishop Blauch that Polly Anna would marry a Christian Hostetler on the Tuesday before Thanksgiving. Yost had insisted that the timing was bad. I could make no sense of his decision unless he feared getting caught with Joseph in an early winter storm. The crops are all harvested except for some corn that he left standing for cattle feed.

Yost had made comment, "I wonder who she dragged in this time," and I had to walk away fast so as not to make angry reply. Yost knows full well that Bishop Blauch reports this family of Hostetlers as given to industry; this Christian is said to be a credit to his family. If Yost did not want to be reminded of past troubles, that is understandable, but it is not fair to Polly.

Poor Polly Anna, my dear sister; even yet, Yost speaks ill of her. I only know relief that she has found herself a man. I wonder who helped her manage her hair on her day. When we discouraged her from thinking on Jonas, I feared we put the lid on her only opportunity. It shames me that I still have such dislike for him. He looks like there is something out of kilter; I do not know what. When his mother died, his hand felt slippery; he did not make grip at all. I was anxious for Polly Anna the whole time she lived with us. Momma had never said ought of caution to any of us girls. Now I think, what if one of mine should make a mistake? With Polly Anna married, no one can question whether there is a problem. Not even Yost. I must remember to call her Polly from now on.

Yost's words brought me back to the barn. "Be gone, Woman. If you do not have time to grab a coat, you do not have time to stand here and catch cold." He mumbled more words to the horse. Tender words. I had been dismissed. I headed back to the cabin, stumbling on a tree root and catching my balance. A black crow flew between trees, carrying something in its mouth.

I was not as pleasant as I should have been when I returned

to the cabin. Joseph fretted, but I could not give him attention. Yes, he is our boy baby. Yost leans down into my shoulder and says, "This is our *first* boy." I have not told him, but I am almost for certain that another little one is taking form. Almost the same day I dried up, I felt a stirring. Momma never said ought of what to expect with the body, but I am learning to pay attention. Of course I cannot make prediction as to the boy or girl nature, but I notice a tenderness; and with Joseph weaned I cannot blame him for my tingles. I needed a rest from giving suck, and Yost could not object, for we have ample cow milk. Even the tubers underground take time to store up for another year.

Joseph came two days before Christmas a year ago and has been a welcome diversion from the trials of losing Marie. I do not mean that I have found rest, but some of the strain has passed away. Yost is right: it is good to have the cradle full. He loves to wrap Joseph in woolen blankets and make their rounds in the stable. As Yost passes with his bundle, he reports that the animals gaze up and stamp and baa and squeal. He says that Joseph shrieks in turn and bubbles a white froth. I tell Yost that it is now too cold for these barn trips, that Joseph will turn blue at the lips. But Yost says, "Oh, no, Woman, not this boy; animals are part of the boy's red, red blood." I can ill afford to upset Yost; I dare not ask why he never took regular exercise with the girls. I must be content that he takes interest in one of my little *bobbels*.

Yost does not like it when I live in the past. He looks with disgust—the same way I feel when he picks his nose at the table—and mocks me, "If only this, if only that." He talks in his high voice and then laughs his big laugh. It does not profit me to dwell on what might have been, but I need for there to be more of a *beschluss*. I need an end. Brother Isaac's words circle around me: "Heretic . . . reject." Those words from the book of Titus buzz at my head; I try to swat them away. In truth, some of his words I did not hear at all, for Joseph stirred in my arms and needed settling. I did not want his presence to be a botheration to others.

I do not like the way Brother Isaac stares at me. I fear he knows my doubts. When he preaches of the peace and contentment that come to those who adhere to the teachings of the church, he looks directly at me. His blue eyes burrow right inside. I did not know that blue could bore thus; I thought only brown. Yost's. Or now, this Prince. Yesterday I tried to rearrange my *halduch* and make it more loose in front as Isaac spoke, for I felt on display. If only I had not worn the purple one; it has been snug ever since my days of feeding Joseph and still seems tight. My mistake began in the morning when I did not like the way the dark green cape looked atop my green dress. I knew better than to ask Yost what he thought of the greens. At the last minute I said I had spilled, and I made haste to change to the purple. That is not entirely true about the spilling. Then I called attention to myself while a brother was preaching, all because of a foolish concern about appearance.

Perhaps Isaac does not guess at my thoughts, but I fear he knows I am not always at peace with Yost. I do not remember saying anything to his Sarah, but I worry that I may have blurted. I cannot help feeling a sorrow for Reuben. How can we expect to win him back if we never eat with him or have business dealings? And what if he is *not* a heretic? Oh, that he might *want* to be restored! That would make everything easier for everyone concerned. His two precious children, too young to take stock of these events. To think that they might be left outside the circle. And Anna also. I cannot forget.

It has been over a year since Reuben was excommunicated, and still there is no repentance. In all that time we have not seen Reuben and Anna nor their children. I am surprised that Lizzie does not ask about Bevy. I do not know what she must have heard. Neighbors report that Reuben drinks heavily, but I do not know how anyone can know for certain since there is to be no mingling. If only he showed some sign of sorrow. When he argued on his own behalf, that only worked as salt in Yost's open sore. And then when he would not withdraw, we had no choice but to expel him. Reject. When the church is despoiled and no longer pure, we must put the bad from us. As Brother Isaac says, the church must be kept blameless, else we will not be fit as the spotless bride of Christ. Isaac is right; no man would taint himself by taking a wife with a bad reputation.

But what if we have done more ill to Reuben than was done by him? What if this ordinance to shun may be the wrong *beschluss*? Yes, I know the teaching makes us Amish what we are. I know that Brother Ammann saved us from the drift. The teaching goes all the way back to Christ and the apostles. I know, I know, I know. Still, I am not at peace. Yost will not speak of it further. "There is nothing to be accomplished by digging up old gravesites," he says. He had already banned Reuben from his life; the church's action but made it official. Sometimes I wonder if Poppa was wrong about me and my fine head. I do not seem able to concentrate for any length, whereas Yost knows in an instant the height and breadth of every matter.

I cannot forget the day Reuben's soul was released from the church's grasp. That is not the way to think, for we all long for his return. How the goose bumps came to life on my arms when Brother Isaac announced, "The brethren and sisters are to remain seated." What words of dread. It was a relief that Lizzie and Susanna went outside with some of the older girls during the proceedings. I could not bear to have had their eyes on me or heard their questions afterwards. I knew this decision was coming, the same way a bad tooth takes on more and more of an ache until it all but begs to be jerked out. Yet I dared hope for a miracle. One day I prayed for a mighty transformation on Reuben's part; the next, for someone who might be withholding information to be forthcoming. Even if the earth had rumbled, I would have welcomed the turmoil if that could shake something loose. But on that Sunday all we could do was weep for Reuben's soul. In truth, I wept for us all, for Yost and Polly Anna. Even for myself.

I believe Brother Isaac has wept his share as well. I do not know why I think this, but that is in part why I do not like his stare. "A man that is an heretic after the first and second admonition, reject." His voice stayed subdued until he said with a scorching: "Reject," the way a spritz of boiling apple hits between the eyes. Then the deliberateness with which he said, "Being . . . condemned . . . of . . . himself." It gave me the shivers. He said each word as if it were an entire sentence. I thought he would never finish. Oh, I wish I could forget.

Lizzie is old enough to hear every word—I suppose Polly did too—the back and forth between Yost and me. I wonder what Lizzie whispers to her dolls. She is such a tender one and believes all she hears. Is every mother partial to her firstborn? I want to teach her aright, yet I stumble much too often. How will I ever explain all that I do not know?

3.

$\mathcal{R}$ EUBEN

May 1812

Yes, it is true. We have traversed hill, stream, rock, and mud to arrive in this Ohio land. We are commencing our second week of habitation along the Trail Creek, as it is called. We are here. What a fitting name for our stopping place, for it was most of five weeks—Anna kept count and said it was thirty-three days—that we lived on Indian trails and followed creek beds. Although we left Somerset County early in April, it might have been wiser if we had gone two weeks earlier. But we would have traded downpours of rain for colder weather, even snow, and that in an open wagon. The last days took longer than anticipated because of thick mud that caused our wheels to bog down; the weight finally became heavy enough that the right rear wheel broke.

We are indebted to Tobias' foresight, for Anna's father had made an extra wheel before we began the journey. Thus it was that we were delayed only long enough to unload our belongings from the wagon so that the new wheel could be attached and pressed into service. From then on we traveled in a heavy cloud of prayer. Anna's, not mine. "No more spares to spare," Tobias said. When I think of all that could have gone wrong and did not, it is cause for much rejoicing. Even from me. All the seeds we carried for garden provision and for crops—"the seeds of our future," Anna says—stayed dry in leather pouches. I did not lose heart on the journey, but the first night here I laid down in the weeds and cried from exhaustion.

When the Livengoods first made mention of a possible move westward, I had serious reservations. Tobias and Esther are both in their sixties, and I feared they would slow our pace and be a burden. In truth, I did not want to listen to Esther's complaints. On the contrary, their companionship lightened our load. For the better part of the journey they traveled in the open wagon with Bevy and Jacobli. Tobias drove the team, two of his horses and two of mine, with Jacobli at his side. Jacobli is only four, but he gained skill in knowing what size rocks to watch for that could cause trouble.

Esther sat with Bevy on the bench at the back of the wagon, directing through tight places and filling the air with hymns of our forefathers. I can hear Bevy's favorite over and over,

> If thou but suffer God to guide thee,
> And hope in Him through all thy ways,
> He'll give thee strength whate'er betide thee,
> And bear thee through the evil days.

This hymn and our new location, even the journey itself, have given me a renewed outlook. It is time to begin again. But I dare not hope too much.

Anna and I traversed on foot most of the way, although Anna would, on occasion, take a rest in the wagon. Her feet gave her trouble, becoming sore from exposure to dampness and cold weather. The moccasins gave comfort but retained their moisture after she waded through water; from then on they were useless. She took to sleeping with her feet to the fire and said it made travel the next day easier. She will not let me look at the bottoms. Esther predicts that Anna is well on her way to a bad case of rheumatism, but Anna says nought. Without her I would still be in Somerset County with judgment lined up against me.

Our path took us across southern Pennsylvania, over to Wheeling; from there we made camp several days before crossing the Ohio River on a flatboat. We continued in a northwesterly direction on a trail called Zane's Trace. It is said that ten to fifteen years ago the government hired a gentleman by the name of Ebenezer Zane to clear a path through the forest. Since our wagon is not as large as the Conestoga wagons that have come through these parts, we had little difficulty navigating narrow spots. But our horses were sometimes too weak to withstand the rush of water. The Tuscarawas gave the most trouble. I staggered many a time. While crossing, the horses became terrified, snorting and tossing their heads and all but stopped in their forward progress. Once Smith and King caught fright, it infected the others. I saw our plans drift downstream with the wagon.

Tobias was of great assistance. He and I took turns unleashing and leading each of the horses through the waters and to the bank on the other side. I returned to carry each child separately. Then Tobias and I went back, making passage together for Esther and finally Anna on our shoulders. I used my right and he his left with Esther; then we reversed with Anna. I do not know how he managed; I know how lame my shoulders felt. The wagon had drifted and been tossed some distance, but we were able to retrieve it and drag it back to where we set up camp. My breeches were stiff from the soaking; I could hardly bend to make a fire. We stayed three nights in that spot until I had repaired the wagon and made certain that Tobias was rested. My impulse was to press on with greater urgency, but Anna was right to insist that we let our muscles dry from the inside out before continuing. My shoulders finally lost their numbness.

Work along the Trail Creek is no less hard than the burden of travel. But we are here. Rain stays our constant companion these last few days. Yet there is such a large measure of thankfulness to have reached our destination that we overlook inconvenience. It took little more than three days for Tobias and me to erect this log cabin which serves as our shelter. It is small, only a dirt floor and a blanket for a door, but we have a roof of bark laid on poles, weighted down with other poles laid crosswise. We count it a blessing to have a roof rather than the open sky or a grove of trees that had been our canopy day and night. With time Tobias and I will help each other build separate cabins that will have more substance.

We met other travelers and felt some relief to know we were not the only ones. People leave the eastern settlements for many reasons. All the enticement Tobias needed was word of cheap land: only two dollars an acre. I can see him make a chopping motion, the fingers of one hand held tight, hitting the palm of the other. "As simple as slipping a knife through butter," he said. "Such an easy way to make gain." Prices for grain have been poor back East. But we sold our acreages for more than twice what we hope to pay for land here. For the time being we have each taken squatters' rights and made our first choices until we can be certain about a final purchase.

I believe that Anna's parents also saw this move as a fresh start for Anna and me. Ever since the shunning began, her parents have ignored the church's teaching. When we visited them, or when they traveled to our place, they never altered our patterns of eating together. According to the teaching of the ban, I should sit by myself at the end of the table, but they made clear, that was not to be. Esther's eyes blinked rapidly at the notion of separation. I had never seen her show such vexation. Now I cannot imagine life without their steadfastness. Tobias is not my father, but I could not ask for a better replacement. Moving to this new wilderness allows us to put these church troubles aside. Of course there are people here in Ohio who know the history I carry in my knapsack. But for now I am content to think on a new start. We are here. This is not the Garden of Eden, but it is not a fiery hell either.

There has been an awkwardness between Anna and me with this shunning. Since I was excommunicated and she not—no one sought to find fault with her—she is expected, as a member in good standing, to shun me as well. She stays as warm as ever, with one exception; she will not allow any consummation. We lie side by side and she permits my touch, but when I want on top, she half-sobs and says we dare not. "It will not look right. Everyone will know, if we have another baby," she says.

At first I grabbed her tight and forced my way, but there is little pleasure when she is crying. "No, Reuben. I am so sorry. Why does this have to be? Yes, Reuben, I want what we cannot have. No, Reuben." And then, "No, no, no." There is no pleasure, only a vicious release. I can grab a tree for that purpose. She says we will love but stop short. That is when my hatred for Yost consumes me. I would like to see him abstain from his wife. *Told* to abstain. But as Anna says—I have heard it too often—my hatred of Yost changes only me. It affects him not one whit. I do not know if Anna and Esther have talked about our stopping short, but for now I will let things remain as they are. I do not mean to minimize Anna's strong arms about me; she keeps me steady in the head. But with more time in this new country—by the time we have our own cabin—surely she will change her mind and allow me satisfaction. Surely.

Since arriving, I have fulfilled one vow. While walking through the wilderness, I thought often of the children of Israel and of their sojourns. Pilgrims and strangers in a foreign land. I thought of the man Ebenezer Zane, of his work and his given name. And so it was that one day, not long after our arrival and before daylight was fully gone, I called Anna to my side and bade her watch as I carried a heavy white stone—it looked to be made of limestone—and placed it atop a large mound overlooking the Trail Creek. I said quietly, "Here I raise my Ebenezer. 'Hitherto hath the Lord helped us.' "

Anna said not a word but touched her apron to her eyes. I waited for her to correct me, but for once, I had the words right. We stood in the silence of our altar; she took my hand as we walked back to our little family waiting at the campfire.

• • •

Last night the earth shook as we slept, causing a fright for the children and much unsettling for the rest of us. "Father, Father!" called a muffled Jacobli as he pulled the blanket over his head. Anna and I sought to comfort the children; Tobias looked to Esther who seemed as a child again. Babbling. I could not stop her from saying aloud, "The Lord seeks to warn those who tread where they ought not." We all know what some of our people back in Somerset County have said about this outbreak of earthquakes: "They are the voice of God." None of us needed to be reminded.

Tobias spoke quickly, "The bad quakes have been along the Mississippi. We are not anywhere near to that far West."

"Yes, but we are closer than we were two months ago," she replied. She looked at me as if it were all my fault.

Anna reached around Bevy's head and groped in the dark for my hand. Now I wonder how Esther could have sung so firmly from the wagon:

> God never yet forsook at need,
> The soul that trusted Him indeed.

These tremors may have loosened the fears she sought to hide. Last December we had felt a brief jolt of the bed one night, and then a shaking of greater import came in each of the next two months. Those who seek to frighten—back in Pennsylvania—reported that earth and rock spewed into the air far away in the state of Missouri. I even heard it said that the Mississippi, a larger river than the Ohio, flowed upstream for a time. I do not believe that. The quake last night seemed of a larger magnitude again; perhaps that is because it came as we slept.

I do not want to argue with Esther. This rumbling may indeed be a sign of the end time. I do not know. Tobias will have to look to her. We may have put ourselves in grave danger by going West. I cannot say. But I know it was a relief when the sun came up. The world looked much as it had before the shades of light were drawn last night. The tree stumps, left in our cabin for use as chairs, are looser now, though still attached to the ground. Several can be made to rock back and forth.

At breakfast I attempted a little levity. "The Lord helped us during the night, breaking up the earth for spring planting," I said.

Bevy giggled and asked, "Did God use a hoe, a giant grubbing hoe?" I started to laugh, but Anna and the other adults kept their heads to their plates.

"Be still now, Bevy," I said. Even those who stay by my side think I am prone to inappropriate expression.

• • •

There is much to do in this new land, but the days are of the same length as in the former country. Anna gives order to the day's work; she has a mind like her father's. It would be my nature to work at one task awhile, then haste to another job, while thinking on all the matters left undone. But Anna plans carefully, pointing in the direction of the work that has most immediate need. She must lie awake thinking about the next day's tasks, while I fall asleep at once from exhaustion. The air in Ohio refreshes, so different from my last two years in Pennsylvania when sleep often gave me the slip.

We have planted the corn seed although the ground was not worked to my satisfaction. The valley in front of our cabin looks as though it may have been tilled before, perhaps by Indians before they moved farther West. I had thought we might see more sign of the Red Man, but thus far we have met only a few camped along the river. They give no evidence of intent to harm. If we can produce enough of a crop this summer to maintain ourselves in meal over the winter, Tobias says that will be good enough. I am eager to build our cabins, but Anna reminds me that the potatoes do better by a longer growing season. Next week I will fell more trees so they can cure for cabin logs; then I will give a hand to broadcasting wheat and oats.

Our present cabin shrinks every day that Tobias finishes another piece of furniture. He built a table with short legs in order that we can sit on the tree stumps and reach our food. We continue to sleep on boards laid on the ground rather than build beds onto these makeshift walls. When the days grow hot, I hope Tobias will continue with carpentry for the new cabins while Anna and I tend the crops. Anna still aches in the joints and walks gingerly on her feet. She says her hips have crimps in the morning until she moves about a while.

Our neighbors here on Trail Creek display a helpful spirit; no one has turned a back to us. It is as if each party arriving from the East offers another hand pushing against the forest. Several neighbors have made comment that when we are ready to place our permanent logs, they want to be notified. There are Amish families here, as well as some Irish by the names of Shrimley and Edgerton up the valley. Most of the people from Somerset County have taken up residence farther south in the Walnut Creek and Sugarcreek valleys. I believe Tobias is content also to be somewhat set apart from those we might know. It would give me immense satisfaction to put former accusations behind me—Yost, be gone—but Anna cautions me not to expect too much. First, she called me despondent. Now she says that casting off an unwanted reputation is not as simple as shedding layers of skin.

Tobias surely knows the day may come when his character is called into question if he continues to have too much interchange with me. Someone from somewhere will know me. Even on the frontier. Much as I need his association, I dare not come to depend on it. With time he may feel too much pressure to conform. If Anna turned against me—. That I cannot think on. I would be bereft, for the children would, in all likelihood, turn away with her. She has been unswerving. My solid rock. I do not expect her to walk from me. But a meager two years ago I would never have thought myself a victim of falseness either. I should have known; I grew up with Yost.

When I am shaken by these dark thoughts I return to the knowledge that we were kept safe all the toilsome way here. If God were against me, He surely had ample opportunity to cause harm on the way. Wild pigs, sinkholes, wolves. I hear again the words from Esther and Bevy, even if Esther only half-meant them:

He knows the time for joy and truly
Will send it when He sees it meet . . . .

I say again, we are here.

The warm sun in the valley brings me comfort. I am one to stand with my face turned upward in the morning. My body must still have some of the Tuscarawas in it. Today though, there came a surprise. I saw a thin blade of green corn poking through the soil. I looked again and dropped to my knees, for it has not been long enough since we planted our own. I dug at the ground with my fingers, poked through weeds aplenty, and saw the pale whitish-yellow root beneath. I quickly covered the fragile stem and then smiled as I spotted more, all along in a row. Some Indian has welcomed us in advance. Some unknown friend. I will wait and let Anna find this good fortune on her own.

4.

$\mathcal{P}$ O L L Y

December 1812

$\mathcal{T}$his is the most frightful thing yet, to be responsible for the life of my own innocent, baby girl. When Eliza's Marie died, I thought I could never feel more burdened. But when I lay six weeks ago in the sweat of giving birth, biting at my fingers and feeling my seams ripped, I knew this must be error again. I thrashed with such wildness on the bed that Momma instructed Christian to put old blankets on the floor where I could lie without fear of falling. She has washed and scrubbed the bedding but cannot remove all the stain. Everything that should be natural brings upset to me. I do not know what ails me, why I am not as other women.

Not that anything bad has happened in my days as a mother, but I fear what could come, so much so that Christian says the Evil might as well have occurred. I do not seem able to soothe Marie or give comfort. Christian took me as his wife over a year ago and gives me a shoulder to lean on. He is my protection, except when he sleeps. Then he does not hear a thing. When he is awake he speaks slowly and has much patience; I would be adrift without his explanations. We met when I worked for the Abe Hochstedler family and their new baby, Sarah. Christian is a first cousin to Abe, although Christian spells his name with a difference and omits the harsh coughing sound. I am grateful for this ease, although I do not have much occasion to sign my name. We spell the name just as it sounds: H-o-s, then the letters t-e-t, followed by l-e-r. Hostetler. We live in a cabin that was abandoned by someone going to Ohio.

Christian says that when the first man came bearing this surname and speaking with such thick German—perchance clearing his throat as he talked—the immigration officer, one of the English, could only guess at the spelling through the accent and phlegm. That is, no doubt, why we have variations. Christian says he knows of at least six different ways to spell the same name. I am grateful ours is simple; I do not need more complication with a baby crying and tales of women who follow their men to Ohio.

We married last year after the harvest was complete. That is the best time to start a new adventure, after the grain is put by. I do not know if I make a satisfactory companion or not—I did not know what to expect—but Christian makes no complaint. He is gentle, especially since Marie. He is the oldest in his family, just the opposite from me. I was sorely disappointed that Eliza could not be in attendance on our day, but Yost was busy, I suppose. Cousin Maudie stood in Eliza's place, but it was not the same.

How I long to talk with Eliza again. Perhaps she would look on me with more regard now that I have given birth. Momma says they have their second boy; this last one came in June and goes by the name of Lazarus. I cannot imagine Eliza choosing that name, although it has the same z sound, like unto her own. Yost must have liked the story in the Bible of him who was raised from the dead. I wonder what Eliza said when she learned we named our own baby, Marie. Ours does not look at all like the other Marie. This one is of a fair complexion, almost a cast of red in the hair depending on the light. How thankful I am she did not come out with her hair on fire. I have never seen such a sight on a baby, but Christian says there is some of the orange on his mother's side. I do not think he saw me shudder.

Momma disappointed me that she was not enthusiastic about the name Marie; I intended it as another namesake for her. She whispered under her breath, "Poor, poor baby." She thought I did not hear. "Burdened. Such dark memory." I believe an old person does not know how loud they whisper. I hope Momma refers only to the evil days behind. I but wanted a replacement for those happy times with Eliza's girls. Our Marie looks pleasing through the face, although she does not make gain. Momma always spoke of me as the chubby one, but Marie looks nothing of the sort. I take pains not to mention her beauty, not even to Christian. Too often a beautiful child turns out to be a vain adult. Maudie may be such a case; she has been fussed over because she is the only girl in the family. I do not want Marie to think more highly of herself than she ought.

If we must have a baby who cries, at least we have a girl. I would know even less how to do with a boy. Christian says not to worry about the boy, that I would learn along the way just as with Marie. I suppose he is right, but there is less strangeness to handle with a girl. Even with Marie, I am at a loss. When Momma helped with the birthing and stayed yet another week, all fared well. I did not stir about the house but preferred staying in bed except for meals. Momma brought Marie to me whenever she cried. I do not know why, but holding Marie does not bring the satisfaction I expected. I look on her in my arms and cradle her in the same manner I remember seeing Eliza do. The tears come unbidden. I do not remember seeing such disarray with Eliza. Christian thinks the first baby may be the hardest. I shake my head, for I fear the problems will multiply. I am fortunate that Christian does not criticize. He has good ideas for quieting Marie; they do not always work, but that may be my fault.

I wish Momma would come again; perhaps this Sunday they will show up with more hops. She said she would bring more to make my *satz* go better. I have not been able to keep up with the bread-making, but Christian has not complained. I sometimes pretend with Christian that all is well with Marie; the truth is that she cried all the time he chored. Then she fell asleep when he entered the cabin. Nearly every day, late in the afternoon, she frets. Sometimes she screams and holds her arms rigid; she sounds as though I am pinching her. I offer her to suck and she finds peace for a minute. Then she breaks into an even more fierce wail, as if my milk makes upset. I fear I have nothing to give and she will starve to death. I am sore afraid that Marie may slip away because I do not recognize the problem. Yost would call me a *dumbkopf*.

I try giving her catnip; sometimes it calms, sometimes not. I try walking her from the bed to the fireplace and back; then again to the fireplace. I rest her cheek on mine and hum whatever assurance comes to my lips. Sometimes this brings consolation, sometimes not. Christian says to try hops for colic. I will ask Momma. I have not told him, but sometimes I lay her on our bed and let her cry all by herself. If she will not be soothed, I am prone to give up. But her crying unsettles my nerves the more. Sometimes when I need to help Christian by milking the cow, I take Marie to the barn in a basket. She whimpers at first, but the smells and noises distract her to quietness. I do not want her to only find peace in a barn.

Christian has a half-brother who is but a few months older than Marie. That is odd to think on, that this baby brother, Solomon, at the tender age of seven months is already an uncle. Christian's mother died while giving birth; it would have been her seventh. What if it should be my lot, to die thus! Soon after the mother died, Christian's father married again. Now they have three of their own, plus the six at home, excluding Christian, from the first marriage. I cannot train myself to think on a second child, let alone see myself thrashing with a seventh or tenth. Momma says I have too much imagination, that the rest will come with more ease.

I tried a procedure the other day that may reap benefit. My German neighbor, a Mrs. Hinkle who does not hold to our Amish beliefs, says that if you put a silver spoon in a baby's hand and carry the baby to the attic, the child will grow up to a life of happiness and riches. Christian and I do not, of course, own a silver spoon—we are glad for the two made of pewter which are much better than the wooden ones—nor do we have an attic. I tried my own variation. I do not mean that I seek after what will tarnish, but it cannot be evil to desire happiness for another, even if she is my own.

While Christian was grinding corn and Marie had a peacefulness, I took our tiny book of devotion—*The Wandering Soul*, it is called—and placed it on Marie's stomach. Christian treasures this little book in the German; he says a Mennonite first wrote it in Dutch, but our ministers commend it to our youth anyway. I had thought of using our family Bible—a wedding gift from Christian's father—but I knew that would be too heavy. I lifted Marie, while balancing the devotional book upon her, and mounted one of the chairs, thinking to raise her considerably higher than the floor whereon she was born. I held her, lifted there, and prayed on her behalf until she took on too much wiggle to be safe. To be sure, I did not follow the directions exactly, but if this saying carries import, I have pointed Marie in the right direction. I wanted to tell Christian, but then I thought better of it.

Many of our number embark on dangerous journeys these days. This urge to leave the settled flock and seek new land farther West strikes at many. What frightens me is that Christian's family seems especially afflicted. Christian's father has a sister, a Katie by name—I have trouble keeping them all straight—who is married to a Moses Joder. It is some of their children, two girls and a boy, who have removed to Ohio. I cannot imagine releasing three of my own to the wilderness. Even if they were grown. Nor can I picture the journey for myself. What if Christian is susceptible! I could never manage with a baby in the wilds. What if someone entered my cabin to molest my Marie? We might not even have a cabin; we might live, as Yost suggested for me, in a cave where the bears make their home. I could not make do on grass. Or tree bark. What would we do for church? I cannot find one good thing about a move like that. Not one reason to throw everything in shambles. I would never see Momma again. Some evening when Marie sleeps, I must question Christian. I cannot go on without some assurance.

• • •

What a blessedness to know peace again! Even Marie responded with a smile as I dressed her this morning. I believe my milk goes better too. If Marie stirred during the night, I did not hear her. I was as dead as Christian. We could both have been in Ohio. Now I can smile about that. Christian and I had conversation last night after supper, enough to quell the aftertaste of turnips and onions.

"These couples who last year removed to Ohio . . . ." I started slowly, not wanting to show undue alarm. "Did you say they are the children of your uncle Samuel?"

"No," Christian said. He always draws out the o part, as if he is stuck. "Samuel is the father of Jacob and Christian. They went earlier. Those three first explored Ohio five years ago. All three of them moved their families West two years later."

I did not like to hear that a Christian had moved, but my Christian went on. "You know of Isaac Joder, the Minister of the Book? He is my cousin also, another of Samuel's sons. But Isaac has the sense to stay at home."

I grabbed Christian's hand and squeezed hard. "Yes," I said quickly, "I know Brother Isaac from when I lived with Eliza and Yost." I hoped Christian knew that I squeezed for the part about staying at home.

Christian studied the pipe in his free hand. "All right. What you need to remember is that these Joders, gone to Ohio last year, are cousins of mine *and* cousins to Isaac. They are children of Samuel's brother, Moses. Not children of Samuel. You see?" Christian is good to repeat his sentences and make sure I understand. Sometimes I think there are too many Moses on the earth. My father and now these others. Christian shook his head slowly. "I believe a man can survive in the wilds, but it was not meant for a woman and children." I breathed easier for my Marie as Christian's head continued moving like a lazy pendulum.

"But these are all Joders. Where do we come in?" I asked. Now that I had heard what I most wanted, he did not need to take as much time.

"That is right. These are Joders." He puffed his smoke; he says it is a relaxation from hard labor. "I have not gotten to my point yet. You have Samuel and Moses as brothers."

"Yes, I understand that."

"All right. Now these two brothers married sisters. We are getting close." He put his arm around me; I am glad he does not sweat as much in the winter. "My father, Emanuel, is the youngest brother of both Sarah Hostetler and Katie Hostetler who married these two brothers."

"That makes you a first cousin to Isaac by marriage and also a first cousin to those who have gone to Ohio."

"That is correct. Jacob and Christian are my cousins, as are Joseph, Lydia, Catherine." Christian squeezed my shoulder into his chest; his other hand with the pipe pointed with each cousin's name. "They are all my cousins because two of my aunts married Joder brothers. The Joders, that is where the wanderlust comes. Not the Hostetlers. I do not see any hankering in the Berkeys either. And remember, while Isaac is a Joder, he has stayed home."

"No, the Berkeys do not roam," I said. "I could not survive such a trip. Do you know how it frightens me? Every week we hear that another family has left, or we hear names mentioned of those giving thought."

Christian took several short puffs. "Some of that is just talk and nothing will come of it. For others—see if I am not right— some who talk big of distant stars will come back dragging their wagon harness, feeling ashamed or expecting pity. Wait and see."

"Maudie says the turning back has happened already," I said. Christian nodded. I am glad his nose does not spread all over his face as does his father's. "She says that fear of the Indian caused this Henry and Lydia to flee their cabin with their six children, abandon their corn, and make haste to return here."

"I heard the same thing. But do you know the rest of the story? Henry and his family had gotten back almost to the Ohio River when Joseph—that would be Henry's brother-in-law—caught up with them on horseback." Christian blew a ring of smoke that drifted toward the fireplace. "Somehow Joseph persuaded them to turn around again. Said the Indian scare was but a false alarm." Christian had the slow head shake going again and I snuggled closer. "I would not want to cause a brother to go against his better judgment."

I nodded as best I could, pressed against his chest. "Did you hear also? Is it true?" I asked, "that these Joders—I think the Moses stripe—have a little brother, only ten or so, who has gone to live with the others in the wilderness?"

"That would be John, the last one, Joseph's little brother." Christian paused. "You hear all manner of rumor these days; I doubt that my aunt would allow her youngster to make a trip like that."

I must have repeated five times my relief that Christian had no desire to follow his cousins. "Promise me . . . ." I grabbed his chin with the beard that grows fuller each day. I turned his face to me. "Promise you will not change your mind. There is enough to do right here at home without needing to give the frontier a push."

Christian smiled and ran the bottom of his beard over my forehead, across and back. His stubbly beard tickled and got in my eyes, but I closed them in safety. "We should be glad someone wants to move on, Polly; some day there may not be room for all of us to farm here. They say the land goes far beyond Ohio, even beyond Iowa."

I put my hand where he likes it. He smiled broadly and said, "Come." He takes all my worries away except when he steps out of the cabin. He does this every night, one last time before going to sleep. I hear his long whistle in the dark. I know it is coming, and yet it surprises me. He slurs his whistle slowly up and then down, however long it takes to empty himself. I do not like it, but I have not said much. I do not want Marie to be alarmed.

Christian came back in and pulled the latch shut. "Frost in the morning," he said, "for sure." And he was right; we had a heavy one this morning. He had stoked the fire so it would last most of the night. I do not mind putting on another log after I feed Marie one more time. By then Christian is snoring and hears nothing. I am the one who must keep alert.

I did not get around to telling Christian what else Maudie had to say. I never make mention of the Zugs, for Christian knows they have a Jonas who paid some interest when I lived with Eliza. Maudie had three pieces of news. For one, Jonas has found him a woman; he married a Beiler girl up in Mifflin County. Maudie thought he had earlier gone there to find work. If I had opportunity, I would take a peek at them. I am relieved that our cousin problems did not set Jonas back forever; now my rebuff seems of less consequence.

Maudie also had news that Jonas' sister, Rachel, has married Levi Speicher. Jonas used to talk about fishing in the Casselman with this friend, back when they were lads and could find excuse from work. Here is the third item: Jonas has bought land in Ohio. That is what Maudie claimed. Right there with the rest of them. I wonder if it is true. Maudie says a brother to Jonas lives with those cousins of Christian's. I think she means the cousins who are children of Moses. Maudie did not think Jonas had actually moved, so perhaps his timid nature holds him back.

I cannot imagine Jonas on the frontier; he seemed to always be looking over his shoulder. I have Eliza to thank for giving me warning; she knew what was best for all. I wonder if Yost might not be a wanderer though. There is much, much to think on. I am relieved to have my assurance from Christian. Of a sudden, the winter ahead does not look as long. Now I will put all my strength to bringing Marie satisfaction.

5.
J S A A C
June 1813

*L*ady's saddle has been my home for little more than a week and already I am certain: I am not meant to be a circuit rider. My bottom portion goes to sleep as I ride, and when I dismount I feel paralyzed. Perhaps I will lose weight from all the jostle. Sarah has sent ample supply of dried beef and apple, but the cakes do not keep and are long gone. I ate them as if I needed to keep up with John. Only he looks as thin as ever. I try to think on the opportunity to see my mother and father again, but that does not compensate for leaving my babies. My thoughts fly to Sarah, abloom once more.

Life flows with its own unexpected current. First, I did not want the Kiss. That has been four years. Now the Lord has called again. And yet again. Once made a bishop, I could not refuse this trip even though Ohio has no appeal. Bishop Blauch said Ohio needs tending. He did not mention Reuben by name, but I am certain we both have questions. Benedict is much too advanced in age to withstand these rigors of travel. That left me. I no longer have my own wishes but must do the church's bidding. It no longer matters whether or not I think I am the man. My crops are planted and others will tend them in my absence. It may be all of two months before I return. Two months. At the very least, one. All manner of trouble could transpire while I am gone, and I would remain in the dark.

Sarah says my advancement was not a surprise, only that it came so early. I thought my age, my youth, would bar the gate. I am but thirty-two. Much too heavyset for my age. I thought my reluctance would be apparent to all. But no one found fault with my service, and only one or two made mention of my youthfulness. Our River congregation needs our own bishop; with that no one can disagree. Who else was available? The floorboards creaked at my weight as I sank to my knees under Bishop Blauch's heavy hands. Those hands pressed more tightly than a new hat.

He reminded me to be on the lookout, to warn others when I see the sword coming. I do not like to be the one in authority. For me, the planting and building are not grievous. The baptizing and conducting of Communion do not present a problem. The weddings even give a bit of celebration in the fall. But the instruction to pull down and break off. That is where I want to look the other way. Why can others not see that I am weak when I have to give admonishment to obey? I am altogether human and prone to error, even when others look to me for answers. But I cannot speak of my misgivings to Bishop Blauch; he might think I blasphemed against the church's authority. I dare not be a travesty.

As if I had not fears enough for myself, here I ride with one so young. He is Moses and Katie's youngest. John, by name. My first cousin. His eyes pierce the underbrush long before I can make out the right direction to look. "It is only quail," he says, or, "a skittish doe with her young." He is eleven but given so much height that he seems older. Skinny where I am fat. My Jonathan is nine and would barely come to John's waist. Uncle Moses says that John has begged for most of a year to ride to his brother in Ohio; Moses thought he could bar the door no longer.

We make an odd pair: I would rather keep to the ease of home while he leaps for the journey. I should look to protect him, but he is the one who gives me assurance. He rides with a long straw tucked under his hat. I do not know why. He yells, "*Gnuddla,*" whenever he sees droppings, as if he needs to warn the horses. He will spend the summer with his family on the frontier and then ride back with someone who returns to Somerset in the fall. His Blackey has a strong gait and follows Lady's steps as if they are of one mind. Sometimes I let John lead. Already I dread riding back by myself; that was the part that gave Sarah most concern.

His companionship makes the travel go faster. After the first two days we had exhausted each other's supply of riddles. Then I chanced to think of one more: what is it that will come but never will arrive? John is still working on that. Now we have settled on our own made-up games. It started with "I spy," but now it has advanced to "I'm thinking of." By asking questions as to color, use, and so forth, one person tries to guess an object that the other has in mind. I stumped him with my shaving knife. He claimed he had never seen one. That is hard to believe since I am sure his father makes axe handles on occasion. Another time I had to give up and insist that he tell me his object. I had identified the color, but that did me no good. It is just as well that I gave up. The yellow stamens of a pink peony.

When we stop at night, John jumps to tend the fire, while my body welcomes the chance to recuperate. When I lie on my back, my muscles protest until they get the kinks out. I must be sitting on Lady with too much tightness; I do not know how to make myself lighter. Getting up from the ground is an even worse problem. I roll and stagger. I grab my back. I am an old woman.

While John pokes at coals before we sleep, I take opportunity to warn one who holds such promise. "Some of our young men follow the wrong summons to leave home. They hear an appeal to join the army, but they do not know what fighting is all about." I cannot see John; he has pulled his hat down over his eyes. "Joshua's Ben is the latest; I fear we may never hear tell of him again. Joshua can but wait with the fatted calf."

"I heard that Ben wants to go to York."

"Yes, there is fighting north of the border. Some take up arms along Lake Erie also. But, John, listen." I would move closer to him if movement came more easily. An owl calls in the distance. "Fighting is not for our kind. The battle is not as exciting as it seems."

"Father says we suffer from the Embargo Act." John's voice is high-pitched and clear in the heavy night air. He has not undergone the change, even though his legs stretch much longer than mine.

"Yes, that is true; we lost markets overseas. But taking up the sword does not bring peace. We need to stay clear of those British." An owl answers. Or is it the same one?

A log rolls off the pile and John shoves it back with a stout stick. He stacks up all the burning pieces to feed on each other's flame.

"It is all politics, John. Wanting gain for one country at another's expense. Best to stay clear. Our people fled persecution in the Old Country; now we are expected to fight wars in this New World. Someone always looking for an advantage. You know about the Revolution, do you not?"

"I have heard some," John replies. He fans the flame, waving his hat.

"Ask your father to explain all that our grandfather endured. The government of this country thought that if we Amish and Mennonites would not fight, then we must be on the side of the British. That was not true. But our people lost the right to vote for a time. We would not further the revolutionary cause."

"You said the British were the problem." He does not sound quarrelsome, but he does not miss anything either.

"Yes, of course, the British. But also the French. Both fought to control trade. Our government too. Any time a man wants an advantage at someone else's loss, that is the wickedness of man's heart. It does not have to be countries that rely on the sword."

I pause while John rearranges logs; sparks shoot high into the night. I wish for time to instruct my Jonathan and William in this way. At home there is too much work to tend to. My Jonathan is obedient, but William bears watching. John settles again and I continue, "Man cannot serve two masters. It cannot be done. There are those who want to accommodate. 'Pay just a little to the government,' they plead. No, John, that only feeds the fire; do you see?"

"You mean those who pay special taxes?" John watches the smoldering end of his poking stick. He swings it in an arc.

"Yes, that is part. Already in Europe some of our people paid a military tax so they would not have to fight. Now in this country: same thing. Some of our number were teamsters during the revolution; some hired substitutes to fight for them."

"That is like paying someone else to sit on the bully."

"You have it right, John. If you cannot sit on the bully yourself, and we dare not, then you should not ask someone else to do it for you." If only some of John's elders were as quick to seize understanding. I roll onto my side; that is the only way to lift this belly. "Same thing with voting. Some of the brethren say we must exercise our right to vote or we will lose it from neglect. Duty, they call it. There is even an Amish minister—calls himself a preacher—from Chester County who wrote down his ideas and circulated them among our people last year. He encouraged people to vote in the national election for a man he called a peace candidate. Do you know? Your father—? Did he vote?" I should not pester a child, but the night is dark.

John does not answer. He busies himself, drawing designs in the dirt with his smoking stick. "Never mind," I say. "I will ask him myself. Here is my way of thinking: how can I be sure that this DeWitt Clinton will stop the war? He was splashed in the newspapers, even the one printed in Somerset County. We will never know what may have been because our President, James Madison, defeated him. But I know this"—I raise my voice, as if I speak to the back bench—"I could not bring myself to vote. Nor could I encourage the membership to do so." I am not in the habit of criticizing other ministers, but this voting business is serious. An owl hoots. "Too many unknowns." I cannot find a comfortable spot. "I would not want to make a mistake and vote from ignorance. Only in the church can we know how we are to live."

"What is this about a Test Act?" John asks. He yawns and tilts his head back onto a large rock. "Father says there may be another."

"That is what our people suffered during the revolution. It amounts to a test of allegiance. 'Accommodate,' some say." My voice sounds harsh, as when I admonish William for carelessness. "Listen, John. Only one deserves our allegiance. *Gott allein.* Never forget that. *Gott allein.* My father—you remember Samuel, do you not?" John does not reply, but I continue. "My father, newly married, had to declare—along with all other white men eighteen years and older—had to declare loyalty to Pennsylvania. Not to the King of England. The truth is, Father cared not a bit for England. Neither could he sign his life away to an earthly government. Do you see?"

I am sure John is listening. He is a bright one. He crosses his legs at the ankles. "What did Father do? Simple. He would not cross to either side of the road. He did not sign. But because he would not sign, he and many others were told they could not vote or hold office. There were consequences aplenty: he could not serve on a jury, he could not transfer real estate by deed." The night sings with crickets. I wonder that John asks no more questions. "That is why some whisper, 'Accommodate.'" I lower my voice to a mumble. "Consequences. That may have been what propelled Father to be an adventurer. He despised the clutches. Despised being told what he could and could not do."

I stop. I have never compared my father's resistance with my own not wanting the Kiss. I will need to ponder that as we ride tomorrow. Tomorrow. That is the answer that John has not yet thought of. For now I am intent on finishing my instruction. "No, John, it is not for us. We must stand firm."

John shifts his head on the rock where he props himself. I go on with the rest of what I need to tell my sons. "Too many of our young people follow their own free will before they join the church. They become familiar with the ways of the English: the language, the fancy dress. Then it is hard to change back when they settle down: to use only the German, to wear the simple garb. Their parents suffer the most. They are the ones who wail, 'Where did we go wrong?' Oh, John, listen. Honor your Moses and Katie. None of theirs has left the fold, even though some have ventured to this Ohio. Would that mine should turn out as well."

Another log falls to the ground, but John makes no move. I cannot see his head under his hat, but I must have put him to sleep. No one has criticized me for erring on the side of dynamic. How I miss Sarah. How I must ensure my big boys' obedience so my young ones will follow as well. I prop one hand on the ground so that I am able to shove myself to stand. Lady raises her head and I reassure her. I add more logs and rearrange the stack. A fire is my comfort. I do not allow myself to hear the sounds of beasts in the night. I cannot get settled tonight and sleep keeps its distance. My thoughts toss about. I do not want to be too strict. Neither dare I keep house too loosely.

• • •

Lady will see me home. And the Divine Protector. I have killed a wolf. I was as surprised as she to be so close. The tale that red surrounds the eye of the wolf is no longer a tale told by others. It could have been a dream, but when the jolt at my shoulder stopped, there lay the dead wolf. Nearly at my feet. I do not remember reaching for my shotgun hooked to Lady's bridle. Nor loading it, taking aim, firing. Nothing. Sarah is right; the Lord cares for His own. I was too unnerved to dismount and inspect my deed. I forced Lady to control her nervousness and ride on; I imagined the dead wolf's brothers in pursuit. Not until many miles separated me from my victim could I stop for rest. All night, flat on the ground, my muscles stayed tight. When the day's grayness mercifully lifted at last, I felt as if I had slept with my eyes open, jumping at every noise.

My other large fright came during the night of thunder. That was the second night of my return home. I did not want to retreat. Yet I could not go on. Huge rumbles broke around me, followed by large crashes. Again and again. Finally, smaller ripples and a pounding rain. I could follow the thunder across the sky, starting behind me on the left and rolling across overhead. One procession after the other. I have been in worse lightning storms, taking shelter in a ditch while the earth lighted up around me. But this thunder was as fierce as twenty wolves at my heels. Sarah will not believe how loud the cracks were. I crouched all alone, trying to calm Lady, saying promises I did not believe. That night I would have done whatever God demanded. Even gone to see Reuben.

Now, to see my own lane, to know how the crops fare—if they have been spared these downpours—that is all I seek. I return a carnal man, dwelling on the things of the flesh. In truth, so much homesickness descended upon me that I shortened my time in Ohio to three weeks. Not that Bishop Blauch had determined a set length for my stay. But I had thought beforehand that a month, perhaps two, would be satisfactory. Now I know in truth. No bishop from Pennsylvania should be expected to have oversight of the flock in Ohio. The journey requires far too much. As for those on the frontier, they are prepared to stay. That much is clear. Their removal to Ohio is not a trifling fancy, not something they dabble in. They need their own minister to look to their spiritual condition.

I do not know why my father does not fill the breach. He shirks his duty. Yet I could not say that to him. He is my father. His reddish cheeks look more hale than I remembered, and he talked at length of his crops and his grandchildren. Jacob has six; Christian, two. But when I spoke of home, he showed little interest in church matters back East. He barely asked about my children. Neither he nor my brothers know ought of the war, even though it is being fought not far from them. They are too isolated to hear official word. They have turned their backs. What is worse, they do not seem to care. They do not see the extent to which they have tied their hands at cross-purposes in order to make ends meet. Everywhere I went, I saw a lack of serious regard for the rules and regulations of the home church. Those in Pennsylvania who accused the ones moving West of fleeing the church have hit upon the truth. I would not have believed it.

My brother Jacob is an example of laxness. He did not hesitate—did not even blink—to say, "Everyone is his own authority here. No one need listen; we are too busy to keep
check on another's soul." He said the word *soul* almost with a
sneer. When I reported Jacob's words to Father, he took off his
straw hat and wiped his brow with the back of his hand. That
is all. Then he put his hat back on. No defense, no excuse.
Nothing. I grant that some independence may be necessary
for survival. But when the individual spirit sets people up as
their own final word, that portends deep trouble. I could not
have imagined this lukewarmness. My own kin. Christian, my
other brother, has more of a right spirit about him. He is serious about the pilgrim walk in a strange land and may be a
worthy candidate for leadership. But Jacob. And Father. I
would not have believed it.

Wherever I went I tried to speak a brotherly word of counsel and encouragement. "Hold fast," I said. Some received the
message. Others have given themselves over to their own
preservation. Bishop Blauch will not be reassured to know
that opportunities abound in every settlement to drift to the
Dunkards or the Mennonites, even to German Reformed
groups.

As I ride I do combat with my thoughts. I fear that I am my
father's son. My guilt assails me. I did not carry out my duty.
I did not go see Reuben Hershberger. I know where he lives.
I could have gone. But when I was near to Trail Creek I made
excuse that those people did not attend our meetings in the
Walnut Creek area. I further defended my weakness by telling
myself that there was not time to make a personal call on each
family. But I know the truth within. I was afraid to speak with
Reuben. Afraid not for physical harm, but afraid to boil the
blood. This is the third, dread fright of my trip. I did not know
what to say to Reuben. I am not the man. My church does not

allow me not to know what to say. When I mentioned Reuben's name to Father, he gave me a blank look. The same as when I reported Jacob's transgressions. As if Father thought me a meddler. I let the subject drop. I convinced myself it was not a pressing matter. What seemed an easy solution then, hangs with me now like a severe sorrow. I fear that my looking away caused the thunder to roar.

I tell myself that I can visit Yost instead. But why? What will I say? Why go to him? He will think me a slackard for not having gone to Reuben's door. I am not the man for the difficult tasks. It is true, we banished Reuben from the Garden; we did that much. But having cursed him to the ground, what have we done but placed a flaming sword over our heads? I fear we did not accomplish the proper *beschluss*. Some would say he was not adequately reduced to his belly. He can still come and go with his life as he wishes since he has escaped to the West. I maintain that we are not commanded to take another's life. We have left Reuben with little to partake of but the dust of the earth.

I do not ever want to make this journey again. I must convince Brother Blauch. We cannot expect to throw a harness from a distance. I may see Father again—I do not know—should he return to Somerset for a visit. But I said goodbye to Mother—that I know for surety—till we meet on those heavenly shores. She has no appetite and looks sickly. Numerous times she said, "This is my fifty-eighth year," as if that were sufficient.

My travels eastward have taken six days thus far, and before another week passes, I hope to rest in the cradle of Somerset County. To be with Sarah. I am grateful to Moses Detweiler; he explained how I could cut short my journey in the vicinity of the Ohio River. I departed from Zane's Trace for a day and found more of a straightness. I must take care not to push Lady too hard; she pulled up lame once, misstepping in high water. Every stream and tributary is a troublesome snare, for all is swollen. My dry clothes stay in my pack while these wet tents cling. I will not change until the sky gives hope of clearing. I speak to Lady of fresh hay at home, but I am the one who needs encouragement.

I miss John, his ears set to listen for me, his questions, his lone straw flopping under his hat. I have had to make peace with bear and skunk, even a rattlesnake, but I have not come to peace with the journey itself. With why I must ride. I know how to survive—to kill a wolf without thinking—but I will not truly rest until I feel my wife and babes next to me.

• • •

"We are home; we are home!" I said to Lady. I let her gallop down the lane, knowing there was no longer need to conserve her strength. Every day since—this is the eleventh day—I give thanks. Sarah says I am beginning to walk as if my legs will stay together instead of flop on an open hinge.

I do not tire of looking on my family and farmstead. Sarah has grown noticeably. She says with a tired smile: only three more months. She makes a small notch in a log by her wash bucket every time the moon is full. All my little ones look more precious than I remember. The four girls and the baby boy have all made advances; the boy even takes steps. And when I look on my two oldest, Jonathan and William, and then look at how they managed the corn crop, it is hard not to allow a trickle of pride. Jonathan is far advanced in his response to duty; he carries through far better than I. The Lord has watched over His own, and my fields are clothed with crops.

Sarah says that Jonathan and William pulled weeds in six rows of corn each day, except for the Sabbath of course. The two oldest girls took responsibility for two more rows. These are not short rows; they stretch to one hundred yards. Jonathan, my apple. He may never have John Joder's height, but he has the right spirit of tending the earth. William still needs a collar—he is not of the same readiness—but he is yet young. When I tell stories, William's eyes open wide and stay thus. I speak of bear and fox, but I have not mentioned the wolf.

Some of the burdens that pressed on me while traveling have now shrunk. It was not until I stood to bring God's Word to His people and looked again into the face of Yost, that I remembered my failing. Sarah says I repeated myself about serving only one master. I lost my place in my sermon. Yost appears unmarked by time, but Eliza is the one bowed down with cares and burdens. I try not to stare, but she makes me think on my mother. I cannot say why. In Yost's place I see Reuben's eyes. I hear his words of three years ago, "I am innocent." Each Sunday Yost will remind me of my lost opportunity: I did not go to Reuben. He sits outside and I did not visit.

The war got no smaller while I was away. Now I hear that Pennsylvania has its own militia. I pray daily that there will be no call to compulsory duty. I do not like to be on the side of individual liberty, but in this case it may be a help rather than a hindrance. If conscription comes, I predict even more exodus to the West where there is far less organization. Now I understand the appeal: less government. Less church. Ohio is the place to go to be lost. My resolve not to ride to Ohio again has not changed. When I can once more sit in the saddle, I will ride to tell Benedict.

As I stand to preach, I am reminded also of the naysayers with their complaints about our drab church services. *Staid* is the word they use. How sad, that certain of our people go to church in order to be revived, even entertained, with emotional expression. Sarah assures me that most of our people are not swept on this stream. I reply that we cannot allow one more soul to sink. Here I am, a bishop, and I do not know how to retain our young.

Yet with all these problems, there is far greater reason for gladness. I am home. I will never again take anything for granted. Sarah says she will fatten me up—not that I have grown thin—and for once I do not mind. I begin my benediction with the same words I used in the wilderness: "Now unto him that is able to keep you from falling, and to present you faultless before the presence of his glory with exceeding joy." That is the promise. Even though I have seen far too much falling and far too little faultlessness. Starting with myself. I do not claim to understand the mind of God, but I believe that God reigns no matter where we roam.

6.

J O H N M.

August 1813

I am far from my mother and father and have a new home, a new woods, and now a new name. Yes, and new cousins. We live as brother and sister, but really, they are my nieces and nephews. While riding here with Isaac I tried to imagine saying, "Call me Uncle John." That did not seem right then, nor does it now. So how can this all be?

I cannot thank my tallness enough. Joseph says I could pass for eighteen. "With a boy's face," he adds. I am a gangly one, but I still have no whiskers. Some day I will have a brown, nearly black, beard like Joseph's, and I will scratch underneath like he does when he thinks. He tilts his head back, pulls his mouth up tight, and turns his lips down in a thin quarter moon. Then his fingers move fast, like they scratch an itch. But really, he is thinking.

I am only eleven. But I am over halfway to twelve. And when I am twelve, I will already be in my thirteenth year. Really. Father says not to use that word, but here in Ohio it does not matter. I like that. Father says we should speak the truth the first time, without question. Then why must I say I am only eleven?

About my name. The other John is the reason even though he is only two. His father, Joseph, is my brother. But Joseph is thirteen years older than I and has lived twice as long. I have another brother, Jacob, back in Somerset County who has lived almost three times as long as I. Joseph writes everything down: everyone's birth date and where, what kinds of crops planted and where, how they fared. He showed me. Even his tools. Everything is written down, what he bought and where. I like that.

When I got here, all of a sudden we were two Johns in the house. Barbara started using Big John and Little John. Joseph put a stop to that. He said, "My son will not be called little anything." I like Joseph; he knows exactly what he thinks, even if he has to scratch. This is what he came up with on the names. He said to Barbara, "Our John will be John J. from now on. The J. is for me, for Joseph." Then he put his hand on my shoulder. "This John, from now on, is John M. The M. is for his father, Moses. We do not need an initial for me, but if anyone asks, I am Joseph M. also. How does that sound?" He reached to shake my hand like a man.

"What about baby Samuel?" Barbara asked.

"He will be Samuel J. Same thing." Joseph spoke more tenderly. Everyone tiptoes around Samuel for he is sickly. Only a year old and Joseph says he has never been well. His twin, Eva, eats and babbles for both of them.

That is how I got my name, John M. Joder. I like it. I will take it with me when I return to Pennsylvania. But for now I am in Ohio. Life is much harder than I expected. Father tried to warn me, but I did not think he knew. He has never been here. Father would be surprised at the walnut trees; they are huge and everywhere. Really.

Joseph says, "Adapt. If you want to survive here you must adapt. If one crop fails, try another. Always adapt." He seems to know, and I believe him. But his words remind me of that word Isaac did not like: *accommodate*. Isaac said it like it was a dreadful cough. I do not think the words mean exactly the same, but I wonder how both men can be right.

Joseph says I work hard and am quick. He told my sisters that I shock oats as well as a grown man. He would not say that if he did not mean it. Catherine and Lydia looked to their own men, Moses and Henry, and they both nodded their heads, although Henry had to think on it awhile. I learned to be fast with Father. Sometimes I had to run to keep up; that is why I have long legs. The last thing I wanted to hear was, "Get a move on." That is for the cows.

About John J. Barbara reminds me that he is only two. One day I caught him with his thumb pressed in the shell of a bird's egg. I am certain it was a cardinal, for their eggs have brown speckles on the gray. John J.'s tiny thumb was thick with the runny insides. I scolded him, which is not good for getting along. John J. does not listen to me. I told him about the beautiful red bird that comes out of this drab egg, how it has black markings all around the bill and eyes. Rather like a beard. Even the female has little dabs of red in the wings and tail. I told John J. that the bird's parents might have to abandon the other two eggs, for the nest would carry our smell. He giggled like it made him happy and went crawling away on his hands and knees as if he could not walk. I wonder if I should report this to Joseph, but I do not want to be a tattler.

I have heard that the same male and female cardinals stick together all their lives like married people. I doubt that is true. Sometimes I see a male bringing grain; other times the female makes trips. I believe birds have a way of talking with each other that we know nothing about. I like that.

• • •

I did not expect this. I came to help Joseph and give aid wherever needed. I wanted to see Ohio, but I did not want to be the man of the house. I am still only eleven. For the past five nights I have lived here with Lydia. Her Henry has died. That is what I did not know could happen. Lydia is left with six children, my cousins. They still call me John M. Even though Lydia is my sister, she seems a stranger. A looney one. She is next after my brother Jacob so she is an old one. She peels potatoes like Mother, around and around with the knife, so there are long curly strips that she fries in grease for breakfast. I am a little bit afraid of her.

About the children. Michael had his tenth birthday this summer; he is my best friend. We sleep together and do all the chores. Then there is Esther; she is seven, but she brings a blanket to the table even though it is August. The blanket is dirty and brown and sits on her lap, rolled up like a cat. She drags it with her wherever she goes. Outside too. The other four are stair steps: Moses is five, Simon four, little Henry— that is what Lydia called him—became three only a day before his father died, and the baby, Lena, is somewhere between one and two.

Here is the arrangement. Michael and I are to manage the livestock and keep the weeds down. Joseph and Moses will take charge and bring others to help with the harvest. I wonder if Joseph forgets that I plan to return to Pennsylvania next month. I do not want my parents to worry if I stay longer. They will hear of Henry's death, for his younger brothers all live in Somerset County with the parents. Word will get back. Perhaps one of Henry's brothers can come give relief. I did not expect to want to be back home with Father.

The death was bad enough, but now there is Lydia. She does not seem right in the head. Catherine comes often—we could not manage without her—but she goes around with furrows in her forehead. I know it is serious. Lydia says nothing. Here is how it happened. The tree went the wrong way, snapped backward, and Henry could not jump fast enough. Michael ran to the neighbors to get Abraham Zug. Michael says the top of his father's head was smashed and blood ran from his mouth. When Michael and Abraham returned, Lydia lay with her head on Henry's chest. She kept crying, "Henry, Henry." Her fingers had to be pried loose. Michael cried when he told me. The night Henry died—we all gathered at this cabin—Lydia kept calling Henry's name. He was dead. It was all she could say. "Henry, Henry." Her voice was all wobbly from crying. Then she would shriek. Little Henry came to her and took her red, chapped hands in his tiny ones. He tapped on her chest with the heel of his little hand and said, "Momma, be still." She has not said a word since. She walks about silently, fixes food, dresses the little ones, but says not a word. She is a spook.

About the water. Several times I have seen Lydia fill a bucket at the well, walk to Henry's grave along the edge of the pasture, and pour water on his burial place. It is near to being a mucky flood. I do not go close for fear I may sink in the mud. Sometimes I think: what if Henry's bones come floating above ground? Maybe a knee will poke through first. There is more, also to do with water. I have seen Lydia take a full bucket to the top of a nearby hillock. She sits down under the tree, flutters her skirts, and slowly pours water down the hill. She rearranges and sits in different directions, doing the same pouring. I could not look any longer. I must tell Joseph; he has already removed Henry's shovel and pick. I do not want Michael to see. I do not like to think that Lydia has become a witch.

Joseph goes about very sober. He does not scratch as fast under his beard now. Instead, he pulls and tugs. I have seen him and Catherine give each other looks when Simon picks on little Henry. Lydia says nothing. Someone will have to step in. I can do the field work, but I do not want to give spankings. I did not know so much trouble could happen. I cannot leave Michael here by himself. Sometime I want to ask him what happened last year when their family tried to return to Somerset and Joseph intercepted them. But now is not the time.

I am sorry that I never cared much for Henry. He was too slow and had to have the whole story repeated. Everyone else had laughed at the joke, and he needed to have it explained. At the funeral my uncle Samuel from Sugarcreek—Isaac's father—said that Henry was a diligent worker and wanted to get ahead for his family. There was some disarray about the funeral. I did not hear it all, but there were questions as to who should be in charge. Lydia would not talk, so Catherine and Joseph made decisions. Joseph said this Samuel Joder had not preached since he moved to Ohio. Joseph wanted Abraham Zug to preach, but Catherine reminded Joseph that Abraham had only been a deacon in Pennsylvania. Or something like that. They settled on Samuel. I could not tell that he showed any rust. I am glad they picked Samuel because I like Isaac. Blackey and Lady rode well together. Isaac is long-winded, but he talked with me on the trip as if I were an adult, something my father never has time for.

I wonder if Joseph ever thinks about being a minister. It is not something we choose, but it seems to come with a naturalness for us Joders. Some day I could be the one standing up, with all eyes on me. That is less frightful than watching Lydia. I do not know what she will do next.

7.

YOST

September 1813

I must get more land. I must accumulate more with three boys to provide for. Another farm, more acreage. John Schrock gave $527 last year for the Tadger estate. That was only 248 acres. Better land costs a pretty penny for only a third or half the number of acres. I must keep alert to get what I need. Someone heading for the Promised Land may want a quick sale.

We are fortunate to have disposed of Reuben to the Great Adventure out West. No farm, no settlement, no state was ever large enough for the both of us. It was a relief not to have him around, interfering and making the rest of us uncomfortable when Father died. Now I no longer need be on my guard for what Reuben may be trying to pull out from under me. I think he has the sense to stay away from making claim to any inheritance. But with Reuben I can never be completely sure. I wonder what land he found in Ohio and how much he had to fork over.

Henry has been entrusted with dividing Father's estate. Henry always seems afraid of me, even though he is the oldest, but I believe I can trust him. Father had already divided up most of his parcels, so there may not be much land for the taking. Nothing like those brothers of his who moved to Ohio and have over a thousand acres between them. That is enough to make me consider pulling up stakes. Father never knew the total number of acres he owned, but I was grateful that he looked out for us boys. Land was cheap when he first moved to Meyersdale. He only had to give $15, maybe $25, a hundred acres for land west of the Alleghenies.

Eliza is finally producing boys. Last March we added our third. Joseph, Lazarus, and now Gideon. Only six months old and he is a hefty one to pack about; he will take up his share of space when grown. Eliza says the boys are too close in age. I do not see a problem; more than one a year is almost impossible. If we wait too long she will start having girls again. I say this in jest, but she does not smile. I try to make life more jolly, but she prefers to wallow in the valley. I had no idea she would become such a worrier. I wish I could put her mind at ease. Her latest tune is that I am too much given to idle trampings, that I do not pay enough heed to the crops. She is impossible to figure out. All the time she complained that I worked past dark on the new house. Now this. I say to her, "Woman, the harvest is yet a month away. What do you want me to do, blow on the corn silk?" She cannot allow herself one little smile.

She thinks I go to the Casselman and come back empty-handed with no catch of fish. She does not know that I tramp among the Indian graves. She would not believe it. Or if she did, she would find that another cause for worry. Ever since Father's last conversations about the Indians, I have felt a fascination. I keep returning to this Indian Burial Ground but a few miles from here. I have never liked walking in cemeteries, not near my mother's, nor Marie's, and now, not near Father's fresh site. I do not stay long at the Burial Ground either. I cannot make sense of their arrangement, but it fascinates.

191

Thirty mounds covered with stone. They doubtless used a different manner of thinking. I wonder if the largest mounds mean more bodies piled high or people of greater significance. It is a mystery.

Last spring and into summer, when Father helped build my new log house, he told these stories. Father did all the chinking and daubing. He dressed all my large beams. I had dug the cellar the previous winter, so that was finished. Father seemed healthy enough and content to live with us those months. I never thought he might be wearing down. How particular he was at making level the beams for the loft. While we worked together at night—I used daytime for the crops—Father told tales of family members I had never heard of. Of course I know the story of the Indian massacre of some of my relatives; I will pass that on to my boys when they are older. But these other tales—Hershbergers mingling with warriors—well, it is good that Eliza did not hear them. It turns out that Reuben is not the only strange one in our family.

For one thing, there is an uncle—my father's youngest brother—a Peter by name, still living. I remember we never had much to do with Peter and his family, but I thought the age difference of twenty years accounted for the absence. Out of nowhere Father said, "Peter does not believe it is right for the individual to own land." I stopped pounding or sawing or whatever. "You heard right; he will not buy land." Father sat down to take a rest. I put aside my foot adze. I could not trust myself with a sharp-edged blade when Father said something that disturbing. I remember his words exactly. "Peter says land is a gift from God for all to enjoy. He rents whatever is available and makes do."

"What is he, an Indian?" I asked.

"As far as anyone can tell, Peter has had no recourse with Indians. Yet, he comes up with a line of thought like unto theirs."

I queried Father at length. He had no knowledge that Peter had ever contacted the great-uncles who survived the massacre. Father also had no answer as to how someone could be a farmer and not care about ownership. Then Father said another thing that stopped me, "Peter belongs in the city."

I watched Father walk back to the shaving-horse; his pants hung loose in the back, he limped on his bad leg. Eliza says we should have noticed that Father had lost weight. Catherine claimed that Father was very thin when he returned from living with us. All I could think on was the horror of what he had said. Assigning a brother to the city was akin to turning him over to the Evil One.

Father also talked about those great-uncles of mine, David and Daniel. They survived the massacre but never were the same afterwards. They had too much contact with the Indians, even lived with them, and got turned in their thinking. Father's brother Amos is almost as hard to explain. He has too much of the itch. Never content to stay in one place. Father said he lived here awhile, then in Berks, then back in Somerset for most of twenty years. Then he moved his family to the state of Kentucky, then to Ohio. Father said that when Amos lived in Kentucky, he and his sons owned over 1500 acres.

Amos cannot be faulted for desiring land, but the trouble came when he married an orphan girl. He was almost thirty. The orphan part is not a problem, although thirty years is very old for marrying the first time. Here is the stopper; he got mixed up with the Dunkards and they made him a preacher. This Amos went to a Dunkard church service and got caught up in the emotion. Father said—he wasn't there, of course— that Amos flung himself at the minister's feet, crying, "Save me, Lord Jesus. Save me, please." At that very instant, lightning struck hard, splitting a tree right outside the building.

Amos jumped up and commenced shouting gibberish. Father wondered if his brother's words were Indian talk. Now two of Amos's sons are preachers with the Dunkards; one of them travels on horseback, evangelizing and planting churches. All of that carrying on and I never knew any of this.

I will keep my boys close when they are grown; I will use land as my bait. A farm ready for each of them. For as many boys as Eliza can fetch, I will have land waiting. Today they only care about climbing the outside ladder. That was part of Father's last work here. We attached short pieces of board up the outside of the house so that the boys can reach their bed in the loft. There is room for ten of them up there, unless they are all as big as Gideon is going to be. Eliza does not trust Lazarus with climbing and insists that I reach both the older ones up through the hole in the loft floor. I will humor her until Lazarus figures out how to get up and down when she is not looking. If only she would let herself smile a little. She is always afraid of something. Even with Father's sudden departure—after he had gone back to live with Catherine—I insist that we have not known more death than any other family. But Eliza will not listen; she still pines for Marie.

Sometime I may tell her of the other oddity Father spoke of. He had a sister, three years his younger, who completely disappeared. "How can that be?" I asked him. He had never mentioned this child, not even when Marie was taken.

"No one knows what happened," he said. He covered his mouth, as if he were ashamed of his few jagged teeth. "It was in the heat of summer; Maggie may have been five."

"Maggie?"

"For Magdalena. She was just little. Tiny little." Father had pointed to a spot barely above his knee. "Her older sister, Katherine, was to have been keeping watch. But she had nothing to report; she heard nothing. No scream, nothing. We scoured the woods for tracks, any unusual sign, a part of her dress, but found nothing."

"But people, children least of all, do not disappear without cause." I had never heard of such irregularity. "What did you do?"

Father shrugged his shoulders as if nothing could be done. "We do not know what happened. She may have wandered into the woods and been devoured. We do not know. Black bears roamed frequently. She may have gotten lost, fallen asleep, walked further in a wrong direction, ended up at a stranger's door and known nought where she came from. We do not know. It is a mystery that we will never know."

I wanted to ask Father what he thought about Marie's death now that three years had passed. If he had any misgivings about Reuben's guilt. I could have asked, but I did not. Now Father is gone. It is better to let the past be past. I believe that is what Father would say.

All these family stories make Reuben's strangeness look less out of line. I do not mean that I would welcome him back. Only that with time passing, life goes better for me. Eliza says I saved all my bad temper for Reuben. If that is so, then with Reuben gone I do not have so much evil appetite to curb. I do not know why Brother Isaac stares at me when he says we are all born with an evil nature. But Eliza may be right. A noose of anger has been lifted from my neck.

8.

$\mathcal{F}$ RANEY

April 1814

I have known how to spell my name in English, Franey Zug, already four years. I am but ten years old. For two months now I have been alone with Father. The aloneness does not frighten, but every time someone leaves, there is need for one less place at the table. David is 19 and of the age to marry, Father says, so we should be glad he has found his girl. I do not know why he could not wait until fall as others do, but Father says it is better to marry than be tempted. There is something not right about a wedding in February. It is too cold, for one thing.

I still feel a sickness for Rachel and Levi; they have been gone five long months. Gone to that Ohio, like so many others. Father calls me homesick. That cannot be, for I am at home. He should send to them to ask if they are homesick. I wonder if Rachel sheds tears. She is the only sister I have known, except for Gertrude, my best friend.

Father said he could see it coming, Rachel's day, with Levi working here all summer. I do not mind that she married Levi; he was nearly a brother already because of Jonas. Last summer Levi would reach in his pocket and give me a piece of maple sugar candy; then tell me to go play somewhere else. That is one of the signs I should have paid attention to. I looked at Rachel and she smiled her silly jiggle and said, "Yes, be off a little while."

When we have church, I still look for Levi's hat. His has a wider brim like they wear in Mifflin County. All the other men have hats from here, with the rounded crowns pointing out. Each hat makes a wheel and Levi's has rolled out the door. I like the way the hats sit on pegs, lined up in exact rows, even if one is missing.

I do not like that Ohio. Too many of my family are being swallowed up. First, baby Eli. Then Jonas bought land; he said it was close to Abraham's. That brought no gladness. Eli is not my baby, but I gave him care and he seemed like my own. Then one day—the sky was very gray; not one speck of blue— Abraham returned, fetched Magdalena and Eli, and before I knew it they were gone, ripped away. Now we hear they have another boy and, just last month, added a baby girl. I do not know if I will ever see them.

At least Jonas has had a change of heart. I clapped my hands when he sold his old Ohio land last year. But coming to his senses did me no good. Who should he sell to but Levi Speicher. Before I could turn around twice, they were gone: Rachel and Levi and their precious little Evangeline. There I was, rent asunder again. I hate that Ohio.

I said to Father, "It is not right that we should suffer all this loss. First, Mother. Now these others, walking away on their own feet." Father says not to pout; he will not cast a shadow on any of them, not even on David.

I do not trust Jonas even though he has sold his old Ohio land. I believe he speaks one way and looks another. He lives with Mary and their baby only a mile away, but every time they come to visit he talks of going back north where Mary's family lives. Every single time. Sometimes twice. Father says Mary may not be happy here—she likes the wide open valleys—but he says not to mention it.

Now that Rachel is gone, I sit with Mary when we have church. I am getting a little wiser; I do not pay their Jeremiah as much heed as I might otherwise. He spits up and I do not like his slobber on my dress. Sometimes though, I lean my head on Mary's shoulder and put a hand on Jeremiah's blanket. Mary is almost as big as when she carried him.

I am glad I do not have to sit with the aunts. Aunt Martha made a handkerchief for me; that is the only nice thing about her. When the church sitting gets long, I roll two corners to the center, tuck in the flaps, and have a baby wrapped up to swing that is all my own. Or I fold and tuck to make a rabbit with long ears. Even a mouse with whiskers. Mary does not say anything, but she does not notice because she gives all her attention to Jeremiah. The handkerchief has more softness than most of our cloth; Aunt Martha calls it linsey-woolsey. In each corner she stitched a flower: a pansy or a peony. I like the yellow pansy the best. I did not know she could make anything so pretty.

There is one good thing about our shrinking family: less work. Father has decided not to plant flax this year. How I hate pulling the ugly parts from the good fiber. I said as much to Father and he scolded, "No, Franey, we are not to hate anything, not even hackling." I suppose he is right, but I do not like cutting my fingers on stickery old burs. It is such a tiresome job; Father spanked me once for not being more careful. He made me bend over so he could strike the backs of my bare legs. Then I learned that hickory stings more than bleeding fingers. Father says we will ask Aunt Martha to spin new clothes for me as I have need. That is a second good thing about her. I should be glad that she keeps me from all that pulling and pulling and binding and drying and breaking. I hate that work.

I help Father with the cooking when he calls, but I would rather read. I feel guilty when he has to call a second time. Jonas found a copy of a book called *Pilgrim's Progress*. I have read it twice from cover to cover and am beginning again. There are words I do not know, but I skip over and hope they are not important. I have asked Father if I might be allowed to take schooling next winter. He has not said yes—his face does not change one whit—but neither has he said no. When Jonas comes to visit, I get help with some of Pilgrim's words. Mary can read also, but she takes no interest. There is the "Slough of Despondency." Is it *slouw*, like a dog's howl, or *sloo* as in school, or even *sluff*? When I asked on the meaning, whether it might be the same as all my family moving to Ohio, Jonas looked startled and said, "Yes, that may be it."

I should like Aunt Martha better, but she had the smell of grease about her all winter. Perhaps it is not grease, but it is something that got hot and sat around too long. She frightens me with the stories she tells, especially the one about the little girl Frieda. That name tells me right away I will not like it. Aunt Martha said that this little Frieda died because she was curious. She climbed a fence where she was not supposed to go, and a bull came along and got the best of her. "Do not make the same mistake and think you can run fast," Aunt Martha said. "Your legs are no better than Frieda's and she was trampled." Aunt Martha looked as if she could see right through my dress. "All because she ventured where she was not meant to go." Aunt Martha's face gets dark, dark brown when she tells stories and her lips pucker with, "Shame, shame." I turn to go, but she is never done. "Let that be a lesson, Franey."

Aunt Katie is no better; she always looks stern and likes to boss. One time I walked in on her upset with me. She was saying to Father, "This girl is not learning the ways of a woman. How will she manage when someone asks her to marry?" I think Father heard me tiptoe to the corner bench, because he said nothing. Perhaps he had no answer. Most of the boys at church are stupid. Daniel walks around with his mouth open, catching flies. Gertrude already has her eye on Matthew, and Aaron's pants are too short. David said it is not Aaron's fault that his mother cannot keep up. I will stick with Father and hope he stays well a long, long time. I do not want him thudding at the fireplace like Mother.

Father makes shoes for people; Jonas calls him a tradesman. Sometimes when people ask Father to do their cobbling, they leave behind a smoked ham or they offer a blacksmithing job in return. Father seems more satisfied now than with all that old farm work. We still have our horses, a milk cow, chickens, and a mean rooster. I love eggs; I could eat eggs three times a day. I do not mind searching for them in the hen house, even up in the rafters. And I love to go with Father to the tannery; he knows everything about leather. When we get home he knows how long to dry the different kinds and how to stretch them. I watch him work; even his mouth pulls to help stretch. I hold the leather when he needs more hands. I wish my arms were stronger; I cannot hold tight enough. I would be happy to be a tanner when I am grown, but that is not what Aunt Katie has in mind.

The last time we went for leather at Little Crossings we used the new stone arch bridge to cross the Casselman. No one was around, so Father stopped the horses and studied the design at some length. He used words like *keystone* and *buddress*. I think he means *buttress*. "Notice how the stones overlap; no stone sits entirely on top of another." Father says this is an old, old method, used even in the Old Country. I like the design, but when we started across I did not want to look. I heard the clackety of horses' hooves on cobblestone and felt the wagon lurch. I leaned into Father. When I came out from his coat, I could see the river under us on both sides.

Father says the bridge is not as high as I think, maybe only a hundred feet from the river. That does not mean anything to me. I only know I did not want the horses to get excited and start jumping. Aunt Katie had said the bridge would collapse when the boards were taken away. I like the bridge, but I do not like what it does. Father says the bridge is a very important part of the road leading West. He says the land goes far, far beyond Ohio.

When we were safely home, I tried making my own arch with rocks. The stones were not as flat on their edges as they needed to be, and their curve was not smooth. When I asked Father if there would not be advantage in having our own bridge across the stream behind our house, he called me a little dreamer. He smiled though, so I think it was all right. I wonder how streams know where to pick their way, which rock to tumble over, where to make passage. Father says not to pay those questions heed. There is much that we are not meant to understand.

I try to be content, but sometimes I cannot help but think about Ohio and that little girl, Frieda. Today I saw the moon in full daylight. I am sure of it. I do not know where it usually hides or where the sun goes at night, but I will ask Father to explain.

9.

$\mathcal{P}$ O L L Y
December 1815

All my pretty ones! Two precious little girls. Taken. Does the heart know nothing but sorrow? I can bear no more. I rub the sleeve of my dress so much so that a patch of grime grows dark near the elbow. Two weeks ago I gave no thought. Christian says we were lulled into a complacency. When we loosen our guard, the wolf strikes. Oh, that this Evil might have been prevented. Poppa says not to gnash the teeth; we cannot fly against the will of God.

The wolf came this time on feet of illness. They call it diphtheria, this disease that afflicts the young. Not only the Amish young, but others as well. What did I do to deserve such treatment? I look to our John each morning and night for telltale signs. He is only six months and stiffens when I pry open his mouth and try to inspect his throat. But he is all I have left. Two Maries and now Barbara gone. I cannot leave John untended. His nose has always been too big for the rest of his face—like his grandfather's—but he is all I have left.

I try to look inside his mouth with haste, before he knows that I have come to poke. Or I look when Christian stands by my side. Our heads bump into each other, but we have the two sets of eyes. Christian holds John's arms so he cannot flail, but nothing calms our fears. Even Christian is distraught. As soon as I step back from looking I begin to doubt. Did I overlook a patch? The light is poor. Did I miss the grayness? Was there a yellow patch? I am all knotted up. I take John to rock and nurse until he quiets. I fear this attention to his mouth will mark him for life. Christian has always had trouble with mucous in the morning. He must spit or swallow backward to rid himself.

Nothing can bring back my Marie and Barbara. I would do anything—change their names, be more earnest in supplication—if it would make a difference. I see their faces and the sweetness of their tiny fingers. Barbara had the fat little hands with dimples where the knuckles should be. She was well on her way to being two years old. Much the easier baby. Marie, the big sister, had her third birthday in October; that seems long ago. Back then, life passed with such peacefulness. We did not know what could transpire. Momma was right about the name; it is all my fault. I did not think that what Eliza endured could be mine as well.

The girls started with coughs, first Marie and then Barbara. I thought these were but trifling colds and would pass away. We have been through the runny nose and the red ears and survived. This time Barbara sneezed often. Short little snorts, rather like a cat. Often three times in a row, one right after the other. Her body shook with each sneeze; then she looked up at us and wrinkled her nose. Christian and I saw a cuteness in it. How vanity overtook us. At first. A few days later she pulled on my skirts and gave little gasps as if she had trouble breathing.

I jumped to the other end of the rope. I scolded Barbara. I thought she was trying unduly to get my attention, to keep me from my work. Momma had said not to spoil the child. If only

I could take back that sharp tongue! Barbara burrowed her sad, blue eyes in my skirts and grabbed tight fists of apron. Now Momma says not to break the switch on myself. Pining will not bring them back. Yet I cannot rid myself of my blunders. Both my pretty ones!

When the coughing and sneezing persisted with both girls, I asked Marie to open wide. She cried and said it hurt in the jaws. With Christian's help we got her to open and stick out her tongue. Then it was that we saw a thickness about her throat. I know it was an ugly yellow; Christian called it gray. The color is of little consequence, except that we must know what to look for with John. Within a few days Barbara became more fretful also. Christian forced her to open. We saw the same ugliness as in Marie. By then neither girl would eat. I sometimes slipped a bit of broth or tea into one or the other, but they cried in loud fits. Barbara would say, "Hurt. Mouth hurt. No, no, no." I scolded her for saying no. I did not think we were going to lose them. I was afraid, but I did not believe it could happen.

Marie was puny as a baby; we always had to coax her: "You cannot live if you do not eat." When the sickness came, I thought she was becoming contrary again. One night, oh, I do not want to remember. One night Marie sucked in great gasps to breathe and get air. I tried to give comfort by rocking her in my arms. I sang hymns, all that I knew. I held her close to me. All at once my chair stopped in its forward rock. Marie's head had fallen quite away. I screamed for Christian. There was no staying of the head. Her eyes rolled back. I did not know she could die in my arms.

We buried her the next day. Because Barbara was still ill, we did not want to venture far from the house. Christian dug a spot that is but a short walk behind the pine grove. Three days later he dug a second grave by Marie's side. The Lord saw fit that these sisters should make their bed together underground, just as they had in our cabin. When I go out back to take scraps for the chickens I see the two little mounds. Only a few months ago the girls ran and jumped on the same spot.

With the second death Christian takes unnecessary remorse. In my delirium after losing Marie I clung to Barbara. I said to Christian that we must yank the offending matter from her throat. "If we can but remove the evil," I said, "then Barbara will have safe passage. We must do this work for her." Christian shook his head, but he took a spoon anyway. We now have four, all made of pewter. Christian tried to loosen what was stuck. I assisted, as best I could, by holding down Barbara's tongue.

I have said to Christian many times that we should not blame ourselves for this loose thinking. We were muddle-headed, having just buried our firstborn. Christian stays grim; his color is all gone out. I tell him to smoke his pipe, but he will have nothing to do with it. "Say nothing of this to anyone," he whispers. I have been careful not to tell Momma of our effort. Christian gnaws at a chicken bone long after the meat is gone. He chews on a piece of rope. I will need to hide it. I hear him outside at night. He does not whistle anymore but sounds like a sick dog that needs to be put out of its misery.

At first our probing seemed to give Barbara relief. She took a longer breath than we had heard for quite some time. "Good, good," I said. "If you could just get under enough to pry the yellow out." I should not have given encouragement. Christian tried again. This time we heard the rattle. Barbara was gone. The eyes staring, just like Marie's. How can I ever forget? Christian put down the spoon and fled the house. I was left by myself with another dead baby.

Somehow Christian drew himself together and fetched Momma and Poppa. "Look to what is left," he said. I pulled baby John to myself and held him all night. I wept and he whimpered. I could not look at the dark covered form in the corner.

I thought Eliza would come to me in my sore need. But Momma reminded me that Eliza was with child. They now have their fourth boy; he came one day after we buried our Marie, two days before we let go of Barbara. I tried to find happiness in their news. We still have our John. Eliza and Yost could not have brought their children anyway, subjecting them to this dread disease. Many of our people near at hand did not bring their children to the funeral, especially not to Barbara's. Word spreads that this may be a disease passed from one to another. Christian and I may be at risk, but we watch only for John.

Momma has been stronger in the faith than when she lost her first grandchild five years ago. She tells me to stop my rubbing. "This is sickness," she says. "We know not whence it comes, but we take what the Lord sends of good or ill. The first Marie's death, that was pure Evil. That could not have been of God."

She tried to comfort me by remembering the three signs of innocence for Hans Haslibacher, the Anabaptist who suffered long ago. Christian remains skeptical, but for Momma there is refuge. She reminded me of how red the sun was the evening after we buried Marie. She says the same thing happened with Barbara's burial. I have no recollection, but Momma insisted that the sunsets both nights were of a brilliance. She says the sky was streaked with bright red running through patches of pink and blue. She had to remind me also that Marie's head dropped away in death. That is another sign of innocence, just as with Haslibacher. For Momma his tribulation was a witness to a wicked world, just as our suffering must be endured. Christian says not to think on it more. Then he grabs the rope. He says we must look to John and hope that he may be spared. I have vowed I will never scold John, only give discipline from a peaceful spirit.

We must hold fast. The other night I was given a vision. I looked out our tiny window and saw two huge hands clasped in prayer, the thumbs tucked inside. I do not know why the thumbs were hiding. Perhaps that is John crouching, and Christian and I are to form a canopy to keep him safe. I cannot bear to lose another.

10.

J O N A S

October 1816

*J*am getting to where I have a good eye for trees. I used to think a tree was a tree, just as a potato was a potato. Trees provided shade in the summer and then disrobed. If evergreens, they kept their color all winter as a relief from drabness. I used to think there was only one kind of oak. Now Levi has shown me different kinds so that on a given day, I look only for black oaks. Then the next day it may be pin oaks that I seek out, or bur oaks, or what have you. I do not limit myself to oaks, of course, for there are ample forests of elm, ash, and maple, even beech. Yes, beech is a good one to keep count on with its smooth, gray bark.

On this, my second trip to Ohio, trees have been my shelter as well. I ride Sam over all manner of terrain, but whether traversing a steep mountain slope or ascending a gentle, rolling hill, I see trees on either side, marking my path, shading me from sun and hail. Only when crossing river beds am I left unprotected. Even then the trees on the bank ahead beckon me as if to say, "After you pass through rolling waters, we are here to dry you and give you protection again."

I am in my tenth day of riding back to Centre County, and I will gladly trade this saddle for my wife and boys. Only two more nights—barring the unforeseen—and I will sleep with my Mary. She is big with child, but I will put my arms around her. It has been most of six weeks since I saw her or Jeremiah and Adam. I could not make this trip without Shem living close by to give Mary and the boys support. Sometimes I feel guilty leaving them behind, but guilt is no newcomer. I still have the same hands.

I subject myself to all manner of Evil as I ride. Sometimes the wind roars overhead. I could know death in the teeth of a hungry, red fox. I could drown at the bottom of a muddy river. If I allowed myself to think on all of the possible terror, I would never have swung my leg onto Sam. A few short years ago I would never have started a trip of this magnitude. All was different then. Polly was all I wanted to swing my leg onto. I have not forgotten her entirely.

These trees give me a way to take stock. I stand at the foot of a great white oak and think to measure how many of me there would be, standing one on top of the other, to reach clear to the top. I am shorter than most men, but I figure it would take ten to fifteen, maybe twenty of me, to reach to the top point of an oak. I do not deserve the favor of a God who could make such a tree. I do not deserve how things have worked out—groveling in sin with my head barely off the ground—but I have responsibilities to tend to. I cannot turn back now.

These trees add to my sustenance. The walnuts I do not bother with, for the outer casing leaves such a blackness that my fingers stain everything I touch. I have known enough of that. The hickory nut, however, is a prize that I gladly collect; even the chestnut is a pleasure to add to my knapsack for cracking at night. I watch for an abundance of squirrels, and without fail, that is where I find the harvest. I put a few pieces of hickory in my mouth and see how long I can ride until the nuts, skins and all, have disappeared from my mouth. I do not allow myself to chew or swallow any morsel whole; that way the game lasts longer. If I make enough of these trips, I will measure the miles by the number of nuts I consume.

I seek diversion as I ride, for I am afraid to think too much on what I have just accomplished. I have bought land again. Father says I was impulsive the other time. I was visiting Abraham then, out of curiosity. He pointed to a plot of land right beside his that was for sale. Abraham said the opportunity might not come again, and I bit. In less than a year I realized how foolish the transaction had been. Too many others moving to that same location along the Walnut Creek. Too many bad memories of Abraham. I regretted the haste with which I had sunk money into the ground. But again, my bumbling soon became smoothed over. I expressed my change of mind to Levi, and he was quick to make offer.

Now I must ponder how to avoid telling Father about Rachel. And to think that I could be living there in her stead! Levi is pleased with his location, but I fear for my sister. She looks white in the face, like she has seen a ghost, and her brown hair falls in *strubbles*. She says she has not regained strength since their baby was born two months ago. She grabbed my arm and entreated me, "Say nothing of this to Father and Franey. It takes longer than usual to make recovery; that is all." Levi says the birthing, Rachel's third, took place over parts of three days. He wears a brave face when he tells how he feared neither mother nor baby would survive. Rachel continues with spotting; I noticed a foul smell lingers about her. Like unto rotting potatoes. Levi thinks it must be afterbirth. I did not offer encouragement when he said he wished for a good powwower. He mentioned Reuben Hershberger, but he lives some distance from them. I do not like the idea of Reuben bending over my sister, but I could not say that. Abraham's Magdalena helps with Rachel's work, even though she is busy with four of their own. Their Eli, the baby I knew a short time, has passed six years and seems more than twice as old as my Jeremiah. The way Abraham tells it, Eli has been carrying buckets of water for two years already.

Rachel has no choice but to accept help; her strength is gone by mid-morning. Her condition gives me pause with regard to telling Mary of my purchase. Perhaps the frontier is no place for women. Abraham's neighbor Lydia is a pitiful case. Her husband, Henry, was smashed in the head by a falling tree. I would be no better if left bereft with my children to tend. Whenever I mention Ohio, Mary scratches herself. She knows I never lost interest, but she was not pleased at all to hear of my plans to travel again. Her father, Shem, speaks of the frontier, however, and that gives me encouragement. I do not mean to move immediately, but if our way becomes clear, we will have title in hand. In truth, there are several parcels in my name. I bought them from James Madison no less. I do not mean that I had direct exchange with the president, but he owns large tracts of land which are being divided up and sold to whomever produces the money.

I will seek to reassure Mary; my new land is located near to where Benedict Schrock has made purchase. That is north and to the east of where most of the Amish first made settlement. Schrock grew up in Somerset County and is one of us. My land is more isolated and has not been identified as part of any township yet, but Wooster is the county seat. With Abraham taking more leadership in the Walnut Creek church, I wanted to keep some distance from him. Mary knows all too well how family members in the same church can cause trouble; Shem has had his share of quarrelsome relatives.

I like the Apple Creek that flows nearby, clean and clear, but not broad enough to cause harm. Creeks run every which way. Schrock says there is talk of building canals close by. What a boost that would be for marketing farm produce. I spent all of a day walking through piles of leaves on my property, stepping off plots of tillable ground. Sometimes I still cannot believe it is mine. It will be a challenge to clear. But I would rather use my axe to fell trees, even if they are huge, than to break my back digging ditches in a swamp. Schrock speculated that Indians must have grown crops in the swamps at one time. I must remember to tell Mary that the Indians have been gone for several years.

Everywhere I ride I see our debt to the Indian. The trails we use were once theirs. Before that, large herds of buffalo had their way. Abraham says they grazed in the vicinity of Walnut Creek. I had never seen tall grass like that; buffalo grass, they call it. Why an Indian would want to kill a beast of that magnitude—one buffalo can weigh two or even three thousand pounds—is hard to understand. I would get my hides and food from smaller game. Abraham says we should not try to understand the ways of those different from us.

Some days I have trouble making sense of my own deeds. Not that I gave Abraham any reason to question. My mind leaps back to events that are too dreadful to think on in the full sun. How could that have happened? How could I have convinced Mary to trust me? And Shem. I intended to tell her all. After we were married. Sometimes I still wish for there to be someone who knows. Someone other than Sam. At one time I thought of telling Levi. But that is not to be. He has enough to worry over with Rachel's condition. No, telling is a weakness I must not succumb to. Mary would take it very hard. And I am not prepared for all that might transpire if she knew. She would tell Shem, first of all. And I have Jeremiah and Adam to think of. Sam passes nothing on. And the trees help with their distractions. But with Mary I must hold the reins tight. I could not bear to cause her harm or lose her. How Levi keeps his wits with Rachel's illness, I do not know.

Mary has much patience with the boys. On Sundays when I am in the house longer and I tire of their play and chatter, I am quick to resort to a harsh word. I have had to put a switch to Adam when quiet is not soon restored. But Mary has a way with the boys—she sends them outside to whistle with their thumbs—so that my edginess is reduced. At least they are no longer babies; my hands become woodenish with the little ones. I will soon need to make peace with another crying baby. Mary knows better than to ask me to help. I do not deserve her trust. The number of people I dare not fail multiplies each year: Father, Shem, Mary and the boys. A new baby. Franey too. I cannot let any of them down.

In another month it will be four years since Mary and I married. I will never forget those first weeks: visiting family, setting up our own household, touching her black, black hair. I could not get enough. I cannot imagine that Father ever considered not milking the cow in the morning. I was rather a bumbler at first, but now it goes better. I did not mean to frighten Mary with my haste; she said my eyes looked to explode. Now I protest when she pulls up the cover at night, even in the summer, but she thinks Jeremiah may be watching in the dark.

There have been misunderstandings, to be sure. She did not like my walking through the house with my boots on; she called it clomping. She did not like some of my barnyard noises and wanted me to wash up more before coming inside. When she gave me the silence and turned her back, I made the necessary changes. She works miracles with the food. I do not know what she does with the cornbread, but there is a flavor she calls a Beiler surprise. I cannot think what herb it might be. And she makes little pie crusts in the shape of half moons for our valley, and she fills them with fruit: the apple, cherry, whatever we have. If she knew I am this close to home—one more day—she would be busy baking. Her garden looks like Eden itself with the weeds chased away and the rows laid out in order, just as Mother did. I will promise her that when we move there will be fewer stones. More fertile land for her string beans. And no snakes; she does not like them at all.

I will convince her that we can manage without her parents. I used to think that I could never desert Father, but I have grown accustomed. I will miss Shem. He is a solid manager when it comes to farming, but he also thinks on spiritual matters. They have made him a minister for us in Half Moon Valley. He does not get ruffled easily and always has an answer. One day I blurted my doubts about salvation. Shem and I were standing at his cistern drawing water for household use, and my words escaped before I could pull them back. "How can we know if we will make it or not?" I asked.

Shem did not hesitate. "We cannot know," he said. "None of us can be assured of our standing. We can but submit ourselves to the will of the church." He removed the rope from around the full bucket, and we began filling jugs. "We can only hope to partake of the divine nature some day." Then he commenced a long tirade against those groups that have more of a revival notion and that promise security. "There is pride in thinking we are safe now. We cannot know until we get over yonder."

I mentioned my neighbor Andrew Weaver who speaks with such conviction about the healing peace of knowing his sins have been washed in the blood.

"Stay away," Shem said. His face turned a crimson, but not from exertion with the water. "Those are Church of the

Brethren people, given to that kind of individual assurance."
He bit at his thumb. "Do not dabble in dangerous waters."

I nodded and have not mentioned Andrew since. Even as I
ride I can feel my hands shake at Shem's distemper. That is
why I need the trees to distract.

Sam steps on a branch; it makes a sharp snap beneath us.
Soon it will be dark and I must look for a spot of pine needles.
Oh, to be home again, to feel Mary by my side. It is not sleep
I crave, although a feather tick will be pleasant now that it is
cooler. It is Mary. When we lie on our sides she curves her
body inside mine. I run my hand over all her shape and pull
her softness to me—even with a new life forming. I did not
know if she would let me touch her belly swollen with Jeremiah, but she seems to like it. By now though, she may
protest at too much rough and tumble. Another twig snaps.

"Mary? Is that you? Is that your voice? Mary?" I do not
know why I say these things aloud. It is habit to say things to
Sam. Most nights the wind makes too much noise, but now I
miss it. Of a sudden, there is too much quiet.

"Mary? Is there trouble? What is it? Is it one of the boys?" I
dig my heels into Sam's sides. He skittles sideways. My heels
do not relax, and Sam speeds up to a full gallop. He cannot
hear Mary's voice the way I do.

I bend low to Sam's dirty mane and whisper into his sweat,
"Get us home! There is trouble. Mary has need." I am startled
at my words, but something bids me make haste.

"The chimney, Sam! I did not clean it as I ought last spring."
Now I see it all. The weather has taken on a chill, and Mary
has added extra wood on the fire to keep the boys warm.
"Mary!" I hiss. "Do not seek after too much heat." Sam's ears
lay low. I must remain steady so Sam does not take a spill. I
grab the reins tighter. "I am coming, Mary. If you can but hold
on another day, I will be home. One more day. No! Stay your

hand from that log. Use the extra blankets instead." Why was I not more careful before I left home? I knew to take precautions; yet I left things undone. I am still *schmutzig*. What will Father say? Shem! I have put others' lives in jeopardy again. I will do anything if they are spared. This once. I will tell someone.

Sam's legs stretch. I despair. He cannot keep this pace for another full day; we will arrive too late. There is a bad scene: white ashes with red coals glowing. I do not know if the boys got out. Mary could not have carried both at once in her bigness. She may not have smelled the smoke in time. If only Shem came by and saved her. Saved us both. No, the ashes speak clearly. I see the men at church shaking their gray beards. "He never had the head. Too rash."

"Mary, I am sorry." Sam's ears quiver at my words. "It was not necessary to make this trip, to make it now. I could have waited as you wanted. Oh, Mary, can you forgive?" My eyes are wet; I wipe at them with a hand.

Sam slows in his tiredness; he must wonder at the pace. He may not notice the absence of wind. Why was I so set in my ways? Ohio could have waited. How many people must I ask for forgiveness? Whatever I touch goes awry. My neck hurts; my back strains from holding tight to the same position. There is no wind save that from Sam's flight. The trees are almost bare, the same ones that were fully covered when I rode to Ohio. All is changed, stripped, laid bare.

I ask Sam if he can ride through the night. I promise a brief rest if he can then continue. I pat his side; my hand must feel like the scrape of a dull knife. Half a moon shines. We can be home by tomorrow evening if we do not stop long. Whence comes the Evil of this night? "Oh, Mary, I wanted to do well by you. And Father, by you too. Why can I not find what is good?"

The trees stand in clumps in the distance, tall and silent. Like dark shrouds. These great oaks of my journey.

• • •

There was not the grief that I had thought. Oh, there had been grief all right, and the looseness in my belly still runs like a fever. But the loss was not as I imagined. A fire burned only in my brain.

Three days ago Sam and I rode up to my house at dusk. The four walls stood, even as I had left them. A lone candle flickered through the oilcloth paper at the window. Smoke from the chimney drifted in such a thin line that I had to squint my eyes to see.

I entered the house and there was Mary. All my fears had been unfounded. I did not at first see the faintness about her, the droop of her black hair. The boys came running and, in my joy, I missed seeing the difference. Not until I pulled Mary to me did I realize that she had taken on a smallness again. She seemed limp; she did not return my crushing embrace. I leaned back and grinned into her face, "The baby? We have our baby!"

But Mary turned her face from me and rested her head on my shoulder. I stroked her black, black hair. Then her sister, Elizabeth, walked toward us, shaking her head. I looked again on Mary and could not change the direction of my thinking. "Is it another boy?"

Jeremiah and Adam pulled at my leather breeches and pounded with their little fists on my thighs, "Father! Father!" They knew nought of my neglect with the chimney.

Through their noises I heard Elizabeth's quiet voice say, "The baby is dead."

"What?" I said, pulling back from Mary and turning her head in my hands to face me. I kissed her on the lips to wipe away her sadness. I kissed again with more tenderness. She did not respond. "How? What happened? Tell me!" I said to Elizabeth.

Elizabeth pulled the boys away to go outside and welcome Sam. Mary, shrunken and subdued, sat by my side to tell her story. A week ago she had noticed an absence of stirring within. She knew not what to think but mentioned it to her parents when they came for their nightly check. Her mother placed a hand on Mary's belly for a very long time, long enough to ascertain that there was no movement, not even one feeble kick. The boys went with Shem that night so that Elizabeth could tend to them; Mary's mother kept vigil at our house. Finally at dawn Mary's pains began, and in the usual fashion our daughter was born, but without breath.

"She never made cry, Jonas. Not once."

"Oh, Mary, I should have been here." I felt clumsy stroking her hair. She was not sweaty like Sam. "I am sorry. Believe me. I should have been here. Perhaps it would not have made a difference, but I could have been here when you had need." I leaned forward and felt too dirty to touch her again. I covered my head in my hands. I smelled Sam on me.

I did not feel sorrow for this lost life. Only a numb grief as all my past burdens slapped at me again. I was glad I had not held this baby girl in my hands. I did not want to know if she had black hair. I felt no attachment, but my scarred pain reopened. I had said I would do anything if spared. I knew I would do nothing.

I turned again to Mary and saw how bruised and unbrushed she looked. "It is my fault," I said. That is all I knew to say.

"Father says we must accept this as the Lord's will, even though we do not understand." Mary repeated the words woodenly.

"Oh, Mary, I am sorry I cannot do better by you."

Mary showed no interest in my efforts at comfort or apology. "I am glad you are home, Jonas. Promise me you will not go far again soon."

I pulled her close. I clung to her. She ended up the one bringing consolation. Her family had stepped into my absence and held her sway. They had buried my child. "You are a strong woman," I said. "I am blessed far beyond what I deserve."

"I do not know that any of us poor mortals has reason to deserve," she said.

The boys returned and made effort to climb upon us. For once I welcomed Jeremiah's chatter, for I had nothing more to say to Mary. I could listen to him without hearing. I did not want to tell Jeremiah about the place called Wooster or about his cousins in Ohio. I had no desire to leave my loved ones, and I made no mention to Mary of my dream on Sam's back. I said nothing, that night or the next, about the land.

11.

ELIZA

May 1817

There are signs of warming all about. Susanna came running, pressing blue phlox into my cheeks and nose. I thanked her for the sweetness. Will she ever lose her baby fat? She patted the baby's head and went running again. "I will find a flower for Maria," she said and scampered off. The first Marie's name, she could not pronounce.

Now we have our second go with a Marie. Only this one is *Maria*. After four straight boys, we are again blessed with a baby girl. I feared we would never be allowed another one. This one favors the Berkeys and brings much pleasure to look upon; her face is round like Susanna's bright, full moon.

Yost was balky about choosing *Maria*, but not because it is the old way of saying the name. "Has there not been trouble enough, first ours and then Polly's?" he asked.

"This one is a robin in springtime. After all the snow and dread cold of winter, here comes God's faithfulness, warming the air with promise."

Yost shook his head. "Easy there, Woman. That bundle is another mouth to feed. Warm air means another summer of hard work. Are you ready to roll up your sleeves?"

"Do you see them rolled down?" The words came out of my mouth unheeded. I am not as subservient as I should be. "My sleeves stay rolled up every day, out of reach of flour when baking and water when scrubbing." I cannot make any adjustment in Yost's nature. That is his way. But I can sometimes distract him with a warm cobbler. "Did you see how the rhubarb flourishes?"

My worry is that I may be a bad example for Lizzie and Susanna. Brother Isaac preached again on the blessedness of a woman submitting to her man; Isaac's blue eyes looked right at me. I want to be a beacon for my girls. When I speak contrary words I only cause heartache. Yost wants boy babies to help tame the fields; he does not see that there is any work of substance in the house. He had the last word, "Matthew, Mark, Moses. They all have a better sound."

Lizzie is ten and gives much assistance with the housework. She is quicker with the pie crust than Polly ever was. We have replaced almost all of our pewter and wooden bowls with clay dishes. Yost likes the potter in Meyersdale and trades our cream and butter with him. We even have earthenware crocks to keep the milk cool in the cellar. With Lizzie's help in the house, Yost thinks I should come to the fields more often. He says he loses time because he has to repay his brother Daniel for labor. Last summer when I trimmed the hedge bushes short the way I wanted, I said nought before the deed was done. He could not make critical comment *and* complain that I only worked inside. Susanna helps me with the boys. She likes to tramp with them when they explore along the Casselman. I warn her to watch for evil eyes in the forest. She has a sound head on her and will make certain that Lazarus does not trick Henry into eating dung again.

Several months ago we had word that Polly has her second boy; I am happy for them to replenish their supply. I tell

Yost that we must make effort to pay them a visit, but he acts as deaf as Joseph was for a stretch. All the death that Polly has had to endure. Mercy. One child was bad enough for me; I cannot imagine losing both my big girls. I do not like to think there is a curse on our family, but I never leave Maria in the house alone.

Yost and I had our differences about the dog also. He has been convinced for some time of the need for a watchdog. I do not mean to argue, but I questioned whether we had scraps enough. Yost gets the switch out if Joseph tries to leave the table before his plate is clean. I also have heard of dogs that carry disease. As soon as I saw the vein get fat under Yost's beard, I regretted my questions. "Woman, is that all you do? Think of things to worry about? There is no better protection against the beasts of prey: a bear come to molest the pigs, a wolf intent on chickens, even a coon attacking the corn crop." He looked at me as if I knew far less than Henry. "The bark of a dog has scared off many an offender." He paused, then charged ahead. "Our first Marie would still be with us if we had owned a dog."

That was uncalled for, opening wounds that we all wish to keep shut. He does not know that a barking dog would have made a difference. I felt like saying that Marie would be another mouth to feed, but I stifled myself. When Yost's mind is made up, the matter is closed. Soon we had our dog, a brown and white collie, possessed of a friendly nature. Yost announced that his name was Blade; I do not know where that name came from and I did not ask. I got my Maria; he got his Blade. Yost works the boys much too hard, so I am glad for any diversion that comes their way. I pet Blade behind the ears if Yost is not around, but I do not like him jumping in my face and smelling at me.

In the spring Yost put Joseph and Lazarus to cutting brambles. The boys had brave hearts to begin, but I did not like to think of my six- and five-year-olds, hacking at wild rose thorns all day. Joseph has always been slight of build, and I fear for him. He looks like he wants to cry at times but knows he dare not. The next two have more meat on them; Yost calls them his little oxen. I fear that Yost means to make Joseph walk and hold the reins this summer while the horses pull the plow. Yost says he is merely doing as his father did. If Joseph dallies too long in the morning, Yost grabs the long hickory stick. When he made my new broom, he laughed his big laugh and polished his paddling stick as well. The stick stands in the corner like a king. I wish I could throw it in the fire.

When I gather boldness to question his methods, Yost reminds me that children are to be brought up in the fear and admonition of the Lord. "Yes, but you will make a stubborn horse if you beat him too much," I reply.

"Do not put ideas in the boys' heads," Yost says. "I will make them *want* to obey."

Joseph gives quicker answer now that Yost has removed the wax from the boy's ears; most of the yellow had turned a dark brown. I could not bear to look when Yost dug with a nail, but it has made such a difference. I tell Yost he no longer needs to bellow, that we are all within his range. He ignores me and says to Joseph, "You must have had bees in there." Lazarus takes it up in singsong, "Joseph has a bee hive. Hivey, gelivey. Joseph has . . ." until I shush him.

Here is the worst part. Yost has changed his tune about Ohio. I cannot find stomach for the thought. "Land is cheap," he says; "I am missing out." At first I thought he only sought to stir my blood; he has always been opposed to people departing. But now, each of the last two winters he makes plain that he contemplates a move. I do not know how long I can resist. His desire for land could lead to wrongful pride, but I have not dared say that.

I hear the same stories as he, all filled with exaggeration. I cannot imagine packing our brood, all seven of them, in a wagon and setting off for a place we have not seen. I try to reason, "We have labored hard for what is here: our first grapes last fall, our new house, a healthy build of manure on the garden. Why abandon all this to start again on a rockiness somewhere else? The stories glitter like shiny packages." I do not mean to argue, but I feel such tightness squeezing at my chest and taking my breath away. There is small comfort that Yost has not yet gone to look. Sadie has extra cause to shudder because Daniel made a trip last fall.

Momma says my health stays fragile, but Yost pays no attention. In truth, I feel stronger now than when Joseph was born. I have dismissed that dreadful cough, and except for pain in the back—where I have to grab to steady myself—I get about as I wish. I do not gain weight, but neither do I have a setback every time I give birth. More *bobbels*, that may be my only defense against Yost's threat to uproot us all.

Something happened late last spring that still troubles. I think of it when I see the strawberries bloom again. My lower back gave discomfort after Lizzie and I had spent the morning picking strawberries. I thought I could not straighten up. We had such an ample crop that year, picking every other day, bending low for hours. We dried enough to last well into the fall. I am partial to red, juicy berries with bread and milk atop. Yet as I lay down for a brief respite that afternoon, I admit to having wished that the plants would get mold from too much rain, or that the birds would take on more industry. Lizzie heard me make utterance as I tried to relax my back. I asked her to rub the tender spots. When

Yost does that, his hands have so much roughness they bring me to tears. I tell him I am not pie dough.

Lizzie's little hands felt like angels ministering. I sighed and moaned in the pleasure of her light touch, when suddenly she cried out sharply, "My hand! Momma! I cannot unclench my hand!" I rolled onto my back so I could see what she described. Her right hand had stiffened like a claw in a benumbed position. "It hurts, Momma! It hurts with a badness!" she said. Her voice sounded like when she was a baby.

Of course I know of grownups who describe a feeling of power in the hands. I could not help but think on Reuben and the time long ago when he had tried to cure Lizzie of her livergrown. I hesitated to touch Lizzie's hand. "Rub it," I said, "or shake it. Rub gently and see if the stuckness goes away."

Her eyes spread wide in their darkness. She slowly tapped with her good fingers onto her stiffened hand. "It makes a tingle," she said. Then, with the stern voice of an adult, she said, "Deadness depart!"

"Quiet, my child. Do not say words. Rub slowly. The hand will come back." I did not know, in truth, that it would, but I have learned that children need encouragement.

Lizzie pressed and rubbed with her one hand on the other. Then I pulled myself to sit up and put my hand on top of hers. "Is it better?" I asked. "Is there more of a naturalness?"

"Yes, Momma. What is it? What is it that put the chill of death in my hand?"

"Squeeze it," I said. "Make it squeeze again; then relax. It must have been a cramp. I do not know, poor baby; I do not know what made that clenching. But it is gone. You are my big girl." I scootched closer to put my arms around Lizzie, and I held her as I have not done for years. The four boys have kept me much too busy. And now the baby. She nestled into me, and I brushed the hair from her eyes. "You will be fine, Lizzie. God loves you, dearest one. Always remember."

"Yes, Momma. I hope it is not that I was bad today. Do you think I was bad, Momma?" She has always been earnest about doing what is right.

"No, child, I do not think so. The hand is not a thing to fret over. And say nothing to Father about this," I added. I do not want to hear from Yost again about Reuben touching Lizzie in a harmful way.

She put both her arms about my neck and would not let go until I reminded her of my bad back. "Lizzie, there are potatoes to peel. Come help."

We worked with our backs to each other: Lizzie peeling the skins—the potatoes are old and knobby—and I, removing the bad spots and cutting the chunks that remained into the kettle. I remember doing this with my mother. I turned halfway to Lizzie and said, "Some day you will have a daughter, and you will show her how to peel." With a potato in one hand and water running down my arms, I hugged her again. I do not show enough affection for my big girls.

Neither of us said more about the hand, and I do not know of any repeat incident. She often seems subdued, however. Not vacant, like Polly, but more on the quiet order. She may be one of those who enters womanhood early. I was only eleven. That is nature's way, but if her hand has unusual touch, that cannot be good. I do not know how to stand in the way. If it comes to that, I may have to rely on Yost.

12.

YOST

February 1818

A pit is the answer. I will catch that bugger who comes as a thief in the night. Where my sense has been, I do not know. All the chickens I lost in the fall and Blade never barked once. Doubtless there had to be a human hand that knew him by name and could walk past undetected. That is what a long winter is for: time to lay waste a robber. I will wait until the ground is thawed; then dig a hole six or seven feet deep, a square one, just inside the gate. By day I will lay planks to cover so the boys do not wander in by mistake. By night I will remove the boards, an open invitation to anyone who enters with cross-purposes. Then I will keep my ear cocked for the sound of a human frog croaking. Better yet, I will keep watch in town, even at church, for who has their neck stiffened off to the side. Four feet square, that should do it.

My body stores up too much rest when it snows all winter. I get fidgety and commence doing things that do not need doing. I shot two deer in December; then I got a bear last month. Now we all have new mittens made from bear skin. Eliza says I should take up carpentry, but I am content with the chairs we have. She is the one who wants more. Or different. I remind her that we have a chest for blankets. Why do we need another? The more furniture I make, the more belongings we will need to move. She will not hear of it. I tell her that in Ohio I would have plenty to do, all winter. That is the best way to stifle her pining for a dry sink.

When it grows dark before supper there is little to do until bedtime but tell stories. Gideon falls asleep in the middle and then shows his upset the next day. Telling these stories reminds me of Father; I know the exact places where he would pause: "'Great-Grandfather survived the voyage on mice and rats.'" That always required a long stop. I explain to the children that this is their great-great-grandfather. Not John Jacob, but the one before that: Jacob Hershberger, our first ancestor to come to this country, sailing from Rotterdam in 1736 on the Charming Nancy. Or was it 1738? With a good wind behind, our people could cross in ten weeks, but when the wind turned fickle and the trip stalled for twice that long, that is when many starved.

Here is another line my children like: "'Great-Great-Grandmother had too much fat on her to squeeze through the cellar window.'" Susanna claps her hand over her mouth. "That is why I married your mother; she can slip through tight places," I say.

"Yost," Eliza says, "stick with the true story." My children squirm and poke at each other.

"The truth of why I married you or the truth about Great-Grandmother?"

"You know," she says.

Gideon edges closer on my lap. "But Gideon falls asleep when I tell long stories," I say.

"No, Poppa," he says. "Not tonight. I stay awake tonight."

"Promise?" I ask, running my hand through his straight brown hair. His forehead goes high into his hair like my father's did.

"Please tell us, Poppa." The others inch closer and settle themselves at my feet.

So I begin my story. Only it is Father's story. His grandfather landed at Philadelphia and took his family north to settle with other Amish along the Northkill Creek. Everything was fine. Fifteen, twenty years passed. William Penn treated our people well. Same for the Indian. Here is where I wait to make sure the children listen. "The year is 1755." I switch to a voice that is pitched high like Henry's. "'It is mine,' say the French." Then I use Lizzie's deliberate voice, "'No, it is mine,' the British say." I explain how they argued about land between the Alleghenies and the Ohio River, how both countries tried to get the Indian on their side. I tell how the Shawnee and Delaware tribes finally helped France defeat General Braddock. I remind Joseph that land is very important; it sometimes must be contested.

"The Indian turned bloody," I say. "I do not know if the Frenchmen made him think he could do as he pleased or what. But for the next three years the Indians along the Blue Mountains were very evil. White people built forts to protect against them."

"The Indian was here first," Eliza says, interrupting.

"Yes, that is true. The Indian may have been taken advantage of by those who encroached. But there was land enough for all back then without killing. It would not bother me to have an Indian next door. He minds his crops; I tend mine."

"What did the Indian do?" Susanna asks. She bites at her fat fingers.

"Did you not have supper, Susanna?" She shrinks away and I continue. "They attacked people; the Indians raided the property of white people. They murdered little children."

"Easy, Yost," Eliza says.

"I tell what happened. These are Father's words." I wait to see if Eliza will contest me further. "Some would say that with that much killing all around, Great-Grandfather should have picked up his belongings and found a safer place. I do not criticize."

"Why did Great-Great not leave, Poppa?" Susanna asks, stretching forward again.

"I do not know. It is not an easy thing to pick up and go." I feel Eliza's eyes on me. "Perhaps he thought he would be spared. That is the way we are. We do not think we will come under attack, because *we* have harmed no one."

I explain how things went better for awhile. Until the fall of 1757—was it 1756?—when they had an apple-*schnitzing* at Jacob's place. The young people stayed late, with games and such. After all were gone and the family slept, the dog began to bark. Here I pause. "Never ignore Blade if you hear him at night. But take care when you go to the door. Jacob's son, Jacob—he may have been 18 at the time—went to the door and peered out." I put my hand like a hat with a brim above my eyes and look at each child. "Suddenly he felt a pain in his leg. Jacob got back inside and shut the door fast. All the family roused; there may have been a dozen Indians standing outside by the bake oven."

"Is that why Great-Great-Grandmother was in the cellar?" Lazarus asks.

"Be patient. We are not there yet. The younger boys, Daniel and David—they are my great-uncles—reached for their guns, but Jacob, the father, would have none of it." All my children keep silence. "Old man Jacob said, 'We do not take a life in order that our own might be saved.'" I look at each child again. "David and Daniel did not like that one bit. They pleaded with their father. Rather like when Joseph and Lazarus do not want to stick more sourdock." Gideon giggles.

"The next thing they knew, the Indians had set the house on fire. That is when the family all headed for the cellar. Are you with me, Lazarus? Take your thumb from your mouth; you are not a baby. There they huddled in the cellar, timbers burning above them. They poured their whole crop of fresh apple cider on the flames that broke through. As daylight came the Indians left, doubtless thinking the family all dead. But one lone Indian lingered behind. Only the family did not know it." I pause, as Father would have. "Now we come to the cellar window. Why do you think I put a window in our cellar?"

"Yost," Eliza says.

"Here is where Great-Great-Grandmother had a problem. Some women get too fat in all the wrong places. I do not know how she squeezed out, for she was a heavy woman."

"Maybe the boys pushed on her," Joseph says. He pretends to shove with both his hands.

"Yes, that may be. Rather like convincing a sow to get on a wagon." My boys giggle and Susanna hunches forward with her hand over her mouth again. The tip of her nose sticks out between her thumb and index finger.

"The younger Jacob had a leg wound too," Eliza says.

"Yes, it was not a speedy exit on several counts. But remember, one Indian lingered. He alerted the others, and they returned to capture all the family except for the youngest, David. That would be like our Henry; the smallest has the fastest foot."

"You mean Maria," Lizzie corrects. "She is our youngest."

"Well, yes," I say, "but she does not run yet. Here is the point, and the bad part. The Indians caught David too." I pause. "The Indians killed three of our family. Jacob, the son with the leg wound, and one of his sisters. I do not remember her name. The Indians killed them in a bad way; they tomahawked them."

"What is that?" Lazarus asks.

"Never mind," Eliza says. "Do not dwell on the gruesome."

"To be tomahawked is an honorable death, according to Indian custom," I say.

None of my children asks more, but their eyes could catch bugs. Finally Lizzie asks, "Who else? You said there were three."

"It was your great-great-grandmother." I look at Eliza and omit the part about the repeated stabbings. "As if she had not suffered enough, delaying her family, watching two of her children executed." I remember how I felt when my father related these events to me. I had wanted to go out and right these wrongs. My children sit still; every one of them is as quiet as Gideon, asleep in my arms. Sometime I will tell my boys about the first Marie's death, about watching for Evil where you least expect it. But not tonight. I often wonder what Lizzie remembers of that night. She may well have heard something.

"The rest of the story goes like this," I say. "Neighbors arrived when they saw smoke. The barn, smokehouse, all ruined. Your great-great-grandfather and Daniel and David, all taken prisoner. Jacob managed to grab a few fresh peaches which he presented to the chief. This found favor because the clubbings and abuse were not as heavy for him. But his beard was removed and his hairs plucked out as with a chicken. They pulled out hair atop his head also, but left a patch that they braided and stuck feathers in."

"That is the same kind of humiliation our martyrs of the faith endured; that is what we sing about in church," Eliza says. "All those who suffered for what they believed."

I shift Gideon's dead weight to my other arm. Lazarus looks as if he will wilt next. I hurry over the remainder of the story. How the Indians trusted David and Daniel more than they did Jacob, as if they knew the old man plotted to escape. How that is what he did when the warriors were off on a raid. He had kept track of his whereabouts and fled at night. For days he crossed mountains and waded streams. He hid by day and walked by night. Somehow he recognized the head branch of the Susquehanna. I tell my children how Jacob built a raft, using wild grapevine to tie logs together. He floated down the river, caught fish to eat, lived on nuts and tender bushes. When he got to Fort Harris he was too weak to pull himself up to a standing position. As Father had explained it, Jacob tried to attract attention but was too weak to call. Fortunately, a short distance below the fort, a man happened to be watering his horse at the river and saw a strange object floating downstream. He reported this to the commander who had a special glass for seeing far distances.

"How many days had he traveled?" Joseph asks.

"Weeks. Not days." I want Joseph to know that humans can endure much difficulty, much hard labor. "We think that Jacob traveled by raft for three or four weeks. We do not know for sure. The commander gave him food and ordered him to rest his body before he proceeded in the proper direction. Imagine what his friends back home thought! A ghost, perhaps." My mind wanders to my father's little sister who slipped away and never returned.

"What happened with his hair?" Lizzie asks.

"His hair grew back, but sparse and very white. My father was twelve when Jacob died." Or was it thirteen?

Eliza stands to bed down Maria. "That is enough storytelling for one night," she says.

"Jacob remained a gentle man in his latter years, but he became easily agitated by outdoor noises: a rap at the window, too much wind in the pines," I say.

"It is far past bedtime, and we have heard more than enough to keep our heads busy all night," Eliza says.

"Tell yet what happened to Daniel and David," Joseph says. "We will not sleep if we do not know."

I turn a chuckle into an extended throat-clearing. Eliza picks up Henry off the floor and puts him on our bed. "Each boy was adopted by a different Indian family. David was taken in by an older Indian who treated him as a son. When this old man died, David attached himself to an Indian brother of the old man. That is their custom. David did not want to leave the strange ways. We do not understand how that can be." I will make certain that none of my boys develops an attachment to anything but the land that I give him.

"You will have to carry Henry to the loft," Eliza says.

Of course I will carry him. I always put him to bed. She knows that. Tonight I will not need to threaten him with sleeping downstairs with the girls if he does not stop squirming and kicking my sides. He likes to pretend that I am a bucking horse when I carry him. "I am almost done. The war went on for seven more years before the Indians had to return their white captives. When Daniel and David had not shown up, Jacob went to the big city of Philadelphia to request help from the governor. Daniel finally returned, but he was never the same. He hardly knew German any more; he could only say, *'Mein nam ist Daniel Hershberger.'* Think of the fear he must have put in his father's heart, for Daniel looked to be an Indian when he first returned."

Eliza stands at the foot of the loft steps, shifting Henry in her arms as if waiting another minute will make a difference.

"Always give heed to the company you keep," I say. "Otherwise, what first seems odd may come to be familiar; before you know it, the strangeness may be hard to shake off." Joseph, Lizzie, Susanna, all solemnly nod.

I carry the sleeping Gideon to the loft, then return for Henry, then Lazarus. I have built a stairway inside, firm enough to hold me.

Sleep comes slowly, but not because a tree branch scratches at my window. I think about all the strangeness in my family. My father's generation and older: David, Daniel, Peter, Amos. Then there is Reuben. I must remain watchful so that none of my boys becomes afflicted. More land, that is the answer. The more land that I accumulate, the more I will have to sell for cash when I convince Eliza to move. I will work the boys hard, starting with my name-sake, Joseph, so their minds dare not wander. I do not want to be careless and overlook the signs as Father did with Reuben.

13.

$\mathcal{R}$ EUBEN

November 1818

Yes, Anna is right; this is the most bountiful crop of apples we have known here in Ohio. Six years already. Six growing seasons. We have the Indians and a strange one by the name of Johnny Appleseed to thank for this abundance of apples. They planted the seeds from which we now reap benefit. Most of the younger Indians have moved on West. Only a few harmless, old codgers live along the stream beds. I know of no problems between the Indian and us white settlers, but it is just as well that the Red Man has found other habitation.

As the stories go, this Mr. Appleseed wears unusual apparel, a coffee sack with holes for his head and arms, and lives from settlement to settlement. He is a strange one, but he is welcomed by all, exchanging apple seeds for his nightly sustenance. His divergence from what most people consider to be natural gives him appeal. If Anna were to put me out, I might be able to exist as a vagrant. But I do not seek a life of constant travel. I wonder if half of what they say about Appleseed is true. I wish I could chance to come upon him and see for myself. It is said that the Indians looked on him with great respect, almost with a superstitious regard. When he bruised his foot from stepping on a patch of thorns, he sought out a blacksmith to apply a red-hot iron to the afflicted sole. His line of thought was that a burn would heal more readily than a wound. I understand his reasoning, but I could not voluntarily subject my body to such pain. It is all I can muster to accept the affliction administered by others.

The apples we harvested are ideal for making hard cider. Tobias fashioned a wooden frame with a crank, and I fitted pieces of metal which act as the teeth so that the apples are torn and ground apart. It is a glory to see that juice run out the bottom. Anna and the children love to drink it fresh. When the cider has sat about for a few weeks, it takes on a zip that suits my taste even better, bringing to mind the cherry bounce we drank in Pennsylvania.

Anna says I consume too much, and I should be more careful around Jacobli and Bevy. I see no harm in a small pleasure that relaxes my muscles. She knows full well I have little else to enjoy. I make no headway in changing her mind about our private relations; surely she cannot think it fair to deny me hard cider as well. Surely. That has become a bitter word. To please her, I constructed a large, oaken barrel and fashioned it with holes in the top to allow the air to circulate. Into this I poured the fermented cider until it was near to full. Come another year, this will be vinegar for Anna's use. She tries to say that at the rate I take from the top for drinking, there will not be time enough for the cider to get heavy and sink to the bottom as vinegar. I put my arms around her thick waist and ask her what she would do with fifty gallons of vinegar.

These hands are my salvation, giving me ought to do. I have taken up the task of fashioning wooden bits. I make a point, and make it exceedingly sharp, so that when it is driven into a piece of wood and then turned or twisted in a steady fashion, it chips at the wood block until a hole is drilled. Tobias used my innovation for putting crosspieces into the legs of chairs, adding much stability with the extra rungs. If I had ready access to more metal, I could make an even sharper drill with a twist that would be good for digging much larger holes. Tobias says there is a man over along the Walnut Creek who makes augers. I would like to see this man's operation. I used to tell Yost that one day I would make my own.

With farm prices dropping I must find some way to supplement our income. Last week I gave far too much for a new horse. I tell Anna that we might as well use the corn crop to make whiskey, for it fetches little income on the grain market. Six years ago when we came, we thought we bought cheap land for $2 an acre. Now people move in and are almost handed property for half of what we paid. Some of these new immigrants, these Mennonites who have come from Switzerland in the last year, have settled north of here in what is now called Wayne County. They can buy eighty acres for $100.

This Wayne County seems progressive in many ways; people have worked together to build a cabin that they use as a schoolhouse. We have nothing of the kind here in Holmes County. How I wish Bevy and Jacobli could learn in that way; they are just the right ages for schooling, twelve and nine. Jacobli has always had the quick head; he likes to count the rings on the trees we cut. I do not know why he enjoys gagging himself, except that Bevy tattles and Anna gives too much attention.

I use my hands for healing also. When asked. There are no doctors about, so people seek my assistance when they become desperate. There is no consistency; some of those who made plain that I was unfit for the church still come knocking at my door. One man would not shake hands at the funeral but called me for his daughter's sake the next week. Another wanted me to look at a sick cow, yet he also followed Abraham Zug's instruction.

How can they accept my touch and yet build a barrier against me? Do they not realize that the healing done through me comes in the name of the Lord? When healing travels through my body, I can feel my strength depleted just as Jesus knew it when someone in the crowd touched the hem of his garment. Aunt Barbli taught me those stories from the Bible. How Jesus rubbed clay together and then touched a sick one with that clay. How he spit into his hands and then took of that spit for healing eyesight. Yet some persist in thinking there is witchcraft in *brauching*. Now I understand why they call it pow-wowing, as if the Indian word makes it a bad thing. When they are determined to keep the door shut, they find a way.

They pulled the string across the door when Esther died. That was four years ago, not long after we had word of my father's death. My father turned his back, choosing to side with church people rather than believe me. He might as well have kicked me in the teeth. I try to forget him. Around the time of Esther's demise, effort was made to organize the Amish here in Ohio. Anna and I had not made clear our intent to be part of the church. We were fence-sitters. In truth, we had not found the disorganization on the frontier to be a problem, except that Anna had concern for the welfare of the children. We had one leg on either side, hoping that those in charge would ignore my past and expect us to join, while at the same time being wary to put the question of welcome to a test.

The events that transpired to put me out happened after Esther's funeral. She had taken a sudden sickness and died within a matter of days, leaving Tobias all alone. We gathered at his new cabin for the funeral; with the large crowd I was glad we had built that extra room to the south. At Anna's insistence I seated myself with the other men. It would have showed a lack of respect not to have attended, and to have stood outside would have confirmed my alienation.

Some there were, like Tobias, who greeted me with natural friendliness, but some others did not see me. Foremost among those: Abraham Zug, minister with the Walnut Creek group. He preached, but he did not shake my hand. I wonder if he knows I was called to his sister's aid. Others followed Zug's example; they stood within two feet of me and gave no notice. Even turned a shoulder. I am tired of being treated as a leper at the gate. That night I said to Anna, "I am not wanted; the leadership made that clear. I will not enter an Amish church meeting again; I will not subject Bevy and Jacobli to the scorn placed on me."

She did not disagree with my conclusion but cautioned me about casting all the blame on Abraham. "He is the Lord's anointed. Why do you point the finger at him?"

"Because he had it within his reach to accept or reject. That is what a leader does. The others are sheep."

"Perhaps he had strict orders to follow. From back East." She hung up her good black dress in the wardrobe closet that her father had made.

"The sheep leading the sheep leading the sheep. Is that what you mean?" I asked.

"He is the Lord's servant." Anna folded a handkerchief and put it in the top drawer of the chiffonier Tobias had made. I watched as she deliberately put her best things in storage.

"Why are you defending him when to do so puts you out?"

Anna would say no more. I know that Zug's treatment of me only added to her other loss, like watching a groundhog dig atop her mother's fresh grave. I tried to console her. In the midst of our uncertainty and my anger we have clung to each other.

A day later she asked, "What of the children, Reuben? What will we say?"

240

"It is time we tell the story. They need to know the truth, for they will hear other versions. Perhaps they have already heard fabrication." I expected Anna to make her additions and corrections, but she said nothing. She stood on the opposite side of the bed, her back turned. I knew the time had come for me to offer her freedom. "We have been wrong to hope that hearts might be changed. The different setting makes no difference. There is no 'surely.' I am sorry for you, Anna." I wanted to fold her into me. I could not say the rest that I needed to say. I did not want to be a vagabond. "If you want to catch a ride to church, perhaps Zug will stop his wagon for you." That was the best I could do.

"Reuben," she said, as if chiding Jacobli. "I am not like them. I will stay with you." We cried and held each other tight that night.

A few days later, after Anna's grief had lessened, we gathered Bevy and Jacobli about us on the bench with the sturdy back that Tobias had made. He must have known that our family would not need a longer bench.

"Jacobli and Bevy," I began, "your mother and I have something to say." I cleared my throat to remove the roughage.

"Will there be a new baby?" Bevy asked, kicking her foot against the bench.

"Yes, yes! We want a big family like others have," Jacobli added. "I want a brother." He snuggled into his mother's bosom.

I looked to Anna for encouragement, but she seemed sunken, pinching her nose between her thumb and finger. I tried again. "No, children, you do not understand. You are too young. Our family cannot be like others." Now Bevy leaned into Anna also, as if she knew that I was the offender. "Back when we lived in Pennsylvania, a bad thing happened. I bore the brunt. But I did not do it." I did not want to sound pitiful, like a whiner. "Do you understand? Someone had to be blamed. There was no one better than I."

"But Father," Bevy said, leaning forward, her small arms crossed in front of her, "that is not fair. Why did you not tell the truth? You always say to speak the truth."

"I did, Bevy. I told them I was innocent. I tried to tell them. But in their rush to find someone, they found me." I did not want my children to see my tears. I am no good at convincing adults. I do not know how to reassure my children.

"What was the bad thing? What happened?" Bevy asked. Jacobli looked at me, frowning, as if he did not believe me.

"I do not want to go into that," I said. "When you are older, there will be time. But I want you to know, if you hear stories about me, they are not true."

Anna roused herself enough to brush back her hair from her face and shift Jacobli's weight on her. "Your father is a good, honorable man. Always remember that, Jacobli. And you too, Bevy. Remember." She looked at each one. What sorrow. What burden sagged on her face. "There are some who needed an excuse, an object on which to pour out their spite. Sometimes when we are overcome by a great loss, something we do not know how to explain, we scavenge for an answer, any answer. Your father suffers unjustly for the sake of another. Who it is, we do not know. But someone roams free because of your father's shackles."

I covered my eyes with one hand and pinched the corners tight to hear my wife give explanation on my behalf. My tender children. Innocent.

Anna reached to put a hand on my shoulder. Jacobli bent forward with her, as did Bevy. I felt their small hands on my shirt. Anna had said the words my children needed to hear, had said the words I needed to hear. The words I had desperately needed my father to say.

I leaned forward and put clumsy arms around all of my family. "Because some think I am at fault," I continued, "they do not want me in the church. Your mother and I have decided not to press the matter further. We will wait for the guilty party to make confession."

Jacobli put his head on Anna's shoulder. She said, "We would like to have more wholesome exchange, but it is not seemly to force ourselves. We must wait for the Lord's own good time. Some day . . . ." She paused to gain control. "Some day, there will be mercy." She waited again, then said with more certainty, "If someone offers you a smile, Jacobli, be a friend. But if someone does not want to open the door, Bevy, do not push; find another way."

The children clung to their mother as if they still doubted my goodness. I wanted Anna to say the part again about me being an honorable man, but she did not. "Find another way" has become our motto. It is not my nature to find another door, but I must try.

"Do not judge another by his boots," Anna said. "You do not know why someone does as he does. We are to love those who make us miserable." Her voice quivered; her eyes were glassy. "We can still be happy in our little family." She wavered. "We have Grandfather yet, and we have our new cabin. Next spring we can plant calla lilies like Grandmother did."

We have tried. Tried to be as noble as Anna sounded. But it is not easy, and I fight the bitter taste. There are some who would do better with cobs up their butts. Abraham Zug is one. Yost is another. No one has come to talk; no one has asked what goes through my mind. They do not care. They only want me to stay away. Until someone is sick and they need my hands. What am I to say?—"Forgive them, for they know not what they do." I think not. The strong cider and whiskey put a lid on my troubles so that I can sleep. When I waken, I think perhaps this is the day the guilty one will come forward. When that does not happen, I try to be content with my cows and grain. My hope of augers.

We had another incident that set us back soon after Esther died. This one was first an embarrassment, then another grief. A few weeks after the funeral, Tobias went back to Somerset County for a visit. He was gone all summer, and I was beginning to think his cow that I milked steadfastly might be mine. But one day, as the leaves turned colors, he came back with a new wagon and a new woman. This is his third wife. The one before Esther died giving birth; Anna never knew her. This one goes by the name, Salome, just like my younger sister. But here is the strangeness: she is but two years older than Anna. This Salome is 42 and paired with Tobias near to 70.

"You know what people will say," Anna said, grieving again for Esther. "That Father took pains not to be the bereaved one again."

"People will talk; we know how that works," I said. "We can do nothing to change their tongues. Ignore them. That is the only way. We will practice a little shunning of our own."

Salome has been the source of leading Tobias away. We met her one time. That is all. He rides over to visit on occasion—the children miss him—but Salome will not come our way and we no longer go theirs. How different from when we made journey and lived with Tobias and Esther. Doing what is right in the eyes of the church must be of utmost importance to this Salome. God rest her soul, for I would like to pitch it in a heap and smear it with cow manure! She cannot deviate one jot or tittle, and Tobias follows like a tottering ram.

Anna says we must give thanks for the good years we had with her parents. She still sings the songs of faith with Jacobli and Bevy: "Hope in Him through all thy ways." I want to puke. Anna has told each of them that when they are of an adult

mind, they can choose to be part of God's church. I remind her
that could mean my children would need to shun me. Anna
will hear nothing of the sort. "By then," she says, "surely we
will have new light."

"New light!" I mock her, but she turns back to her knitting.
I do not say more. I will let her believe if she must. I need her
to believe, for I cannot. I do not expect light from Zug's church.
I never did ought against him. But he must needs follow the
dictates of the church back East. Asking Zug's church to grant
mercy is like asking a bumblebee to spread soothing balm.

I doubt that Abraham knows I was called to his sister's
home. I could be wrong, of course, since Ministers of the Word
know all. Three years ago Levi Speicher came riding for me.
The same Levi who called me to help his father with snake
bites when we lived yet in Somerset County. Only this time he
lived over on Walnut Creek and came on his wife's behalf. I
recognized him as a boyhood friend of Jonas Zug. Levi had married a sister of Jonas—Rachel by name—and therefore a sister
of Abraham. I did not know until I arrived with him that Levi's
farm was right next to Abraham's.

Once there, I could not see to leave until I had made effort
to heal. But I fear my faith was weak. I kept thinking that at
any minute Abraham would stick his nose in the door. Aunt
Barbli used to say that after Jesus healed someone, he would
say, "Thy faith hath made thee whole." If faith is the measure
for the sick one, then it must play a part for the one laying on
hands.

Levi's wife had given birth earlier and never regained
strength. She looked gaunt, even deathly, with a head like a
bird's. Repulsive is the word. Thin, bony arms. Her hair had
fallen out. I did not want to touch her. I asked Levi if she knew
her numbers, but he said she had not learned past ten. Counting backwards from fifty to three would have been the best

remedy for her condition. I repeated the only words I knew to say to stop the hemorrhaging: "Jesus Christ's dearest blood, That stoppeth the blood, In this help Rachel, God the Father, God the Son, God the Holy Ghost, Amen."

I said this three times, walking back and forth in front of her. But my thoughts were scattered. I should have refused to offer aid. Yet that seemed heartless. I did not stay long and I offered little hope. Levi was a sad figure, standing there with three little children hanging on him. I was not surprised to learn that Rachel Speicher died soon thereafter. I can tell the measure of a man. Levi does not seem like those heartless ones in Zug's church who can look both ways and not know the difference. He may go along on the surface with his brother-in-law, but I do not think he accepts everything he hears.

Anna reminds me that others suffer too. Her positive expression disgusts me. She repeats the words: "When He has tried and purged thee throughly." What can she mean? Throughly. It would be easier for me if she were bitter also. But she pretends to have set ill will aside. How can any other suffering compare with banishment? With being thought too Evil for social contact? When will those who act as though they own the light, as though *they* were the ones who cast light in the sky, ever know illumination?

Yet Anna is all I have. Even if I cannot have her as I want. We seldom touch in bed, but her voice stays gentle with me. There is that much; she has not forsaken me. I wake in the night and want to turn to her in my need. But there would be no point. I spend my nights in torment, my days in doubt. Will I never know reinstatement? Am I meant to die an outcast here, and in the world to come? Sometimes I despise myself and loathe to think on my end. Another man would have known how to avoid such trouble.

14.
J O H N M.
April 1819

"*W*hat should it be: allow two suspenders or stick with the one?" Joseph asked. I looked at him, puzzled. "And those pants," he went on, "what if those hooks and eyes were to give way to a single button, or perhaps two? Would your prayers be heard? Or would they be stuck in the mud?"

I could not help reaching to make certain my hooks were secured. Top one first, then down. That is always the order in which I check. I had no idea as to Joseph's direction.

That was two weeks ago. Now I recognize the devilish grin that sneaks through his beard, especially when we milk cows. Joseph seems young to have such a scraggly heap of a beard; he is only thirty. He does not act old, but he kept himself better before Henry died. Now he has a rough side; grayish specks have popped up in his beard. When mine grows full I will keep it neat, even if I dare not trim it. But that is not until I marry. For now I am barely getting a good start on the chin.

I have come to enjoy these verbal jousts with my brother. At first I did not know what to make of them. I still flounder at times, but I like to have my head pushed. Back home Father only cared about my muscle and long legs. But here Joseph takes me to a high ridge: "What should the church do? Stick with what is known or break over the wall?" Then he walks away, letting me find my own way back down the hillside.

The first answer that leaps to my lips is always, "Stick with tradition." That is what Father would say. And Isaac too. I have learned not to always say what comes first to mind. Joseph would not ask these questions without a purpose. If Mother knew of these mental exercises, she would send to have me brought back East. She does not know that Joseph has some of the rebel in him. She had voiced concern for my safety back in early March. Joseph had come to visit before the spring planting began and to make sure that all was well with Mother. Father died last fall, and we were still making adjustments. Joseph explained to Mother that the wilderness had moved on to Indiana and Iowa. That Ohio was filling up. I wished he would have added that I looked to be a man, that I could take care of myself. I was the one who had to remind Mother that I am seventeen and fully grown.

All I needed was her blessing to relocate. She gave me Blackey as my inheritance. My sister who is closest to me in age got married as planned, only a month after Father's death. I was left stranded, alone with Mother. Now she lives with Jacob and his family, but I had no inclination to stay there. I would much rather work for Joseph than Jacob. Jacob is the old one; I doubt that he and I will ever hold much in common. He is the kind to be content in Somerset County all his life. It is strange how brothers can be so different.

Ever since I traveled to Ohio six years ago, I could not forget the place. I saw heartache aplenty and knew that a pioneer's life is work, work, work. That time I could not wait to get back to Father, but I had not been home in Pennsylvania a week before I wanted to return West. Now here I am on the Walnut Creek. Ohio has not, in truth, filled up, but our settlement looks more and more like Pennsylvania. Joseph brings order to everything he touches; it is only my head that he seeks to disturb. It is just as well that he has not been made a minister; I do not think he would ever let the church have final say in his life.

Several months before leaving Pennsylvania, I joined the River congregation. Brother Isaac had made mention at the start of the new year that parents should encourage their older children to think seriously about a commitment. I did not want Mother to push me, so I spoke with Isaac on my own. He has seemed like a brother ever since we rode to Ohio together. He gave fatherly encouragement, and soon I was meeting with four other young people for instruction. Right on time, my beard showed up. If I were still eleven I would add the word, *really*. I thought that was the best word. Now I see that it was silly; but what is forbidden carried great appeal. My sparse stubble sprouted even better on the journey, and today I no longer need avoid the looks of older girls. I think my tallness frightens many of them. Mother called me *klutzich. Ungeschickt.*

I keep my eyes open. I have done nearly everything early, and I might be one to find a mate at a young age. No one catches my attention here—I am still getting my bearings—but families come and go with frequency. On any given Sunday there may be a new one come for me. I want someone nearly as tall as I, with long fingers—girls with short, stubby ones are stupid. Joseph would laugh if he knew of my preference. He says the hook pounded in the door frame of the barn is exactly six feet from the ground. The top of Joseph's head comes directly under that hook. For myself, my eye looks square at the top of the hook. With my forehead and hair added on, I have an advantage of three inches over him.

Everything has changed from six years ago. I feared for what Barbara would say when I walked in the door. I can eat as much corn pone as all her children put together. Joseph had said it would not be a problem for me to join them; yet I fretted in the saddle at times. I did not want to be a nuisance. I hung outside the cabin when we first arrived, taking extra pains to brush Blackey and give Barbara time to cover her surprise. But Joseph soon came strolling outside with little Joel in his arms and said, "John M., they are all waiting to see how tall you have gotten. Come."

I ducked my head inside their cabin and felt a welcome as if they all expected me. Only John J. seemed slow to warm. He does not show meanness, only a holding back. I doubt that he remembers the smashed cardinal's egg, but I do. Samuel J., the sickly one, died long ago, so Joel takes his place as the baby. Barbara, the girl, is four, another new face for me.

Perhaps Barbara, the wife, was relieved to take me in, as only *one* extra. A year ago my sister Catherine and her husband, Moses, with their boy and girl made room for Lydia and her six. Joseph had warned me that Lydia was no longer able to care for her young, that sometimes her senseless babbling frightened the little ones. I wanted to know how long she had stayed silent, but I did not ask. When I saw her at Catherine's, I still was not prepared. She sat by the small window with her hands crossed and cupped under her bosom. I do not want to say, breasts, but that is what they are, if Joseph were to ask. I reached down bravely to shake her hand, for she is my sister. She stared at my mid-section. Or below. I reached to make certain my hooks were secure. She seemed unable to lift her head any higher.

I wanted to make manly comment. "I am John M., your youngest brother," I said.

"Water . . . a cup of water," she said, still staring.

I stood awkwardly with my hand extended, but she made no effort to reciprocate. I looked around for water to fetch; I wanted to cover my pants.

Catherine intercepted me, shaking her head sadly. "She says that to everyone," Catherine whispered.

I halted, unsure of what to do. All my cousins watched as I fiddled, rubbing my fingers up and down my suspender, standing heavily on one leg, then the other.

Joseph says that the tree that killed Henry took Lydia as well; she has never been the same. Joseph had mentioned Lydia's change of residence to Mother, but he gave no details. How easy my life has been compared with Michael's. The worst things in my past are trivial: sitting on a wet bench and walking in clinging pants the rest of the day. Having little girls giggle at my height. Banging into doorways. Michael and I are friends, but not with the same ease as before when we managed his father's crops. Michael now works for Moses and goes about very quietly. Sometimes I think he tiptoes. I want to remind him of our contests, when we shot snot to see who could let fly the farthest. But that does not seem important now.

Why would a brain take on disease? That is what I ask Joseph. He says it is the human lot to suffer. That is too easy. His answers are not as good as his questions. How can Lydia's thinking be flawed? No one should lose normalcy there. It is good that Mother does not know. I could not bear to lose my mind. *Wahnsinnig.* I wonder if Lydia knows that we watch her and feel pity. I pray not.

I go to the woods on Sunday afternoons when there is time; that is where I think about the changes. Joseph does not mind so long as I am back for evening chores. The ferns grow wild over the hillsides, more so than I remember in Pennsylvania. More kinds of them too. I drop to my haunches or knees if the ground is not wet, so that I can study the patterns. The Christmas fern is a common one, but there are many others. Some with broad leaves, some with spidery-fine leaves, some even with black stems. Some have a little baby shoot off to the side. I used to think that birds could signal to each other, but I have not been led to foolishness about talking plants. They are put here to please us with their beauty.

Joseph had wondered what I thought of changing the spelling of our last name. "We should be consistent," he said. "Either I am Joseph Joder or I should be Yoseph Yoder. People are more and more—I see it at the gristmill or at the courthouse—softening the hard *j* of our last name to a *yuh* or *yo* sound. If that is the case, why not spell it with a *y*?"

"I see no problem," I said. "*Joder* has always been a jar to the ear."

"Some in the church think it wrong to change the spelling; they say we may be following the pull of the world."

I could not think of a wise response so I kept silent, watching the milk from the cow's bag hit the side of the bucket. Molly is the easy one to milk.

Joseph would not accept my saying nothing. "Some would say we are too concerned about what the world thinks if we change."

"The only way to beat that argument is not to change," I said. "Ever." That is what I have heard him say. Molly turned her head to the side; she looked as if she did not approve.

"That is right, John M. That is all that will satisfy some people. No change."

"A name is a foolish point to quibble over," I said, staring back at Molly.

"All the more reason to leave things the way they are. The way they have always been. Is that not what our brother Jacob would say?"

At that I laughed and spit into the straw and dirt at my feet. "We should change the spelling because it makes life simpler. There is no sin in that." Molly moved over a step. I grabbed another teat.

"How can we be sure? It may cause another to stumble. We must be concerned for the brother," Joseph added.

I could not tell if he was serious. His words reminded me of Isaac. Sometimes Joseph pretends to voice another's opinion. I have learned to take pains before I commit myself. "I might not ever make a decision for fear of hurting a weaker member," I said, hoping that Joseph would give me a reprieve.

That is the way the battles go. Sometimes he pushes too hard and pokes fun at what I have been taught to believe is right. "How can we be sure?" is his favorite. I cannot forget the tremble in Isaac's cupped hands, the way they parted on top of my head, pressing down in blessing, releasing water to drip into my eyes, down my nose. Sometimes I give answers to please Joseph because I do not wish to argue. Yet I remember Isaac giving me his hand like a brother, telling me to rise in the name of God. Sometimes I wish I had stayed in Pennsylvania, a safe distance from the questions. But I could not have lived with Jacob. If Isaac had hired me, perhaps. But he has boys of his own. Joseph is bold, but Isaac is near to God.

Another time I turned the tables and asked a question of Joseph. "Why do you stay in the Amish church? Your questions sound like you are ready to bolt."

He hesitated and I thought he might be angry that I had dared ask. I had overstepped and could not think how to back out. Finally he spoke. "It is as good a way as any, John M. There are those in the Amish church who say our faith is the *only* way to peace and happiness. That is where I disagree; that is not my line of thought."

I gulped and teetered on my one-legged milk stool. I did not want to hear that.

"There are different ways to get from Pennsylvania to Ohio," he said. "The way you and I rode—up to Wheeling and the Ohio River, over to the Tuscarawas, and then along the smaller creek beds to the Walnut Creek—that is the way many Amish people travel. As well as people of other persuasions. It is the way familiar to me, but it is not the only way. Is that not so?"

I nodded, then remembered he could not see me with Molly in between. "Yes," I said, softly. I thought of Isaac. I knew he would be very sad.

"In the same way, John M., it would make little sense for me to study the ways of the Methodists and follow their path. I would need to backtrack, or I would miss an important fork. I might get to my destination, but it would take me longer and I would splatter myself with mud along the way. The same is true for the ways of the Dunkards or what have you. They will get there also, but at their own pace and in their own time."

I could not believe I had a brother in the family and in the church who thought like this. I stopped milking. Molly shifted. Joseph seemed to sense my shock. "You and I know this is not what our church fathers would say, nor for that matter what our own father, Moses Joder, would have said. We get the *M* from him, but we do not need to agree on every point." Molly stared at Joseph's back. "Why do I stay with the Amish? Because it is the way I know. It is the safest, driest, surest for me. It is as good as any other. But it is no better."

Later I wished I had thought to ask, "How can you be sure?" But I was not quick enough. I do not know that Joseph's answer can be my answer, but I know it is an honest one.

15.

ℱRANEY

July 1820

Something stirs within that I do not know how to answer.
I do not want to bother Mary, for she keeps busy with
baby Verena. I live here in Centre County these two months
to be of assistance to Mary and Jonas, not to burden them
with troublesome questions. But sometimes my body takes its
swoops and dives, and I fear that something is wrong. One
night I woke in the midst of sleep. All was dark around me
and none of the little ones stirred. The crickets made a frightful racket outside. More than their usual peeping. I do not
know what gave the wake-up call. The tingling through my
chest seemed mysterious, as if a force traveled through my
body. I was careful not to touch myself, for I have heard of
people being struck dead for doing what they ought not. That
would be something Frieda would try.

I lay with a quietness for what seemed a long time. Finally
Verena became restless and Mary woke to quiet her whimpers. I heard a loud sucking and wondered how the milk
knows to be there. How that must hurt, to be the one giving
nourishment. Yet Mary appears serene when I catch snitches
of her nursing the baby. I do not mean to stare. She helps with

my hair when my braids do not want to stay under my cap all day. When Mother died, dearest Rachel gave me aid as best she could. Even David took a turn when Rachel's hands trembled too much. But Mary has better hair pins, stronger and longer, and she has showed me how to tuck more securely. Now I do not have an unruly bunch of hair flopping over my ears by the end of the day.

Sometimes when I brush my hair I imagine going about the house all day with my hair hanging down. It is an awful thought and I do not know why it comes. My hair is thick like the straw of a brown broom; Mary says the kinkiness comes from the braiding. She says my hair is pretty with its light brown shade. I like her for saying that, but I wish my color were not so ordinary. Nothing could be more beautiful than a head of black hair that curls on its own like Mary's. Gertrude has the black hair also, but she does not appreciate its beauty. Not until we were both twelve and old enough to wear the black cap for Sunday dress did I think that my hair looked better than hers under the dark cap. I know we are not to make comparisons, even among ourselves. But now there are these new girls come from Germany.

Church is where I see them: these Amish from the Palatinate. The girls look strange because they do not wear the cap at all; only their married women get to put on the *haubchen*. That is their rule in the Old Country. Here we go from white to black to white again. Elizabeth gets to wear the white cap as a little girl; it looks so tiny when it rests beside her bed at night. Then when we marry, we are allowed to wear the white cap again, a reward, like unto marriage itself. I do not know who gets to decide when we wear which color or why it is different in different countries. Yet we have the same faith.

Mary's father Shem says more people still come from the Old Country. Why they come now when farm prices are bad is hard to figure. He says they stay with a relative or an old family neighbor in Lancaster or Mifflin County for a week or even a month before they decide to go south to Somerset County or gird up their strength to move on to Ohio. Jonas does not like them at all, but there are many things he does not like. Shem reminds him that our grandfathers arrived penniless with torn shirts on their backs, and now it is our turn to make someone else's path straight. Jonas looks sulky when he tells Mary that most of them only speak German and know only a few phrases of English. He rubs the back of his hand on his nose and then wipes his snot on his pants. He says they should do their schooling before they come to America. I do not know why he thinks he is so much better.

Jonas goes about with the big furrow on his forehead. "Better markets," he says, "that is what we need, better markets." He and Shem work together on each other's farms. I believe Shem is the one who manages though, telling Jonas where to put his right hand and when. I am not certain what happened with the hay, but Jonas acted as if it were his downfall. I heard him say to Mary, "I am a varmint. *Schmutzig.* I should be cut off and left to rot." I think the hay was cut and lay wet in the field too long, but that is only a guess. I know there is grave concern about how the horses will make it through next winter. I did not like to see Jonas carry on so. A little regret is to be expected, but he moped about far too long. He pays no heed to Verena. Yet I remember his kindness to me when Mother died.

There is too much trouble in my family. I begged Abraham not to take baby Eli from me those long years ago. Then Rachel left; I never dreamed she would be the one to become sickly and give up the ghost. What could she have done to deserve such illness? Now Father says not to blame Levi for wanting another wife; he could not be expected to give care to three little ones by himself. There is some question about the woman though. We do not get clear reports from Ohio, but Gertrude's mother says that since the woman's name is Miller, she must be of the Brethren group. Our family is all befuddled. Poor Evangeline has a new mother of unknown stripe and now an extra brother from this second mother. We do not even know if they are being brought up Amish.

It is better to think about the children here. I give care to Evangeline's cousins: Jeremiah, Adam, and Elizabeth, who is two. I did not want to come—I had told myself I would never move anywhere—but Father insisted that he would be fine without me and that I could be of more help here. I hope he stays well and does not leave me in the lurch. I fear I am getting too attached to the children. Even with Adam, who has too much of the colt in him. Father never complained about my cooking, but feeding six mouths has been a surprise. I cannot get by with only fixing eggs. They have a Dutch oven built into the wall on the side of the fireplace that I use for baking. And Mary gives direction for the stew and cornbread. But Jonas says, "This is not Mary's," and looks disgusted. It is not only me he finds fault with; he yells at the boys much much, too much.

It is good I am not ready for marriage. One night I heard loud noises from the bed of Jonas and Mary. At first I thought they might be having a quarrel. I expected the bed to collapse at any moment and was about to call out, "What is wrong?" All of a sudden, the noise stopped. Just like that. As if someone pulled and pulled on a cord until it snapped away entirely. I heard Jonas—I think he was the one—make a long, slow moan in his sleep and then roll over. He must have had a bad, bad dream. I am glad I kept quiet, for the next day neither Mary nor Jonas looked one snitch different. I will have to ask Gertrude about it when I get home.

Father holds me back in ways I do not like. He let me go to school for three winters and I learned to read some English and the German, but he says I am not ready to join the church. "Another year or two" is his usual tune. I wanted a second dress for wearing to church, but Father was very set against it. There was more obstacle than not wanting to ask Aunt Martha. "That is sin," he said, "to have more than you need." I am no good at feeling cast down and unworthy. That is for Jonas and the way he carried on about the hay. I do not see the error in a second good dress. It is hard for me to hate myself, so that I, a sinner, will know God's saving grace. I also do not like what this new book says about education. Here in Centre County we young people have been given a book called, *Address to Youth*. Jonas says it was written over twenty years ago. In it a person asks questions of a Burkholder man, questions that are like some of the things I wonder about: "What do I need to do to be saved?" and such. I wonder how we are to read this book with its helpful ideas if we have not been to school. Some things do not add up.

Then there is Aunt Martha. I do not mind that we younger ones are to submit to our elders, but why can Father not see how puffed up she is? When she ate with Father and me at our house, I was made to sit at the far end of the table instead of next to Father as is my custom. She made certain that she and her family had the best places. Now that seems high-minded to me, and Aunt Martha cannot read one whit. While we ate she repeated that same story about the girl Frieda and the bull. Now I know she made it up because not everything was the same. Last time there were storm clouds; this time, two sets of fences to climb over.

Here is another thing. With every church I have ever been in—even Shem does it here—the ministers sit on the front benches. If the first are to be last and the last first, why do the ministers not take a place at the back? Why do they drink from the cup first? These must be silly questions since no one thought to ask them of Brother Burkholder. No one asked why women are allowed to be more humble than men; they are served last at Communion, and they wait the tables at funerals. When I let these questions run about in my head I feel unhappy and given to strife, so I know Father would say they are a waste of time.

Father may be right to hold me back, but I do not like it. When I am old enough to find assurance for my questions, then I will also be ready to think on a marriage partner. Not that I go looking. I must wait to be found. I do not like the mole that grows dark brown on my face between my right eye and ear. David has freckles all over, but Father said my freckles all went together and formed a mole. I have tried to rub it off, but that does no good. I am glad I do not have to look at it, but I know it is there. Another thing bothers. I do not make gain with my height. Father says, "Another year or two," but I think time is running out. I do not want to look like a little girl all my life.

16.
J S A A C
April 1822

*H*ere we are; the quiver full. An even dozen; half of one and half the other. Peter's birth in November evened up the arrows. What a blessed privilege to be the father of this full brood.

Jonathan will be eighteen in another week; he is already much taller than I. He does not put on the meat as I am wont to do, although both of my big boys partake of food as ravaging wolves. Where it goes, there is no sign. Would that I could eat as they do, but I only get shorter and rounder. Feeding us never ends for Sarah. She begins again as soon as the last meal is consumed. She has the three girls, twelve and older, to give her aid, but I fear her body may be wearing low. She says with fervor—I have seen her lower lip tremble—that twelve is a goodly number. I cannot argue, what with the twelve tribes and twelve disciples.

I fear I may be attaching myself to a thing of excess. I have taken to working with wood this past winter. Last fall I built a small woodworking shop behind the house where I can keep my tools all in one place and have space to store wood for drying. I am partial to the smell of cedar. This spring when I help my boys with the planting, I would rather be in my shop. Sometimes I go there for the exaltation of seeing beautiful birch and beech. I do not think it is a sin to look and enjoy. I made a new washtub of white pine and a bigger, oak butter churn. Now Sarah wants a saltbox. Recently one of the little ones asked what heaven would be like. Without stopping to consider, I said, "Like my shop, full of sweet-smelling wood from the forest." It is not an answer fit for Sunday morning, but there may be truth in it. Sarah says I give too much elaborate explanation when I preach. I do not know what she means. Now that I understand more fully what I memorized in those early days, I cannot help but expound.

As for those who admire my handiwork, I tell them that wood comes as a gift from God. This spring I finished a chest of drawers for the girls' things. Now each of the five oldest has a place for putting her what-nots. Eva had the pout at being excluded, but I reminded her that she is only five and has room with her momma's things. When the chest was finished, I carved Sarah's initials, S. B. J., in the top. She came out of her melancholy and hummed all day when she saw it. I felt better than if I had engraved my own name. Would that we could just as easily carve our godly heritage into the flesh of our children. Would that Sarah could refrain from finding fault.

We have had yet another innovation, right here in our home this past winter. School. Matthew Fortney was willing to give instruction for several months; in return, we fed him and gave a small recompense for his effort. Sarah expressed concern as to what others in the church would say. In the past she would not have worried thus. I reminded her that there have been schools among our people in Ohio for three to five years already. We do not have to be the last at everything. Not that we should take Ohio as our guide. Far from it. But I feel certain our children can learn the basics of reading, writing, and ciphering without compromising our dear faith. I do not consider this an unnecessary change. We are to be *in* the world, but not *of* the world. That is the gist.

I did not want to give preference only to my own, so we invited our neighbors' children, the Brennemans and Peacheys, to come as well. Some thought it was considerable commotion for our small house. The Peacheys came but twice and then stopped. William said they were all slow on the number drills and that Sam Peachey could not sit still but roamed about the room. As it turned out, John Folk heard of Fortney's work and asked if his seven could come, so everything worked out for the best.

I fear that William may be involved in sput-making with regard to the Peacheys'name change. Ever since they abandoned the *Bitsche* spelling, Mahlon Peachey has complained that some of his children, especially the boys, received heckling about the old pronunciation. That is the problem when our German words get mixed up with the loose English. I queried William at some length, although Mahlon did not name names. William, of course, thinks I pick on him. It is not my nature to think ill of anyone, certainly not my son. But we do not want to give comfort to the Devil and his cohorts. We must stay alert. I must keep house.

I still have no relish for conflict. When I think back on my first trip to Ohio, I was certain it was my last. I said as much to Bishop Blauch. Sarah thinks I must not have said it clearly enough. Duty. Duty took over. I have lost track of the tasks I first said "never" to. I do not mean evil deeds. I mean the good that I did not want to do. All of the certainties of youth get swallowed up in life's vicissitudes. Years ago I only wanted to be a farmer. Now I know not to say "never."

I make the journey to Ohio two or three times a year, and I

have my regular places for stopovers. There is a tavern keeper in Wheeling that I have developed a friendliness with. He does not appear to be an evil man, although his nose is smashed sideways. I am glad I do not need to know his story. I wish, however, he could refrain from selling to excess. On the other hand, he has refused to take payment from me a time or two when I have spent the night. He says, "You are a godly man. My house is blessed to have you enter." Another time, after I spent a Saturday night, he asked me to preach to his patrons before departing. It seemed an unlikely setting to impart God's Word and yet, who is to say what seed may have been sown?

Life in Ohio appears much more settled than ten years ago when I first made visit. For one thing, stagecoaches carry mail back and forth. Father took me to see the hand mills for crushing corn. We also stopped at the sawmills where wood is processed. I have not seen it, but he says there is a wooden frame building in Green Township. Father does well for an old man near to seventy. My prayer has been answered and he has returned to his duties as a minister. Poor Mother has been gone already eight years. I made note of it in my Bible: March 27, 1814. But her spirit hovers over the large field stone that marks her bodily departure. Every time I visit Ohio, I go to her resting place. I am much too fat to sit on the ground with my legs crossed as I would like, but I perch on a nearby rock and think on how she taught me to get along with my fellow man: "Give two coppers for every one you get."

Her death brought her surcease of sorrow. That is not a thing to be mourned. But what troubles in the gut are those premature deaths that usher in unending sorrow and leave people's lives upturned, exposed to ill winds. Baby Marie Hershberger's death. I cannot forget. Already twelve years have passed. Would that we knew the what and wherefore. No one has made confession. Not Reuben. Not anyone else to absolve him. Most people have forgotten the terror of the deed and of those left in its wake. Yost's eyes do not trouble me as they once did. But I do not forget.

I have done nothing to bring about redemption. I have not sought conversation with Reuben. Not once. The first time in Ohio my neglect came from my eagerness to return to Sarah. After that I only needed to repeat what I had done before. Repeat my nothing. Now I tell myself: it would be strange to show my face at this late date. I do not go to Reuben. That is my sin. I have confessed my failing to my father. I do not know why I told him, for he is in no way responsible. But I needed to speak with someone. He showed little concern; he only reported that Reuben is shunned. Father did not know how it came about but thought it might have been at Abraham Zug's instigation.

Father reminded me of other untimely deaths of our own people other than baby Marie. He said that many have suffered injury rather than death. Long ago the Indians massacred three Amish, relatives of Reuben and Yost. What I did not know is that on that very night, shortly before dawn, my own grandfather, living in the same vicinity, also suffered attack by the Indians. Ever after, Grandfather's right hand was crippled, the fingers curled under, unable to be stretched out straight. I do not know why Father waited so long to tell me; the story could have been lost. Father said he was only three years at the time.

What happened is that Grandfather was out early, chopping the day's supply of wood. Unknown to him, a group of Indians and a lone Frenchman lurked nearby. Father said this Frenchman—I do not know how his origins were determined—fired at Grandfather. The ball of his rifle hit the head of Grandfather's axe as he was about to strike a downward blow. The ball then bounced off Grandfather's right hand, mashing the fingers all along the big row of knuckles. By comparison I am fortunate to have suffered little. A full quiver; a ripe, albeit fat, body. Grandfather had to live with an odd-looking thumb, sticking out bereft from the stump of his hand. I always remind myself to be careful when I use my shaving knife; I have not nicked myself once in my shop.

I wonder why the Indians did not attack Grandfather further. We do not know. Some would say we are not meant to ask why. That seems sufficient, for it avoids unnecessary speculation. If Yost were to ask me why three of his ancestors met death that day, whereas only one in my family was crippled, I do not know what I would say. I do not think he will ask.

When Father asked what is the hardest part of being a bishop, I answered without hesitation: "Keeping watch over the soul of another." Father asked nothing further. He knows I was not shaped to confront. I would much rather do good for another—help him shock his oats, give him my best milk cow, if necessary—rather than make investigation regarding a darksome matter in his life. I read an old, old letter—perhaps written in 1703 or 1705, the date is besmudged—addressed to the elders and ministers in the churches in Germany. It might as well have been written to me. The instruction remains the same: preserve the old customs. Do not make unnecessary change to new and unusual things.

Yet when I take counsel with other ministers here in the East—regarding matters of discipline—and I hear their certainty, I shrink away from heavyhandedness. Each Sunday when we ordained brethren greet each other at the front of the church, we shake hands and plant the Holy Kiss, as our brother Paul instructed, each on the other's cheek. The very Kiss I would gladly have spurned. Without fail, at these high moments of Christian love and fellowship, my thoughts leap to what Evil may be flourishing unnoticed. Could there be a stained one among us? A kiss of betrayal? A Judas? I try to cast out this line of thought, but it haunts me like the gray wolf I killed long ago. Is it I, Lord? Sucked in by the smell of wood?

When I was young and first made a minister, I thought that if we faithfully preached the Word, people would obediently follow. I took the burden of admonishment upon myself. To that end, I memorized Scripture. Oh, how I struggled. But now I see that we cannot force good works or like-mindedness with Christ onto others. Would that we could. Sarah says that if I hold the reins too lightly with anyone, it is with our own children. I do not know what she sees. Not Jonathan. Perhaps William does not tell the truth about the Bitsche name. I remind Sarah that we can only bend the twigs in the right direction.

I take comfort in the Scriptures, for I believe there is an answer to my every doubt. Paul told the believers at Corinth, "Be perfect, be of good comfort, be of one mind, live in peace; and the God of love and peace shall be with you." I try to include every point of import in my sermons, even though Sarah says I could do better with less. I am not perfect. Far from it. When I preach and recall later what I omitted, I am distraught the rest of the day. Then it is that Sarah comes to my aid. She reminds me that God's Spirit takes control of my feeble words and showers them on all who hear. I pray that she is right about such grace and power far beyond my doing. I can but kneel in awe to be a servant of the Most High. Even if my heavy body stumbles when I rise again.

17.
ЄLIZA
September 1822

My nights have taken on more fretfulness again, but I cannot place the blame on Lydia, born this past July on the twenty-seventh day. She is the first to make entry in the light of morning and has been our easiest to care for. I have wondered if we even have a baby; she comes with such smoothness.

I am the wakeful one. In the middle of the night I lie there, waiting for Lydia to cry. Yost says I get as ornery as the cows when they are not milked. He has said that now for ten years. Ten births and Lydia makes eleven, with the cradle robbed but once. I could not manage without my grown girls. I look on them, Lizzie with the dark eyes and Susanna still on the chubby side, and I marvel. They have done all the garden work this summer—enough squash and beans for two winters—and are in the thick of drying apples. We have long strings full of their endeavor hanging from the loft. For Yost, what matters is that we do not need to find help outside the family when a baby comes.

During the night I think Lydia's cry will come at any minute. My mind drifts: Yost's plea for Ohio, the boys and their naughty quarrels. I do not know where Gideon got the word, *pecker*. I think on brave Momma, gone from us now two years. And Reuben, the lost brother, gone to Ohio. So far as we know, he and Anna have had no more children. No one brings us word, and Sylvia would have no reason to know. Yost, of course, will not speak of Reuben. How I would love to see their Bevy and Jacobli; I wonder if they call him Jacob yet. If Bevy and Lizzie stood back to back, I wonder which would be the taller. I know that if Reuben and his family were to walk down our lane today, I would make haste to kill the fattest duck. I would invite them to sit down. There would be places for all at the table, and we would give thanks. But not Yost. He would find excuse to absent himself before he would make room for his brother. He would douse water on the fire to delay the roasting of the duck. It cannot be right for brothers to be at odds, but with Yost there is no softening. Brother Isaac's words go unheeded. I know he looks directly at Yost about loving the brother, but Yost does not hear. When I glance across the benches, I see his head bent low, his eyes shut, heavy from the past week's work.

When I finally fall asleep, Lydia wakes. I should not complain that she sleeps for long stretches at a time, but I am glad that Yost is a solid sleeper and does not notice my restlessness. I do not know why my weeping assails me again, like a sad refrain. It may have been that awful dream. The summer carried so much humidity that my eyes felt heavy, even before I took to crying. My fingers were swollen; my ankles grew big. I believe my grief still stems from the first Marie; she would be twelve if she were with us. Almost a woman. Our new Maria is turning out well. She loved to suck at the sweetness of honeysuckle this past summer. Even Yost admits to her contentment—the name has not been a curse—although he pays heed only to the boys. They are the ones who do the hard work, he says. I want to draw all my children close like a hen with her chicks, but few of them will fit under my wings. We know not what they may encounter of pain and loss in this world of woe. Poor Polly. What sadness she has borne. Of her twins born in April, only one survived. Leah, such a pretty name. The other twin, named after me, lived but two days and then was called home. Eight precious ones for Polly and three gone already.

What troubles me of late is my dream of Jonas Zug; I still see his shirt flapping open at the top. His eyes, a light green, almost silvery color, like a cat. I could never trust eyes like that. I have not seen him in years, but on Sunday when our neighbors John and Sylvia Schrock came calling, she made mention that Jonas and his wife have a new baby, born one day after our Lydia. Sylvia has a brother Shem who is Jonas' father-in-law; she keeps track of all the relations and reports that Jonas has the five living children.

Two nights later I dreamed of Jonas. It is bad enough to have the wrong man crop up in what little sleep I get; worse yet, everything about him set my nerves on edge. He was at church meeting—I know because of the benches—and he had on his black Sunday dress coat, the *mutze*, with the split tails. But the top of his white shirt flopped wide open. His chest hairs spilled out, bristling like those of a wild animal. I am surprised I did not cry out, but Yost made no mention. His snoring makes such a clatter. Not even Yost's chest cover carries as much thickness as Jonas' did. And Jonas is puny in size by comparison. When Jonas got up, he walked with a limp. Sylvia had said nothing about an injury. His eyes darted every-which-way. I do not know what ails me that I should dream thus: the disheveled shirt under the Sunday coat that signifies full obedience. It makes the bumps rise on my arms to think of such unnaturalness.

Yost and I did not treat Jonas well when he was setting his sights on Polly; I know that now. Still and yet, theirs would not have been a fitting marriage, what with them being cousins. Two horses are better when taken from separate stock, Yost always says. I did my best to be a mother for Polly; I was convinced she had inherited much less sense on her shoulders than I had on mine. I would tell her, "Leave the basket on the table," and she would walk out the door with the basket under her arm. She often lacked a clear idea which end was up. Her hair—. Such disarray. When Polly mentioned a face at the window and a brown jacket, I doubted she knew whereof she spoke. But Yost was quick to seize the import. The years have given no reason to think otherwise, but they are laden with heaviness. What if we have been wrong?

I take small solace in my daily work; it is better to busy my hands with apple butter than to be distraught over Jonas. Momma was right: fewer crows can roost if the nest keeps moving. Yost has been more content this summer. That is a blessing. He only brings up Ohio to remind me that I have denied him his wish. In truth I believe he is less certain of the wisdom of a move but cannot admit thus. Now he says to make preparation for the hog-killing. That is welcome news, for I have been without soap for nearly two months. I gathered several empty crocks for catching the lye from the fat. Yost says we will use the wood from the large hickory he cut last spring to make the best ashes.

It is good to be part of the cycles: sowing, reaping, and returning to dormancy again. I see the early change in the maples, already losing some of their green. Our nights are cooler also. It is all from God. Even with the ease of care for Lydia, I am ready to let the fields lie fallow. Yost says that plowing the soil without seeding makes the soil richer. I wish he understood the full truth of his words.

18.

$\mathcal{F}$ RANEY

December 1823

$\mathcal{A}$ helpmeet. It has fallen to me to be Peter's helpmeet. I still answer to Franey, but my last name is now Troyer. A year ago I fretted that it might not be mine to ever be a wife; even Gertrude grew tired of listening to me. Now everything looks different. I am only nineteen and already the recipient of abundance, a month by Peter Troyer's side. I am not a girl anymore. I am still short, but not a girl. I first heard of this Troyer family when I returned to Father from working for Jonas and Mary.

Peter is far more than I could have hoped for. If truth be told, I knew not how or whence to hope. I dreamed of a man like Father: quiet, but always knowing the right thing to say. Peter is that and more; he has teeth and he does not grunt. He has ever so fine hair, almost as black as Mary's. Nothing like my thick patch of straw. He says he does not even notice the mole on the side of my face. His ears seem small, as if they have not fully developed, but he does not like it when I look at him too long. He asks if I am studying a corpse. There is something about his lips; I cannot explain. They are small, rather like a woman's, but they have their attraction. The shape, perhaps it is the curve in the upper lip that causes me to tremble.

The first time he kissed me was the Saturday before we were to marry. He does not push the rules as do some. I had gone with him to his horse, and when we were on the other side of the barn, he pulled me to himself with such a fierceness that my breath was all but taken from me. When he bent down and his lips grabbed mine, I thought my innards would drop out from all the commotion. Now I have grown more accustomed to his onrush, but I still like to tease and ask if everyone kisses like this in the Old Country.

I shudder to think. If Peter had not come across the ocean. Or if we had not had opportunity to make acquaintance at our Sunday evening singings. We are both the babies in our families, but Peter is not short like me. He is also not a singer like Father—that has been a sore disappointment—but I have learned to overlook his rumble. He knows to sing softly and does not interfere with others. Father no longer has breath enough to be the *Vorsinger* and lets the younger voices lead out. Such a child I was to think I would marry a good voice. Peter has played his harmonica a few times. I do not know how to tell him that I do not care for the sound; it is too twangy, and he plays much too fast.

This past summer it became habit for Peter and me to be paired at the singings. Then he started making visits on Saturday nights. Father went off to bed early while Peter and I sat under the large weeping willow and found things to talk about. He liked to tell about his home in Germany—they seem much more advanced—and I told about having my family ripped from me: Mother, Eli, even Rachel. When the cool nights came, we sat inside by the fire and talked with a quietness so as not to disturb Father. Sometimes Peter took hold of my hand—he has black hairs on his fingers too—and we sat thus, watching the logs burn. It is strange how a fire can attract; there is nothing to watch but the sizzle, sizzle. The logs hissed in the same way that Peter says the name of his hometown, Hesse. Peter liked to take the back of my hand and trace his finger over one of my veins, holding it flat for a long time. Then we laughed quietly when he removed his finger and the vein popped back up, fatter than before. His hands are much, much bigger than mine. Gertrude kept track of Peter's visits, but I was afraid to count on his interest for fear of being let down.

Then one day the deacon rode in; I thought he came to see Father about cobbling shoes. But when he approached the house and asked to have a word with me, I realized that Peter must have carried through. I put my hand flat against my chest because I could feel the pounding want to leap forth. Deacon Ropp was all business; I did not even think about offering him a drink of water. He asked if it were true that Peter and I had talked of marriage. I nodded with an earnestness; no words would come. I gripped the chair underneath me with both hands. Then he asked if I were still pure, and I trembled with gladness to answer my squeaky "yes." We talked of a possible wedding date, and Deacon Ropp said he would convey our wishes to Bishop Isaac and make public our plans to marry. The Sunday when we were published, Peter and I did not attend church, but after that we did not need to be secretive about our intentions. I wanted to burst out to everyone—even sitting in church and looking across the meeting room—there he is!

Now we have visited our relatives on both sides, and Peter and I have our own house set up. With every visit we came away richer: quilts and other bedding, several buckets, tools for Peter. Father gave us Jesse, the cow I always milked at home; I have to think to say: the cow I milked at Father's house. I asked Peter if I could still be the one to milk Jesse. I thought he was going to laugh aloud, but he said he guessed no harm would be done. I try not to be sad about leaving Father all alone. How I worried for years that I would be the one bereft. Peter and I have more cast-iron utensils and clay pots than Father ever owned. I practice to see which works best for cornbread, which for mush.

Before we married I had opportunity to talk with Jonas' Mary. They and their five little ones came from Centre County a week before the wedding to visit Father and help with preparations. The new baby, Stephen, is over a year old; Jeremiah is now ten. He does not whine as I remember from three short years ago. While Mary helped me bake pies for the wedding feast, she asked if I was ready for the duties of a wife.

I gave strict attention to the apples—I did not want to slice a finger—but finally said, "I pray for a right spirit." That was not nearly all I wanted to say, but I did not know how to ask the questions. I was afraid Mary would soon be distracted with Stephen, so I blurted, "What should I know to do?"

"Think of the other first. If you remember that, you will not err." We busied ourselves, cutting chunks of pumpkin to simmer. A while later she added, "Remember, he is your man. Remember that when you are tired and wish for sleep. He has needs. More than you. You want his happiness above all."

Now I am certain as to her meaning. When I have to be prompted, I feel guilty about my selfish nature. But Peter is kind; he does not want to cause hurt. I am grateful that Peter loves me in return; he makes it easy to obey. Brother Isaac made frequent mention of the words from Ephesians: "Wives, submit . . . as unto the Lord." Those last four words carry heavy import. In the manner that I obey Peter, I give evidence of my faith. There are rungs for everyone in church; we are all on a ladder. The church must follow Jesus, and I look to

Peter. A husband is like an extra head for me. I know my numbers better than Peter—he has to count by ones rather than think in fives—but a man has a different kind of knowledge. My reward for obedience is that Peter loves me as much as he loves his own body. I do not know of any man who would be inclined to pound his head against a tree, especially not a thorn locust. I know Peter was not happy last week when he nicked his index finger with the axe, chopping short lengths of wood for kindling.

Peter fared better when he chopped the chicken heads—we had separated the twelve fattest for slaughter—for the wedding feast. He followed the tradition for the groom and came to Father's house on the Monday before the wedding. All the menfolks from both families—except for Jonas (Peter said he mysteriously disappeared)—gathered outside to watch the chopping. We women shooed the children inside to be out of the way. I have watched Father, and I know how the chicken jumps when the head is severed, like a bird taking off in flight, only to flop to the ground. Just when I think the chicken is dead, it jumps again in a heap or flutters its wings.

Father reported later that Peter did his work cleanly. "Not one miss, Franey; each head, one stroke." I clapped my hands, for it is considered bad luck if the head is not severed with only one chop. When I commented to Peter about his skill with the axe, he passed it off as if it were nothing. But his eyes had a bit of the glimmer in them. Like when he plays the harmonica. I remember how quiet the menfolks were after the chickens were killed for Jonas' wedding feast. Father would not say what happened, but I know something was amiss.

Our wedding fell on the first Tuesday after the harvest was complete. Peter used great diligence to make certain his father's crops were put away in a timely manner. His father follows the old ways of Europe and does not appreciate all the rush-rush he feels in this new country. It has been only three years since Peter set sail—then only 18—with his parents, four sisters, and a brother. The two oldest brothers had come over a year earlier and sent word back to the father, encouraging him. I had never seen a rush light, like what they brought from Germany. It has a wrought-iron holder and gives much better light.

The air was crisp on our day and I wore my shawl some of the time, although I did not want to cover any part of my beautiful blue dress. I wore it to church again last Sunday. After all the exhortation from the New and Old Testaments and from the book of Tobit—Isaac is not one to skip—Peter and I were invited to come forward if we still wanted to complete the undertaking we had begun. I waited for Peter to begin his rise because I did not want to appear more eager than he. We answered Bishop Isaac's questions; first Peter and then I. Before each question the bishop cleared his throat—there may have been smoke from the fireplace in the air—and Peter says I cleared mine as well, although much more quietly. One time Peter hesitated and I had to poke him a little; he said later he was thinking of something else and fell asleep on his feet. I asked what he was thinking, but he would not say.

Only two people caused any dampening of the day. Aunt Martha had already asked her meddlesome questions: "What will your father do by himself?" and "Do you know how to keep flour sacks drawn up tight so the bugs do not molest?" At the wedding feast she came to me and pulled on my tucks—they were already in place—but I was determined not to let her spoil my day. Peter calls her "a gabber," like one of his aunts back in Hesse. I think he means *gabbler*.

Jonas sat all glum for most of the week. I was too occupied to give much notice, but Father says Jonas did not visit much with the menfolks. I reminded Father that Jonas has had his sulkiness for some years already. Father shook his head. The older he gets, the more his cheeks cave in where his teeth should be. He said Jonas showed no relish for being near the Casselman again, took little interest in Father's new bee-hives, and cared not a bit that the Miller brothers had swapped farms.

Jonas was our *Vorsinger*, although custom would expect a relative of the groom to do this task. But Peter's relatives are few, and none of his brothers fare better with the singing than Peter does. So it fell to Jonas. I have always loved his voice, tender and clear, although he has developed a bit of a rasp.

Father questioned Jonas' song selection. "They do things differently in Centre County," he said. His eyes looked as sunken as his cheeks.

"Do you mean the first song?" I did not want to admit that I had not thought about all of the words.

"First song, #5 in the *Ausbund*. Make no mistake, it is a good song. But I have never heard it sung at a wedding before." Father began to hum.

I joined in and then sang the words to the refrain:

O God of love and truth and pow'r,
Thou art our God in every hour:

"Yes, Franey, you know it well. But did you hear how mournfully Jonas sang that fourth verse?" Father spit into the fireplace and then sang,

He sees the secrets of the heart,
Our inward tho'ts perceiving,
A thousand years roll by for Him
As yesterdays are leaving.

Father spit again. "I could not help thinking, what is the meaning of this? Jonas sang slowly, which is as it should be, but the despondency did not seem fitting." Father shook his head again. "The first song at a wedding."

Later, while eating supper, Peter and I talked of Father's upset. It is much better talking with Peter than with Gertrude. We could not decide whether Father's distress was with Jonas' being downcast or with the lack of uniformity in songs sung from one county to another.

"He should move from one continent to another," Peter said, a piece of cornbread stuck in his short beard, "if he wants to see differences among the Amish. My parents have to adapt to all manner of change. The American way is always preferred." I did not like the way Peter sneered when he said preferred. "Why do we not say that those from the Old World should be listened to? That is where our people started. America is but a tiny baby."

I must have had a startled look on my face, for Peter stopped talking and took a long drink of water. I do not know what ailed me, but I said, "Is that how we should all drink water too?" He downs everything in his cup at once, so that his head tilts back farther and farther. I see his Adam's apple jerk with each gulp.

Neither of us said anything for long minutes. He turned away in his chair so that all I could see was his dark hair in back, falling over the collar of his shirt. The potatoes on my plate turned cold, and I could not eat another bite.

I began to rise from the table, but Peter grabbed my wrist and said, "I am sorry for my outburst."

"Oh, no," I said, reaching to place my hands on his shoulders. "I am the one ashamed for not giving more thought to the difficulties you immigrants face. We old folks in America treat you with the new blood as if you must always conform."

I had been foolish to prefer small sips of water, but I still did not like his "tiny baby."

Then Peter stood, stumbling out of the chair in his rush. We found each other—his lips never lose their hunger—and we were dearest friends again, even husband and wife. When we give each other pleasure, he says my eyes get bluer than the sky. I beg him to stop, but he holds me tight and will not let go. I would much rather lose my breath with him than have that sickening feeling of animosity over how to drink water. And to think, I was the one who started it all. I shall not provoke him to anger ever again.

I do not like to think of Father getting crotchety in his old age, but more and more he says, "This is not what I remember as a boy." Or he comments that the Amish do not all think the same anymore. "How will we maintain unity?" he asks. He shakes his head and says, "Too much diversity . . . too much." The differences do not seem like matters of consequence to me. People tie their hats to matters of custom that carry little import, here or in the life to come. Yet I do not want to argue with Father. I shall do all in my power to keep an old man's days free from unhappiness. He is 67 and if he were to die soon, I would regret that I had not waited longer to marry. I do not want Aunt Martha to be right.

I said nothing to Father about the drawing Mary gave me. It was not a wedding present. For that purpose Jonas and Mary gave us our own Dutch oven; this one sits on a three-legged stool and can be placed right in the fire. The drawing, however, has no solid reason; I do not think Father would approve. Mary gave no explanation but said someone in Lancaster County had drawn it. She wanted me to have it. It is done with two colors, a dark blue and a rather soft red, and has flowers and two birds on it. I covered my mouth with my hand, for I have never seen anything with so much prettiness.

I did not ask how she paid for it or if Jonas knows about it, but I placed the drawing inside the back cover of our new family Bible, a gift from Aunt Katie. I do not think Father will look there, and if he does, I will have to make something up.

I did not even show the drawing to Peter until after we were married. I was relieved that he kissed me when he saw it. The two birds face each other with beaks almost touching and flowers arranged all around them in large scrolls but with tiny details of petals and stems. Hardly a day goes by that I do not peek at the drawing. Our church preaches simplicity and usefulness, but I feel happy inside every time I look.

It reminds me of the loveliness of sunsets, especially with winter coming on. The fields look all flattened without their crops, and the trees stand naked except for the pines and pin oaks. Against so much bareness, the sun goes behind our mountain like a fat, red ball. Sometimes the clouds form a bright outline where the sun has disappeared, putting a glow on all that has transpired. I tell Peter it is God's benediction.

When I close my eyes after dark, I can still see the colors in the sky. And I remember the two birds with their beaks close together. The words from the wedding prayer run through my head: "It is not good for man . . . to be alone." How wonderful to think of myself as Peter's rib, although a small one. "Let their hearts and minds be stayed on Thee . . . ." What if Peter had stayed in his Hesse? I want him to see that we can blend the old and new. And if we should be blessed with children, I will clap my hands. I could not wish for more.

19.

YOST

August 1824

All right, I am making the sink, the dry sink she wanted. I have found some poplar left over from the benches I built last winter. I did not have adequate time before, which is what I tried to tell her. But now I will fashion the finest that a woman could want: a wooden basin five inches deep, standing on four, thick legs with a plug at the bottom for a drain hole. I will show her; I will make it better than what she wanted. Underneath I will build a shelf for the water to drain into a bucket. I will finish before the harvest begins.

I forget myself. At times a blur comes over the last few weeks and I catch myself thinking that she is still here. That *they* are here. Eliza, my good woman, died almost three weeks ago. Many days when I walk in from choring I try to prepare myself: she will not be at the hearth. I do not want to see that it is true. Susanna carries on bravely; just last week she turned sixteen. The next girl, Maria, is only seven, so there is little help. Susanna picked up much of the slack after Lizzie left us in April. I do not know how to help Susanna carry her burden. I could not sing for her birthday last week although Joseph tried. She seems sad beyond her years, but at least she does not weep.

Who could have predicted? My wife and eldest daughter, both taken in a span of three months. I do not see any purpose. What good can come from this? I suspect that people laugh at me again, as when Evil caught me unaware with Marie's death. I do not like to be gawked at. Lydia is only two, and Anna but turned four. I am at a loss, how to dress them or what-have-you; I leave that to Susanna. Catherine offered to live with us awhile—that is good of a sister—but I do not want to impose on her if we can make do by ourselves. Now that I am over the first shock I try to think who in the community might be eligible. I go up and down each section of land from here to Meyersdale; I name every available woman. The list is short.

At 42 I am not a young man, but I can still see the hinges on the barn from the doorway of my house. I can still hold my own with a plow. I have land in my name, a goodly amount. But I must find a helper. I cannot wait a year as Catherine advises. My dire need should make it possible for people to overlook my haste. I will go to another county, Mifflin or Berks, for a woman if Bishop Isaac exacts too much strictness. I do not want to have another run-in with him. If anyone criticizes, I will line up my nine motherless children.

A brownness stays at Eliza's grave. Scarcely a weed or green blade grows from the mound of earth below which we placed her body. I do not stay long, for I am not one to moon over what is done and cannot be changed. Yet I miss my woman. Lizzie's fresh plot is completely covered with grass and weeds, and the little stone that marks the first Marie is practically lost, grown over. I did not expect to be guardian of our own Hershberger Burial Ground.

Late at night I cannot avoid thinking on Eliza's passing. She had taken to coughing spells around the time of Lizzie's death.

Her hacking, as well as Lizzie's, was not pleasant to walk into. Back in March already I was glad for longer days and warmer weather so I could stay outside and work. Eliza's coughing was similar to the way she carried on after Marie was smothered; that was fourteen years ago, I have been reminded by the bishop. At first I did not make much of her coughing. Who can blame me? Susanna says Eliza was coughing already before Lizzie died. I do not want to quarrel with her about the timing. What I will say is that Eliza seemed to get better in late May or early June when the days got hot.

In those early summer weeks a melancholy persisted about her. But again, that was not entirely unusual. One rainy day when I was confined to the cabin, one of the little ones—I believe it was Anna, for she is the one who prattles—called to Eliza for assistance. Eliza continued kneading the dough, even pounding it with her fists; from all appearances she was unaware of being summoned. Finally when Anna's shrieks became insistent, I called out, "Woman, pay attention, will you?" My voice had enough of a shout to release her from her daydreams. But even my rebuke could not cure her wandering mind; she went about pitting cherries or whatever, as one present only in body. In truth, I do not think she ever overcame her disconsolation at Lizzie's death.

Yet it came as a surprise in late July when I realized that she coughed more and spit up a horridness. Even globs of blood. She carried a tin cup with her and kept it by the bed at night. I knew she was frail, but I did not pay attention as I ought. How was I to know that it was serious? I do not know what I would have done differently. She complained of feeling hot; when I touched her brow it was like putting my hand to the coals. Many times she placed her hand on her chest and said she felt sharp pain. I do not know the first thing about what to include in a poultice, except red beets. There was no one to call. I encouraged her to take of my whiskey—even a tablespoon might have helped—but she turned her head away.

As it was, I might as well have been in Ohio. We went to bed as usual that night; I told myself I needed to be of a toughness and get my sleep, for the next day we would shock more oats. I put her coughing and shaking of the bed from my mind. I had to. I did not awaken until little Nicholas tugged on my arm, "Father! Father! Look to Mother. She is not right. She feels cold and makes no answer."

Nicholas had also been in the house when Lizzie died, so it is not surprising that he often cries out in the night. I do not know if it is nightmares or what. Eliza always took care of that. Joseph has agreed to sleep with Nicholas to answer his calls, and Henry now shares a bed with Lazarus and Gideon. I do not want Nicholas to turn into a weeping woman, just because he has been exposed to untimely death. Perhaps there is no age when we are old enough for death. Lizzie's was no easier to stomach than baby Marie's. For one thing, there were seventeen years of attachment to Lizzie, whereas we hardly knew the first Marie.

It is the same as when I lose a horse. The night that Prince, my work horse, could not make it up onto his legs anymore, I wanted to lie down with him and pat his head, bring him comfort. We had been through years of plowing soil, upending rocks together; no other horse could obey my command as Prince did. By comparison, when we had a colt that lived only three days last spring, it was not a drawn-out sadness for me to dig a hole. He was a pretty one all right, just like the Marie we lost. I was never able to talk at any length with Eliza about the loss of Marie. She would only commence crying. But I will never forget the baby's dead eyes, staring. The wickedness; the pure Evil. How Reuben can have no conscience, how he sees straight to comb his hair, I cannot figure. And no, I will not go to him.

With Lizzie's death Eliza and I had little profitable exchange. As usual, she latched onto an idea and would not be swayed. We have lost numerous Amish young people recently; even Brother Isaac's oldest boy back in late winter died of a sudden one night. Eliza called it punishment for the bundling. "Yost,"—I do not like to recall this—"we should never have allowed Lizzie to spend so much time at night with Ben and Rebecca's Moses. We should have put a stop to it." She became entrenched on the subject as one possessed.

It is true; there were Saturday nights when young Moses' horse, going out our driveway, woke me up. It would be near to daylight, and I could not return to sleep. Eliza lay there, claiming she had not slept at all. She whispered, "This must not go on any longer."

I hissed back, "Woman, this is the way our people have always courted." She knew as well as I that Lizzie and Moses took the same course we had followed, as well as our fathers before us. Few there are who abstain. I have not instructed a one of my boys, but they will know how to do when their time comes. The custom, of course, goes back to unheated houses in Europe. There it was a necessity, an innocent custom. A young couple, seeking each other's favor, would lie down together fully clad. How can a courtship practice of this long-standing, suddenly be grounds for divine punishment? Other groups, the Germans, the Dutch, the Welsh, all have practiced it, not just we Amish. If death were God's punishment for this so-called sin of bundling, we Amish would have died out long ago. Yet Eliza used the occasion of Isaac's son's death— Jonathan, I believe is his name—to hearken back fourteen years, saying we had not allowed Jonas Zug to court Polly on our property, so why were we slow to protect our own daughter? I was tempted to say, "Because Ben's Moses is a sensible young man," but I stuck with, "It was good enough for my forefathers; it is good enough for my offspring."

After Lizzie's death, Eliza was even more torn apart and convinced of the Evil. "My firstborn taken in the flower of womanhood," or some such. I was partial to Lizzie too, for she had my dark eyes. But Eliza carried on about how the forest that surrounds us is full of wickedness. She could amplify her line of thinking as no one else could. I do not mean to debase her memory. She meant well, and she was a good woman. I tried to succeed with the crops—I always sought more land— so she would not need to worry. But it made little difference.

She grasped after loose straws, rather like Bishop Isaac. I am sorry for him, losing his son. At least I only lost daughters. Not that there is a difference; Eliza always tried to say I made a distinction. Not so. Losing a child is not something to wish on anyone. But Isaac and I had a difference of some unsettling. Now I believe his son's death has finally put caution in his mouth. He should have thought twice last fall, early in November to be exact, when he approached me about my relations with Reuben. I was out mending the split-rail fence, but I dropped everything and we went to the barn to talk. He has the fattest face I have ever seen; it is almost a circle. I know he is the bishop and looking after the flock is his duty. But I never thought, never would have given one iota of credence, to the possibility that there would be just cause for a bishop, any bishop, to come to my door. Now especially, after all these years.

I told him I had no intention of making amends with Reuben. "The fault lies with him," I said. I could not have been more clear. "Until he confesses to having taken the life of my child, I will have nothing to do with him. Nothing. Is that not what the church teaches regarding infidels and sinners?"

I thought that would be enough. But the bishop asked—he was as contrary as Bishop Blauch long ago—if I was assured of hard evidence in my denunciation of Reuben. He emphasized the word, *hard*, as if it were important. I managed to stay calm and slipped the brim of my straw hat around and around through my fingers before I answered. "Life does not always bestow hard evidence." I emphasized *hard* also. "When we cannot be completely certain, we use our best judgment. Let the finger fall where it may." I could have added that that was my father's position. I should have added it.

There has been a strain between Bishop Isaac and me ever since. He came to my place right before Communion. That is too farfetched, that he considered me unfit to partake because *I* nursed anger. He expected me to ride to Ohio to seek correction with Reuben. For something Reuben did. *Himmel!*

Unfortunately, Eliza got wind of Isaac's visit. Gideon, it was, spilled the news. He is my strongest work hand, so I could not be too hard on him. She pestered me, "Was the bishop here? What did the bishop want? What did the bishop say? What? What? What?" I told her it was a private matter between him and me, and it would stay that way. She persisted, "It was regarding Reuben, was it not?" When I would not budge, she walked away muttering. I long ago grew accustomed to her sighs. She always said I was the stubborn one.

The bishop and I still shake hands, to be sure, but I cannot trust him as I once did. I was relieved that he did not deliver the long sermon at Eliza's funeral. He took part in the service, of course, but removed himself from major undertaking. Ever since his son's death he has less to say on many occasions.

If I went to Ohio I would never look up Reuben. Never.

With circumstances such as they are now, however, I give more thought again to a possible move. Before, when I made brief mention of the subject, Eliza became distressed to the degree that it was impossible to hold a conversation. "Spare me the shades of Ohio," or some such. I do not mean to make light. She meant well for her children. Now, however, I pay more attention when I hear that good land is still available. Daniel has gone. Reuben has gone. Not that that matters. What is to keep me here but nine children and the lack of a wife? I must make careful selection: a woman with an openness to being transplanted. And one who can handle Nicholas. He has had his sixth birthday but cries more than the two little girls put together. Worse still, I cannot get him to mind as the other children do. Every time I get out the strap—the hickory stick does no good at all—I see Eliza's gray eyes interceding.

Last week the older boys and I worked in a field far from the house when we heard the dinner bell. We had already partaken of the noon meal, as Susanna had brought it to us. So why was the bell ringing? I could think of no reason but trouble. I sent Joseph to the house with haste. He returned shortly, saying that Nicholas had rung the bell, thinking it a game. Susanna had stopped him as soon as she could and spanked him forthwith. Later when we all returned to the house, I doubled Susanna's punishment of Nicholas with my own, leaving no doubt.

The next day we returned to the fields to pull more weeds in the corn—our last go-round for this crop. Again in the afternoon the bell rang: five clear dings with those echoes that linger in the ears. I told the boys to pay no heed; I could picture Nicholas' little hands tugging on the rope. We worked on by hoe and hand; the sun was very hot and there was not a breeze to be had. Once more in the distance we heard the sound of the bell. At this I thrust my hoe toward Lazarus and instructed the boys, "Stay at your task. I will put an end to this tomfoolery. If I need help, I will ring the bell myself; then you must come."

I walked with haste into the clearing at our cabin—some of the time, I admit that I ran, fearing that I had waited one time too many—sniffing for smoke or some other sign of serious trouble. When I ascertained that there was no culprit larger than Nicholas, I slung him over my shoulders like a sack of feed and hauled him off behind the shed where we stack wood.

It is not necessary to say what I did next, but the Good Book is clear, "He who spareth the rod, spoileth the child." I did not spare. It is true that Nicholas has little to do with me ever since; he hides behind the largest sugar maple when I come in from the fields. Even as I work on this sink he keeps his distance. I ask him to fetch me more boards, and he sulks. But he will come around. He must if he wants his own land one day. Some time he will thank me for not allowing his willful nature to take root. If I must be a parent alone, I will not have it said of me that I am a slacker when it comes to discipline.

PART III

May 1826 — May 1844

1.

$\mathcal{R}$ EUBEN

May 1826

Yes, it is true; I have put another notch in the tree. There are fourteen cuts in the biggest hard maple behind our cabin. For each spring that begins another year along the Trail Creek, I mark the passing with a shallow cut of my drawing knife. Some of the early cuts I have had to redo as the wood has a way of filling in its own gashes. If only other wounds would heal themselves.

Fourteen years seem a long duration, yet represent a brief span for all of time. I have been on this earth over forty years and known exile for most of my adult years. When I was a lad and heard stories from the Bible, I was fascinated with the children of Israel. Brave souls to wander in the wilderness for forty years. I could not imagine licking dew off the ground or finding sustenance in a strange, white manna that fell from heaven. Corn mush was all I knew.

Our children know no other life than to have a father viewed as a criminal by the church. An *unrepentant* criminal. Bevy will be twenty this summer, a full-grown woman, and Jacobli calls himself a man at eighteen. He has big ideas about how to make Ohio better. "Get more organized," he always says. Then he announces, "My name is Jacob." I try not to squelch his enthusiasm; I was young once. Anna thinks Jacob does not respect his elders. "How could he?" I ask, and she hushes quickly. I do not tell her how he mocked, "Beware the enemy, seeking whom it may destroy." He said it when the milk bucket tipped over; then he said it when he ripped open his finger on a protruding nail. Each time his puckered brow spread into a foul grin. If Anna knew, she would blame me for teaching him to undermine the church. What does she expect?

Jacob and Bevy have interchange with other young people who live along the Walnut Creek; no one has told them to stay away from the Amish singings. Anna still says she hopes our children will marry Amish. I cannot understand her thinking. Why she wants to put the children to the test of deciding whether or not to shun me is a puzzle. We still dress Amish, perhaps from habit; in many ways we think the same. Yet it is the Amish who have placed me outside, left me to beg beyond the city gate. How am I to beg when no one comes close enough to see my need? Everyone else is free to go about their normal living, while Anna and I are left to wait for some un-known trumpet-sounding. No one is going to come forth with truthfulness after sixteen years. Yet I am to sit idly and cogi-tate on what I have done wrong.

The worst part came a year ago when we could not attend Tobias' funeral. Not me, not Anna. His last wife, Gertrude, did not even send word at the time of his passing. It was as if we did not exist. We guessed at what had happened from the number of horses and wagons going to and from their cabin. Bevy and Jacob were willing to make inquiry and brought back news of their grandfather's demise. It was some conso-lation for Anna that her children could pay their respects. As Bevy said, "I want to show remembrance; he carried me across the Tuscarawas."

Gertrude stayed in Ohio only a few more weeks. The next thing we knew, a large wagon, piled high with chair legs riding upside down, went past our farm. She made no effort to communicate with us or with her husband's grandchildren. Just made off with the goods. The children learned later that she moved back to Somerset County. She left not one keepsake for Anna. I will wager she did not distribute their goods among the poor. All the tools and farm equipment, everything was cleaned out. I would like to see her wield Tobias' foot adze or his froe and mallet.

Anna had the gall to say, "Perhaps this is as Father intended: she should have all."

"We do not have to be stupid," I said. "The only good part is we have rid ourselves of Gertrude." Anna acted as if she could not hear. "What will happen to his cabin?" I asked. "That is my sweat on those logs. I tamed his land as if it were my own." I might as well have talked to the chinks in the logs. Anna studied the toe of my sock, held up to the light, as if mending were the most important consideration in her life. "Do you not care?" I yelled. "Does nothing matter? Do you not realize? Your marriage to me—this foul, worthless scum of the earth—has robbed you of your inheritance?"

Anna's needle stopped its in-and-out motion. Her eyes, like those of a mournful owl, looked at me sadly. "It does no good; I cannot let myself think on it," she said. "What good does it do to rant? Only a wild man curses. And you are not scum."

That is my saint, my Anna. I wish she would get angry, if only once. If only with me. And stop her talk about new light. This staying calm all the time, as if our tortured wait is the Lord's will, this is not natural. I try to goad her; even the least discouragement on her part would give me some satisfaction, show that she agrees that our treatment is not right. Can she not say that? I want to drill holes in my feedboxes, smash all my buckets. But then I only hurt myself. My name will never find release. I am sentenced for life. Labeled dead, while given freedom to walk about. If I stay drunk, people can nod their heads and say, "Just as we thought."

This spring we got our answers about the cabin. A new family, Peter and Franey Troyer and their baby, came from Somerset County. Either the Troyers have not been told of my Evil nature or else they do not put much stock in obeying the church, for they have shown more neighborliness than most. We have been cautious in our response, because Franey is a sister to Abraham Zug. I picture Gertrude laughing, thinking that innocent people paid her good money to live next to the snare of the wicked one.

Jacob is my best source of information. He calls Zug a strict holder-of-the-line, set to enforce all the rules from back East. All he lacks is being made a bishop. One day last fall Anna and I had gone to the woolen mill at New Carlisle. We walked in to do our business and were comparing the various bolts of cloth when I became aware that an Amish man at the counter had turned in our direction. That is what I do not like about public places: feeling another's gaze settle on me. I am made to feel guilty for being alive. This man in his dark blue work coat that all Amish men wear, turned his back to me. "Put the cloth back," he said to the merchant. "Perhaps another day I will have incentive to buy." He walked out the door without looking to either side. It was Abraham Zug; his nose has gotten redder and bumpier. I would not expect him to ask me to fashion an auger or brace bits, but I shudder that he will have nothing to do with a store where my presence has spread contamination.

Anna's face looked shrunken, as if from the force of a slap. We made our purchase and left. But Anna hobbled noticeably as we walked to the wagon. She sat silently on the seat beside me; for once I had no desire to talk either. Zug's venom spreads within me; I cannot rid myself of its poison. I have examined my skin for white spots; I find nought. The longer this isolation continues, the more I see myself as bad within. I have even wondered if I did the foul deed without comprehending. But Anna—. Anyone can see she is blameless.

Time will tell with the Troyers. Peter has been quick to ask questions: where the nearest mill is located, how Tobias managed his acreage, which crops went where. I believe Peter knows how we are regarded by the church. Surely. Franey asks Anna for advice about the baby; Franey could almost be another daughter for us. We have not known this back-and-forth spirit since Tobias remarried. I found Anna weeping over the peas one day. She said it was for joy. For joy of a friend. Those are unfamiliar words for us. I warned her, "We must not expect it to last. Brace yourself against the day when Zug reminds his sister that shunning is practiced here." She nodded, sniffling and wiping her nose with her hand, her stiff fingers fumbling at the green pods.

With Yost I have learned to live with coldness; I care little about our estrangement. Tobias had told me about Eliza's death, two years ago—right before I built the smokehouse. My first thought was a faint satisfaction. Not that Eliza had died, but that Yost was being punished. I do not expect that he saw it that way. Anna had wanted to send a word of condolence; some word, she said, that might open a door.

I scoffed. "Eliza went to her grave still thinking me responsible for her baby's death. And you think there may be an opening now?" Sometimes I think Anna has lost all her wits.

Now we hear that Yost has found another wife; Fanny Beiler by name. Jacob snickered when I said, "Fanny! That is all he ever wanted." Peter says she comes from the same family as the woman that Franey's brother Jonas married. Peter sometimes gets his relations mixed up—he knows all about metals in the Old Country, however—so I will wait to see what Jacob hears.

I asked Anna, "Are you going to send to congratulate Yost now that he has found another slave to tend to all his seedlings? Perhaps a word of condolence to the new woman would be in order. Something that might open a door."

"You do not become yourself," she said, "to speak of a brother thus."

"He is not my brother. He has put me out of the church. Remember?"

"You have the same mother and father as he."

"That means nothing."

"Is that what your mother would say?" Anna asked.

She knows how to touch what little tenderness is left. She is right, of course, but I cannot revive a kinship whose blood has been stopped. If I were younger I might try to do something to change Yost's mind, but I am getting too old. Forty-one years! Sometimes I do not even care to make amends. Let him think what he wants. I only want the ache to go away. To be restored. We will see about these Troyers.

2.

$\mathcal{P}$ O L L Y

August 1828

I know not what to make of these boys. I try to bring them up in the fear and admonition of the Lord, but they seem bent on mischief and destruction. Christian says to let them be boys, that they will grow out of their tomfoolery. I try to remember that Christian was once a boy, but when John and Andrew stray so far from the good that I mean to instill, I despair of ever giving proper instruction. They recently told a tale to David—he is not yet ten and has always been on the frail side—a tale full of fright and terror, enough to interrupt the soundest sleeper. I have spent too much time weeping over my three lost girls and have not given the necessary attention to my big boys; it does not seem possible that they can be thirteen and eleven already.

I have been given six years of healing since Leah's twin sister, Eliza, died at birth. Born one minute and dead the next. Every six years a bad thing happens to one of mine. That is the length of time from when my Marie and Barbara died of diphtheria to when the babe Eliza never survived her birth. I fear I should not have named her Eliza, although why there is a shadow over the Elizas and Maries of this world, I do not know. I pray that the Lord's timetable is not about to exact another loss. These death calls come also for our neighbors, the Beachys; only for them the horn sounds every third year. First the little boy, then an older daughter, then the father, next a middle girl, then a baby from a second marriage, then the grandmother, now the second husband. On and on it goes for Mollie, as regular as a clock.

Christian points out that the six-year intervals do not work out with an exactness for us; there have been other deaths in between. He is right to count my niece Lizzie, as well as her mother. My dear sister Eliza. Gone from this world of sorrow. I cannot bear to think of Yost lying down with another woman—I see his enormous, dark eyes—but I know it is true. I do not want to question the Lord's plan. We heard that he and his new wife, a Fanny, had a baby girl late last winter. The infant's name was reported to be Ursula, but that must be a mistake. I have never heard of such. Poor Eliza. What would she think?

This frightful tale told to David must come from the unseemly boy nature. I first got wind when he came to me today—his reddish hair makes his eyes look as if they have gone wild—and asked, "How did Negro Mountain get its name, Momma?" I have lived in Somerset County all my life and have heard variations of how the name came to be. I said, as my momma always did, "No one knows whence the name comes. Do not bother yourself."

David jerked on my apron strings. "Is it true?" he asked. "Andrew says there is still a Negro up there groaning. He says the Negro is half-dead but is so big and strong that death cannot take him. Is that so, Momma?" His rowdy hair needs to be cut. His Hostetler hair. When he came out all slippery and his hair dried out, I knew he would face certain trouble.

"Of course not, David," I said, turning from the blackberries with my fingers dripping red juice. "People do not live forever and ever. Only when they go to heaven. Where did Andrew get a story like that? Never mind, I will speak with him myself."

"But, Momma,"—David half-wrapped himself in the loose flap of my apron—"Andrew says if you go near the shadow of Blowing Rock, you hear a groaning." At that, David gave a miniature imitation of a growl, almost like Christian with a fierce pain in his gut.

"David, be still! And stop your moaning! Andrew but seeks to speed your nightmares. Pay him no mind."

David started to speak more, but I went to him, wiping my hands on my apron—the dark brown color does not show the juice stain—and I covered his mouth tight with my hand. "Enough, David, hush now. Think no more on this tale; put it from your mind. Foolish thoughts profit no man anything. Now go, fetch cream from the milkhouse."

When Andrew and John came from the fields, I stopped them on the porch and reprimanded them for passing on frightful stories. John bowed his head; he is always the contrite one. But Andrew paid little heed; he kept stretching his suspenders so that his pants hung far down.

When the children were abed, Christian only grinned at my worries. He does not know how he looks with five of his front teeth fallen out. Christian will only be forty next year, but he stoops as one twice his age. He strains when he throws hay to the horses. Some nights I fear he will not muster strength to walk from table to bed at the day's end. Or even remove his smelly work pants. I do not like the way he walks with such a hunch in his back.

On these hot summer nights everything feels damp and smells musty, as if we live in a cave with water dripping from the ceiling. I breathe a prayer for all my little ones when I make my nightly checks. Leah's body, all alone in her narrow

bed, has a softness. I must keep my only girl safe. I run the
back of my hand over her cheek, and she opens her lips as if
to make utterance. Only a sigh comes forth and she sleeps on.
I try to smooth her hair, clammy with sweat, away from her
eyes. My boy babies have grown away from me. John and Andrew take their regular places at the table but seem like
strangers. They would laugh if they knew I think on their safety each night. David always sleeps on his stomach—his red
hair tamed in the candle light. My eight-year-old, Joel, lies
next, his little-boy-sprawl like that of a jagged S. I tug gently
on his feet to make his legs more comfortable, but he frowns
and tucks his knees more tightly into his body.

Christian says it is better for the boys to sow their wild oats
before they settle down, but I do not like these tales that
frighten. I know well that dreadful story about the Indians attacking Braddock's men while they were fleeing, leaving that
Negro man half-dead. It does our children no good to dwell on
such. There is enough fright for me, thinking back to when
Eliza's Marie was smothered. And to think, that was among
our own. That happened to my very sister. How Reuben can
keep quiet all these years and have a wife live with him who
makes food at his table and hears his snores, I do not understand. I am glad he moved on to Ohio so I do not need to
worry about meeting him or having my children come across
his path. That is one story I do not want David to hear: how I
had to be the one who looked out the window.

Christian maintains that the story of Reuben's wrongdoing
should be passed around for the edification of us all. He says
the boys need to know what can happen if they get entangled
in Evil ways. I insist though, the part about my living with
Eliza and Yost at the time, my children do not need to know
that. Christian says they will hear of it. I do not like the way
he looks so certain.

• • •

After days of scorching sun and sodden, drenched air, it was a relief to go about in the mid-day heat of a clear blue sky. But such a rocky beginning to the morning! I still try to wash away the memory of those pups' eyes bulging. If only my little ones could have been spared. We waited outside the house this morning for Christian and the big boys to finish choring. I had the food baskets packed—several cucumbers for each of us—to take to the fields, when Joel called from behind the house, "Momma, Momma, come look!"

I put down the water jug and went with haste; something about his voice made me instruct Leah to stay by the baskets. When I arrived, David and Joel stood there, bending over a bucket full to the brim with water. In truth, Joel jumped up and down as if ants infested his pants. At first I did not realize there were objects floating, but as the full measure of this horror made its way to my head, I seized Joel's arm and jerked at David's shoulder to tear them away. "Oh, terrible of terribles!" I cried. "Do not be so caught up with ugliness. Come! At once! Both of you!" I had a better grip on Joel but had to call David repeatedly, even returning to pry him from the spot.

I do not understand what prompted Christian to take such dire measures. He had remarked yesterday that the pups— born two days ago to Shep—looked sickly and that he was afraid for them. But I never thought he would take matters into his own hands. Not in that way. He even allowed John and Andrew to participate. I can see Andrew throwing a pup into the water and holding its head down, watching the bubbles gurgle and foam. Where was Christian's head?

"Quiet!" I said to Joel and David. Joel was still leaping about. I sat on a tree stump and fanned myself with the fingers of my hand, pulling Leah into the shelter of my arm.

When Christian and the big boys came, Christian spoke slowly—that has never changed. "The pups were sick. They seemed not to know how to suck." I often take comfort in his deliberateness, but now his speech dragged out my torment. Joel hung onto his father's pant leg, swinging around and around in circles. "Shep will have other pups. John, be sure to give extra food to Shep. Sometimes the first litter does not go well."

Joel stretched his neck back to look at his father. "Next week, Father? Will there be new pups next week?"

Christian placed his hand on top of Joel's light brown hair, smoothing his locks to one side. "No, Joel, not that fast. Be patient. Perhaps another year." Then he looked at me as if nothing had happened out of the ordinary and said, "Is all in readiness?"

I scuffed the toe of my shoe in the dirt, making a broad arc, and quietly said, "Yes." I never uttered a contrary word to Christian about the pups, but surely he knew I could not have been in agreement. But it is not mine to say. I remember how Eliza peppered Yost with questions, repeating Scriptures: "Judge not, that ye be not judged."

It was a relief to spend the day threshing flax. The hard labor and the dry air helped me forget my upset with Christian. I still hear the sounds of the day: the thwack, thwack, thwack of the flail against the rock—too many thwacks to count. The swishing of grain as it fell from the top pan to the bottom and then into the sack. My arms ache from all that shaking back and forth. Earlier in the week Christian and the boys had pulled the flax by hand and left it stacked in the field to dry. Yesterday they loaded the sheaves on the wagon so that today we could pile atop and drive to a cousin of Christian's who has a large field rock used for flailing. It is low and flat, large enough for two men to work at the same time.

When we were first married, Christian did this wearisome work with one brother or another, but now they have all removed to Ohio. Paul was the last to go. Christian misses his kinfolks, but he is too hunched to give thought to moving us all. As more and more of our people move West, Ohio does not have the distance it once did. Nor the fright. If I were to make count, I might find we have more cousins in Ohio than in Pennsylvania. I have even thought if there were some way to get to Ohio without making the tiresome journey, I might be as satisfied to live there as here.

Simon and Verena and their host of children made the day go better. We women carried the sheaves to our men, while Christian and Simon did the flailing. The older boys spelled the men for brief periods. But the youngsters soon got their fill of separating the grain and winnowing it—David has no strength in the arms. Sometimes Verena and I exchanged places with the young ones, for they did not always take sufficient care in separating the grain from the chaff. I hear Christian and Simon break into a chant to keep up their rhythm. Christian's voice is higher than Simon's, "Shlop shoe, shlop shoe, shlop shoe, shlop shoe." On and on. Thwack, thwack, thwack. Christian says he will use some of the flax fiber to make us new ropes.

In the afternoon we spread our quilts under a nearby tree so that the babies could get their rest. I am not certain that Leah slept, but at least she shut her eyes. Flax is the most tiresome crop to harvest. The straw will take more weeks of drying. Then the children will help me with all the scutching and heckling. The best part comes last: the spinning and weaving for next winter. Even Eliza said I was good at the spinning years ago. Making the cloth is like sitting down to eat the apple after all the pruning of trees and stretching high to pick. The reward of our very hands.

Joel could not forget the morning's ugly start and asked at supper to see the dead puppies. "They are gone," I said matter-of-factly, although I did not know exactly how or where Christian had disposed of them. "Your father said there will be other pups."

"Put them away." That is what Christian has always said about our lost babes. "Put them from your mind, Polly." Neither of us has said ought, but I believe our family has reached its fullness. Part of me is glad; no more extra pull on the legs. As it is, my leg veins stay a fat, ugly purple. But also I feel a sadness. We cannot go back and make another start. We cannot be young again. Christian is too old to touch me with tenderness. He looks on me, but his young eyes are gone. Leah is the one given to comfort me now with her snuggles.

The bright sun gave sustenance today, beaming through the blue, blue sky with its puffy white clouds. I do not know how we would make do if God had not set the light in the firmament above. To go about with a flickering candle or a smoky lamp would be a wearisome life. The natural light of day, that is for the best. Evil comes creeping in the night. I do not want to shut my eyes and dream about dead pups tonight.

3.

JONAS

June 1829

*M*y own tree has been topped, my very head. My father, for whom I carry my name, dead after 73 years on this earth. It happened less than a month ago, May 15, almost my forty-second birthday. How the wind howled that night. Father's death was not unexpected, for who of us can expect *not* to die? Yet when the Grim Reaper struck with his sickle, who could say that the very hour had been anticipated? Now the burden falls to me. I must carry on. But I grow stale in this Half Moon Valley. I used to think: wait until Father is gone. After that, go West. Now I cannot leave with the busyness of summer work upon us; the hay will soon need to be cut. I cannot bear to leave this crop behind. I go back and forth in my mind. I carry too much burden.

Father's departure will go hard for Franey. When she left for Ohio, she said goodbye to more than the Casselman. She headed West the same year Shem moved there with his family; that was three years ago. I do not mean that they live at the same spot. Franey and her German husband chose Holmes County, along the Trail Creek. But not the same creek where Abraham resides. Father heard that Franey and Peter's farm-

stead sits right next to that of Reuben Hershberger. What awkwardness. I would not have wished that for Franey. What if
meeting him were unavoidable? Mercy! For years I have not
allowed myself to think on Reuben. Now I wonder if he has
grown melancholy. We would make a pair.

Shem has moved to that other settlement in Ohio, Wayne
County. The same place where I have my land. Church trouble; that is why he moved. I went along to help transport his
belongings and had occasion to walk my land and take the
measure of what I had purchased years ago. His creek is the
Little Sugar; my land is along the Apple Creek. Much change
has transpired in thirteen years. The roads are better with
wide clearance and straight, even better than much of Holmes
County. The people are not crowded; they have given careful
thought to laying out their farms. Shem points out that Wayne
County is flatter, lacks the hilliness of Holmes County. I have
never seen such straightness. One road goes one direction, say
northerly, and then comes to a corner just as two walls meet
in a house. Then another road goes off to the east, but it is also
straight, not curved. Wayne County has the look of prosperity compared with Holmes County, all winding and heaped up.

I cannot decide. One night I think we will move to Ohio,
perhaps as early as fall or when we have a little income from
harvest. Father's wagon, my final inheritance, sits along the
row of evergreens like an enticement. Mary favors a move,
but I believe it is because she longs for her father. She seems
afraid to say as much; she says instead—accuses me—that I
have grown despondent. She says I need more pepper on my
potatoes. The next night—back and forth—I am fully convinced to stay put; there is nothing to be gained from the rigor
of a move. We would subject our children to unimaginable
worldliness. Shem says he had to go to help restore the proper strictness, but I do not know if rules are possible in Ohio.

Shem knows much more about the faith than I do, but I am left to maintain a strictness for my children with the German language. I must teach them to strive against the modern push toward individualism. Jeremiah and Adam and all the rest must learn enough English to do business among those of the world when they are grown. Yes, that is true. And Shem did not see a problem with using Pennsylvania Dutch for everyday conversation. But we must retain the high German for worship and instruction. For certain, with the hymns. That is the only way to teach *Gelassenheit*. Shem's face grew red with fervor when he explained that the English do not understand what is meant by overcoming self-will. He said we Amish will lose our deepest values of hard work and giving aid to the brother; even our plainness may go if we use a language that does not express the teachings we hold dear.

Shem is also a stickler about shunning. He went into great detail, all the time chewing on a piece of dead skin in his mouth. He picks at his fingers until they bleed. He said there are Amish in Wayne County who have a more liberal spirit than is faithful. This came to light over how we should treat people who go back and forth between the Amish and other groups. Jacob Nafziger, a Mennonite, lived among our Amish in Mifflin and asked to join the church. As would be expected, our ministers, including Shem, sought counsel with each other and told Nafziger he would have to be rebaptized. The Mennonite faith is not complete, so it follows that Mennonite baptism would, of necessity, not be complete. Shem explained it better than I, but that is the gist.

Nafziger became a troublemaker and said it would violate his conscience to be rebaptized. Then what did he do but move to Wayne County and pull the same trick out of his pocket, asking to be a member of the Amish church again. The Pennsylvania ministers got word that the Amish in Wayne

County had accepted this fellow as a member without being rebaptized. That is how it goes. A long row. Back and forth. I do not care for these church disputes. Not at all. There is too much indulgence in Wayne County. A bishop there by the name of Daniel Mast, over with the group at Oak Grove, shows great laxness. I do not know if Shem can help stem the drift or not. Many meetings, back and forth. It is sorely sobering when our ministers cannot agree. I did not like to hear Shem go on and on about shunning. If Mary and I move we will need to take great care, even among our own. Shem said the frontier needs more people who will give heed to the admonition from the brethren back East. They are the ones who know best how things should be done. I ask Mary, "Then why should we leave this Half Moon Valley?"

When we returned to Somerset County to bury Father, I saw his old horse gear made of hickory bark. The apple orchard had grown scraggly. I felt relief and sadness at my father's grave. Relief to have him gone, but sadness to look, as it were, on my own demise. My hands and fingers have raw cracks that will never heal. I thought it would be easier to fess up when Father was gone. Now I no longer need worry what he thinks of me or my boys. It matters not how I carry the name. Yet I want to uphold Father's memory for my children. Lift up all the fathers in the faith. My godly heritage, my leg to stand on. That is what I want to pass on to Jeremiah and Adam, even to Elizabeth and Verena, Stephen, Mary, Dorothy, and Simeon. All eight.

I carried the damp air of the Casselman back here to this Half Moon Valley. There is nothing good to say for this place. Nothing good but the limestone land. I know I must leave. I think I will go. But I do not know when. Nothing turns out right for me. My children bring no pleasure. A baby in my hands has always brought discomfort. Now these big boys squirm out of my grasp. I do not mean to frown all day as Mary accuses, but Jeremiah has never known when to stop talking. He tells Mary about the snake in the henhouse sucking eggs—he speaks with wide flourishes as if he is Abraham—and then goes outside to repeat the same story to his sister. Only this time there are four snakes sucking. Adam would rather wrestle and cause a commotion than keep the sickle moving on the rye. And Stephen complains that his shoes are too tight. I explain that Adam has not outgrown his shoes yet and that tight shoes are not an excuse for almost letting the mare get away. I have shown extra patience, reminding him that we can ill afford to lose a horse. When he takes on that stoniness and looks the other way, I ask if he has money to replace the horse he wants to set free. I want to jerk him about to face me and give answer. But I have shown restraint.

Even Mary seems given to stubbornness at times. Last fall she hounded me, wondering when I was going to repair the logs on the east side of the house where the rain came in. I already had it in my mind to do—I needed more clay—but not at that exact time. I snapped a reply; I did not have the tools for chinking or whatever. The job got done before it turned cold, so it was not a matter of consequence. But I did not like her hammering at me. When Simeon was born, also a year ago, she insisted that we should give him my name. Part of me found pleasure in her pleading, but a stronger portion knew I did not want a namesake. Now with Father gone she talks again of a little Jonas, but I have no interest. I tell her we have had enough; every other year a baby, except for the one we lost. She reaches her arm around me at night, but I feign tiredness. Then I am the one left awake while she drops off and rattles in her sleep. How different from my youth when I yearned to touch a girl. Any girl.

I carry the burden of the rift between Father and me in his last years. Not that we were ever close, except perhaps when Mother died. And not that we had words. But in recent years we sat around the hearth at John's place, and I felt no part in the goings on. My body was there, but I did not feel attuned. Father gave rapt attention to John and David as they discussed their crop rotation; he asked questions about sorghum and warned about the dangers of machines. I sat there, scratching what is left of my hair on the sides and back. One time I rose from the table and told Mary to collect the children, hours before we had planned to return to the Half Moon Valley.

Once on the wagon she asked, "What is it, Jonas? You seem to be many places at once and nowhere in your entirety."

I shrugged my shoulders. Then it slipped out. "I do not care much for people." Before Mary could ask for particulars, I went on at length about how David wants Father to give advice, but then goes home and plants as he pleases. As if that were my bone of contention.

Father was not one to hold grudges, but his will made no mention of Levi or the three older children born to Rachel. We hear that Levi has left our people and moved away from Abraham, farther north in Holmes County. That is another drawback with Ohio; I do not know what I would do about Levi. How could I shun him? I could not set aside those years of fishing with him as a lad: the catfish, the suckers. His parents treated me as a son. Yet I must be firm in following Shem's leading; he is my only remaining guide.

Father was not a wealthy man by any count, but such as he had, he shared freely. I remember when the Hans Weaver family lost everything to fire, Father gave them a hog and a sheep. I was near to tears as a boy, for I did not see how we could spare those animals. That was long before Abraham had left home, long after I had heard, "Worthless runt." But Father was right: life went on for us much as before, and the Weavers made recovery with greater ease. My own children will not find me to be nearly as generous; I clutch things to myself.

Father's will gave evidence of careful thought, like unto his whole life. To those living at a distance he gave small items: devotional books, a Bible and coverlet to Franey; the mantel clock, another Bible, two flannel shirts, and four pairs of stockings to Abraham. Of course they will each get proceeds from the sale of property and livestock also. Father gave me a featherbed, one chest, and two tables, built more solidly than much of the old that we have, as if he knew I would not want to move our delapidated furniture. John got most of Father's farm tools and gadgets: his scythes, axes, barrels, guns, what-have-you. To David he gave all his materials for leather-working, plus the grindstone, the bellows, anvil, and three sets of pantaloons.

Only David knew of Father's latest work on leather. I am not much for ornament, but Mary and the other daughters by marriage—even Peter—received a saddle skirt, tooled with flowers or feathers, some with leaves or vines. Shem might consider them too much of a show, but Mary is quite taken with hers. It seems beautiful to me also, the work of Father's hands.

When I was a young man, I longed for my share of the goods. I could not wait. Now I have been given Father's wagon, but I feel poorer rather than richer. I do not move on West. I wait. I have spent all my life waiting for a better time, for the right moment. Now I have no excuse. Nothing will ever be easier. I live here awhile; I buy land there. I am never at home. I am like a fungus grown forlorn, in search of a rotten log.

4.

JOHN M.

May 1830

*I*have known that this cup would not pass from me, even
that I did not want it to pass, as surely as I have known
that I would be a farmer. I could not seek after this calling. I
did not even mention it to Katharina, lest I manifest too much
pridefulness and reliance on my own knowledge. Yet I knew.
I only waited to know when. God calls His servants through
the church in God's good time.

There have been anxious moments; I cannot seem to do
anything about my perspiration when I preach. More troublesome, I have been cautioned concerning pride; some of the
brethren have made comment that haughtiness might be my
besetting sin. I do not mean to think more highly than I ought,
but my head has always stretched far above the other boys.
My school teacher expected me to do my sums swiftly, to un-
ravel the difficult puzzles. Farming came with ease also, not
unlike Joseph's success. I do not hesitate to experiment with
different seeds or rotate what I plant where. Yet I must remember: the meek and lowly Saviour humbled himself and
became obedient, even unto death.

When my desire to minister came tumbling toward me, I

felt an awkwardness I did not expect. Like unto holding my firstborn in my hands. Elizabeth is of my flesh, but the fit has not been immediate. I waited all these months for her birth, knowing she developed within Katharina's womb; then suddenly she was here. I debated whether to hold her flat in the palms of my hands or to cradle her in the crook of my elbow. Such a red, scrawny thing. *Zerbrechlich.* Neither way seemed natural. I did not want to show any uncertainty. That is how it has felt to be a minister in the Amish church. I wonder how I will answer the questions that are sure to come. Or what their exact nature will be. Yet I know I am called to do this work.

Four of us stood in the lot that day; I was the youngest at 28, but I looked down on all the rest. To be named as a candidate we each had to be mentioned by at least two people as a worthy servant, when the voice of the congregation had been taken at the spring council meeting. I wonder if Joseph named me. All those times of milking when he prepared me for this with his interrogation. The official qualifications, of course, come from I Timothy. I had memorized the list: blameless, husband of one wife, vigilant, sober, of good behavior, apt to teach, not greedy of filthy lucre. The only stipulation that presented a stumbling block: the requirement that the candidate not be a novice. Some may have trouble giving me the natural respect due an older man, but I walk as circumspectly as possible. When I stand to speak, I remind myself to slow down. *Ruhig. Sei ruhig.*

Two weeks after the council meeting the church gathered to learn the Lord's will. I was more anxious than I cared to show. Before leaving home Katharina had difficulty quieting baby Benjamin. I could not give attention to Elias' questions about how Bacon knows to turn right. I have shown Elias often enough how to pull on the reins.

The four of us named took our seats at the front of the meeting room. The few windows that could open stood ajar, for we have had early, oppressive heat, and a stuffiness soon prevails in our small houses. On a table in front the bishop placed four *Ausbunds*. One of them contained a slip of paper with the words from Acts, "And they prayed and said, Thou, Lord, which knowest the hearts of all men, shew whether of these thou hast chosen." I knew those words by heart.

The hymnbooks were all a similar, drab-brown color, with heavy bindings and bearing equal amounts of wear. At first I did not want to look at the books, but when I did, my eyes stayed fixed on the second one from the right. A shaft of light hovered there. I have wondered since if the other men did not see it or if they chose not to look. I had to drag my eyes away.

The bishop—he has a sad droop in his left eye—read our names. I did not like it that he pronounced mine *Joder*, the old way, but I did not want to be distracted. All in the congregation knelt behind us, praying silently for God's will. The time of examination took what seemed like hours. Finally, bodies and floorboards creaked, dresses rustled, old men sighed, as the members sat again. I could not see the light anymore and I began to doubt. Before praying, I had been certain.

The bishop invited the four of us to each select a book. No one, not one of us, moved. I heard a woman sniffle in her handkerchief; several old men cleared their scratchy throats. I did not want to be the first to make selection, but I had also determined not to be the last. I wanted to do the Spirit's bidding. The eldest brother among us stood shakily and wobbled forward to the table. His hand stopped over the book where the light had shone. My heart plunged. I could not look. I tried to slow my rapid breathing; all was over.

When I raised my head again I realized that the first brother had selected the farthest book on the right and that another brother had already picked the book to the left of the one I wanted. Soon there would be no choice. I stood quickly—much more quickly than I intended—but once up, I could not sit again without advancing. My hand shook—and to think that I had been amused at the first man's wobbles—as I reached for the remaining book on the right. I sat down, making a loud thump with my rear end as I forgot how low the bench was. The last brother stood to take the last book.

The *Ausbund* felt cool in the sweaty dampness of my palms. All that I had rehearsed beforehand to assuage any possible disappointment—that the results were not the last word, that there would be other Sundays—counted as nought. I wanted that slip of paper. I do not know if any of the others felt the same desire as I, or if some wished to drop the book and run. I ran my hands over the smooth leather, felt the wear on the corners. I could not imagine hiding in the Palatinate in a cold cave or dungeon with these songs of the faith, these stories of our brave forefathers.

The bishop opened each book in the same order in which we had selected them from the table. He looked half asleep with his eye drooping. We all knew that when he found the slip of paper, he would look no further. My chin sank to my chest, my eyes closed, as he reached for the first book. I heard him untying the bands around the *Ausbund*, rustling the empty pages. The bishop handed back the book to the first brother. A short time later the brother beside me sighed, as if he had completed a day's work.

I opened my eyes and stretched forth my book as the bishop's hand reached toward me. He did not fumble at all. It was as if he knew also, in spite of his eye. The book opened and there was the slip of paper. I do not know why, but I cried. In that moment of solemn calling I cried. Not sobs, but quick, salty tears. I blinked rapidly to bring some control. I heard women weeping; men coughed and stirred on their benches. I wiped my forehead with the large handkerchief Katharina had made for me. I wiped my eyes and heard the bishop say, "John M., if you can accept this service, you may rise to your feet. I give you my hand; stand up." I stood tall and felt like an awkward youth again, looking down on the elderly bishop. His rough hand clasped my smooth fingers. He looked up at me with the kindliness of a grandfather and reached to put his hand on my shoulder. I did not hear his words, but I know he told me all my duties. Then he greeted me with the Holy Kiss and shook my hand some more.

I had to bend to each of the other candidates in the same manner. Then the other ordained brethren present each greeted me with a kiss, some speaking encouragement, some looking through watery eyes. All the men in the congregation followed in line, shaking my hand, whispering and mumbling words. The women followed in the same manner. When Katharina came we looked at each other as if we did not know each other. We have all watched the same procedure before; we all know how to do. But I did not know how I would feel; I did not expect the tug of fear. I did not expect to weep again when Joseph came by.

When at last the service was over, I walked alone to fetch the horse and wagon. I have never felt that alone. Not when riding to Ohio on Blackey, not when eleven years old and straddled with Henry's responsibilities. I wondered why I wanted such churchly duty, why I had never counted the cost. There would be problems. Some would not like my leadership; some would think me unfair with them, too lenient with others. I had never entertained these thoughts before. I do not know how I knew of a sudden. I was about to eat of the tree of knowledge.

Katharina, her eyes swollen, reached our three oldest into the wagon, Elizabeth, Barbara, and Elias, and handed me the

baby while she climbed up herself. She seemed shaken also. I
returned Benjamin to her without saying a word. It is good
that at such a time as that I could go through the motions out
of habit, telling the horse to commence without needing to
think how to do. Bacon led the way home. I sat in a blur, my
thoughts stayed on each of my little ones, praying that they
would grow in godly character and holiness. I could not abandon my responsibility to rule well my own house because of
the gravity of being a shepherd to others. Little Elizabeth tried
to be motherly and quiet Elias' jabbering questions. I did not
know what to say to Katharina. What had happened is not like
a corn yield where it is safe to exalt. We were all changed by
what had transpired, but we did not know in what way. Only
time will tell. Even at life's end we will not know for certain,
because we will not know what might have been had the slip
of paper been tucked elsewhere.

At last I dared to look at Katharina, and I pulled her and the
baby to me as the reins flopped loosely in my hand. She rested her head on my shoulder and I squeezed tight at her waist.

"Will you help me in this endeavor?" I asked, pretending to
watch the road.

She did not lift her head, and I could barely hear her reply.
"Yes, John, I will be what you need." I thought I heard her
sniffle. "When we married, I knew this might happen." She
paused again, then turned her face into my shirt. I could barely hear her words. "I thought more years would pass before
we came to this."

I loosened my hold on her. She straightened, and I saw a
sadness in her eyes. I imagined her thinking, "Let this cup
pass." I had not expected this. I had never considered what my
being named a minister would mean for her. Well, of course I
had, but not in the same way. Not with the burden of the call
suddenly heaped on my shoulders. She must have felt alone

also. It would not be easy for her: to know much and be allowed to say little.

She seemed to know my uncertainty. "It will be all right, John. You have my support. Whatever that requires." I looked long to make certain of her sincerity. A strand of hair had strayed from behind her ear. I wanted to lean over and kiss her on the lips. Sink into her softness. But the children were behind us; I knew they watched, wide-eyed. They had seen a year's worth of kissing in one day.

Katharina is almost seven years older than I, taller than most women and given to moving gracefully. I have always liked the way she walks as if she glides, barely touching her feet on the ground. She does not have the long fingers that I wanted, but that did not seem important when I found her. She came to Holmes County from nearby Tuscarawas when her father decided to move away from the Grand Canal work that was taking place in his backyard. I do not know if he feared unsavory contacts with men from New York, or if he knew his sons would be tempted to take up the offer of construction jobs at $7 to $10 a month plus board. Whatever her father's reasons, I reaped the fortune. Joseph raised his eyebrows when I told him she was 27, but he never asked questions. He knew that I knew that she was the one. Her fairness complements my average brown hair. Her face burns easily in the sun. At first I thought she had no eyebrows; they are exceedingly light on her skin.

There was a time of youthful indiscretion when I took her on the mountain. We had hiked a distance, out of range of ginger root and trout lily to where only an occasional violet survived and beds of trillium flourished. Katharina shivered beside me in the crisp, spring air and I sought to keep her warm. I suggested that we pause on a large rock, and she did not resist my embrace or what followed. I did not intend that it should happen, but intentions are only part of life. I know that now. Afterward I felt shy to look on her, and we descended with more than a little haste. Now I minister to the flock and she is a minister's wife.

There are those who predict major changes to come in the Amish church. I would have to be blind not to know of conflicts between the church on the frontier and the church back East. How could I forget the hard hack of Isaac's warning not to "Accommodate," the contrary counsel of Joseph's "Adapt"? I do not believe these differences will become divisive. As long as we brethren look to God's Word, we will know the way wherein to walk. I trust that Henry Stutzman wishes me well; he also recently has been made a minister. I have always felt at odds with Katharina's brother. The first time I saw his freckled face and stubby fingers, I knew I did not like him. I cannot explain why—he said nothing offensive at our wedding—but I am ashamed to admit that I am glad he lives down in the area of Farmerstown. It is almost as if we have a mutual agreement that we will never be friends. That is not how things ought to be.

I think often of my blessed mother back in Somerset County. *Geliebte Mutter.* Has she dared to smile at word of my ordination? I doubt it, but perhaps her worries, that the frontier would lead her baby astray, have abated. Better for her to receive our news than for us to hear last week of another loss in Mother's family. Her nephew—my first cousin, Christian Hostetler, married to a Polly Berkey—has lost another child. His fourth loss. A twelve-year-old named David who carried the red hair that runs on Mother's side. There were no details as to the cause of death.

That is the task I most dread: bringing comfort to the bereaved. Especially when the young are taken. I have few answers. Why some families are hit harder than others with death's scourge, I do not know. But I will do the best I can to minister, with Katharina by my side. She is my best sounding board. I know I will make mistakes: a word too hastily spoken, an unseen error. But even with my so-called inclination toward pride, I am ready to do the Lord's work. As surely as the light shone on my book, He will show the way.

5.
J S A A C
November 1832

*J*have regretted all these years—eight already—that I did
not help build the coffin. I did not trust myself with a
hammer in those days of grief, but I insisted the men use cherry to fashion the box. I had twenty medium lengths, dried for
several years, that I had been saving. For what, I did not
know. Perhaps a robe closet for Sarah and me. Some people
whispered later as to what purpose was served by burying
him in the beauty of cherry when pine would have served as
well. I do not regret it. I wanted my firstborn housed in the
very finest. If it was a mere mortal desire, so be it.

Not a day goes by that I do not think of Jonathan and remember. The lamb offered up. Sarah says it was smoke in the
lungs that took him. No other ram appeared; no other caught
in a thicket by the horns; no substitute. Each morning I now
make supplication: "Here am I." I tremble that the day may
again require wood, fire, a knife. I have learned to fear God.

Before I went through the valley and shadow of Jonathan's
death, I could not see my shortcomings. Not that I viewed myself as perfect in every respect, but I was content with my
spiritual progress. One of the grave dangers of being made a

minister. This truth, I try with diligence to impart: how easy it is to blind ourselves. But it is in the mount of the Lord that we are seen. My name should have been Abraham, for my learning has been that of the father, not the son.

A week ago I was given the additional burden of a namesake. William, my oldest living son, saw fit to name his third child, Isaac. I do not count myself worthy. This is not my first grandson; there have been two others, plus the five granddaughters. Even as the Lord promised to the first Abraham, so He has multiplied my seed—eight stars in the heavens. There is a difference with grandchildren, not the same burden of responsibility for Sarah and me. But we remain parents also, even though Peter thinks himself grown at eleven.

He watched my stallion, Star, my replacement for Lady, mount the mare. His eyes got big; he looked away and then back quickly. His thoughts seemed to wander far from shucking corn. He looked to be a mixture of sheepish and shy, as if he had already tasted of the fruit. Gone was the innocence of childhood when he had first observed the same act. That time he had come running for my help and thought there was trouble. I had not wanted to explain, had not wanted to say the cumbersome word, *copulate*. I still do not know how to talk to my boys. "There is a beast in us all," I said. "And a small portion of beauty."

Peter reminds me every day of Jonathan, his short forehead and pointed nose. He has the same obedient nature and a willingness to work. Some of my boys—William, to be sure—grumbled at long days in the field, but not Peter. It is as if he wakes wanting to tend the soil, taking satisfaction in pleasing me by lifting another shovelful. He reminds me also that at one time, I, too, only had thoughts of farming. Sarah says not to succumb to the idea that his end will be as sudden and premature as Jonathan's. She calls it superstition. She bids me not dwell on the state of Jonathan's soul. "We cannot know," she says.

There is much I could have done differently. Before Jonathan took to coughing that winter and became too weak to stir from his bed, he was gone from home on many a Saturday night. We thought he was courting and did not want to inquire unnecessarily as to his whereabouts. He was our first. I did not know to keep watch. I knew, but I did not know. Only since his death have we learned that our Amish young men were prone to travel into Maryland on Saturday nights where their pattern included smoking, drinking, and much carousing. Sight comes only on the mount of the Lord.

Even when I heard rumors of these sad developments among our young, I dismissed any connection between Jonathan and such activities. In the years since, it is no longer possible to keep the eyes and ears shut. His friends have made confession of participating in this folly. I failed. Whether because Jonathan was my firstborn and I had no experience, or whether his obedient nature made me think he knew where to draw the line. Sarah says a parent is always the last to know. She puts her finger on her tongue and rubs; she says she feels a hair but cannot find one to remove. It has become a habit.

For these eight years I have wrestled with Jonathan's eternal state. There is no Jonathan to ask. I can but seek to give instruction to those who remain. I want to say to Peter, "Strive for the beautiful," but I fear I may overlook the beast again. Whatever I say or do never seems enough. Sarah says not to doubt that my answers to an 11-year-old will take root and be a sure defense. When I am downhearted, she takes on boldness. But she licks at her fingers.

How we yearn for peace, even in the Amish church. Among those of us ordained, the tensions increase rather than take their ease. Two years ago we had a meeting of ministers right here in Somerset County. The following spring we traipsed to Ohio. I treasure the times when Father and I—we still do not agree on everything—broke bread with the other brethren and gave thanks to the Almighty for leading us in the right way. Can it be wrong to seek after peace? The larger the membership becomes, the more the differences grow among us. We talk and think we have matters cleared up, only to find again that not all can hold the line. It is good that Bishop Blauch is no longer among us to see such contention.

Now we have problems when relatives marry who are nearer to each other than second cousin. We ministers have agreed not to depart from the old customs. Then what happens? A year later we hear of discord and dissatisfaction among our people, a desire to loosen the cords. I fear that our talk among the brethren is not accomplishing a thing. We *grabble* over the same matters again and again. Some of the weaker vessels are prone to ignore the teachings of those of us who are older. Perhaps they see that our gold and silver is tarnished. That our sons are lost.

Mennonites seek to join us but do not want to be rebaptized. What are we to do? We began our conference with earnest prayer that the Lord would rightly show us His will. All of us sought to be of one mind—I am certain of it—even as Paul admonished, "...let there be no divisions among you; but be ye perfectly joined together in the same mind and in the same judgment." The trouble came anyway. Opposing parties gave their reasons; each side used the Holy Scriptures and the *Martyr's Book* to support their claims. Sarah says the word is *grapple*. In my heart, I believe we *grabbled*.

Even as we sought diligently to keep unity, I felt uneasy. There I was, the son of a minister, wanting to maintain the old ways; yet my own father has more of a liberal spirit. Some may discount my words because they know of Samuel Joder on the frontier, how he departs from some of the sacred teachings. Yet he is my father, and I cannot accuse him of seeking personal gratification. Some think the new churches in Ohio should see the light as it has always fallen to us in the established settlements. Then the ministers in the West rail that we do not understand how it is to live on the frontier. Still others say we are too intent on bringing about peace in our own power, rather than allowing God's spirit to work. Too much grabbling.

Our Somerset conference ended with all thirty-five of us agreeing to maintain the rebaptism of Mennonites and Dunkards. If they want to join us. How can we accept a Mennonite baptism when we would never wash feet with one or observe the Kiss of Peace? But one year later I was one of the bishops called to Ohio to set right those churches where problems of enforcement continue. How am I to tell Father to rebaptize a Mennonite? If it goes against his scruples—is it *scrubbles?*—I am tempted to think that in his case it does not matter. But in order to keep unity, someone must ask Father, and others like him, to seek out another bishop who can do the rebaptizing without burdening his conscience. It is all heaviness: the frequent trips, the constant toil of showing others the way. We need more leaders on the frontier like Abraham Zug; he sticks to the straight and narrow.

Our people do not understand the *Ordnung*. That is the source of our trouble. Church members think the *Ordnung* is just a set of rules whereby to hedge our living. That is not the way to think. The *Ordnung* must be lived by the Spirit, not by the letter alone. That is what I preach, but I am not certain the message soaks through. When we dwell in the spirit of the *Ordnung*, we have peace and contentment, even a feeling of liberty. For then we are not fighting the selfish powers within.

I say it again and again. Some of our people misunderstand
and think we bishops and ministers *make* the *Ordnung*. That
is not so. We only try to uphold the *Ordnung*. Some have left
the church saying we draw the line on fashions or styles. No,
no, no. We only attempt to hold the line so there is stability
and equality among us.

If only we could all be like my Peter. He is still a tender age,
but if only we could all give up individual wants and seek to
be one flesh, even one mind and one state. Sarah says it is the
work of the Devil that causes me to dwell unnecessarily on
my wasted opportunities with Jonathan. She says I repeat myself. Too much. I cannot rid myself of his memory. The Lord
had to rip him from me so that I not lose sight of my own
human condition. Yet all the time I pray mightily for the souls
of others.

Sarah says to stay my thoughts on Hans, our adopted son. I
am careful not to take undue satisfaction in his regard, but he
has lived with us now nigh to two years. I first heard of him
from Michael Kurtz, a young man who came to our settlement
by way of the Baltimore harbor. When traveling across the
ocean he learned to know this Hans Hooley. No one knows
how Hans was allowed on the ship, not even Hans, for he had
no money to pay his passage. Because of his poverty he was
bought as a slave by a Baltimore nurseryman who needed a
workman. When I heard of an Amish boy suffering such fate
I said to Sarah, "This is not right." She encouraged me and I
rode Star to Baltimore—it was close to two hundred miles—
and hunted until I found the boy. Then it was only a matter
of paying his obligation and bringing him here to live with us.
Now he is a free man and can live and worship as his own parents must have intended. It does me good to know I have
brought freedom to another; that is what I would want for any
of my sons. Oh Jonathan. Ripped from me.

How we strive to find freedom for the soul! Scripture teaches that it is only by the blood of Jesus that our redemption has been purchased. Now I have learned to watch my step, even when I walk in the way. I pray for grace enough to approach the mercy seat. I feel old beyond my fifty-one years; my white hair sheds easily. Sarah teases and calls me "the hoary head." I think of Father nearing 80 and shake my head. I do not understand how he perseveres. Perhaps that is what pushing back the forest has done for him.

When I cast about for appropriate words that speak to my soul, I remember what the Apostle Simon Peter said to those of like precious faith in his second epistle, chapter three, verses seventeen and eighteen: ". . . beware lest ye also, being led away with the error of the wicked, fall from your own stedfastness. But grow in grace, and in the knowledge of our Lord and Saviour Jesus Christ. To him be glory both now and for ever. Amen." I can only echo, "Amen." And again, "Amen."

6.

$\mathcal{F}$ R A N E Y

January 1834

"What is it that will come, but never will arrive?" That is a good one for Noah—our eldest, almost nine—who loves to bring home riddles from school. He tosses back his head—much like Peter does—and laughs. I never tire to look at him. This winter he has filled in the gaps from his lost baby teeth and has two fine rows. He is blessed with Peter's black color of hair, the same hair that hides its natural waviness these cold days. In the summer, when the air gets heavy with moisture, his hair takes on the sizzle.

Peter and I have grown tired of "What kind of stones are found in water?" and "Which candle burns longer, those of tallow or of wax?" Almost immediately Noah asks, "Are you stuck? Shall I say?" Peter and I act dumb and Noah says, "They burn shorter, not longer." We laugh and hear again the one about throwing butter out the window. Mary, with her green eyes that Peter calls blue, is not yet four, but she giggles and repeats, "Wet ones," or "Burn shorter." We laugh when her voice trills, "Butterfly." We laugh, but the winter days drag on. How much better for the children to play and work outside. Daniel tries to do whatever Noah does, even though he is pudgy and slow. Last summer they taught Dodger how to fetch; another time they tied old scraps of cloth on the cats' legs and watched them prance.

Noah loves the cold weather. He would rather go to school than anywhere else, even church, I fear. This winter it is no problem to get him to help Peter with the morning chores, for Noah does not want to be late. The school is only two miles hence and, unless we have a huge snow, Noah trudges by himself. We have not sent Daniel to school, but each night Noah drills him, starting with his numbers to ten. I remarked to Peter that Noah could be a teacher some day—he sounds like Abraham Saylor back in Somerset—but Peter cautions me. We know not to encourage that, for Noah's knowledge might go to his head. Last summer Peter got aggravated with Noah for boasting to Daniel about how many lightning bugs he had captured. Peter finally told him to catch some wind in his hands and put that in a jar. I am not alarmed; as long as Noah learns what is useful, there will be no problem with education.

I do not believe he will get this new riddle though, for it takes more understanding. It is one Father taught me when I was little—every Amish child learns it sometime—but I may have been older than Noah. How I long to hear Father's voice and see his eyebrows raise themselves. I never studied his eyes—they were the same shade of green as our Mary's—but now when I think of him, I picture his eyebrows giving his forehead the lift. I see his mouth stretching sideways as he pulled on leather.

Here I am, blessed with a tender husband and four dear ones, and I still long for Father and the old days back in Somerset. When we headed for Ohio—how I despised that word as a child!—I knew that I would never see Father again. Now he has been gone from this world and its cares over seven years; we can but hope to meet on that distant shore. I catch myself sounding like Aunt Martha more and more. But I have not once frightened my children with tales of Frieda. Our life here in Holmes County is much easier than what I knew growing up, yet I wish I could sing again with Jonas as of old. How safe I felt at night with Father in the next bed. Now it falls to me to give protection, to be the one who knows the answer is "Tomorrow."

Father would not care for our family meals, for they are sometimes a noisy babble. He was never talkative, so when he said something, I listened carefully. He used to say, "When you talk, you only repeat what you already know; if you listen, you may learn something." I like to remind the children of Father's other motto: "Think twice before you speak once." Father became cranky about the affairs of the church in his old age, but that was not really Father.

I wonder if our winter will ever end. Peter calls the long nights tedious and cracks his knuckles. He had picked out all the black walnuts a month ago. He tries to be patient until I have healed from Veronica. Huge drifts of spotless snow pile up behind our cabin, and the hills are much prettier all covered with white than when wearing their drab, December colors. But there is not much to do except huddle by the fire. It is good to have rest from all the summer's work, but I would much rather be cutting off asparagus or fixing a fat squash. I am eager to see if my purple and yellow iris will survive the cold weather; I planted the bulbs in groupings at each corner of our cabin.

Peter has fashioned a marble roller for the children; he says it was his favorite plaything in the Old Country. But we only have eight good marbles; the wooden ones do not roll smoothly. Bump, bump, bump, bong; that is what I hear all day. As Peter says, the noise is *obstrusive*. Three of the green marbles are glassy and have a spiral inside; I wonder how someone caused that to happen. Bump, bump, bump, bong. The children never tire of the noise. Peter will look for more marbles when he goes—if it ever stops snowing—to the general store in New Carlisle.

In each of the next months one of us has a special day. First, there is Noah's birthday in February, then Daniel's in March, mine in April, Mary's in May, and Peter's in June. Veronica, our baby of little more than a month, will have to wait until the leaves have fallen again for her celebration. I named her after Mother, but Peter insists that the baby is named for me. She is a precious one like each of the others. I do not mean to bring undue attention to anyone, but a little sugar cake to mark the day of birth does not seem like a thing of excess. The cake does not need to be loaded with candles as some do, but it is right and good to be thankful for each life. I remember one time when David and Jonas hoisted Father on his day.

Peter says I am too sentimental about the old and what is past and gone. He is right: there is much in Ohio that gives satisfaction. He laid new wooden floors in our cabin last fall; the old ones were splintered and warped. Now the new treads go about their quiet ka-zum, ka-zum when I rock Veronica, instead of the rickety hummp-thunn, hummp-thunn, hummp-thunn. Veronica helps me pass the winter days with all her feedings. She is a little nibbler, wanting to taste often but not for long at a time. I trust I will not have trouble as with Mary. Something was not right with my breasts; after only a few months my nipples became cracked and painful. I do not know how she survived. We had plenty of cow's milk, so I dipped clean wads of cloth into a pan of milk and gave her the cloth to suck. She has always been skin and bones, never walks but runs everywhere. She is our sparrow, and Daniel our fat robin.

Considering that we bought the cabin and land unseen—on the word of Gertrude Livengood—we have known good fortune in our purchase. Peter puts two fingers over his mouth, shakes his head, and says, "We could have ended up with a cave, for all we knew." This Gertrude was far from forthright about our neighbors, the Hershbergers; we thought she could be trusted since she was Amish. I offer excuses for her: perhaps she did not want to speak unkindly since they are her relatives by marriage. She may have been frazzled as a young widow, intent on a quick sale. Peter shakes his head and smacks his fist in his open hand. Whatever her motives, we made purchase. If we were to buy again, we would be more deliberate in our decision-making. But that is hindsight.

Not that we have a problem with Anna and Reuben themselves; they are good people. But our being neighborly with them puts us crosswise with the church. We do not seek to display or make a show of our friendliness, but neither do we turn back in our lane to avoid meeting them. Now they have another burden to bear; their daughter's husband was killed by a mad dog this past Christmas day. Bevy is left by herself, mothering two little girls—a sad, sad story. To have such sorrow happen on New Christmas Day must double the pain. There was never dispute for Peter and me; neither of us could ignore Anna and Reuben's sadness for their adult child, as if they were not people or had no feelings. Of course, my brother Abraham did not like it that we paid our respects, and he had to say as much.

I believe he is too puffed up for his frock coat. We are not in his district, and he does not have jurisdiction over us. (Peter once called it *genuflection*.) Jurisdiction is the wrong word also, but Abraham makes the church's rules seem like a court of law. If I am not careful, I will sometime blurt to ask him who tends to his soul. Abraham says I do not understand the gravity of what Reuben did. He looks at me as if I am still a little girl. He stares at my mole. I am small, but I am not a little girl.

I was too young to know what happened when the Hershberger baby was killed, but something seems amiss for one to be punished all his life for what he steadfastly claims he did not do. Abraham sits there with his nose too big—bumpy with red spots—and says, "Well, Franey, you may not know the whole story." He brings the tips of his fingers together in a circle and asks, "Have you considered that?" I feel discomfort living contrary to the church's teaching, but I cannot bring myself to anything less than neighborliness. I teach my children, "Do unto others . . . ." If Reuben were guilty, surely his shame would have exposed him by now.

I know we should not have favorites among the ministers, but John M. has a more kindly manner. I have heard others come near to a shout when they preach, as if they are Daniels in a fiery furnace, putting fear in our children's eyes. Veronica stirs in my arms—her hands make tight fists—amidst such carryings on. John M. stands tall, even stately—I do not mean that he acts kingly—speaking about the importance of humility. That is why Father long ago said I needed to wait to be baptized. More *Gelassenheit*. I would like a dose for Abraham. John M. makes humility sound appealing, not a burden at all, but a joy to serve the brother in the church. "God resisteth the proud but giveth grace unto the humble." I cannot imagine Abraham saying that verse; he would mumble or botch it, somehow.

I come closest to this nakedness before God, this yieldedness, when I wash feet with a sister. Last fall at our Communion service I chanced to be paired with John M.'s Katharina. I felt awkward—perhaps it is shame—as I pulled down my stockings on the church bench. If I were a young boy my eyes would wander too; but we are not to question Jesus' example of washing his disciples' feet. The bare floor felt cold to my feet as I walked to the front where we women waited our turn at the bucket on the left. I prefer to wash the other's feet first, rather than be washed right away, but it does not always happen that way.

Katharina motioned for me to sit, perhaps because of my heavy condition with child. She knelt at my feet. I stretched a foot over the bucket, and she gently dipped her hands, pouring cold water over the top. Then she took a towel while I lifted my foot as high as possible, yet maintained modesty with my skirts pulled under. I did not want the corner of the towel to dangle in the water when she dried my crusty sole. We did the same with the other foot. Here was the minister's wife saying she was no better than me. Of course I had washed with greater care the night before, using Peter's knife on my toenails, but Katharina was willing to bend to me.

We traded places and I stooped as low as I could with my belly swollen before me. I hope Katharina did not see me hesitate when I saw the red, boney tops of her long middle toes, rubbed almost raw. I do not see how her feet could bear that constant scraping under shoe tops. I would ask Peter to find another cobbler. I barely dripped water on the top of her foot for fear the water would run down and sting. I do not think the meaning of the act is dependent on the volume of water. I made a light dab with the towel.

When both her feet were dry, we stood to one side of the bucket and clasped right hands, giving each other the Kiss of Peace—I on my tiptoes—first on one cheek and then the other. I thought again of her toes and how she never made complaint but bore her suffering silently. *Gelassenheit*: "Reside quietly in Christ." She does not engage in useless talk, as do some of the women. I put my free arm around her waist and, with a sudden impulse, gave her as much of a hug as I could with the baby between us. That is not part of the regular ceremony, but when we pulled apart, we looked each other in the eye. Hers are a very light blue with the dark pupil in the center, much like mine.

Katharina did not seem surprised at my sudden impulse but said the usual, "The Lord be with us," and I whispered, "Amen, in peace." No one knows about the toes, except John M. of course. I hope he knows. But no other man. Certainly not Abraham. Katharina and I are sisters in the faith, a cord knotted tight with a towel of mercy. A holiness. I do not understand what happened, but now when we greet each other we look again deep into each other's eyes. I wish we did not live at such a distance from each other; she must feel lonesome as a minister's wife.

I trust that Peter will never be made a minister, although it could happen to any man with a clear conscience and a good reputation. I have wondered these long winter days what it would be like to be entrusted with the care of all the members, to ever be in readiness to bring God's message. I do not know why I linger over such thoughts because it is not for me, a woman. Noah might take to it with ease when he is older, for teaching and preaching must be similar. Of course it is not for me to guess how the Lord will lead. We can only seek to bring up our children in the fear and admonition of the Lord so that when they are fully grown, they will not depart from it. Even when Veronica needs me during the cold night, I can be content with my lot in life. I marvel at her dainty, long fingers, at the work she will one day do. Cooking, cleaning, raising her own. Nothing can be more important than preparing her to be yielded to her life's purpose on this earth.

7.

Y O S T

May 1835

I heard a good one today. Samuel Weaver over along Kill-
buck Road is called Gooka Sam. That fits him all right.
Every time I drive by his place he stops his plowing, milking,
undoing his britches—what have you—and gooks. He waddles
to the door of his barn with his mouth hanging open, gawks,
and waves great big. Gooka Sam, that is perfect. As if he has
never seen a wagon before. If I had that kind of time to wave
to every passerby, I would consider myself fixed with land
aplenty.

That is one thing good about Ohio; the nicknames hit the
mark. Back in Somerset our nicknames set apart one John
Joder from another. Here, middle initials help keep people
straight, but there is more of a woolliness, a bold spirit. People do not hold back. Gooka Sam!

Dick Dannie is another, or is it Dickie Dan? One of the skin-
niest men around. If you stood him next to a fence post, you
would see two crooked posts. But his head is as thick as Ohio
mud. I have never encountered such a gooey mess. Dick Dannie told someone that his wife's face was as pretty as a pansy.
Now she is stuck with Pansy Mary. What an oaf! There are

people aplenty in this world who would do well to keep their mouths shut. A woman can expect to attach her name to her husband's: Jakie Anna or River Joe's Susan. That is natural. But Pansy Mary beats all.

With over one hundred of us Amish families here in Holmes County, and all of us using the same Bible names for the most part, it follows that there will be duplication and confusion aplenty. It is hard to keep everyone straight, unless you know the father and grandfather. Eliza would think that some of these nicknames border on meanness, but they serve their purpose. My new wife's name—some try to make jokes behind my back—comes handed down from variations on the original Swiss name, *Verena*. *Fanny* and *Frances* are the American forms and follow from *Veroene* to *Veronica*, and from *Frohnia* to *Franey*. When it comes to first names, some people are too quick to take offense. After all, I am *Yost*, come from *Joseph*. For those who switch from *Joder* to *Yoder*, I do not know what to think.

Fanny made certain that our two new ones would not get their names mixed up with others. Ursula is seven and Alexander has just turned three. Their names still sound strange, I will admit, but I tell myself, they are only names. Inside, my new children breathe as my flesh; they are Hershbergers. I am fortunate to have Alexander coming along late; I will need his help when I am in my sixties. How is it possible that I will some day be an old man? I have had to make considerable adjustments to Fanny's ways, but I do not want to get started on that. I was near to desperation with nine of my own. What a relief to find her. Fanny said that she had saved all her energy for me. I assured her that she did not need to hold back. She was only halfway through her thirties when we married. I tell you, I like this woman, even if she borders on boldness. She knows how to finagle her way all right. Some say it takes two mothers to raise every pioneer family, but I know cases where it took more than two fathers. So who is to say where the toughness must lie?

My biggest reservation has to do with some of Fanny's relations; I do not like the way this Jonas Zug keeps cropping up in my life. It is creepy. That is a new word Gideon taught me. I cannot say why Jonas disturbs me—almost as much as Reuben—except for the unsavory memories. Fanny is a cousin to Jonas Zug's wife; their Beiler grandfathers were brothers. Here is the rub. Fanny hears that these Zugs have moved to Wayne County. It should not bother me; I should not complain about the splotches on her side of the family. She reminds me that I have a deep thorn in the flesh for her to contend with. She wanted to know everything about Reuben and how the first Marie's murder took place. I told her the whole story. One time. No more. After rehearsing all of that I was agitated for a week from letting my mind dwell on that infidel again. Fanny knows not to ask about Eliza; that part is said and done. Except that Maria has turned into a whiner, just like her mother.

Our own move came about after Gideon had moved to Ohio all by himself and apprised me of this land available for purchase. I begged of Fanny one more time and finally found satisfaction. After eight years of marriage she agreed at last. This is what she said: "No more little ones and I will go." What could I say? I could not believe her the first time she announced this, as if it were all decided. She said that she had birthed the right number: one of each kind. Now she tells me to act my age. I did not know that abstinence goes with being over fifty. Still, I like this woman. She is a wily one. We came here a year ago to the edge of this village called Mt. Hope. It is not a land flowing with milk and honey, but I have no regrets.

My children are a bundle to keep track of. Besides Gideon, Susanna lives here in Ohio and has made me a grandpop three times; this last one, finally, a boy. Shortly after I found Fanny, Susanna married a brother of Levi Speicher; that is another place I see this Jonas Zug shadow, for Jonas and Levi were like brothers. I find no quarrel, however, with Adam; he reports that Levi left the Amish for a time but now has returned to the fold.

My Joseph and Lazarus stayed behind in Pennsylvania. I always thought Joseph a weakling, but he delivered a boy on the very first attempt; I find satisfaction that he stays on the home place. Lazarus surprised me; I wanted him to come along—he is unattached—but he turned obstinate. That leaves five young ones of my own, plus Ursula and Alexander. As far as I can make out the two sets have meshed, although no one gets along with Nicholas. I do not know where his unruly nature comes from, but I am beginning to think he cannot be broken. Fanny says, when you have as many as Eliza and I did, there is bound to be one bad batch of dough. I shake my head. Not in my Hershberger line.

Ohio has not been as wonderful as I expected. Much about Holmes County commends itself, even though it was named to honor a Mr. Holmes who was an officer back in the War of 1812. The land is twice as productive as what we knew in Pennsylvania. Wheat, oats, corn, it matters not. Even Irish potatoes. One of those is almost more than I can handle at one sitting. I have all the supply of wood I could want for building furniture. We even have a postal service as close as Millersburg. Gideon claims that in a few more years the mail wagon will come to Mt. Hope, but he exaggerates. Whatever we need is near at hand. I know who to contact for a sawmill, a wagon shop, the tannery. All of these connections took time, however, and left me a little discombobulated. At Little Crossings all we had was a grist-mill and a tavern.

Our church life has brought easy transition, although some questions trouble. Making the move allowed me to get out from under Isaac's feeble leadership. We drive the team a little farther on Sunday to be under the instruction of Henry Stutzman at Farmerstown. No one has said ought that we choose to drive out of our district. Henry is younger, but he preaches the Word as it is meant to be heard, with a good wind behind it. I cannot make out some of these timid ones. John J. Yoder—I believe that he is Joseph Yoder's son—has recently been made a minister. I could incline my ear in his direction, but Fanny resists making yet another change.

Wayne County, that is where the trouble sprouts. For one thing, they have a dangerous element coming from Europe; there are people from Alsace-Lorraine in France, some from Switzerland, a few from the Palatinate, others from Prussia. I do not know where that is. These immigrants arrive by a much easier route of passage than did our forefathers, coming by way of the Hudson River to Albany, then to Buffalo by the Erie Canal. These canals have made all the difference. A traveler can traverse Lake Erie to the Ohio and Erie Canal, until it brings him right to Canal Fulton. Smack into Wayne County, the Devil's snare.

It is just as well that this new rabble has not continued south to Holmes County. What have they done, these people from Switzerland, but built a log structure which they call their church meetinghouse. If this is not following the style of the world, I do not know what is. Yet these people have the gall to call themselves Amish. And to think there are ministers who go along with such newfangled ideas. I have given my children, even the grown ones, strict instruction to stay away from this Sonnenberg meetinghouse.

I do not trust Nicholas; he might go there just to upset me.

We of course stay clear of Reuben, even though he is here in Holmes County also. I understand he is near to being a drunkard. Whether that is entirely true matters little; reputations are not dredged up. I have heard people tell of going to fetch Reuben—still caught up in his powwowing—only to find him intoxicated. Strong drink has its place; I do not mean that abstinence is necessary. We would not make it through the hot summer without the gallon jug in the fields. That is how I hire extra help to swing the cradle and shock sheaves of oats. But debauchery is another matter. On that I have no disagreement with Henry Stutzman. I have had to warn my own Henry, however, about tobacco; it soon becomes a reliance. I doubt he remembers that I smoked on occasion when he was a lad. But Eliza complained because of her cough, and after her death the pipe lost its appeal. Henry would be better off not to give the tobacco a start.

I would prefer for no one to know that Reuben and I are brothers, but I cannot escape that contamination. Too many old-timers from Somerset know my roots. That does not mean I need to send a rope in his direction. Even if Bishop Isaac once thought that wise. *Himmel!* After all these years—over twenty since Reuben left Somerset County—I did not expect him to try to make contact. But knowing that word of my own whereabouts gets around, I prepared myself for the worst eventuality. I had warned Fanny of what to do.

Sure enough, one Sunday afternoon last fall—it was a day for visiting—I contented myself with some additional sleep. The summer had required heavy work with our move and with getting crops established in short order. I find I cannot push myself in the fields as I once did. I heard a horse in the driveway and roused myself toward the door, as would be my custom. But something brought me caution even in my groggy state, and my hand shrank from the latch. I can smell that man. I went to the window and saw an old man tying his horse to a tree. It was like looking at an image of myself, except that he has more of a belly. Fanny says I am too heavy, but she has nothing to complain about. As he started toward the house and removed his broad hat with the low crown, I saw the white in his hair. He is old. He still wore the black, round-tailed coat with the standing collar.

It is good that the path to my house stretches for a distance. Otherwise I would have stared too long and not had time to call Fanny. "He is here," I said. "Do as I have instructed."

She is a sharp one, for though half asleep herself, she guessed at my meaning in an instant. She says our likenesses left no doubt but agrees that the aging has taken a greater toll on him than on me.

Before I could give reminders she snatched a shawl and bonnet and was out the door. Part of me wanted to linger at the window, but I knew not to take chances. I climbed the stairs to the loft—that next-to-top step gives slightly under my weight—where Anna and Lydia played with Ursula and her rag doll. They acted as if it were news for me to climb to the loft. "What gives?" they said, one right after the other.

I acted indifferent to their clamor. "My past has come calling," I said. "I need a high place to rest." They looked at each other, perplexed. Ursula started to go downstairs as I settled my back on the large bed, my hands clasped behind my head. "Stay," I said, pointing a finger in her direction. She does not always obey, but this time she listened. The girls resumed their pretend world, haltingly at first. The rag doll goes by the name of Priscilla. Anna and Lydia have dolls made from ears of corn with kernels taken out for eyes, nose, and a mouth. The air in the loft was stuffy. I am glad I am not a girl and do not need to sleep up there at night.

I tried to envision the proceedings outside. I had to wait much longer than seemed necessary for Fanny to do her work. Finally I heard someone in the house; I sat up, hissed, and put my index finger to my lips. The girls stopped their chattering. I listened to make sure there were not two sets of feet, not two voices below. When I could ascertain that the walk was Fanny's—she takes short, quick steps—I clambered down the stairs.

"Is he gone?" I half-whispered. Of course I knew he was, even as I went to the window and heard horse's hooves retreating.

"Yes, Yost. I told him not to bother again." She set about to cut off the ends of turnips as if supper were the only thing.

"You said what?" I was surprised at her boldness. "What did he say? Tell me all."

"There was not much. You two do have the same eyes, dark brown and searing." She looked at me as if she were examining me for the first time. "He asked if this was the Yost Hershberger place and I replied that, yes, it was. Then he asked if I was Yost's wife and again I nodded my head. I did not introduce myself. Did your mother have the high forehead or was it your father?"

"Then what? Go on." The vein in my neck throbbed. To think that Reuben had been right outside my door. "Put those turnips down." It was deathly quiet in the loft. "Stop listening," I yelled, my voice extended upward.

"He asked if you were here." Fanny wiped her wet hands on her outer skirt. "He said, 'Is Yost here?' and I said, 'No, he is not here.' I said it, just as you instructed."

"Yes, it is true. The Yost he seeks is not here. You did well. He, doubtless, wants a Yost who will say, 'Never mind the past; we all make mistakes; come in and rest your feet.' No, that Yost is not here; that Yost will not be arriving any time soon." I lowered my voice for it was still quiet in the loft. "If Reuben wants attention, he can go to the preacher and begin to make amends."

"Then he said—." Fanny came close and grabbed my wrists. I heard the devilish melody in her voice, even in her guarded tone. I wondered if she had looked as fetching to Reuben. "He looked over yonder to the barn and said, 'Is that Yost's horse and wagon?' and I answered truthfully, 'Yes,' for I did not want to tell a lie."

"That is all right, Fanny. It *is* my horse and wagon." I had not thought he might ask on that. "What then?" I whispered.

Fanny pulled me outside to get away from the quiet upstairs. "He turned his back and appeared to be surveying all the parts of the farm: the apple orchard, the trees still full of leaves." Fanny swept her arms wide as if she needed to show me. "He looked at your fences, at the stubble in your fields. I did not know what went through his mind or what he might say next. I tied and retied my bonnet to give my hands some business. Then at last he turned again to me. I thought—." Fanny examined me again. "There was a redness about his eyes that had not been there before." She paused. "I could not be sure, for I do not know him well. He is old. Did you see how he walks? Are you certain that you are older than he?" I motioned for her to continue. "His eyes looked like yours when you have been around goldenrod too long."

"Get on with it. What else did he say?" Fanny can be like that. All women seem prone to supply endless details when only the facts are needed.

"I cannot get over the similarity of your eyes. He looked at me and said, 'Tell him that Reuben was here.' I nodded and said I would. Then as he slowly walked away—promise me, you will never walk that slowly—the time seemed long, and I wanted to say more. But I thought better of it. Then, as he reached his horse, I commenced in his direction and half-shouted, 'You do not need to come again.' He looked as though I had taken his horse whip and struck it across his face."

I pulled back a bit from this woman. My wife. I had not instructed her thus, but I did not criticize her embellishment.

"He said nothing more, but slowly mounted his horse. I heard his scratchy, 'Come, Boy, easy now,' and his horse turned. He does not have thunder in his voice as you do. Has it always been that way?"

I shrugged and motioned for her to go on.

"I watched him down the road; he sat slumped, not tall and straight as you do, Yost. I hope that last part, about not returning, was all right. I know we had not planned thus, but it will be easier if you are not jerked about by reminders. Did your father's voice grow scratchy when he was old?"

"Yes, Fanny, I might not have said it, but I am glad you did. He knows where to go to admit his wrong. If he only has in mind to proclaim his innocence again, that is not something either of us needs to hear."

I asked Fanny if there were any signs of alcohol. She shook her head and said Reuben appeared to be clean with no smell of whiskey. I should have known; he would not appear other than to put on a show. I do not know why I feel as if I have escaped something, but I am certain that Reuben will not return. The part about the tears; I do not know. Women exaggerate.

I have often wondered what I would do if I met Bevy and Jacobli. Jacob, it is now. Likely I would not recognize him. We might have already met at New Carlisle and not known; I hear he is married and a father himself. Fanny says the women at church have it that Bevy is remarried, but not to an Amishman. No one can blame me for that. I still think of them as children, running about under foot with Lizzie and Susanna. I might give the right hand of fellowship; I do not know. It does not seem fair for them to be burdened with the sins of the father.

I believe that if children are brought up properly they will have no desire to depart from the true faith. That does not explain Nicholas' first sixteen years, but he is an exception. Perhaps he saw too much of death at a young age. I will not coddle him, that is for certain. If Eliza were to see him now, coming in late on Saturday night and sleeping all the Sabbath, she would be brokenhearted. The good Lord knew to spare her any more tribulation. And the good Lord knew to spare me from an early moldering in the grave.

Fanny keeps me young. She insists that I do not catch everything that is said, but I do not know that I have missed anything important. God did not mean for these small infirmities, the stiff knees, the occasional wax in the ears, to slow me unduly. I have an eye on another parcel of land that Henry may need soon, the way he spends time at the Mishlers. For me and my family, we are barely making a start here in this Ohio.

8.
⅃ S A A C
March 1837

*L*ike the psalmist of old, I eat and drink my tears. "Why art thou cast down? . . . why disquieted? . . . hope thou in God." I seek for solace at morn and setting sun. It offers small consolation that God's instrument, David, also knew downheartedness.

My sorrow comes at the hands of some who have also brought me greatest joy. My next to oldest, Mary. Why oh why? She has a mirror hanging in her house. The first time I saw myself full, I did not know what to do. Such roundness! Mary is good to her five little ones—she has no deficiencies as a mother—but why she allows this mirror right inside the front door is beyond my understanding. If the mirror were along a back wall it would not trouble as openly.

That is not all. My son, Zachariah, a member in good standing here at the River congregation, takes after my skill in woodworking and has built a walnut wardrobe for his wife. That alone does not cause a problem. But he added yellow and red paint on each of the corners where he fashioned a flower and leaf design. Red and yellow. I do not know where he latched onto the paint. Perhaps at Little Crossings. But why did he use such loud colors? Even if that is what his Sally wanted. I had encouraged his early interest in wood. I never thought it would come to this. My own love for cedar. I did not mean to start an unnecessary thing. Would that we understood. Now we see only in part. My own flesh and blood following after worldly styles, blind to the traps that beset on every hand. I thought my fortitude had already been tested sufficiently with the death of Jonathan.

I was in such a shaken state from my children's doings that I could not eat before facing the other ministers. I did not want to go to the meetings. Not that I have ever enjoyed these deliberations. We brethren have been beset by so much discord that we had to gather again to present a unified position. I could not excuse myself on some pretext. My new woman, Barbara, helped me not at all, promising to keep an eye on the boiling sugar. Many of the brethren came from a great distance. Five from as far away as Johnstown; five from the Glades. Of course there are the three of us here at the River group. On many matters we reached agreement, and my soul was unburdened for a few days. But now, less than a week after the conference, I have looked into the faces again of those whose souls I carry responsibility for. I feel again the heaviness. I cannot keep house. My own children deviate, right and left.

I know what to say—it is what I believe—yet when I stand to face Ezra Peachey with his red nose and splotchy face, and when I think of Samantha Horst's cabinet of glass dishes, I am overcome by despair. How can we ever come to uniformity in practice? My insides shake with the softness of Barbara's apple jelly. Everything seemed clear as we thirteen brethren discussed and were in prayer together. Wherever sin resides, we must pluck it out. I know that. But now all is untracked; the right words have fled. I do not have Sarah to give me advice. I do not want to offend anyone; that is my trouble. That has always been my trouble. I am not the man. I had thought that as I got older it would be easier to speak with firmness. That may have been true for awhile, but now just the opposite seems true. I cannot blame it on Barbara's cooking, not even on the liverwurst.

I helped with an ordination at the Conemaugh congregation and met this woman, Barbara Kempf, a Stutzman before she first married and a widow of four years. She is short in stature and almost as round as I; perhaps that is what misled me. I believe even my children do not know what to do with me now. They may be whispering behind my back. I cannot keep track of all of them—my children, step-children, grandchildren, what-have-you. When Barbara and I first married we had five of mine, three boys and two girls still at home, plus Hans Hooley. Add to that Barbara's five from her first marriage to Nicholas Kempf. In addition, this Nicholas had been married twice before he married Barbara. She brought with her the two youngest girls from his second marriage. I believe there were thirteen under our care when we started our union. Here is what I cannot say to anyone. Barbara does not know how many Kempf grandchildren there are. I cannot believe her haphazardness. I thought we should make effort to find them, to know who is where. What is what. She laughed more gaily than I cared for and said she had enough bread to bake without looking for more hungry mouths. That is a severe thorn.

When I gathered with the brethren I could not bring myself to confess that some of my difficulty comes from my own quiver. Six have married and settled in our River district. I would not for a minute ask any one of them to move away. With many people transplanting to Ohio and beyond, it has been a satisfaction that my own children have chosen to stay.

But some of them will be slow to accept the discipline as we ministers have set it forth. Very, very slow. They would likely prefer to be under their grandfather, Samuel Joder's voice. God rest his soul. It came as a comfort to learn that John M.— my young companion on that first trip—had part in my father's funeral. We often do not agree, just as Father and I did not. Still, John M. is my cousin.

We ministers came to firm decisions on twelve items. Pride in ornamentation, that is the stickler. When I stand to preach I see numerous silken neckcloths, one a turquoise blue, another a flaming orange. Some of the sleighs driven to church this winter have been painted with two colors. Red next to black or bright blue with purple. There is even more foolishness in the afternoons following services. Some of our young drive their sleighs excessively. I know my Benedict and Peter were in that number. Yes, my once obedient Peter. I pray for spring thaws to bear away these heavy snows with their temptation. The list goes on. New styles creep into houses; those hanging cupboards at the Schlabachs.

My walk is complicated because Barbara does not see the harm in these displays. I chose a wife with too much haste. I thought I explained before we married that my position as bishop makes for precariousness. I thought she nodded with understanding. But she remains slow in redirecting her thinking. The same slowness that my children manifest. I would not call her obstinate, but she does not see the gravity. As she tells it, her father always wanted to be among the first to try the new ways. Adapt. Accommodate. Now she resides in my bed. She is eighteen years younger than I. Perhaps that is where I made the mistake. I have chosen poorly. Some may have snickered at my haste, but I have always preached with the Apostle Paul that it is better to marry than to burn.

Sarah, my dear wife of thirty years, died over two years ago.

I still get the tremble when I dwell on her passing. I did not think she would expire first. It may have been consumption. Whatever the cause, she is gone. There is nothing to be gained by questioning the Lord's timing. How I miss her cakes with burnt sugar. She always knew what to say to encourage me. It is a mystery how a wife can become a commonplace, as ordinary as an apple or corn fritter, until suddenly she is gone. Then the appetite for the fritter takes over. Sinking my teeth into the apple is all I could dwell on.

Time does not stop for us; Barbara and I have added our own Elizabeth. I have never seen such golden hair. She is a blessing. Nicholas Kempf had sired an Elizabeth also, so we call this new one, Betsy. The name borders on the modern, but we cannot change it now. I agreed before I had thought of all the ramifications. Barbara says her grandmother on her mother's side was called Bessie, so perhaps the name is not as new as I thought. Betsy toddles about, one bright pastime in my old age. Now Barbara says there will be a playmate come summertime.

I wish we had been given fewer girls. Yet I cannot call them a plague. Only a problem. I was one who helped set down in writing the ninth item: "With regard to the excesses practiced among the youth, namely that the youth take the liberty to sleep or lie together without any fear or shame, such things shall not be tolerated at all." All these girls. Under my roof. But I could not give up this Betsy. I remind her not to pick her nose when I tell her about David and Goliath. She has no understanding of a slingshot. It is the older girls who give burden. This bugaboo of courtship. My Eva has just turned twenty and has young boys visiting at night. I know, because my sleep is disturbed when I hear the stones thrown on the roof. I cannot get back to sleep because I imagine the whatall. Then we have Barbara's string of girls: an 18-year-old, a 16-year-old.

Two more after that. I have not even mentioned my Anna, a mystery at the other extreme. Twenty-seven and unattached. I do not know what ails her.

Some of the ministers held firm that the only way to put an end to the unsavoriness of an unmarried girl with a baby is to hold the girl's parents accountable. They insisted there have been cases where the mother knowingly prepared the bed for her unmarried daughter. I thought that preposterous and said as much. The brethren stared at me. I regretted making a stir. Such abomination! I do not think Barbara would do such, but now I worry on it. I do not know how to talk with Eva and warn her of dangers I cannot describe. I cannot talk with Peter either about his recklessness. My good intentions are never enough.

My church dealings have never been sufficient. Not once did I contact Reuben in Ohio. My effort with Yost was tardy. Even puny. Now I must preach regarding all these disciplines before our spring Communion. I dare not forget a thing. Barbara says nought whether I repeat myself. I wonder if she pays any attention. We remain sorely divided on the teaching of the ban. Some say the church has been kept pure by putting Reuben Hershberger on the outside. His is the name that always surfaces. Few there are who remember him, but he is our primary example of unconfessed sin. Would that my hands were clean. It has been twenty-seven years ago already. The same time that our maidenly Anna was born. The first year I was made a minister. I did the best I knew how, with Bishop Blauch's help. But it was not enough. I should have been more forceful in bringing about reconciliation.

Some people take the other side with regard to Reuben. They maintain that by putting him outside we have hardened him in his ways. They point to his reputation which has gotten back to our community: drinking to excess. These same people who do not even know Reuben speak of the brothers as if they know all the facts. As if they were present when every log was thrown on the fire. These know-it-alls—Sarah would rebuke me—only cause more splinters. They speak with a mighty voice—I do not want to name names—"Do this," or "Say this word of truth." It is true: decline has set in among us. Sadly true. I have prayed for boldness, but it has not come. My laxness shames me. Bishop Blauch used to say, "Watch and pray." I have prayed for peace, and I have kept watch. I weep to think what sorrows may lie ahead. As if losing my firstborn and my first wife are not sufficient.

I can but return to the psalmist and say: ". . . hope thou in God: for I shall yet praise him, who is the health of my countenance, and my God." That is what I will say when I stand to preach about all twelve items. That is all I know to say.

9.

$\mathcal{P}$ O L L Y

July 1838

*S*he buries her face in the palms of her hands and wails, "My heart is still in Somerset County. Please take me home, Momma." She is too old to cry like a baby. She is sixteen and very comely, but her cries twist me apart. She is the pit inside the peach, clinging to me. When she is sad, my very insides hurt. She is all I have left, and I have gone and made her unhappy. She hides her dimples because her mouth is pulled tight and all her face knows to do is frown. She does not know that we have nowhere to call home.

If anyone should be given to tears it is I, for I have worn the black dress like an extra layer of skin. I save my sorrow for when Leah is out of the house; even then there are other ears. Maggie and the baby. I do not mean to disturb. My own dear Christian left us two years ago, only forty-seven when his time on this earth was finished. I should have known his demise would come early; his stooped frame showed he was not meant for the rigors of this life. At the last he was afraid to get out of bed for fear he would fall. His slippage started with a gradualness. Just as darkness slowly drops its mantle over us at night, so it was with Christian. First, we realize it is getting dark. Then we know it is almost dark, but a little light remains. Then of a sudden, the sky is black. If only he could see this grandchild.

Daniel was born at the start of the year to my John and Maggie. Not one speck of red hair. How Christian and I hovered over baby John's mouth years ago; now he has his own son. This past spring they decided to move to Ohio. John bought land a few miles south of Berlin and inquired if Leah and I would be of a mind to come along. I think he may have been surprised at my agreement. I do not know what possessed me, but Ohio no longer seemed foreboding. Where else could I turn? With John leaving—my oldest and my steady one—I knew not what else to do. I think Maggie is less than pleased; I did not mean to be a burden.

At first Leah seemed agreeable. But as the time drew near for our departure, she drooped more and more. I did not think it right to turn back before we started. I begged her to be of a willing spirit and seek to find good in the newness. She wailed, "But, Momma, there is no one for me." I reminded her that she had cousins aplenty, that three of her father's brothers lived in Ohio. It made no difference; she was too young to remember the uncles.

Her whining taxed us all as we traveled; numerous times Maggie looked at John as if she expected him to quiet his sister. I did not mind the trip with its bounce, except for the nighttime. Who can close the eyes when the woods gives forth such fierce noise? John teased that I slept more in the day, sitting upright, than I did at night. Such a racket and buzzing with frogs and crickets; even owls manifested their busyness. I set myself as the night watchman. I know that wildcats stalked. I saw cougars slithering about. I saw every eye set to harm us.

I thought that after we settled Leah would adapt herself and think less on what she had left behind. But that has not happened. She admits that the Big Dipper looks the same in Ohio, but she will not smile. John says I have spoiled her. I want to say to him: you have not lost all that I have lost. Everyone else builds bigger and bigger tables. Mine gets smaller and shows more vacancy. I do not know if Leah and I could manage on our own. She has never grabbed a cow's teats. I have surprised myself with what I am able to do—even churning butter—but Leah only knows to look pretty. She is my ornament.

The troubles increased when Maggie blamed me for using milk that had already curdled. I tasted nothing bad. Then John claimed this Ohio soil was not as fertile as he had expected. He has had setbacks with hay and oats already. He says people are moving on farther to Indiana and Iowa; then he looks at the clock on the mantel as if he might load up, come morning. I do not want to tell my married son what to do, but he needs to have more patience. I point out that Christian's brothers are all prospering. The signs are everywhere: new barns, a wash house, glass windows instead of the greased paper, even a new house with stucco and stone for Paul. I tell John we need sheep to get ahead, but I make no progress with him.

Here is the truth. I could not bear to move back to Pennsylvania. Some people's tongues busied themselves far too much when I decided to move without a man of my own. Those same tongues do not need more fat to chew. We have heard nothing from Andrew and Joel who stayed behind. Andrew has a head for farming and will be able to fend for himself; he promised to stay ahead of the weeds. But I fear to think on Joel. Eighteen, and all he can talk about is going to the far reaches. He scoffed whenever I said that he needed a wife. Every sentence of his began, "When I get to Oregon . . ." or "If I lived in Oregon, I . . . ." The boy has no sense. I entreated him, "Just because a place exists does not mean you have to go there. Oregon will survive without you."

His blue eyes twinkled as they always do when he looks for mischief. "Momma, wait and see. Some day you will get a letter and it will be posted from Oregon."

Joel has all the gumption that my David lacked. I asked John the other day if he agreed that something was not right with David's blood. John said he did not want to talk about it. I knew there would be trouble when I first saw David's patch of red hair. My sickly one died when he was but eleven. Christian found him crumpled in the barn one evening when he went to chore. I thought David had been in the fields with the other boys; Christian thought he had stayed inside the house.

Something was not right. If he bumped his nose, the blood rushed out. When he spit up, he reported a reddish-brown substance that came out in chunks. I believe he picked at his nose more than he knew. We tried all manner of treatment to stop the gush. We laid him down, tilting his head back and holding it thus. We poured water down the nape of his neck, but he jerked from the coldness. On a hot day he went out of the house and let the blood run onto the ground until it ceased its flow. He could barely crawl back inside, and he begged Andrew to give him a hoist into bed. I urged him to eat more meat and potatoes, but all he wanted was milk poured over fruit. He stayed skinny; I do not know what we should have done. We do not know how long he lay in his vile, red vomit, sprawled in a pile of shinnamon hay. Christian kept saying, "His fall was soft, his fall was soft," as if that is all that mattered. I had to milk our two cows that evening. We laid David's remains beside his three infant sisters; now Christian lies there next. I could see no reason to stay in Pennsylvania with five graves at my back. The owls shrieked mightily in that grove. I asked John recently if he thought his father knew in advance that his time was coming. John said he did not want to talk about it.

I fear I am not wanted here. Maggie does not like it when I roll a pinch of bread into a ball and let Daniel suck on it. The bread has no mold. Where is the harm? She made up that story about curdled milk. Come winter she will welcome the beans that Leah has helped me string. I do not know what will become of me if John's feet get itchy. Or Leah. Indiana is not the answer. I long for my Christian, for those days long ago when he sat down and explained things to me.

I may have to rely on his brothers if my own children fail me. All his relatives here in Holmes County have given us welcome. They had what they call a Hostetler reunion the other Saturday. I have always had trouble remembering Christian's relations: who comes from what branch. John does not get everything right either, for we have disagreed about some of the cousins. He insists that his uncle Paul has three boys and not four.

"Then where does Obadiah fit?" I asked.

"Never met an Obadiah," John mumbled, rubbing his left shoulder as he does when he finishes something.

"I know there is an Obadiah, for when I first heard it, I thought of my horse when I was young and working for Eliza."

"Never heard of it," he said. John can be that way when he dismisses what I say. That is the way he responds about the sheep. "Wolves kill sheep." That is why I have not told him all. When everyone else is occupied, I like to pull out my pouch with the coins from the sale of my household items. I like to make count.

I got to meet a cousin of Christian's who is a minister, John M. Yoder. What a stately one. He has a certitude about him that I do not see in my John. We do not live in his district, but

I told John—my John—that sometime I want to hear this John
M. preach. There is something unusual about him that I cannot explain. It believe it is in the eyes. They are not like Yost's;
with him I did not want to go against his wishes. With John
M., it is different. His eyes have a blueness that holds me in
their grip. Yet right in the middle of their firmness there is a
kindliness that makes me want to nod in agreement.

At the reunion John M. wanted to know all about his mother's funeral. She died only a month before we left Pennsylvania. John M.'s wife, Katharina, suggested that we sit down to
talk. She must have noticed my neck developing a crick from
twisting upward to John M.'s height. We sat under the shade
of a young elm, and I was able to describe everything. His
mother had lived over fourscore years. John M. wanted to
know which minister preached the first sermon and which
the long one. I named all the pallbearers, although at first I
could not think of George Semler's name. Jakie Mast's John
built the coffin of walnut; I was certain of that. John M. did
not recognize the names of some of the women who had laid
out his mother's body. All in white of course. He says he has
lived in Ohio twenty years. And to think, he was the young
lad traveling to Ohio on horseback with Isaac that we heard
about long ago.

The only funeral I can remember that was bigger than John
M.'s mother's was that held for Bishop Isaac, our cousin, last
summer. Again, John M. showed much interest. He and Isaac
had done church business together at recent ministers' meetings. I wish my own John took more interest in relatives and
in the church. He does not ask questions. He thinks I know
nothing of importance. He only wants to say what he thinks,
rub his shoulder, and look at the clock.

Isaac was fifty-five at the time of his death. When I was little, fifty-five was considered a goodly number of years; now I

am getting close to fifty. Yet my poor Christian tottered at forty; something ailed his bones even if John will not talk about it. I cannot remember ever seeing as many wagons and conveyances assembled at one place as there were at Isaac's homestead. Many more than when Eliza's Marie died and we thought that was a multitude back then. The hostlers for Isaac's funeral must have had eighty to a hundred horses to care for and keep straight. I tried to explain to John M. about Isaac's new wife, Barbara, how she did not look to be much older than some of Isaac's children. The black clothes did not fit her. A month after the funeral she gave birth to a baby girl, Hannah. A new baby and all those other children; I wonder if anyone knows how many there are with all the steps and grands. At least when I lost Christian, I did not have a baby sucking.

Isaac's going came of a sudden. We had such a wet spring that year; every day another bucket of rain. Isaac made countless trips by horseback to visit a church beset by troubles across the border in Maryland. As it happened, he returned from one of those journeys in a continuous downpour and took to his bed with shaking chills, even tremors they said, from which he never made recovery. I hope I did not give too many details for John M. and his wife; my John says I elaborate too much. I mentioned that some had noticed a sadness about Isaac in his last year, saying that he preached the Word with full understanding but lacked some of his early fervor. John M. did not seem surprised; his blue eyes looked back solemnly at me, and he nodded when I remarked that none of us is safe from the Devil's slings and arrows. Many think that Brother Isaac was never the same after his oldest son died. And that was years ago.

That is the same way it was for me with Christian and David. The heavy winnowing. I wonder if we are given omens for good or bad. I remember being sore afraid in that cabin where Eliza and Yost lived with the dark mountain behind, the trees overhanging. I am not one to believe in witchcraft or other sorcery, but there seemed to be signs everywhere. Black crows swooped. When I was first a mother my hands shook that I might do something with a child that would bring a dire result. I try not to blame myself unduly for past blunders. Christian did not like it when I spoke my premonitions; he thought me foolish. But if I could have spared one tender life, those warnings would have been blessings. I am slowly learning not to think unduly on the sorrows that pile up like snowdrifts. We take what comes, the hollyhocks with the blizzards. To do otherwise is to fly in the face of our Lord. I remember Poppa warned about that years ago—or was it Momma?—long before I had any notion.

I ask John, my John, if it is too much to desire that one of my girls should survive. He shakes his head. So many of our young people are lost to the church back in Somerset. No one whispered ought against Bishop Isaac when he died, but everyone knows the problems had increased. Too many of the young get interested in the attractions of the world and drift away. I cannot let my Leah return to that snare. Not another blunder. She helps me with the comforters. That is one good thing. They are simple to make with wool filling between two layers of fabric. I brought scraps of wool along that I had spun in Pennsylvania. Leah ties the short pieces of yarn together; her tiny fingers work much better than mine. I am waiting to tell John the other part that my heart is set upon. I want my own loom. I see a place for it to stand, over along that south wall. That is why we must buy sheep.

What I have in mind is to make coverlets. The hard part would be the carding and fulling; John would have to help with that. I have seen coverlets that come from Mr. Wise's woolen mill down the road, and they are beautiful to look upon. One had light and dark shades of blue put right next to each other. It was a glory to look on. I can do just as well here at John's. It will take me longer than the people at the mill, but I can do it. If John will only make sure about the sheep. I will remind him that there is always a market for wool. And Doughty Creek has plenty of room for sheep with its wide valley. I know a thing or two, even if Maggie says that Daniel will not quiet in my arms.

I will show John that I am not a burden. I have plenty of coins to buy a loom. And sheep. Andrew still owes me money for that land. But I must convince John. Then I will start with one shade of blue.

10.

$\mathcal{R}$ EUBEN

April 1841

$\mathbf{Y}$es, it is true; Anna and I have had birthdays again. Last month, only four days apart. We are getting on in years and the white hair has taken over. My belly sags. I have almost reached the age of Father when he died. At 56 I think I am old, until I remember that Anna is 63. Nothing sobers me so quickly as advancing years. Not that we have engaged in excessive gaiety during the past thirty. Perhaps my last curse will be a long life. Shackled.

I fear for Anna; she gets more and more crippled in the hands. Already when we first moved to Ohio she noticed stiffness in her joints. For a few years she had no more problem, and we decided the difficulty had passed. Now there comes a worsening again this past winter. I catch her mumbling, but she does not realize it. One day it sounded like "death, sweet surcease," but she would not admit to it. A piece of cloth slips out of her grasp. She cannot stretch some of the bones in her fingers out straight. It is a pity to look upon. She gets nicks because she cannot properly grip the knife. I tell her I do not mind peeling potatoes or apples, but she wants to persevere as long as possible.

She has tried any number of remedies: goat's milk, copper bracelets, and has allowed me to rub my spit on her swollen hands. I do this with the forefinger of my right hand while counting in my head as I rub: first three times around, then five, then seven. When I am done rubbing I blow with great force, so much so that the blood rushes to my head and I must stop when faintness comes. I have also said words over her pain, the old standby:

> Christ's wounds were never bound.
> God, the Father; God, the Son;
> God, the Holy Ghost.

She shakes her head, "It is not for me, Reuben. Do not trouble."

I never thought she disapproved of my *brauching*, but she must not be fully convinced when the practice extends to herself. How I wish to be a source of healing for her, of all persons. Perhaps it is not meant to be. She takes her own concoction: equal parts of sassafras bark, burdock, dandelion, the root of dock, some dwarf elder, and boils this mixture in water until it is half of what she starts with. I hear her mumble—"boil, boil, boil"—as if she stirs a witch's brew to drink from her small tin cup before each meal.

Peter Troyer says there is a young man, Levi Speicher's oldest son, who has studied the medical books and calls himself a doctor. He would be a nephew of Franey's. That is all well and good, but what makes this so-called Doctor Frederick's practice any better than my own? Fancy book-learning? Peter says that many flock to Speicher's home over near to New Carlisle. What do they think? He is the new Jehovah? Anna says not to waste my breath; she does not like it when I growl. Well, I have my books too. John George Hohman's *The Long*

Lost Friend is now published in English; not that the English matters to me. That is my most reliable book. And the book that Aunt Barbli gave me: Albertus Magnus' *Egyptian Mysteries.* It is good for healing charms—although some people do not like magical words—and tells me all I need to know about herbs. Anna put her foot down, however, on *The Sixth and Seventh Books;* she called that black magic.

I remind her that some have called *me* Evil. Who decides where wickedness resides? I do not doubt there is an evil force in the world causing people to do bad, but sometimes evil takes up residence in the front parlor of people who call themselves good. Anna has no response to that. We have not been to church in thirty years. No new light has shown itself. Most of the time I see no need for the church, but I believe Anna would be there in a minute if the walls came tumbling down. I wonder if she regrets her decision to be shunned rather than to do the shunning. She points to the song sparrow in the highest branch and says that is where she wants to be. I do not know what she means. Up high? With the birds? I tried long ago to give her freedom.

When Yost first moved to Holmes County, I sought to shake his hand. Anna encouraged me, and I will admit, I thought his anger might have cooled. As I rode to his farm there was not a cloud in the sky. It was one of those clear, fall days when all is well with every creature. Part of me shrank from the going; I do not like to disturb a rattlesnake's den even when the sky is blue. Yet the den persisted. No one cared ought about me, except that I had defied the church's will. Doing nothing for thirty years had gotten me nowhere, so I went. I went as a brother, but Yost would not show his face. I received the brushoff from his new woman. I went home to the jug.

Some days I think we should move on. The National Road, the same one that went near our place in Pennsylvania, has been finished all the way to Indiana. They claim the passage is easy, but I hesitate over Anna's joints. Another long journey and all the packing of particulars might push beyond her limit. My burden would follow me there as surely as it has settled on me here in Ohio. Bevy says I should leave the Amish; I ask her, "Since when do I belong?" I have thought of affiliating with the German Reformed or some such, but I am washed through and through with Amish blood.

Bevy has recovered from her sadness and married again, this time to an Otzenberger. Michael Otzenberger. His people, the Swiss Reformed, came to the Trail Creek area ten years ago. They are quick to organize, for they had their own building, a church building, over in Winesburg within a few years. Bevy seems well-satisfied with their worship and beliefs. She says they are not so serious as we Amish; their clothes can be of bright colors and they are allowed musical instruments. She made a point to tell Anna that the hummingbird goes for the red flowers. She said red with a loudness and laughed merrily. Bevy has a small reedlike contraption with holes. When she blows, it makes a piercing noise which is hard on my ears. She says she likes it. She also says that on every Sunday, Amish youth are in attendance; many find the differences appealing. I cannot be convinced: the noise, the separate building for church services. That is a far different songbird.

I have done like many others and built a larger dwelling, although no one asks to have a church meeting in my house. Anna wondered why we needed bigger, just the two of us creaking and rattling about. Now we have the two stories with a porch all along the front. That is what I wanted, the porch. I like to sit at night and look across the fields where deer come to feed. I rise before the cows are up—I often cannot sleep— and watch dawn come into my valley. It is not the Garden of Eden, but it suits me well. From my porch I put out sunflower seeds and watch the cardinals snap at finches and chickadees. In the back of the house I enclosed a pantry for food storage and added another bedroom. When our children come with their own—seven grandchildren for us—Anna is glad for the extra space. My Hershberger line, brief as it is, will continue; the other week Jacob and Louisa had their first boy, Solomon. Jacob still remembers how much he wanted a brother.

I was not allowed inside Yost's house, but I noticed that he has built with bricks. I could not see my way clear to sink that much money. I used instead a method of half-timbering as they do in Europe. Michael showed me the proper mixture, using mud and straw between the timbers and covering with a plaster. I have never seen a young one grunt and grimace as Michael does, but his results are sturdy and pleasing to look upon. Now we have our castle. Anna wove together rag pieces—blue, green, and brown—for floor coverings. Finished wood for flooring suits me plenty good—I remind her of our first dirt floor here in Ohio—but she likes the carpet, so I oblige. I need to take more care with my boots when I enter, and then we get along.

Our Jacob surprises us with his involvement in the affairs of Trail; all the village men know him and make easy exchange with him. I will admit, he got my vote for road supervisor. As long as he does not get entangled in the politics of the nation, I believe his interests can be kept safe. He has married a Swiss Reformed girl also, a Liechti. She has come his way for now, but if he continues to dabble in county affairs, I doubt they will stay Amish. Far be it from me to warn him. Long ago I had wished for schooling for my children; now Jacob speaks of school for his little ones as an expectation, not a perhaps.

I am the one who changes not. I sit, waiting to be freed. Jacob makes a name for himself, but mine cannot be cleared.

I am glad for him but sad for myself. I make matters worse rather than better. When I came home from Yost's house and from his woman spitting words at me, Anna tried to reason with me. "Go to bed," she said, as if she forgets there is nothing for me to do there but sleep. I went to the barn instead. For several days I made my nest, knowing little else but the need to relieve myself. The putrid smell of urine and vomit surrounded me; I cared not. Anna said later that she did not know what to do besides keep the cows milked. I believe she finally hid my jugs.

I might still be drinking, except for the snakes. They came in my sleep, and I could not fend them off. I have not been the same since. A heavy rattle and thumping woke me; I sat up on the straw, my hands braced behind me. A thick, brown rattler—diamonds blurred into black rings—wrapped itself around each boot. I yelled mightily, "Let go!" I shook to disentangle my feet. The snakes clung tighter than jewelweed; there was no ridding them. My yelling—"Let go my boots"—only made the snakes rattle louder. I sank onto my back; I hugged myself; I cowered. Then I saw the others, three more, stretched in a row, hanging from the loft above, their heads pointing toward me, their tongues whipping. The fattest was in the middle.

I covered my face with my arms, screaming, "No, no, no! By all the heavens, no! I did not do it."

Sometime in the midst Anna came to me, wiping a wet cloth over my sweaty forehead. She tried to soothe, "There, there, Reuben, it is nothing." She rubbed my socks so hard that I could feel my feet tingle again. "You have no boots," she said.

I licked my dry lips and asked for water. I tried to slow my breathing. Something moved across my stomach. I raised my head and saw a viper ease its way over my chest. Its eyes stayed tight on me; its wetness slithered over my body. "Get off! Get off!" I yelled, flailing my arms and hands.

Anna was no help. "Quiet, Reuben. You see things that are not here. Calm yourself, and it will go better."

She says I carried on and on until I spent myself. She brought a pallet to the barn and spent the night, hearing me thrash in my sleep, trying to shush me. When I woke I remembered there had been snakes and Anna had walked among them, stepping over them, ministering to me. She brought fresh spring water and broth. She offered me her crippled hand to walk to the house; I went slowly on my own. Her eyes carried so much sadness; I do not know how she endures.

I sat, rocking on the porch. My porch, my castle. "I am sorry," I said to Anna. "That will not happen again." And it has not. Yost has made me a leper, but there is no excuse for the ruin I could bring on myself. I still drink on occasion, a shot of whiskey, but I cork the jug and put it away before I drink. I have but to close my eyes and see Anna, my deliverer, walking with her long skirts in the viper's den.

Jacob says there is a movement, started back East, to prohibit the use of alcohol. They call it a temperance movement, these people who promote total abstinence. That is nonsense, refusing a man the right to his own still. If a man cannot control his own use, then perhaps there is need for a law, but it is far better for a man to set his own limits. Abstinence will never take root, except perhaps among fat ladies who drink tea and want to lord it over others. Was not this country founded on individual freedom? I wait for freedom. Perhaps we all wait. Yost is not free, for he is trapped in his beliefs and misconceptions. Anna is not free, for she is married to me.

The closest I come to freedom is when I feel the cool earth between my fingers. Every spring the air brings promise.

Every dawn the air on my porch warms my old, crusty face. I test the soil. When it cakes into mud balls I know it is still too wet to work. I stomp, impatient, with dirt stuck on my boots. Will winter never end? Then, of a sudden, the miracle happens. Soil sifts through my hands; the wetness has gone out. I stand up and splash water on my face. I am free to grow things again.

I do not have much; my name is not cleared. But I have Anna, my children, and their children. And two good neighbors, Peter and Franey. No one has sought to take any of that from me. At night I can sit on my porch and be at peace with the insects. As long as there are crops to grow, Anna may be right. It is not too late.

11.

JONAS

May 1844

A Mr. Tyler tried to sell me lightning rods the other day, said I needed them to protect my buildings. I did not run him off, but neither did I give him a sympathetic ear. It is hard to understand, but some of our people are buying.

I said to the gentleman with the fancy boots—two shades of brown—"If God sends lightning to strike my barn or house, I would not want to interfere in the Almighty's doings."

"My good man," he said, "don't you think God wants you to take care of your possessions? You've worked hard for what you've obtained. Wouldn't your God desire adequate protection?"

I could but look this English man in the eye and say, "I will trust that God knows best. I will not stake my safety in a steel rod."

He did not know when to stop. "Why is it then, that you put a roof on your barn?" He stood there with his arms folded, as if he owned the place.

I did not want to quarrel with a stranger, so I busied myself, securing a fence post. When he saw that he made no headway, he got on his horse and took his leave.

On Sunday I told Shem about this exchange; he suggested a better response if I am approached again. God told Noah to put a roof on the ark, but He never made mention of lightning rods. That is a good answer. I was right in refusing to put my trust in the things of this world. Some go about selling what they call insurance. All it is is a piece of paper. You give the man some money—he comes every year—and then if you have a fire, he gives you money to rebuild. Of course if you do not have a fire, you are out the money. We have no need of that, for if one of us has a loss, the rest in the church will come help rebuild. Shem says we are each other's insurance; we have no need to rely on the world. Shem is right: those who fall for this trap not only throw away their money; they also abandon their souls to the wickedness of an insurance company. A sure sign.

I have witnessed other disturbing changes in the ten years since we have lived in Ohio. The soil is more obedient from our taming, but we are losing our way on every hand. The world creeps in and plants its darts. I try to work Simeon hard, but I suspect he is among the Saturday- night carousers. There is too much idle talk and frivolity, the kind of foolish joke-playing that accomplishes nothing useful. I found a rhyme in his possession; the Pennsylvania Dutch could not fool me:

> Drink ich—so shtink ich.
> Drink ich net—shtink ich doch.
> Besser gadroonka oon gshtoonka
> Oss net gadroonka un doch gshtoonka.

I confronted Simeon as to why it was better to drink and stink, than not to drink and still stink.

He scoffed and said, "Father, it is only a joke. It will not hurt you to smile."

It is not only among the young; even with the adults there is horseplay and too much wasting of time. Some think it amusing that Truman Schweitzer swallowed his cigar when the bishop came along. No wonder our young do not respect their elders, not even the ministers, as they ought. The word of a man of God used to be considered nigh to sacred; people did not question. But now these young folks think they have the right to speak their minds instead of listening and paying heed. None of my younger ones: Mary, Dorothy, Simeon, has a serious outlook. I have completely given up on Stephen. He has too much of the smart mouth; I fear it may be from the schooling. I used to be all for a man getting as much education as possible; I even encouraged Father to let Franey go to school. But with my own children I have come to understand Bishop Blauch's warning about becoming swollen.

One morning Stephen said he was too plugged up to go to church. I thought he meant from the spring pollen. Salome could not keep still, of course, and asked, "Why do you not sneeze then? My hay fever makes me run at the nose."

That is just what Stephen wanted, for he said, "I do not sneeze with my butt."

Mary thinks I am too drawn in upon myself; she thinks we should be more given to talk at the table. What is there to say? She knows what her father preaches. The tongue is like a fire, a whole bed of iniquity. Mary seems to have taken up where Jeremiah left off. We hear that he has his own boy now, back in Pennsylvania. I wonder if the little one will be a talker too. When I take my place at the table it is for the purpose of eating, not gabbing. How can I talk with my mouth full of food? When I have partaken of nourishment, then it is time to get back to work. Why sit and stare at each other? I would rather know more than I say, than be foaming at the mouth with nothing of substance. Those people who claim to know everything about modern gadgets and go on about every little trinket, that is not for me.

Sometimes I notice a severe ache within my mouth. I always avoided looking at Father's cave, but now I have my own troubles to contend with. My pain seems embedded in the teeth along the lower gums. When I first wake, the pain is the worst; I must grind too much while at sleep or hold my mouth with too much tightness. After I am about and have chewed at sausages, my jaw takes on more ease. Shem preaches that the letter of James carries helpful instruction about the tongue. This member can defile the body and no man can tame it. My lips get dry thinking of flames in my mouth or rat poison in my stomach. Yet some people act as if they are deaf, carrying on in a foolish manner and repeating nonsense. *Hinkle dreck.* What a displeasure to God.

Mary says not to worry about the children; that with more time they will find what they need and settle down. Salome, Stephen, even Mary, have all reached twenty and could be married. Yet they are not. Only Adam and Elizabeth have married and each settled nearby; they provide an upright example, but it goes by, unnoticed by the others. I worry that my children tarry in finding mates because they are as addled and ill at ease as I was. Those were dreadful times, my enrapture with Polly; I was all thumbs. My hands knew not what to do. I cannot believe that it all happened. How my thinking fell on the short side. I wonder what has become of Polly.

It is not only my children; some of our ordained brethren give pause as well. It used to be that what one minister believed and preached was pretty much of the same mind as another. Not so now; it is almost as though they do not use the same Bible. Shem says some of them allow too much human thinking. Here at Oak Grove our bishop Daniel Mast holds to the old truths. For the most part. And of course Shem can be counted on. But with some of the others there is grave doubt. One thing after another creeps in: trimmed beards, buttons, winter caps. All of these changes cause confusion and strife. Shem says it is like unto the time of the Judges when each man did as he thought right in his own eyes.

The differences among the Amish are even greater over in Holmes County. Abraham must fret that he has never been made a bishop. I wonder why his nose has gotten bumpy with red spots. In his area of Walnut Creek they divided into two church districts already three or four years ago. There is no sense. People build large, elaborate houses and fill them with unnecessary accumulations; then when it comes to having church they say there is not room enough. Now they have the two bishops: John M. Yoder at one and Henry Stutzman for the south district at Farmerstown. Even a squalling infant could see the black and white between them. Two brothers-in-law. I have heard Bishop Stutzman preach and know that he has written God's Word on his heart.

But Franey—I have not gone to see her once—lives in John M.'s district. He has too much of a progressive spirit; it is as if he encourages people to think that the rules of our forefathers are no longer sufficient, that people can introduce improvements without fear of danger. Shem shakes his head and chews on the gristle in his mouth. "The chastening rod," he says, "I see it coming; that is what the Lord uses when people forget." He says to watch for more signs.

It is frightening to think that the Lord might not tarry long. Widespread hardness of heart. Very sobering. Like unto the gray entering Mary's black hair. It still has its springiness, but there is a patch near the front where she pulls it back tight that has taken on the look of snow. One day I will be an old man, and she will bring me aid. But not yet. It would be far better for her to go first.

In the meantime more families come to Ohio. People say it may not be too many more years before each of these churches, Henry's and John M.'s, needs to divide again. I hear that Levi Speicher and his family are again back in the Amish fold. They live near to Charm, so they are under Brother Stutzman's care. I wonder if Levi would be a person to speak with some day, to unburden myself of things from my youth. But not while Abraham sits nearby.

For now, I will stay low. As Father said years ago, "You can always tell a wise man by the smart things he does not say." That will have to be good enough for me. What I have not said would only make me dumb if uttered.

PART IV

November 1846 — June 1859

1.

YOST

November 1846

There is nothing gives satisfaction like unto this. Nothing. Another year's harvest safely put away. All the bending to plant, the sowing in the spring, tending and cultivating all summer long with an eye on the lookout for the grasshopper. Then comes satisfaction: grain stored for the winter. All from the land. How could anyone desire more?

Even though I am slow to rise, I still like to lie in the tall grass when the day's work is done. I lie on my back with both knees in the air or with an ankle crossed on my other knee. I do not know why it appeals. Well, yes, it makes me feel young. It is a reward to feel the cool earth under my back. I remember when the boys were little I laid thus and surprised one of them. Gideon, I believe it was, but it may have been Henry. Whichever youngster, I can still see him running to the house with his pants loaded.

I could not make it now without Alexander's help. He is a sturdy fourteen and does the work of a man. Not too long ago I could tote sacks as he does. When he marries and goes off on his own, I do not know what will happen. I do not take well to the words, *cutting back*. I am fifty years older than

Alexander, but I am not ready to head downhill. With all of my children married, except for Alexander and Ursula, there is less need for provisions. Yet when land is available, how can I not drop the seed? I pray that Alexander will take interest in my acreage. Fanny and I could dwell here. The old folks. I would gladly help out as needed.

I purchased another hundred acres last fall. Just like that. A snap of the fingers. It still spites me that I let twenty acres slip away—two years ago—across the creek on the south side. I deliberated too long, and the land was gone. I hesitated because Fanny tells me I am too quick to snatch. I plan so far in advance there is no surprise left. When she comments thus, I ask if she is glad the wood is split and dried for the winter, or if she would rather stew about whether we will keep warm. She puckers her lips and says, "Go on with you, Yost." That is what I do. That is what I have always done. She says it is too early to make arrangements with Alexander about the farm, but I will make certain not to wait too long.

Fanny says we have been married for as many years as Eliza and I were in union. I would never have guessed it; the easy years go by much faster. Nicholas, my ornery one, has mended his ways and has three boys of his own. They follow him like ducklings in a row, their necks and chins stuck forward, their shoulders hunched, just like him. Three little Nicholases. But they behave themselves. If the sight of those grand boys were not enough to startle Eliza, perhaps my barn would be a shock. No one around these parts has a finer one. Feed alleys, watering troughs, separate compartments for different animals. Whatever I could think of, I included. Cattle go in the bottom part; some call it a basement. The cow stable has a window and the Dutch doors let in light through the top half, so there is natural light for feeding and choring.

The haymow, now that is a thing of beauty! The whole upper area measures 100 feet by 50 feet—Manuel Blough only made his 40 feet wide—and has room for wheat and oats as well. There is more: the haymow has an opening all along the front, from the floor up five feet so I can fork hay or straw in and out. And the roof—this pleases me to no end—I found white pine shingles over near to Winesburg.

Farmers from all over have come just to see my barn. I do not mind that they gawk. Some of them look skeptical when I tell them the arrangement is my idea, the workmanship is mine. Of course, Gideon and Henry helped place the oak beams—it took six of us to heft them—but aside from that, I look on this barn as the work of my hands. I thought my knees would buckle, holding the weight of those timbers. Someone will be glad for this barn some day. Very glad. This barn will endure long after I have kicked the bucket. Alexander will be sure to remember who built it.

There is every reason to make improvement in the farm setup; that is the way I have made a living, with my nose forward. But with the women it is a different story; they should keep to their bonnets. For them the question of change is not one of survival, only a flimsy following after the styles of the world. These modern currents threaten to sweep into our church with exceeding swiftness. We must all be on our guard. I try to warn Fanny. I am not in favor of her buying undergarments at the store, not when we can use what she makes at home. But I learned long ago to take great care when I admonish her. I do not like to wait when it is time for my supper.

It has always been thus with women: prone to poor judgment and stubborn to the end. Already in the Old Testament Lot's wife brought on her own destruction because of her imperfections. She had no one else to blame. I can see her: a white pillar of salt with her head turned sideways, looking back. Even the angels gave warning: Sodom and Gomorrah would be destroyed and all the iniquity therein. Lot knew to listen; he knew not to look back on all that fire and brimstone. But not his wife. Oh no, she had to look back.

Henry Stutzman is the right man to bring us these stories from the Bible. When I cup my hand behind my ear, I have no trouble hearing him. He keeps all of us at Farmerstown on the straight and narrow. It is true just as he says: many there be who go in and out the wide door to destruction. Sometimes I have trouble staying awake for the whole sermon, but I never miss the Old Testament stories. Just because my eyes are shut does not mean that I am not listening. I have always pictured that first paradise as having the contours of my own land no matter where I have lived. My soil might not be as black as what they claim to have in Iowa, but it is good enough to be the Garden. The serpent knew to go right to Eve, the weak one. Every time the story is told, I want to hear that Adam knew to say no to the woman, but it cannot be changed. She had been warned aplenty not to partake of that tree in the middle of the Garden. That was the fruit that was pleasant to look upon. How fickle, to be taken in by appearance.

Another of my favorites is the story about the brothers. Not Cain and Abel, but the other two: Jacob and Esau. I tell it to my grandchildren—that Gabriel is a sharp one—so they will be warned as well. I always knew that Reuben would try to steal a birthright, some blessing that was rightfully mine. I saw how he set himself, always determined to take advantage. Even if it was only to get the lighter task in the shade, he would try to get a step on me. All his gibberish: God the Father this, and God the Son that. I have known the truth about him as surely as I know my left hand from my right. Always grubbing for more than was his. That spirit of Jacob. I have made certain that he will not walk off with my barn. I wonder if Bishop Henry has had occasion to run into Reuben, for when he speaks of how Satan takes a grip on people, to the extent that they do not recognize the sin within, that sounds exactly like what has happened to Reuben. By being vigilant I may have thwarted him more than I will ever know. What grief we all would have been spared if he would have early recognized the truth of his nature. Stubborn as a woman.

I have never been to one of those gambling dens that Nicholas has confessed to, but Reuben trifles with his soul as surely as do those who riffle through a deck of cards. I had thought that with advancing years he would know his life was coming to a crossroads between confession and eternal damnation. Sometimes I even feel a twinge of pity—that tells me I am getting old—when I think of him burning in a fiery pit. I needed to set aside my grievance with him long ago so that it did not rankle. I cannot choose *for* him. He knows he is responsible, as surely as did Lot's wife way back in the beginning.

2.

J O H N   M .

October 1847

*J*remember when I reached twenty and called myself a full-grown man—old enough to marry. Now Elias has turned that milestone and knows all about all. *Deliver us.* I know less today than when I was his age. Know less with certainty. I learned well from Joseph. All that was necessary for farming. How to think on many questions. All seemed in order with my life: my young faith planted, my commitment to the church, the woman of my choice. *Our Father, which art in heaven.* I have no regrets; I would choose the same again today.

But it is entirely a different story to watch my seed come to these same turning points. Nothing is simple when it is another's decision. My son's choices. I want to be Joseph and ask the questions, but Elias beats me to them. "What is wrong with buttons?" I want to choose for him, but I cannot. Elias' life has emerged like that of a pine cone. First, the yellowish-brown nub, tender and bare, exposed to the cool spring air. Then in the summer heat the nub stretches, its hard scales overlapping around its base. The next time I wonder what became of the young, brown start; all is green, popped out in prickly needles, and taking its place amidst the life of the tree. I thought I watched carefully, but the transformation happened without me.

Elizabeth and Barbara, my two oldest, have joined the church and seem content. Some years ago, soon after I became bishop, I made clear to Katharina that bundling could not be allowed for our daughters; if the pattern of courtship were to change for the Amish, then it would have to start with my family. *Deliver us.* We would lay down the rules. The boys who came calling would leave by midnight. Katharina did not object, for she felt too the need to protect our own from unwanted consequences. But now she has said on two different occasions, "The young boys no longer pay our daughters heed." I have noticed the same, but I do not come to the same dire conclusion. I remind her that she was twenty-seven when we married. I want her to laugh when I say that our daughters may know as well as she: the best comes late. She looks unconvinced, barely smiles, and says, "You do not understand how it is to be the one waiting for a knock at the door." She is right, I do not know. But our girls are only in their early twenties. It seems premature to call the hour late or to think that our rule has caused a problem.

What troubles is that Katharina often knows about these kinds of things. She was right about Rebecca, our baby who lived only a year. *Vergib uns.* That happened seven years ago already—how is that possible?—and we have not had a child since. Rebecca came to us within a few days of my being named a bishop, a time when I still knew all. Around the time of her first birthday she began to fret, crying for most of two days. Nothing we could do would quiet her. None of the usual remedies. Catnip. Diluted willow bark. Katharina was distraught with worry. I was the calm one who knew this was but a childhood illness that would pass as had all the other upsets with the seven older ones. *Vergib uns.* The truth is I felt irritation with Katharina that she allowed herself to get disheveled. I was a bishop in the Amish church. Where was her faith? *Unser Vater in dem Himmel. Dein Name werde geheiligt.*

The night Rebecca died we took turns rocking her. Katharina held her, singing hymns and lullabies; then I insisted she go to bed while I took the vigil. As I rocked Rebecca I placed my hand on her forehead and felt stunned by its heat, akin to placing my hand on a red brick that we take from the fireplace to the wagon to warm our propped feet in the winter. Too hot for the bare hand to touch. Rebecca's hair, dark with sweat, lay matted on her forehead. Only then did I realize that this child lay in the balance between life and death. This seed of mine. I have ministered to many others in their grief. I have said with glibness, the tree that wrestles with the gale is stronger for it. But I did not know how it feels, when the loss is mine. *Vergib uns.* Nothing in my power could pull this child one way or the other. Not being a bishop. Katharina had said that Rebecca was feverish, and I had thought, yes, even as all babies encounter fever from time to time. But we were not immune, after all, to the ravages of disease; my ministry could not spare my child. I offered frantic prayers on Rebecca's behalf, but it was too late. *Dein Wille geschehe auf Erden wie im Himmel.*

I woke Katharina—I do not think she slept—to hold Rebecca while I went to the ice house. We placed ice all over Rebecca's body. To no avail. "I am sorry; I am sorry," I said; whether to baby or mother, I know not. *Es tut mir leid.* Katharina and I wept in each other's arms until the day broke over our house. We found small solace. Since then Katharina does not glide when she walks. Since then I have been more gentle in my hold on life. I do not seize it as one making a demand, for I know now—what I thought I knew then—life comes from the Giver. Every little one reminds me of Rebecca. I need Katharina as much as ever—we do not abstain—but we have not filled the cradle again. I do not know that anything is wrong, except for our spirits. *Und führe uns nicht in Versuchung. Sondern erlöse uns von dem Übel.*

I know less inwardly, yet I must give answer to more and more questions that seek to shake our church. These questions do not come in the friendly quarters of Joseph's milk shed. Some of our people ask for freedom from the *Ordnung*, from *this* tradition, from *that*. Some of them leave the church; then they have their freedom. But do they find freedom? That is what I try to explain to Elias, but I do not know how. Not that he is dumb. Only young. Not that I do not know how to say it. Only that the knowledge may be beyond explanation. He asks, "Why do I need to grow a beard if I want to join the church? I like the feel of my smooth cheeks."

I try to explain that it is not the beard that saves, but submitting the will to the care of the church. That is what gives meaning to the way we live. I am not for empty rules; the tradition itself cannot give life. But neither can *not* living by the tradition give life. Elias does not understand. Perhaps it is impossible for a twenty-year-old to give heed when the world offers so many attractions. *Erlöse uns von dem Übel.* I remember how I could not wait for my beard to come in full like Joseph's. How I could not wait to be made a minister. How the light hovered above the *Ausbund*. But Elias does not think the same way. The church was my safe haven, whether I was in Pennsylvania or Ohio, whether I was with Isaac or Joseph. I knew I was loved as a child of God. I do not know why it is not thus for Elias. Except that he has to reckon with the excitement of a gaudy fair. He yields to the pleasure—he calls it fun—of seeing his face on a photograph. It is not wrong to be tempted. That is only human. But it must be self-condemnation to think to know all. *Erlöse uns von dem Übel.* That is what my detractors said about me, already seventeen years ago when I was made a minister. I thought the oldsters knew not whereof they spoke. I had not yet rocked Rebecca to eternal sleep.

I say to Elias, "You may go; you may leave the boundaries of the church and be free. But you do so at the risk of being lost." He does not understand; he may even think I push him out the door. As a child, he leaped to empty the ashes—"See Father, how strong I am"—but now I cannot make him *want* to do anything. *Dein Wille geschehe auf Erden wie im Himmel.* I can only tell him that he is precious in God's sight.

Here is the sad truth: many join our church out of habit. Out of ease. Only later they decide there is not the meaning they had hoped for. Not unlike the many who come to Ohio and find it is not all they expected. Then people leave the church, thinking the church has failed. Thinking that in their leaving they are no longer bound. I say they have only exchanged their fetters, desiring a chest with deeper drawers, a secretary with a writing desk, instead of being satisfied with what is plain and useful. They want to be successful with a business, so they bind themselves to selling bolts or running a creamery instead of being content as a farmer. I am not against progress, but the people do not understand. *Übel, Übel, Übel.* My son, Elias.

It is a hard time for everyone. Hard to be young and see the choices right outside the door; hard to be old and feel that those coming along do not count as precious the very things that give life meaning. Here I am, seeking to help people in my charge remain faithful. I stand tall before those with rosy, soft cheeks and those with faces lined and tired. God's people still count on me. Some, at least, still trust me; others have their doubts. I am only a vessel for Elias and my six others. A vessel for the lives of all the flock.

3.
$\mathcal{P}$ O L L Y
May 1848

irst, we lost our girl babies. Now we lose our grown children. Dead and gone. March, that dread month that seized Eliza's first Marie, claimed her last *bobbel*, Lydia. This niece of mine that I did not know. Yost and Eliza's last offspring. She died, leaving two forlorn children and a bereft husband, a Lehman. Is there no end? Even with our ease of life here in Holmes County—compared with those dark, uphill days in Somerset County—the heartache and sorrow still fly to us. I trust that Eliza's soul knows nought of this last burden. I am the one left to keep watch on her behalf. All alone.

I paid my respects for Eliza's sake. My tottery legs with the varicose veins got me to the funeral and back. It is not unsteadiness so much as a heaviness. I sit about too much, especially this past winter, and am content to let Judith do the jobs that require heavy standing. Christian would say the flab has taken over. I have extra folds of skin that he never saw, under my chin, around my middle. I do not mind the skin's wrinkles, but I am swollen everywhere. Now I have fat ankles to match my fat fingers. I am too fat to catch anyone's eye for companionship—widowed for over ten years—too old to fill in for someone if death called a poor wife home. Momma stayed thin to the end, but I am nothing but an old, fat one.

When I heard that Lydia died, I wanted to see Susanna, my little lap baby with the dimpled fingers of long ago. I had heard that she had moved here to Ohio, but I did not know where to find her. Now she is the momma—married to Levi Speicher's brother, Adam—and has held four sweet ones to her bosom. She looked to be a good manager of her chicks. I could see the Berkey in her, but she did not recognize me until I shook hands and said, "Polly Anna." Her eyes grew big enough to pop, and she covered her mouth with her hand. We did not have much to say. *"Es kisselt und kasselt"* did not seem right at a funeral.

I was the one surprised to see the years on Yost. I had wondered what his bellow would sound like, but I should not have bothered myself about that. He is much reduced. His eyes, the same ones that leaned down and demanded an answer, had the watery squint to them. But his mind is alert. He recognized me right away, even with all my fat, for he shook my hand and said, "Polly Anna, is it not?" Years ago it was always, "Girl this," and "Girl that."

"Yes, Yost, this is Polly," I said. "We have lost another."

He cupped his hand behind his ear.

I raised my voice, but I did not want to shout at a solemn occasion. "Another death."

He shook his head and looked down at his knobby hands. I do not know if he could not hear or if he was overcome with emotion. His eyes had the red of an old man, and his face was much too yellow with ugly brown patches. We talked no more; there were people all about, and I did not want to make effort to speak above the whispering din. I noticed a younger woman keeping watch over him; I suppose that is his Fanny. She had white lace on the cuffs of her sleeves. Since the funeral I have asked about; Christina Kauffman says that Yost makes recovery this spring from a bad case of the grippe. He has been confined indoors and could not go to his barn for weeks. Paul shook his head gravely and said that Yost has accumulated much, much land. It must be far more than the usual. I wonder what Eliza would think, if it is true that Yost has become a wealthy man.

March is not the only month when we lose our children. Evil comes in the spring as well. *Übel, Übel*. Let me think; Eliza's firstborn, her lastborn, my first two, Leah's twin. They all passed on in March or April. Next year, come May, it will be twenty years since my David departed. Think of it; twenty years. Judith helps me keep track. She is my new sister. Last spring we had word about Joel. He always said I would hear from him in Oregon, but I do not think he meant in this manner. His remains are buried in a place called Marion County, Oregon. We received no explanation as to the cause of his demise, only the notification that he was laid to rest. For weeks I did not even shed a tear. How could I weep for another baby? I can only watch as, one by one, they march away. Joel reached his goal that he never tired to talk of, but I shudder to think what Evil may have overtaken him. Indians, or a herd of buffalo. Even women, wild women. Christina Kauffman says that those who go to the far West lose all sense of right and wrong.

John and Maggie stayed in Ohio only two years before they followed the pack to Indiana. Christina says there are large settlements in Elkhart County and Lagrange. I get no word from John except through those who travel back and forth. He could make effort to write a letter—one of the boys would read it to me—for we now have what is called a postage stamp. They can be purchased at any post office and by licking such and affixing to an envelope, a letter with one of these stamps can be sent to any other post office in the United States. That is how I heard the bad news from Oregon. I am rather surprised that Joel had on his person where to find me. But with John there is no ailment in his handwriting. He did satisfactory work as a scholar. I hear through others that John has four boys and two baby girls. He could write if he would but take the time. One night I dreamed that one of his girls has the red hair. It was a relief to wake up.

When John and Maggie pulled up roots, that left Leah and me as poor, lost orphans. Judith, married to Christian's brother, Paul, came to our rescue. They lived only two miles down the road, still in Doughty Valley. I was relieved for joy, thinking that Leah would be happy living with four boy cousins, but not so. She had set herself to pining for Somerset County and would not budge from it. This went on for several years. I can thank my Andrew, still on the home place, for offering a solution. He sent a posted letter with this question: Would Leah have interest in being a hired girl? He had found him a wife, and within a short time they had their second child on the way. Leah did not hesitate. It was almost a relief to have my pretty one go. Our only delay was in finding a suitable ride for her. I sent with her a tiny pincushion, made from shiny, yellow material in the shape of a heart. I wonder where she keeps it.

Now I have a room all to myself and a chest of drawers that is all mine. I am very fond of the way the sun shines in this valley. I do not feel tight and oppressed as in other places. Paul and Judith have the four big boys at home; I was right about Obadiah being theirs. The boys are all straight and tall like Paul but walk a smidgen off to the side. I hope there is not trouble with their bones. I do not have a closeness with the boys, but that is nothing new. They treat me with kindness, so I do not feel like a back porch added on. I wish Obadiah would not scratch his rear end so much. Paul has much more spunk than Christian, even with his handicap. A hand lost to a bobcat. He rests his stump on the table as if it wants to look at me. I take pains to avert my eyes. Judith and I are like sisters; only she does not call me Polly Anna. I do all the spinning for the family. She let me show her how to make coverlets. She has the quick hands and long fingers—they remind me of Eliza's—and she has a good eye for a design that pleases.

I am ashamed that I do not help with the food, only with the eating. I do not want to be a burden as with Maggie. Judith makes what she calls Indian pone. I wish it had a different name, but it tastes wonderful. When she adds our precious wheat flour it is extra good, even better than johnnycake. She bakes it in a large, deep, iron skillet and places hot coals under it on the hearth. She even puts hot coals on top of the lid. She is very particular about adding fresh coals until the pone is done through. I would not bother with all that getting up and down to tend.

Whenever Judith has extras with pea-shelling or pulling grapes from their clusters—anything that I can do sitting down—then I give help. It is the weight on my legs that starts the throbbing. When the boys have extra field work, I do not mind grabbing at teats either. Paul did not think I could do it. "You will fall and not be able to get up," he predicted. But I have shown, once I get myself situated on the stool, that I still know how to make a cow cooperate. I use Paul's widest milk stool, and I do my getting up and down when no one is watching. The boys give my sheep care, but it is my money that buys the sheep. I think Christian would approve: from sheep, to wool, to coverlets, to money, back to sheep.

Judith teaches me how the old rhymes go in the Pennsylvania Dutch. It seems a pity that I do not have even one grandchild living nearby. Paul calls us old biddies with our child's play, but Judith and I pay him no heed. We like the saying about the two old women: one cuts wood, the other gathers splinters:

> De oldt hockt huls,
> De yoong layst shpay.
> De oldt huckt im fire-eck
> Oon grotzt eara bay.

I do not want to be an old hag who sits by the fireplace and scratches; it is better to be jolly.

When Leah first left for Somerset County I was overtaken with lonesome feelings. Not a child in sight. Leah wrote three letters that first summer; I begged Judith's boys to read them to me. One of them would usually oblige, but I knew if Obadiah skipped some parts. I took the letters to my room and kept them under my pillow. Leah has not said ought of going to visit the graves. Instead she wrote that she had married a man by the name of Johnson. George Johnson. Only she called him Jack. Her letter was full of Jack this and Jack that.

That was another way to lose a daughter that I had not prepared for. She still writes, once a year or oftener, so her loss is not entire. John could write a letter if he but would. This Jack is eight years older than Leah, and she says she loves him dearly. It is embarrassing to have the boys read that part: "I love Jack dearly." Obadiah clears his throat and blushes. Leah writes that they go to a Methodist church, built from stones, in Little Crossings. At first that was as frightening as Joel traipsing to Oregon. But Judith reminds me: Leah is twenty-six this year. I could not hold her close when she was here. It is better for her to be happy.

Paul's boys bring home tales from school; they say that we have been at war with a country to the south called Mexico. I do not like these faraway places. Nor do I see why men must resort to bloodshed; there is enough grief without that. Some seek after land in places called Texas and California. There is too much grasping. Our ministers—John J. is a good one—do well to warn us of the dangers of coveting a neighbor's property. I wonder how much land Yost owns. Paul talks endlessly that he needs to get his four boys set up. Then he repeats himself and says it all again. I do not say anything critical, but I believe we can kill when we squeeze from another. Like unto those Evil ones who take up the sword. I do not say one thing that is reproachful. I do not want Paul hounding me about why I need ten sheep instead of five.

My sheep. I have names for them all, but I have not told Paul or the boys. Let me think. Angelina always walks first, leading the others, and Pooker brings up the rear. I must take care not to get too attached. My eyes are precious for doing the coverlets. I have been given sight for over fifty-seven years, and I must take care not to overtax them with too much close work. If I must lose all my children, perhaps the good Lord will spare my eyesight.

It is strange how the Lord works His will. My children go West or they turn back East. And here I sit in Ohio. Who could have predicted? Not Christian. Yet the Lord tarries, as faithful as the sun that rises and sets each day, as certain as the rooster's call each morning. Even as beautiful as the dogwoods this May. The one in front of the house cannot stop showering us with its splendor. I left the East, the only place I thought safe, to make it easier for my children on the frontier. And to escape death's grip. Ohio was the place to be, to make a go. Now I have but three children left, John, Andrew, and Leah, and two of them are back where Christian and I started. If something were to happen to Judith and Paul, I do not know what I would do. I do not want to end up begging at Andrew's table. I do not even know his woman.

There is much talk of church trouble. Paul says there are too many divisions among us to call ourselves one church. That kind of talk only keeps the pot stirred. Christian would never say a thing like that. If people want to be at peace and stay together, they will find a way. That is what John J. says; he is our new bishop at Pleasant Valley. The Lord will show us the way wherein our steps can be made safe and sure. Our church group needed to divide because we had not space enough to worship in each other's homes, not even in these biggest, two-story ones. Since last fall the lines are drawn by manner of geography. Those of us close to Berlin have formed a district with John J.; we got to keep the Pleasant Valley name.

The other group took the name Walnut Creek Church, over near to New Carlisle. I would have liked to be in John M.'s church—he has godly eyes—but Paul was strong to stay with John J. His middle initial is for his father, Joseph, John M.'s brother, if I have it right. I doubt there is ten year's difference in age. Judith says the Walnut Creek group is larger and has more of a progressive spirit. I do not like it when Paul makes a fuss about the differences. Some things are better left unsaid. There is no need to dwell on splinters when there is wood to cut.

• • •

We almost lost Judith to erysipelas! What an ugly word. It goes through my head like a bad rhyme: erysipelas, hairy-gipelas. My whole life was nearly turned upside down. Last week she showed me her arms, both of them mottled with a red rash. I thought she had brushed against a stinging bush, but she knew not where that might have happened. When the rash did not go away, I mixed sheep tallow and scrapings from an elderberry bush. Paul collected duck droppings for me. Momma always said to use from the goose, but here we have none. I stood on my legs long enough to mix these three: the tallow, the scrapings, the droppings. Then I rubbed the salve carefully over Judith's arms. She said it burned mightily, but she was willing to try any remedy, for she suffered so much itch.

For the next several days her condition improved slowly, and we all took more ease. But of a sudden one night, she tossed in her bed. A fever wracked her body. Paul called me from my sleep; I have never seen him as frenzied. He reminded me of Christian, gnawing on bones when our David died. We put a lamp to Judith's body and saw that the red had returned, only this time in streaks up and down her arms.

My throat felt clogged. I offered to strike fire on her head. Since I had borne twins I thought it worth a try. I struck Paul's corn knife against a piece of flintstone which I held over Judith's head. Two times in two hours I did this repeatedly; then again the next day. My arms were not strong enough to make long sparks, but I did as best I could. It was not until later that I learned the twins must be boys, not girls.

Judith took a turn downward with heavy vomiting, and Paul announced he was going to fetch the *braucher*. In my disordered condition I thought no further; all I cared was that someone come who could restore Judith. Not until they walked in the door at dusk did I realize that Paul had gone to fetch Reuben Hershberger. Here I had seen Yost at Lydia's funeral in March and now, two months later, Reuben walked into our house. For almost forty years I had not seen either one. I left Judith's side and shrank into the background with Paul's boys. I found a chair.

Reuben walked slowly, but as one who has been called. He removed his hat and threw his brown hunting jacket on the table. I stared at the jacket. It could not be the same one that was disputed forty years ago, but it was made in the same fashion. Reuben's hair has turned to whiteness; his cheeks look fuller and he has a belly. But he has nothing of Yost's frailty.

"Yes, this is wildfire," he said, as he examined Judith's arms. "A bad case," he added, pulling a skein of red woolen yarn from his leather bag. It looked to be a good strain of yarn, but I have never made a red coverlet. He proceeded to take careful measurements with the yarn, first over Judith's head, then across her chest and limbs. All the time he mumbled words, low and solemn. I stretched my neck forward to catch what he said. It sounded like:

Fluck and brand, in the night
Fluck and brand, go in the night.

Part of me wanted to warn Paul that this might be Evil, but I could not interfere. What would I do without Judith? I did not want to take her place with Paul. I heard Reuben's scratchy voice:

. . . in the night . . . in the night . . .
Fluck and brand, come no more.

He held the yarn—very good quality, I am sure of it—between his thumb and forefinger, first one hand, then the other. His hands moved swiftly like long-legged spiders, making knots as he measured. I have never seen the like; the fire seemed to draw out of Judith's body in red strands. I have always been certain that Evil comes at night. Now I watched as Evil departed at night. I gasped when I heard Reuben say:

God the Father, God the Son, and
God the Holy Ghost, Judith Hostetler, Amen.

I clutched my hand to my mouth as he repeated the same words two more times and then walked slowly to the fireplace. The way he said Judith's name brought goose bumps. He did not hurry but held the yarn high above the crackling logs. "Tame fire," he said, "take away wildfire." My eyes strained to see; the yarn began to smoke. Slowly it weakened and broke into pieces, dropping into ashes. No one said a word. Obadiah had disappeared outside.

Finally Reuben backed away from the fire, rubbing his hands against each other as if they retained disease. "That should do it," he said, rubbing and rubbing and rubbing. "Call me if this needs to be repeated."

Paul took Reuben's hand in both of his and shook it like a handle, but said no words. I remember times of fright when I could not speak. Paul's stump of a hand rested against Reuben's. Reuben looked uncomfortable and glanced around to find his jacket.

I was overcome—Judith would live!—so much so that I lurched up toward Reuben, extending my hand. "*Danke, danke, danke.* You do not remember. I am Polly from back in Somerset County. I have grown fat. A sister to Eliza, once married to Yost. Now I make coverlets." I babbled, my hand still extended. "I have my own sheep."

I wanted to touch him, but I thought Reuben flinched as he narrowed his dark eyes on me. Paul had let go, but Reuben did not seek to shake my hand. He tugged at his beard as if more wildfire needed burning. His long, white eyebrows curled wildly above his eyes. I dropped my hand to my side, rubbing my dress. I had blundered. Reuben did not look angry nor friendly. He only looked as if he had suffered much.

"Yes, I remember," he said slowly, "hearing of you." He picked up his hunting jacket as gingerly as a hunting knife. "You live here?"

"Yes," I said, trying to swallow. Then the words rushed out in short gasps. "Judith is my sister-in-law. My Christian died. Paul's brother. I moved to Ohio. Leah, my baby, has moved back. All my children live far away." My mouth was dry. "Paul and Judith took me in. A lonely sheep." Obadiah banged the door when he came back in. I wished I had stayed sitting in the chair. "I did not know Paul would fetch you," I blurted.

"Does it matter?" Reuben asked, his white eyebrows twisting like gnarled tree roots.

I wanted to grab his arm. "I have lost five of my own," I said. "I could not bear to lose Judith." My *danke, danke* turned to sobs. My legs ached and I sat myself down. I do not know why I expected sympathy.

He tied his belt slowly, reached for his hat, and spoke deliberately. "We all have our sorrows." Then he turned to Paul and said, "I go wherever I am called." Paul said nothing but walked Reuben to the door.

I remembered Judith, left alone, unchecked since the yarn had burned. I scootched my body out of the chair again. The boys crowded around her also. Her mouth was set slightly ajar, but her chest moved up and down. I grabbed her hand and squeezed hard; I did not want her to sleep too deeply. I touched the wrinkled skin on Judith's arms. I rubbed as if I could make it smooth. The fiery redness seemed already less bright.

I wish I had taken more caution with Reuben. I wish I had kept my name silent. I do not think he liked me. I am certain he saw my hand reaching. John J. may ask for an accounting with regard to our exchange. But it was Paul who fetched Reuben. Yet I wanted to touch him. To give thanks for Judith, to take the sadness from his eyes. Two brothers in two months!

4.
ℱRANEY
July 1849

I love to walk outside in the evening and feel the dampness of grass and earth on my bare feet. I do not like the sharp rocks and straw stubble of the fields, but the paths in my garden are hard and smooth. When I walk outside, I find refreshment from the summer heat after the sun has set, but while there is yet light enough to see. Clothes stick to my body when I am inside our cabin; there is little air to circulate and my kitchen becomes a tomb of stifling heat. When I open the door and leave it ajar, I end up battling flies in the pudding. Aaron, my baby of five, takes my hand as we walk through the rows of flowers.

"What color is this?" I ask, pointing to a bright zinnia. They are just beginning to bloom.

"Red," he says.

"And what is this?" I touch a lighter shade.

"Red."

"Now, Aaron, are these the same color?" I slap at a mosquito.

"No," he says, giggling. He misses on purpose, to hear me explain.

"Remember pink? This is a *pink* zinnia."

"Stink pinnia," he says and giggles.

"Aaron, you are a little *knix-knux.*" I squeeze his hand. When I am with my grown boys, Noah and Daniel, and their wives, I feel old in my bones, but when I walk with Aaron, I am young again. We circle through red and white salvia, pass marigolds in two shades of yellow, and stop at the petunias. "Stinky tunias," Aaron says. He touches the blooms and then pinches his nose tight with his fingers.

"Look at the daisies. Which do you like better, the white ones with yellow centers or the yellow with black buttons?" Another mosquito buzzes at my ear.

"Black buttons," he says, "back bluttons." I wish all choices came as easily and with as little complication.

We reach the row of gladiolus, their lower blossoms unfolding on long, slender stems. Anna gave me of her extra bulbs: pink, white, orange, yellow, and a deep, deep red, all with leaves like swords. Aaron tugs on my arm, but I am not ready to move on. The older I get, the more I love to linger on the lips of a beautiful flower, the more I cherish the tiny arms and dainty fingers of my grandson. How easily I forget how small they begin. The beauty of all God's creation. I cannot get my fill. Aaron runs ahead and will mash the cucumber vines if I do not reach him in time.

"Aaron," I call sharply. "Do you see the celery? The pretty green feathers?" He stops, swivels on his feet, and looks around so that I have time to catch up. I intended to mound up the celery rows, but Peter said it was not necessary.

We have planted more celery than usual. Mary is too young, but I cannot stop her. From the look of rapture on her face, I tell Peter we need to make provisions for a wedding feast. She has all the sparkle and gleam, and not one practical bone in her. She has always been in a hurry—too hasty with the broom in the corners—as if she thinks her life will be cut short. She is quick with the butter churn too, but one day soon, all will be changed and she will be gone to her man. I am not ready. Peter scratches his back on the round edge of a log and looks content. I did not question when the boys left home and married; that is the natural way. I did not feel the tug. But with Mary, I am not ready. I have had nineteen years to prepare, and still, I want to hang on. We named her after Jonas' Mary, and I have thought to pass on to our Mary the beautiful drawing that the other Mary gave me when I married. The two bright birds with their beaks almost touching. But I am not ready to part with it either.

Peter says I should rejoice that death has not laid its scourge on our children, rather than pine when the young want to fly from the nest. He is right. But with Mary my work is not complete. I must take pains to teach Veronica, my girl-woman who reads by candlelight as Noah used to do. And Levi, my silent one who will be twelve this month, but who broods like an old man. When I ask a question, he gives one word answers: No. Barn. Butter. Perhaps. He mopes, even as Jonas did on my wedding day. I do not know where his downward spirit comes from.

Aaron points to the biggest watermelon hiding in the foliage and starts the rhyme they all learned as children:

> *Ains, tsway, drei,*
> *Hicker, hocker, hei.*

That is as far as he will go. He listens as I say the rest, but he will not repeat after me:

> *Tsucker oof'm brei,*
> *Sols oof'm schpeck.*

Hawna, gay weck
Do shtinksht nuch hinkel-dreck.

"Now it is your turn, Aaron." I reach up under my sleeve to scratch and wonder how a mosquito found its way. I have welts on my stomach too.

"Hicker, hocker, hei," he says and looks at me, wrinkling his nose. Noah was the quickest one to learn and could repeat the whole verse without prompting. I thought he might make a teacher, but he is content with farming. He and Daniel have more acres than Peter ever thought possible.

I am the dreamer, even as Father said long ago. Now it is a piano I want, not a bridge. A piano with a little round stool and beautiful carvings. It would be an extra expense and Peter wonders where we would put it, but I have heard one played at Solomon King's and again at John Schwartzendruber's and think it has a wondrous sound. I believe I could teach myself; Jonas claimed I had music in my ears. Then I could teach Levi and bring him out of his doldrums. Peter says they had a piano in the Old Country. I do not mention that it did his ear no good. They also had a music box on their mantel. On occasion Peter still takes out his harmonica and plays a jerky tune. Levi perks up and begs for a chance to play; he can pick out a hymn as if the melody grows from within. The piano would be much better because it does not have that scratchy, tinny sound.

Our church frowns on musical instruments, but I see no harm in them. Peter says I ask too many questions. I say that owning a piano is not the same as drinking in a public inn. Not by far. I do not mean to flaunt the rules, but a piano could be a blessing—I would clap my hands—not a hindrance if used for songs of the faith. I do not mean at worship, but with our family. I would rather that people could choose and decide the harm or benefit for themselves, instead of needing the church to show the way on every little invention. It is Abraham who thinks he must show. A piano would be like my zinnias, a small relief against the hardships. Even against this hot summer with its mold and mildew and mosquitoes. Peter need not worry that I would sit daydreaming on my little stool all day, plunking keys and forgetting to snip the beans. I am willing to wait until after the wedding to make purchase so the piano will not be a hindrance to anyone present. As Peter still says, that would be less *obstrusive*. Not that we know for certain about the wedding.

Nothing fills me with such dread as to hear at the end of a Sunday service, "The brethren and sisters are to remain seated." My stomach growls like Father's used to, and I scarce can sit still. I want to flee outside with Aaron, but I keep my hands folded in my lap. Some people complain of unfairness; others see wisdom in all the deliberation. With John M. we do not hear these matters of discipline brought as often as do those in other churches. He preaches what is important, reminds us to think on humility, and gives scant attention to the gnats which becloud some ministers' views.

From what I hear, Henry Stutzman's church is not the place for me. And to think that he is Katharina's brother. Recently she seems more severely drawn. I believe it is more than the heat that makes the bags under her eyes sag. It must be an awkwardness for her to be caught between a husband and a brother. Several families at Farmerstown have had to confess to owning a piano. Even Levi Speicher, the very one who gave me maple sugar candy as a child. He was forced to get rid of the offending object and make confession before he was restored to full fellowship. That is entirely too much to-do about a piano. Henry Stutzman's line of thought is that since neither Jesus nor the Apostle Paul mentioned musical instruments, they should be forbidden. That is sufficient for Henry's conviction. But for me, if a piano is not mentioned in the Bible, then it must not be a problem. Peter warns me that I might feel proud to have a piano in our home. Well, I would be excited and happy.

I try to imagine Levi Speicher making confession, standing with his hands clasped in front, his shoulders slumped, acknowledging that, yes, he had owned a piano. I hear him plead meekly for the forgiveness of all, promising to walk circumspectly. I cannot see this aright, for in my mind Levi still has the voice of a young man. I see him as my sister Rachel's beloved; yet he must be almost as old as Father was in his late years. I know Jonas has rounded the bend of sixty. Abraham likes to say that we do not sin off in a corner by ourselves; if we have offended God, then we have offended the members as well. It is bad enough to get Abraham started on restitution, but then Peter gets mixed up and calls it *retribution*, and we have to get that straightened out. Abraham says a good confession cleanses us from within, just as the body needs to empty itself of waste. I do not care to hear the details of another's bile, but then, neither do I rejoice anymore when Abraham comes to visit.

With Jonas it is just the opposite. He will not pay us a visit. We were to his home in Wayne County years ago—our little nibbler, Veronica, was our baby at the time—but he will not come our way. We sent special word each time when Noah, and then when Daniel, married. No reply. If only Jonas' Mary could convince him to come for our Mary's day. I am certain that his Mary is not the one to hide her face. Years ago she said that Jonas kept to himself and had little to say, even between the two of them. He would only talk at length with Mary's father, Shem. And then about church matters. Jonas knows we are not getting any spryer; even Peter is forty-seven.

Any one of us could receive our summons at any time. Now should be the time to renew acquaintance, not be off by ourselves.

Father would be very, very sad if he knew how his children have drifted apart. We hear nothing from David back in Somerset. I do not know what prompts one child to follow one path and a brother or sister to take the opposite direction.

Peter says I have become very loose about the rules; he says even in the Old Country they might kick me out. Well, I see no purpose in this weary pursuit of coming to understanding over every jot and tittle. What good does the ban do? What happens to the church's soul when it scrapes the dirt from its feet? *Hinkel-dreck*. Keeping the cracks clean. Peter says I get too worked up. I will admit, I have scratched my ankles until the blood comes. Do these ministers never tire of their deliberations? I believe Abraham gives no thought to what this standing guard does to *his* innards.

When members disagree, it follows that the ordained brethren will have differences. Some say it is the other way around, that dissension starts with the ministers. Whichever way, it seems a pity. We only hear snatches—Peter among the menfolks—and do not know, in fact, what all has transpired. Several years ago a minister back in Mifflin County—close to where Jonas lived those years in his Half Moon Valley—was silenced. Some say this minister used seventy-two unnecessary words in one sermon. I cannot help but wonder who did the counting. Abraham would be one to volunteer. After the silencing people were still not at peace. Much strife followed. Some thought it the right decision; others said, no. The disagreement festered like the sore on Peter's shin that oozes for months. This spring that same Pennsylvania church asked for two senior bishops from here in Holmes County to help them settle matters. Who should go but these brothers by marriage, our own John M. and this Henry Stutzman. Plus two other ministers.

We do not know if they rode horseback as a group or shared a wagon. Peter shies away from asking questions. Henry wanted the silenced minister to be reinstated, whereas Brother John M. spoke strongly *against* the minister. I told Peter there is more to this story than unnecessary words spoken. John M. must carry great weight because the congregation decided to continue the silencing. Yet John M. always preaches reconciliation. He was recently called to Indiana and helped bring about unity over rules and regulations in the churches there. Confusion abounds. No wonder the bags sit heavily under Katharina's eyes.

I still hold my breath that Abraham will do nothing about our friendliness—over twenty years now—with Reuben. Peter says that is another reason to go slow about the piano. We do not want to give my brother a second grievance, or I might be the one made to stand, looking sad like Levi Speicher. Abraham has always insisted that Reuben is a heavy drinker. I have never seen it. These stories get a start and there is no stopping them. Anna and Reuben sit on their porch, rocking back and forth, outside the church all these years. What must they think? I feel such alarm when I look on Anna's gnarled fingers. I sent my Veronica and Levi over to help shell peas this spring, and what did Anna do but send back a strawberry pie. I cannot see how she pinched the edges, unless Reuben did the crust. Yet she never makes complaint, not even when the coons got half their corn last year. I tell Peter to remind me when I am old not to be a fussy one. Not even when I have lost all my teeth like Father or scratched all my skin raw.

All these church troubles make me feel old. It is far better to put my mind to what may transpire this fall. I want all to be in readiness for Mary. If that is what happens. Peter will

410

need to build an extra table so we have work space enough for butchering chickens. And I will put extra care into the yellow mums out front. The maples, our beautiful trees that have grown up with our children, will have shed their colors by November. Mary could climb them with ease when she was little, even in her skirts. Now that Peter has cut off the lower limbs, Levi can only reach to climb by taking a big leap, grabbing hold, and walking his legs up the trunk. By the time Aaron wants to climb, Peter may need to give him a lift. With trees I do not mind their being out of reach, but with Mary I am not yet willing.

5.

J O N A S

December 1851

*M*y left eye has its flutter back. Not a constant movement, but enough to trouble. I sneaked a look in
Mary's hand mirror and saw that it is not the eye flickering,
but the lid that covers the eye. I do not know why it behaves
thus, nor how to make it stop. All these years. Mary says she
has never seen the like; she thinks I should just say the word
and the twitch will cease. That is easy for her to say. Even
when the lid tires of its jiggle and gives me rest, I know not
when it will start again.

These mirrors. They should be done away with. All of
them. I am surprised that Shem has not objected. Mary
nags at me to burn the brush pile behind the house—she
calls it an eyesore—but this mirror is a much more serious
abomination. What would possess a woman to hold a glass
in front of her face and look first sideways, then frontward?
Some even have two mirrors; one to hold in front and the
other behind. What is there to manage in the back? For me,
the back of my head is the only place where I still have hair,
but I do not need to see it. I can feel if need be. It is vanity
to need to look. I had to force myself to glance long enough

412

to take in the measure of my eye. I did not like what I saw. Not at all.

I looked at my teeth, but only briefly. What a dark cavern is set forth in the mouth. No wonder I never cared to look at Father's. The teeth on my left side all along the bottom are the troublemakers, setting my whole mouth on edge. They seem to have raised themselves higher than they ought, causing a grinding on the upper teeth. Mary says I grind in bed; she does not know that she rattles. I move my index finger back and forth on my teeth to soothe them, but it does not help. I have no patience for anything more to go wrong. My eyelid, these teeth, my hair falling out. The rats.

My nerves were worn to a frazzle at the butchering. It was a cold, windy day, threatening rain or even snow. I dressed with an extra overcoat, but the wind still found its way inside my bones. Every time Shem's rifle sounded, my body could not help but give a start. I knew the shot was coming; my muscles tensed. I knew the hog would go down in a heap; still, my body took its lurch. I wanted to disappear in the woods, but all the menfolks gathered for the killings. Shem would have noticed my absence.

Every year for the past five, Shem has gathered his three children who live nearby for this hog-butchering. There is no acceptable way *not* to be present. Shem was as excited as a five-year-old riding a horse for the first time. He walked around all day with the big grin and found no time to chew on his fingers. We butchered seven hogs, the biggest and orneriest. Now Mary has hams and shoulders curing in salt water; we have stuffed sausages hanging in the smokehouse. That is the good part: our own supply of pork for the winter.

But my Stephen did the stabbing. As soon as the hog squealed, down from the first shot, maybe a second, Stephen jabbed it with his knife. Right under the neck. I stared at my flesh as he thrust in the knife. I turned away. Blood gushed onto the ground. I busied myself, bringing more wood to throw under the kettles of boiling water. Child's work.

Stephen has never seemed like my son, but I have not kicked him out. I could not manage my crops without his muscle. He is more boisterous than the roosters; he chatters away like Jeremiah did as a youngster. Yippity-yap. Shem did not seem bothered at all, not even when Stephen drove his knife like a conqueror and slapped his thigh, crowing with glee, "Got us another one!" I could not help but think on my father's hogs that got away when I was a lad. For the first time I was glad for their escape. I could not dwell on the destruction—too much death— even when pulling bristles from scalded hogs. I know we must get our sustenance somewhere, and Shem says it is right that man has been given dominion over the beast of the field. But the unseemly unpleasantness: one beast's life taken for the benefit of another. I could not stomach it.

Mary goes about, overtaken with thoughts of death. Weeks ago she insisted that we make arrangements for a burial plot. She has lost two brothers in two years back in Pennsylvania. She says we must make preparation, or death may come as a thief in the night. I am not anywhere near ready to die. Must she remind me? I see people my age succumbing as a commonplace, but I do not have my house in order. My life hangs like a string of sausages.

In my youth, death was something that visited the old, with exceptions, of course, for a dread encounter with a catamount or an untimely disease, such as what struck Mother. The women wailed all the more when death struck the victim with his shoes on, as if death had somehow bent the rules. In my long middle years, death came as an unwanted intrusion: a distasteful memory, a pesky fly in the house that eluded my hands. I was quick to put the grave from my mind; I had things to do to ensure a living. But now the bottom of the hourglass is nearly full. I cannot keep pace with the hoe as I once did. I spill my hot tea on occasion. Too much shake.

With all the unseemly tumult at Oak Grove we did not know where to look for a cemetery plot. There has been much deviation from the true regulations of the Amish faith. Some of us had to leave in order to save ourselves. We are fortunate to have Shem giving leadership to our small, faithful group, even though he sometimes forgets his thought in the middle of a sentence. Scrub Ridge Congregation is our name. Mary does not like the sound of it, but at least we are not subjected to faithlessness on every hand. David Gingerich gives Shem help with the preaching, and I do the best I can as *Vorsinger*. "I am not young any more," I say to Shem. My voice surprises me at times; I have not air enough to hold the notes. The high ones escape me. I waver with uncertainty, even as I did the first time Father turned and nodded to me. No ease. None at all.

"As the Lord gives strength, so you are able," Shem says. Sometimes he gives little thought. He says words, but his mind is elsewhere. Perhaps with George Keim. I should be glad Shem is preoccupied; he has not mentioned the flutter of my eyelid.

Keim has caused endless trouble. I see no intent on his part but divisive quarreling. The disruption began when his name was placed in the lot at Oak Grove. But before matters could proceed, he raised a big ruckus by saying that if he were made minister, he would baptize new members in the creek, not in a house. In the creek. We have always baptized by pouring. We have always baptized *inside* the house where the church service takes place. What is even harder to swallow: Oak Grove granted him permission to carry out his plan, *if* he became a minister. When I heard of such, I knew the lot would not fall to him. Not with such deviation. This matter first

reared itself back in Mifflin County where Verena resides—
she has fire on every side—but now Keim asks people *here* to
entertain this same recklessness. Something failed mightily—
a true sign of our falling away—for this Keim selected the
book with the paper. Soon after, he was made a bishop.

There have been other signs. We had little choice but to
leave Oak Grove. Shem works a piece of skin in his mouth;
his jaw strains forward. The preaching there leaves too much
room for individual understanding. These Mennonites who
come, they have lost their souls. They follow after business interests, becoming quite wealthy, even collecting interest when
they loan money to others in their church. They have always
been susceptible to the gaudy appearance of success; then our
Amish youth get hoodwinked.

Two of my children have seen the light and stick with us:
Adam and his three little ones and Elizabeth with her five.
Along with their mates of course. But these other four,
Stephen, Mary, Dorothy, Simeon, my younger shoots, these
remain outside the fold. Two of them have left the Amish
church, caught up in the shadowy distractions of innovation;
the other two do not affiliate with any group. How they can
take such a lax attitude, I do not understand. Stephen, the one
who wielded the butcher knife with such gusto, has made no
effort to seal his vows with the church. He is thirty years old
and makes no pretense of looking for a wife. It is as if he
snubs commitment, preferring instead a life devoted unto
himself. It is beyond the pale. Unseemly. I have not pruned as
I should have. Father would be overcome with sadness.

Now this latest blow. Not so much a waywardness but a
sore tribulation. Word has reached us that our Verena, back
East in our Half Moon Valley, has stepped her whole foot full
into the fire. She could have tested to see how it feels with one
toe singed. But no. She has married a man with seven chil-

dren. The last two are but babies, a boy and girl twin. She has chosen aright, following our Amish ways, but no one should adopt that kind of a family load.

We hear of another fellow back in Pennsylvania who got so taken with these new railroads, buying rights-of-way for new sets of tracks throughout his county, that he became embroiled in politics. There is talk that by this time next year, tracks will be laid for passenger trains to come right into our own county. I cannot imagine a black, smoking beast snorting and puffing that close to my land. Shem says to prepare for the worst. He says all of this was foretold in the book of Revelation where it mentions smoke coming out of a pit—like unto a great furnace—with enough blackening so as to darken all of the air, even the sun. Shem says these trains are a forerunner of the end times. Devouring the earth. Another sign.

In spite of all the wickedness at Oak Grove, Mary and I decided to be interred with many from that group. I cannot explain it, except that we had few choices. I believe Shem questions our association. When Mary and I went looking for a burial plot, we were swayed by the peace and repose that the surrounding trees afforded at the Plank Cemetery, over on the north edge of Wooster. A welcome break from the wintry wind. Our reasoning may have been faulty, but we have done nothing to overturn our decision. There is awkwardness aplenty, riding away from the spot where our flesh will rot and decay. Even Mary had nothing to say on the ride home.

Another thing. She has badgered me of late that we should visit Franey on a Sunday. "We are getting old," she says, as if I have not noticed my tremble, her white hairs.

I shake my head and say, "Then we would need to go to Abraham's too."

"Why is that a problem?" she asks, squinting at me. I say nothing more. I do not need to explain that Abraham talks too much and asks too many questions. It is enough to live with Stephen's yap.

Last week Mary came to my aid when I encountered the rats. I had fallen asleep while shelling corn—I often sit down, for it is a tiresome task—and when I woke there was a gray and black scurrying all around me. I had propped myself against the wall of the barn to take my rest. My stillness must have given the beasts reason to think I did not exist; their nibbling and gnawing and squeaking finally woke me up. A squeaking like unto a shrieking din. I thrashed so mightily— Mary says I yelled as if a gray wolf threatened to grab my neck—that she came running. By the time she got there, the rats had resumed their places of hiding. She thought I merely dreamed.

All these reasons to clench my teeth: the rats, my eyelid, Stephen, the smoking monster that clatters on wheels of iron. It is all too much. I do not like any of it. Not at all.

6.

$\mathcal{R}$ EUBEN

September 1852

$\mathbf{Y}$es, it is true; I trudge up the hill each day to visit Anna. I do the talking and she listens. The hill begins with an easy rise but gets steep at the top. I puff and stand with my mouth hanging open until my breath comes back. Off to the west I see my large valley where my corn stands ready to be picked in another month. Black crows swoop among the rows but do no harm. I have watched a lone hawk circle and then fly off into the woods. Always the same hawk, never more than one at a time, flying with steadiness and grace as if the soaring comes from within.

That is the way Anna's soul made its departure, soaring on wings held with the right tautness. She left one afternoon when I was out pulling sourdock in the fields; it has now been three weeks. Her body lay on the bed in full repose, as if angels had ministered. She must have laid down to rest, and while her body was off its guard, her soul took its leave. The quiet and peace about her brought comfort; I could not find tears until I touched her cold body. I knelt beside the bed and held her crippled hand to my head. No more pain. I saw her perched with the songbirds at the top of the tallest tree.

Her death did not surprise me. All summer she had little strength for garden work or kitchen duties. She would go outside with a hoe, only to come inside again soon. I would find her sitting or resting. She often held her hand on her chest. I asked if she had pain, and she quickly withdrew her hand, said only that something raced inside. I believe she was afraid I would attempt another cure. It is a sore point that she did not trust my *brauching* when it came to her own health. I could not change her mind. Neither could I ever change her thinking about us being husband and wife. We were warm bodies for each other in the winter, but that is all. Now even that has been taken.

The church gave no assistance with her flight, but I believe she found her way alone to the bosom of God. How else to explain the peacefulness that spreads through my body when I ascend to her gravesite? The fresh mound of dirt begins to settle now that we have had a few hard rains. Thorny locusts drape their low branches all around, and a soft wind often moves through the trees, whispering through the tall grass. I hear the voice when I quiet myself, lying prone beside her grave. I have pounded the ground with my fists aplenty, but when I tire of my ranting I hear the voice, "All will be well; all, well."

The first time I heard such I lifted my head and looked back and around to see who had joined me. No one was there. No one is ever there. The voice comes through the grass; that is where I hear it. I do not hear it when I sit with my ankles crossed in front of me and face the setting sun. I do not hear it when I prop myself in the nook of a low tree branch and sit thus waiting. I only hear "All will be well" when I am flat on the grass, when I am as close as I can get to my Anna. There is no reason to believe the promise, but I do.

All these years she stood beside me. When I raged, she brought me calm. When I scorned the possibility of light, she stayed steadfast. When I gave myself over to drink, she chided. Now I do not see how I can go on. Or why I should bother. I tell Bevy that I am strong, but I am not. I know where there are bushes loaded with poison berries. I am sixty-seven and have no desire to reach Anna's seventy-four years. I would rather go to be with her. I have lived on her strength. Lived, because she believed. I would prefer to be reinstated—if some bishop would take care for my soul—but if that is not possible, I will watch for the same hawk that helped her find entrance.

I have come to rely on my children. Jacob offered that I could live with them; his oldest is nearly grown; his youngest, but two. I told him I would rather stay on my own as long as I can. I may need Bevy to scrub my clothes from time to time, but there is not much work there. I have fixed my own chamomile for years. With Anna's crippled hands nearly useless, I fixed succotash all summer. When the corn turned too hard for roasting ears, Anna taught me how to grate it and stir it into our mush. I baked it into johnny-cakes.

Bevy's minister came to our farm to say the last words. I had first thought of asking John M. Yoder, for Peter mentions his name with great respect. But Bevy and Michael introduced this man of Swiss Reformed persuasion, and I was well satisfied. We gathered at the top of the hill, the very site Anna had chosen. She always said, "I want to be lifted up when I am gone." So lift her up we did. Not I, in truth, but Jacob and Bevy's man shouldered the weight of the box while the biggest grandsons gave assistance. Peter and Franey did not need to come to my aid, but come they did. One or the other has been here every day since. I do not know how they ignore the church's teaching, nor how they do so without adverse consequences, but I am grateful.

Franey has become like a daughter, although she is older than Bevy. She came the very first night with her condolence, a cherry cobbler or some such, and yesterday brought a pan of turnips. She and Peter even trudged up the hill with us—Franey had to stop as often as I to rest—and spread their wings over our poor, sorrowing family. I told Peter later to take some brace bits for his barn. He insisted that he was the one who owed the debt, that I had done the favor last winter with Franey. She went through a severe valley of illness, but good has come from it. Her daughter, Veronica, only seventeen, takes great interest in matters pertaining to healing. She reminds me of Bevy at that age—a quick learner and eager—the way she leaps up two porch steps in one bound. Their eyes are the same gray-blue color as well, but Veronica has a bit of the red in her hair.

Franey had been subjected to severe headaches for a matter of weeks and asked Veronica to cut some of the thickness from her hair so it would not hang with such heaviness. When this brought no relief, Veronica came calling. In truth, she came begging. She was all in a frenzy, her hair pulled back tight, her eyes about to pop. I asked what they had done with the cut hair, and Veronica said she had thrown it out the back door. I shook my head and explained that if birds pick up hair cuttings and use it to line their nests, the headaches are likely to continue, even worsen. It was too late, of course, to advise that cut hair should be burned.

Veronica pleaded to know if there was anything else to try. Sometimes the girl locked her fingers tight; sometimes she tapped her fists together in an anxious jitter. Anna did her best to calm Veronica. The Troyers had already dipped a cloth in vinegar, wrung it out, and bound it over Franey's forehead, but to no avail. Then I thought to ask Veronica if she knew what day of the week she had been born on.

"Why, Sunday," she said. "Momma always calls me her Sabbath baby."

"That is good," I said. "I will go with you and show you what to do." I could tell that she thought I took much too long in getting my coat and boots, that I moved much too slowly.

I explained to Franey, huddled on their day bed under a gray blanket, that she was fortunate to have Veronica. A person born on Sunday has the gift to cure headaches.

Franey held her head rigid, her eyes fixed on the ceiling, as if to move an inch might make her head shatter. "Please end this bursting," she said. She is such a tiny woman; it would not take much to knock her over. "My head has been set to explode for too long; all that is inside pounds to get out. I vomit to empty my stomach, but I cannot rid my head of this corruption." Franey refused to look at me directly but added, "If Veronica is my angel of mercy, so be it."

I looked around for Peter, but he was nowhere in sight. I gave instruction, telling Veronica how to place her hands on Franey's forehead with her fingertips touching in the middle. The young girl's hands moved jerkily. I explained how to draw them slowly, the one to the left, the other to the right, across the forehead and temples, down behind the ears, finally out from the head into space. At first she was too gentle, afraid to cause pain. But I instructed her to exert pressure. The proper movement soon came with greater ease. In truth, it came from within her. I know now how Aunt Barbli felt when she first taught me. Watching Veronica's hands move, I was enraptured with her natural gift.

I told Veronica to repeat the entire movement so that it was done a total of three times. I also taught her the most simple *brauch* words: "Christ's wounds were never bound. God, the Father; God, the Son; God, the Holy Ghost." When Veronica finished, her lips trembled; she clasped her hands in her lap to stop the shaking. Her shoulders slumped forward. I put my rough hand on her shoulder, "You have a sacred gift, Veronica. Guard it; use it well. Let no man speak ill of you because of your healing." She nodded and lowered her head. She put the back of her hand to her mouth to stop the trembling.

The next day she came to my house, leaping up the front steps in her long brown skirts. She said that within an hour of the *brauching*, Franey had roused and asked for broth. In that brief time the pounding had already taken some ease. Veronica's young face looked full of pleasure and fright, as if she wanted to smile and could not.

"What will I do?" she asked, breathless.

"Whatever you choose," I said. "You can hide your gift under a bushel basket or you can bring relief. Some will find fault." I spoke sternly, as I would if it were Bevy. "Many will criticize, until they need you. You must decide whether or not to do. You will suffer either way." Veronica's face twisted with uncertainty. "But you will also be blessed. It is a gift from God." I watched her trudge slowly, head down, across the road and down their long lane.

Once Franey's cure was accomplished, I wondered what the parents would think of their daughter. I did not want to lose friends over leading Veronica down a narrow path. Anna fretted that this would be the dagger that silenced the neighborliness. She kept asking, "Where was Peter? Why was he nowhere to be found?" But once Franey was rid of her headaches, we heard nought but gratefulness. She told Anna, "The Lord has seen fit to bestow Veronica with the healing touch. Who am I to question the Almighty's wisdom? Perhaps she will make a midwife yet."

Peter shook my hand after Franey's healing. I do not doubt his gratitude. He has said nothing, though, about Veronica, so he may have reservations about her taking up *brauching*. I do not know what he was accustomed to in the Old Country. He has not interfered, however, when Veronica has asked if she can go with me when I am called to give healing. We make an odd pair, riding in my wagon. She fidgets with her hands, picking dirt from under her fingernails. I am sure there are those who talk. She observes my manner and methods and learns my words. She is gentle and speaks softly. While Veronica watches, she often rubs the feet of the person I am attending. She understands much about healing and comfort without being told. Aunt Barbli would be pleased that I have found the right person to carry on the work.

Some day soon I will lie beside my Anna, and there will be no grass to separate. I have thought of going again to Yost; I have considered how I might bypass his woman. Outfox her. Anna would caution me to be patient. As if forty years is not long enough. My anger towards Yost has made its home within me, a dull knife. I had thought that old age might break him down, but I fear he thinks not at all on me.

I do not understand the Almighty turning His back to my pleas, refusing to supply Anna's promise of light. But I am too old to rail against deaf ears. If I were to meet the Lord today, I know not what He would require of my soul. Anna always said that His ways were past finding out. But I do not think His judgment throne would be as hard to reach as the church's.

My Anna. She is not here to warm my bed. She is not here to listen for geese with me from the porch. She is not here to remind me that my worth does not depend on how others regard me. But I know she watches my valley with me. That is why I go up the hill every day. To hear her voice. To soar with her spirit. To listen for her hope.

7.

JOHN M.

June 1853

*H*alf a century plus one. How we mark our lives by the passing of time. Each day. The years. It has been forty years since I first came to Ohio as a scrawny lad. Over twenty years as a minister; over ten as a bishop. When I was young, I did not notice how long it had been since anything, except my last meal. Then I saw Joseph writing things down. The date that he bought a horse. John J.'s first year in school. His orderliness with records; his disorderliness with ideas. Barbara has shown me his two books full of notes. She is as red-cheeked as ever, even this past winter, but Joseph does poorly. He stays in bed and does not look himself, swollen in the cheeks, jowly. He cannot speak. When I first saw him lying down with his mouth sagging to the side like a broken barn door, I thought him a gray corpse lying with open eyes. He spoke no words, but he grabbed my hand tight. I cannot ask him about where to do the pouring. I cannot ask him why my daughters have no callers. I cannot ask him about those who play tricks with time to gain advantage. I cannot ask him why God does not intervene. But I thanked him for gripping my hand tight. I thanked him and held on.

Not all is grim these days. All manner of newfangled pots and pans show up at the store in New Carlisle. Dishes, both clear and colored glassware. There is no end to what little piece of beauty might bring a light to Katharina's eyes, if only for a moment. I must remember to make purchase by her August birthday. Elizabeth would also like a pretty dish with painted flowers. She was a smart one already when young, reminding me daily of Katharina's approaching birthday, knowing full well that if I remembered the one, I would not forget hers three days later.

Time slips away for my daughters. My two oldest approach thirty, but they remain unattached. Katharina and I do not talk about it anymore. I hope I have done right by them, and that when they are old and I am long gone, they will rise up and call me blessed. Elizabeth seems disconsolate at times; that troubles me. I wonder if she is downhearted from hearing people gossip about me. She would make a good teacher with a sharp head for figures. Barbara always manifests a willing spirit; she adds little touches to all that she sews: white lace on Katharina's blue dress, a fringe on the yellow tablecloth. She has threatened to sew scallops on the legs of my next pair of underwear. She is the age of Katharina when we married. But neither girl glides the way Katharina did when I first came to know her. Both girls gladly help their brothers when new babies come to be cared for. Benjamin has the two little boys down the road, and now Elias has a firstborn with another making entry soon. My Katie is over twenty and wants to move to Indiana, but she has no prospects that I know of. I did not think she would be the one with the wanderlust.

Some say these are evil days for our children to be born into, but I see days of opportunity. Less dreadful toil, for one thing. I do not shirk from hard work—no one has found fault on that score—but neither do I think work is the path to salvation. If a machine will do as well and faster, then go with the machine.

I saw a new manner of giving light when I happened to stop at Peter Troyer's to borrow a second scythe for cutting oats. My son Samuel flexes his muscles around his brother John who is only fourteen; I wanted to stop their feud and keep them both occupied. Samuel is what the world would call an eyeful. As the unexpected sometimes happens, it chanced that Peter's neighbor Reuben Hershberger was paying him a visit when I entered Peter's driveway. Reuben looked anxious when he saw me walk up, as if he sought to hide behind a pile of hay. But Peter showed no haste to cover up and purposely asked another question of Reuben to detain him. Visions of Abraham Zug and Henry Stutzman flashed before me. Even John J. The world wobbled for a moment in front of us, but we stood our ground. I saw no heavenly reason to make feeble excuse about coming another day, and we three proceeded to talk about lamps. I think I can trust Peter that this occasion will go no further. I have been surprised, however, at who turns tattler.

I had heard that Reuben makes lamps, the fat lamp or Betty lamp, as the English call it. But I had refrained from further inquiry. Some of my members might think I nosed about to see who has had exchange with him. I can never be too careful. Most fat lamps are made of iron or, more recently, of tin. Reuben was showing Peter a lamp he had fashioned of brass and cast iron. It had an uncommon shine to it. I can picture the light flickering in it, hanging low from a fireplace mantel, but I do not think Katharina would consider it an appropriate birthday gift. Peter said he had heard from relatives back in Pennsylvania that a new substance, petroleum—sometimes they call it kerosene—is being used in lamps. These are called oil lamps. Peter claimed that this oil replaces the rendered fat, burning with less smell and less smoke. I wonder if this fuel oil might not be dangerous in a house; with time we will know.

My chance meeting with Reuben has made me ponder whether candle-making might be an enterprise for my daughters. Something to give them a boost. Elizabeth would catch on to a trade very fast and could handle the bookkeeping. If we had more sheep- and cattle-raisers in Holmes County, then more tallow would be available and not be as expensive. I am not inclined to bother with bees, but Katharina says the best candles come from beeswax or bayberry wax. If Reuben made metal molds for candles, Elizabeth and Barbara could prepare the wax for dipping. It is foolish that this thought persists—Katharina would laugh if she knew—for it would never be acceptable for my children to be in business with Reuben. People would snoop about—Abraham Zug comes to mind—and find out who made the metal molds. There are no secrets in my life. Well, not many.

Here is Reuben, graying over a deed he has never confessed to. If he committed the crime, of course he should make restitution so his soul can be free. But what if he did no error? He looks more harmless than some who sit in my church. His white eyebrows curl and twist every-which-way, but his eyes show no malice, only suffering. I have my share of rebellious ones in church; I see it in their eyes. They seek to overturn every stone, and often, for no good reason. If the object were to see what manner of moss resides on the underside, I could understand the need to turn upside down. But when people only desire that a black stone be made white or a green leaf be turned red, all for the sake of differentness, then they miss the mark. My Samuel, the one whose young body turns heads, displays this spirit. There is some consolation that Elias also thought the same for a time: "Whatever is cannot be right and must be changed." Those who think thus are as stubborn as the ones at the other end of the bench: "Whatever is is right because it has been right in the past and dare not be changed." Now we have this awful row over the manner of baptism. If only God would intervene.

Henry Stutzman thinks I am on the side of changing everything, but he misunderstands. I try to state my position clearly, but some people distort. Sometimes I think he is not capable of drawing fine distinctions. All is right or all is wrong; there is no in-between for him. If only he were not Katharina's brother. I cannot say to her, "Your brother has a narrow mind," but that is how he sounds when he insists that there must be uniformity of practice. "So there is not envying and division," his voice whines. If someone else said the same, I could let it pass. But Henry is my brother-in-law. This enmity goes far beyond my distaste for his short, stumpy fingers. He is a hangnail that I want to rip off. Yes, we must honor tradition. But we must also test the faith under the light of Scripture, so that what we pass on to our progeny has substance. That appears to be too fine a line for him, especially when it comes to baptism.

Every spring the question of procedure rears up. The quibble is not whether to sprinkle, or pour, or immerse, but *where* to do the pouring. Around Easter-time I asked this year's class of applicants if they wanted to proceed with baptism in the house, or if they wished to wait for warmer weather and have the baptism outside in a stream. They consulted with their parents and the strong preference was to wait. So it was that two weeks ago we gathered on Goose Creek and found a shallow spot where each applicant could kneel on small pebbles in the creek bed. I stood in my high boots in the deeper, cool water with minnows darting around me. My manner of baptizing deviated not from tradition; I bent low, cupping water in my hands three times for each soul seeking baptism for the remission of sins.

Before we began, a cardinal called to its mate in a nearby bush. All of nature seemed fresh, even hushed in the morning's coolness. I heard the drip of nearby springs. The ceremony proceeded with all the order and solemnity that we have when inside a building. All in attendance seemed satisfied. I dare say, all would agree that God's spirit was manifested among us. It is from those who were not there that I hear winds of discord and strife. Why must they be offended at something they did not see, something they were not required to partake in?

Furthermore, word has come from Lancaster County—we still get instruction from the East—let those who want baptism in the house, practice it thus; for those who want to be baptized in a stream, let that practice be acceptable as well. This admonition from the committee of ministers in Pennsylvania, allowing room for both possibilities, upset Henry Stutzman exceedingly. He pointed and wiggled his stubby index finger. He said the word "division" like a shrill blue jay whose nest has been disturbed. I do not concentrate on his meaning; all I see is his waggling finger. Then I am upset with myself for getting distracted. "We are not to be carnal and walking as men," he said. Of course not. What is carnal about baptism in a stream? I do not favor individual expression above everything else, but that is how he distorts. I agree with the Pennsylvania call for openness.

Henry called the ministers' meeting last week. I do not know if I can stomach another one soon. When Katharina asked afterward regarding the proceedings, I had little to say. I believe she knows I detest her brother. She reminds me to regard all men with charity. I want to say, yes, there is charity for all. But me. Her eyes look sad. I have watched her sadness deepen ever since the day I chose the book with the slip of paper. I miss her sparkle, her glide.

I sought for clarity at the meeting, explaining that I do not favor disagreement or strife, but that one way to avoid unhappy results is to allow differences of understanding and practice. I remember making strong my point, "Jesus did not say, 'Be ye baptized in a house.' Nowhere is that recorded." I considered saying it again to make sure that everyone heard. I tried to slow my racing mind. *Ruhig. Sei ruhig.* I looked around the circle at each minister. No one looked me in the eye. Henry's head was down; Abraham's eyes were shut. Johannes Shetler dug at his dirty fingernails with a knife. "How can there be transgression when there is no commandment?" I asked. I did not like my querulous tone. No one responded. Their silence, their bowed heads, spurred me on. I knew I was right. "All we know is that Jesus was baptized in the Jordan River."

Henry broke the silence by slowly turning the pages of his Bible. I do not know what he looked for. "Something is wrong when those of us who are called cannot agree," he said. He blew and puffed out his cheeks. He did not look nearly as sad as his words sounded. "You seem, John M.,"—more deliberate page-turning—"given to argument. Correct me, brothers, if I am wrong." No one said a word. Not Johannes; he is a coward. When he had been questioned years ago regarding his horse-dealing, I defended him. Now he said nothing on my behalf. John J. was also silent. I do not know what ails him. Perhaps he *does* remember the smashed cardinal's egg. He is Joseph's son, but he lacks his father's spirit. The large clock on the wall ticked steadily, as if these deliberations deserved no special consideration.

At last Abraham Zug, the oldest among us, roused at his end of the bench like a slow, lazy turtle sticking his head out.

"Our Anabaptist fathers have always baptized in the house," he said sleepily, bringing his fingertips together in a circle. "Only pride would lead one to break with tradition."

As patiently as I could, and yet distinctly, for Abraham's hearing is not good, I said, "Our circumstances are not the same as theirs. Our Anabaptist brothers were being hunted; they had to baptize in secret. *Inside.* They were outlaws. They faced beheading if caught."

Abraham heard every word—I always suspected that his deafness is selective—and said, "Too much learning hinders a submissive spirit."

I slumped back in my perspiration. Now I was at fault for knowing the history of our ancestors, as well as the story of Jesus' baptism. I folded my arms in front of me. I could say nothing further or I would be chided for quarreling. The clock ticked. We would still be in session if I had maintained my silence indefinitely. I had to say the right words. My words were not completely sincere: "I do not mean to stand brother against brother." The clock ticked. "I want to be obedient to our Lord in lowliness and newness of faith." That is what they wanted to hear. It is true; I do not seek discord. But I have lost patience with those who only fear change.

Katharina has always been my best listener; now through circumstance I have allowed her to be taken from me. It troubles me that I get overwrought regarding baptism. I criticize Henry in my head for assigning too much import to the mode and place of baptism. But because of Henry I have allowed baptism to take on too much significance for myself. I have no one to talk with. If only Joseph were well. I have even thought of confiding in Elizabeth, but that would never do. The anger seethes inside, trifling with my soul. I cannot detest a brother. It is not to be. I wish I could excuse myself entirely from these ministers' meetings, but then my ideas would not get expressed. There is no one else to turn to in Holmes County. It is hard to believe that there is room for all of us in the Amish world that we love and cherish.

They threw one more trifle at me that irritates. I should not stoop to dwell on it. I had been informed that the meeting would start at ten o'clock in the morning. I thought it odd—we usually begin an hour earlier—but I did not question. Instead I thought with relief: one less hour to be tied down. When I walked in before ten—I am always early—I sensed that the others were waiting. What is worse, no one rose to give me the Kiss of Peace. No one, not even Johannes. I was caught off guard by the sudden awareness that I was somehow late. A spot on the bench remained empty, and I quickly lowered my frame. That is when I am the most uncomfortable in a small room, when all others sit and I am standing. Unless I am preaching of course. The meeting began immediately with prayer, and with the way matters progressed I did not inquire at the end whether I had missed any early proceedings. Now I fear that Henry may say I left in a huff. I know they gathered early to discuss me. I know it. Well, I do not know, but I suspect. The absence of the Kiss was not an oversight.

I feel squeezed on every hand. Perhaps Reuben and I will some day have more in common than our conversation about lamps. Perhaps I will be ostracized for my pride. Then Reuben and I can go into business together. I do not mean that it is a laughing matter. Only that there is nowhere for me to turn. No one from whom to seek counsel. My God, my God, why hast thou forsaken me?

8.
Ⴑ O S T
July 1854

*M*y strength has gone out from me. Someone came along six years ago and took all my strength. Same way Samson lost his hair. Well, I have most of my hair—Fanny says it falls out on the pillow—but I have no air to breathe. Fanny says I breathe too shallow. How does she know? I breathe what air is there. Then I have to stop and catch my breath.

I know this; I will not allow that little bit of a woman—no, I do not mean Fanny—to tell me what to do. "Scale the wall." Bah. What does she know?

Bishop Henry is right. We live near the end time. Evil, apostasy, people wanting to copy the ways of the world. Now they talk of the need for meetinghouses. Pshaw. We have always had church in our homes. Today our houses are bigger than ever and can accommodate large crowds. Yet people want a separate building for worship. Poppycock. Fanny even seems turned. She says the womenfolk have all the work of serving dinner. Well, that is why they have each other. What do they want? I may have lost my strength, but I can still use my noggin. What next? Do away with dinner altogether? Sometimes

Fanny is the one with the hearing problem. Fanny and Franey. I do not like the way they come from the same name.

With these bank barns that the young men build—barns far bigger than mine—there is seating space to spare in the summertime. I went to Sooey Crist's the Sunday we had church there. Floors were swept clean. Too clean, to my way of thinking. Nothing smells of heaven more than horses and hay. But then they come up with another argument. They say that in winter we cannot meet in barns. Too cold or whatnot. Even an old man like me knows that in winter there are fewer in attendance. Health problems, bad roads, such like. These troublemakers waste everyone's time. All because of selfish whims.

They say we should keep better records in church. Poppycock. Know how many are in attendance each Sunday. How many are baptized. When and where a brother is buried. Such folderol. With a farm, records are necessary; that is a business. But as Brother Henry says, pride in numbers can creep into our thinking. Better to be content with how we live. Not put stock in recording all the details. I have told Fanny: no grave marker for me. Crist said that Reuben put up a white one for Anna. Dates of her birth and death. Doubtless Reuben forgets that Father and Mother managed well enough with flat, field stones. Fanny says that markers will help future generations. It is not for me.

"Scale the wall." That runty-sized woman came to me in my sleep. Who does she think she is? Crist told me all about her. I will stay awake all night if necessary to keep from hearing more false words.

I am not one to dream. Never been prone. Reuben used to make up wild tales of wagons flying through the air. A chicken with two heads. I never believed a word of it. Dreams are not for me. I do one thing at a time. I sleep. I eat. I work. No dreaming while sleeping. Maybe a vision. One time I saw harvested corn piled high like Mt. Davis. Another time I had a nightmare. Stuck to my waist in mud and Fanny could not hear me. That was when it rained every day, and we had mud up our craw. There was a reason. But these words of a foolish woman, almost a dwarf at that, will not take their leave. "Could you not make attempt to scale the wall?" This little bit of a woman—I do not know why she appeared extra small in size—standing all alone at the edge of the woods. I hissed back, "Go away! Scat!" I saw her disappear. Then the next night her tail swished from behind a tree again.

What gives her the right? I know who she is. The body of a seven-year-old but the face of a woman. All the county knows she keeps company with one who has been put out. Even allows her daughter to ride in his wagon. How does that look? Veronica. That same name. Crist knows how people talk. I have said repeatedly: there should be strict consequences for anyone who openly defies the church. Mingling with Reuben, the outcast, as if he needs help. I am the one aggrieved. Can she not see? It was my child whose breath was snuffed. Yet this bitty woman asks me to crawl to my brother. Jump over *his* fence. She never heard the tremble in my father's voice. She should keep her mitts out.

Her foulness lingers like a bad stink, but I do not carry on as Fanny did with the raccoon. She had gone to the milk house late at night to fetch stink cheese. I do not remember the occasion, except that it happened when I was still spry. Before the grippe made me an old man. She still talks about that raccoon. She had opened the milk house door and heard a rustling. I was inside our house, and I could hear her whooping and hollering. Yet she complains that I do not hear well. For the next two weeks I heard, "Dark rings, Yost, dark rings. All about the eyes." Her finger moved in circles about her eyes. "Fat, ugly, enormous." Why does she blame me? I do not know how it got in. "What if I had stepped on it?" she asked.

"What if you had?" I replied. It is pitiful. A distraught woman. I will not stoop that far to carry on about a little woman who disturbs. I do not even know the woman, except from Crist. Of course she is a sister to Jonas. That slimy hand. And Abraham. I will not let her have dominion.

I put off going to bed. That is how I outfox her. I sleep well, for an old codger, in my rocking chair. Long before the sun is up Fanny wakes and patters about, saying she cannot get back to sleep. When she lights the lamp I go to bed. She cannot sleep because she thinks on Ursula and Alexander. Bad choices for partners. Forsaking our ways. A pestilence of buzzards has attacked my children. Lydia, taken long ago; she also wavered. Anna—the one I did not know how to dress as a girl—has one turmoil after another; she has lost four little ones in a brief span. Like unto that Polly Anna.

Susanna has made me a great-grandpop. That is one bright spot. But Joseph has moved back to Pennsylvania. I did not know what to make of that. Still do not. Henry packed his tribe and moved to Indiana. Here I provide land for all my boys. Then they leave. Gideon only comes to borrow my tools. Moocher. Never brought my plow blade back. Nicholas. Yes, he has stayed. He has all the boys who look just like him. High foreheads, every one. Hershbergers. He will get the barn, my beautiful barn. Even if Crist's is bigger. Nicholas looks in on us old folks very regular-like. I could sell another fifty acres to him; he would put it to good use. All those boys. I asked him to blow tobacco smoke in my ears, but it was to no avail. It would go better if Fanny would not mumble. She walks to a far corner of the house and then blames me that I do not hear and respond.

Lazarus. I forgot Lazarus. He complains that I favor Nicholas. Well, Fanny has everything written down. Who owns how many acres and where. I keep a clear account. But I insist, no grave marker. I warn her that I will know if she disobeys. We get along all right, the two of us, for old folks. Things are not the same, but I still have land aplenty, a fair number of grandsons, and a way to keep that unwanted woman off in the woods.

9.

J O N A S

April 1855

*S*o much of my past stirs in my head that I scarce can pour milk on my apple without spilling. I must take more care. We have almost finished the dried apples from last fall. They have no taste, but neither are they spoiled. Mary had to pitch the berries. The milk gives a little life and the crumbled bread makes a full meal. *Bruckle* soup.

Our Scrub Ridge is no more, and Mary and I seek another church where we can affiliate. Because of our searching about I met Levi Speicher yesterday. After all these years of absence I recognized him at once. He has not put on weight about the middle as most of us do, and he still parts his hair down the center. He has enough hair for both of us. Levi claimed that I looked quick enough to catch a fish with my bare hands. I do not think he looked closely, for when I examine my hands I see brown spots and limp, wrinkled skin. And the shakes.

We lost Shem early this year. We lost Abraham last November. So many of godly persuasion passing over yonder. All is in an uproar. I am glad for Shem, that he need no longer walk this world's vale of tears. But we are left adrift without leadership. Mary and I both dread going to visit her mother.

Mary feels the loss of her father's tenderness. I suffer because Shem was my true, spiritual guide.

With the demise of Abraham I felt no sorrow. Only the loss of a family member and a Minister of the Word. But no sorrow. I went to his funeral—that was a major undertaking—but I did not grieve. "Worthless runt" never strays far from my remembrance. I do not think Franey grieved either. She looked well, but seemed shorter than ever. Mary says we are all shrinking.

After the burial Franey insisted that we spend the night at their place before heading back to Wayne County. I did not want to at all. Mary nodded assent much too eagerly, and I had to manifest stubbornness. We had not made provision for the animals in our absence. Mary interjected that Stephen would provide care, but I reminded her that he is not dependable. I had to scowl at Mary to get her to stop. We came home forthwith. I did not care to explain that I wanted no chance encounter with Franey's neighbor.

Before we could make our departure Franey grabbed my arm and said that I did not look well. I was startled by her words and grip; I feel better than I did twenty years ago when we first moved to Ohio. Back then the work was never-ending and the children showed too much rowdiness. I wonder what she sees. She persisted, "What is wrong?" Her hand tightened on my coat sleeve. I could have told her that the mole on her cheek has a hair coming out of it, but I refrained. "What is it?" she said tugging. I shrugged her off. I do not think about the future. She cannot see my toothache. Her questions were as snoopy as anything Abraham might have come up with. I do not want to see Peter's wagon driving in my lane on a Sunday afternoon.

Some at Farmerstown had to be set back from Communion yesterday because of their transgressions. Henry Stutzman did not shirk. Mary and I were made to feel welcome even though we are not members, but it was a mistake to happen in on their spring *Ordnungs-Gemeinde*. I must plan more carefully. I nearly had to shake an unwanted hand. As soon as the first hymn was announced, I knew that this was their preparatory service. But having settled my poor bones on the bench and being situated far forward in the room, I could not take an early leave.

We had started out very early to make the long trip. Henry's church meets much too far away for us oldsters. But where can we turn in Wayne County? Henry emphasized the importance of confessing sin so that we do not eat and drink unworthily. He has a strong way of pounding his Bible; even the table shook. The first time it happened I jumped, but after that I knew what to expect. Yet Henry spoke with a kindly spirit, manifesting no vengeance. He was very clear that if a new way causes disagreement among the members, then it cannot be from God. He shook his head and puffed out his cheeks. Mary seemed pleased with his forcefulness also. "Unswerving," she said of him. But Farmerstown is much too far of a ride.

Our other Scrub Ridge minister, David Gingerich, has gone back to Oak Grove. I tried it there again myself but found little evidence of the members holding firm. For one thing, they use a different hymnal. Our *Ausbund* resides on the benches, but they sing from a book called *Unpartheyisches Gesangbuch*. I could never be the *Vorsinger* for such songs. My voice lacks steadiness, but these songs are much too lively. Some insist that these tunes will keep the young at home, rather than wandering off. That argument grows stale. Their new minister, Andrew Miller from Pennsylvania, has too much compromise in him. These newfangled songs sound like the Mennonites; that is the sum of it. I am glad Father does not need to hear them. Or Shem. If people want to sing Mennonite songs or want to be puffed up, they should join a Mennonite group, not try to drag the rest of us down.

There was an even worse problem at Farmerstown; Yost was there. He sat one bench ahead of me. I had, of course, never seen his balding head, one circle grown bare at the top. He still has more hair than I, but he no longer towers. I paid no heed to the man at first. But he called attention by tilting his head far to the left and whistling through his nose hairs. Then he jerked and half-snorted when he awoke. That may have been the first time Henry pounded. Soon Yost's head began its drop again. I followed the head and not Henry's words. Every time Yost woke, he looked to one side or the other, as if he feared he might have disturbed someone. Of a sudden, I caught his profile: a high forehead that leans far over his eyes, a big nose, a scraggly beard. I jumped a second time; this time at the recognition. I should have known. I had not taken sufficient care about the danger.

My first inclination was to relieve myself, but I held my body tight. That is not easy at my age. I regretted sitting so far forward, but there is no other way for an old one like me. I gave over following Henry's words and made my plans. When Yost tired of his head chase, he leaned far down to pick up his cane, positioned it in front of him, leaned forward again, and rested his head on his hands.

I could think of no alternative but to shake Yost's hand after the service, keep my head down, mumble, and be gone. Why had I not given thought? I knew he did not like me those long years ago. I did not want to stir his memories. What I had not anticipated was his slowness in standing. After we were dismissed, he stayed sitting. He did not move. I may not have much hair, but I can still scat if necessary. I do not mean that I ran, of course, but I saw my way clear to the door, shook hands on occasion, slipped behind others, rather like a giddy young man. A light mist fell outside. That is when I spied Levi. Another surprise. He had come in after me, and I had not noticed. Once we had determined the other's identity, I suggested we talk under the overhang of the horse shed. There I could keep one eye alert, in case Yost shuffled past. I saw him leave, hanging onto the arm of a middle-aged man. A son, likely. I had escaped. Mary made no mention of having met her cousin—I forget Yost's new wife's name—and I did not ask. I must take more care; I do not like close calls. Not at all.

It was not a problem to keep Levi distracted by asking about his son. He spoke at length—I was surprised that he showed no reservation—going on about this Frederick who is some kind of a doctor. This boy has built a new house with an office in it, and people bring their ailments to him. I thought Levi would have misgivings, for this Frederick is also a Minister of the Word. *And* a farmer. Where does he find time for all three? Levi gave no evidence of second thoughts, even though we had just sung, "No pride be holding" and "Self-love you must be hating." Levi did not bat an eye either that this Frederick has a son who expresses notions of going off to a medical school in Cleveland. Things have changed mightily from the days when Levi courted my sister. He still wore his hat the same way, but his lack of concern about spiritual matters does not bode well. I did not feel inclined to talk at length. Too much pride.

We are all getting on in years. Mary says I will have a birthday in another month. Sixty-seven years, she says. She is the one who remembers our children's and grandchildren's dates. I do not see what purpose a birthday serves; it seems like another examination, as if I am being questioned about my life. I can count on her not to plan a frivolous birthday shindig for me. I am in need of nothing, and there is no place for empty accumulation. I surprised her, though, last month. She claimed I had not given her a gift in thirty years. I doubt that is true. She may have forgotten the feather tickings for pillows that I brought home several years ago. Whatever the case, she now has a new coverlet with a woven fringe. We disagree about the color. I call it a dark brown and blue with white threads; she says it is dark red with blue and black and white.

"Where did you get this?" she asked, her hand alternating between covering her mouth and fingering the soft warmth. "Jonas! Where?"

I shrugged my shoulders and kept mum, walking about the room in short circles. The coverlet pleased me exceedingly. "Next year you will be 70 and you might expect something then," I said. I had not thought of that explanation until the minute she asked.

"Look at the weaving, the cotton and wool, warp and weft. Where did you ever . . . ?" She squinted her eyes at me.

I had not expected such insistent interrogation. At first her persistence was amusing; then I tired of her questions. I began to fear that she might not be satisfied until she found out. I had sworn Stephen to secrecy, but when put to the test, I wondered if he would give in to his mother. It had been difficult enough for me to maintain my indifference at her questions.

"Stephen," I had said, "I want you to ride to Doughty Creek; that is where the finest coverlets are made. Get a pretty one for your mother. Whatever you like." I handed him two gold dollars.

He grinned, tossed the coins into the air as if they were worthless, and spat against the barn door. Then he spat again to hit a higher mark. He is a great one for adventure. I do not know if he will ever settle down. He still eats at my table and feels no shame. I was right that this assignment would be to his liking. I had first thought to send Adam; he does business in Holmes County sometimes. But Mary says Adam's ears and his build are much like mine. The ears would not matter because his woolly hair covers all but the lobes, but I have often thought too, that Adam takes after me. Stephen would pass for Shem, except that he has a wildness about him with his gaudy clothes.

"Say nothing to your mother. Do you understand?" I waited until he looked me full in the eye. Then he spat again and belched. "Promise me. Give no particulars to Mary. Not for any reason. Or to anyone else." He nodded and grinned, rubbing his hands together and spitting into them. I suppose he thought this an exciting endeavor to be in cahoots with me.

"Ask for a weaver. Polly, by name," I went on. "She is old, but I hear she does excellent work. Wrap it in this blanket."

That was all the goading Stephen needed. He returned as pleased as I, although I wondered at his choice of roosters and roses for the design. We hid the coverlet in the haymow until Mary's day.

"What does she look like?" I asked when he returned. I fiddled with the coins Stephen gave me for change. A dirty collection of small cents, half dimes.

"Who?"

"The woman. You did say her name was Polly, did you not?"

"Polly Hostetler, she said."

"Good," I said, but too quickly. I made a show of counting the coins again.

Stephen looked at me as if he took renewed interest. He ran his fingers through his pile of hair, front to back, front to back. "Do you know her?"

"No, no. What does she look like? I have heard others speak of her."

"Like every other Amish woman."

"No, I mean, is she old? Does she have gray hair? That sort of thing," I said weakly. Abraham's death had brought back memories of olden times. I put the coins in my pouch. I could not bring myself to ask Stephen if he had returned all the change.

"Why do you ask? She is fat. Old and fat. Her upper arms shook inside her dress sleeves when she reached to pull down the coverlets." Stephen put more chewing tobacco in his cheek. "I told her you grew up in Somerset County too."

"You did?" I said, too quickly again. I pulled a handkerchief from my pocket and carefully wiped my forehead and the back of my neck.

Stephen did not seem to notice, for he readjusted his plug. "She said Somerset is the cradle for Ohio." He slapped his thigh. "She is a crazy one."

I did not ask more. The whole enterprise was foolhardy, as dangerous as going to church at Farmerstown. I cannot afford such carelessness. One day Stephen muttered something in Mary's hearing about "Father, the sly one"; another time he slapped his knee and guffawed about "Father's other interest." I pretended I did not hear. Sometimes my one ear gives me trouble. I have been kept safe for a month. All I can do is hope his curiosity passes. I should not have put myself in a position where I am beholden to any man's secrecy, let alone Stephen's. I am too old for new deception.

I do not believe in luck, good or bad, but I have had my share of both. Mother claimed that I would never be a manager, but I have been successful with wheat and corn on a par with those around me. I have tried to stay in the shadows. I hid in the shelter of Shem's assistance. Now I must depend on my Adam and Stephen. It is no wonder I have the shakes.

I watch and wait to see what others may yet do. I wait for others to die. Mary, even Franey. I wonder if I will be given as many years as Father. That would be six more. Sometimes I use his cane made of the finest hickory. Abraham's widow passed it on last fall. I did not remember that Abraham inherited it from Father, but that is what she said. I did not get a good look at Yost's cane, but I am certain his is a sturdy one. I have heard it said that he owns much land.

Six more years and I will be seventy-three. Even my grandchildren see that there is something wrong. They dart around me giggling. They stare at me and then run. I believe they run away and laugh. My bald head. My shaking hands. Six more years of wondering if there will ever be *beschluss*. I know now I cannot go to Yost. Nor do I have the stomach to see Reuben. Those other words of the song, "Kind words then be you bearing," I cannot see my way clear. It is not for me. Far easier to despise myself.

10.
ℛ E U B E N
March 1856

Yes, it is true, my neighbors are both gone. I could not
save either one. I could not save Anna four years ago.
Now in two months' time Peter and Franey have been taken.
Yost too. I am not one who clings, but my stomach churns
from all this upheaval. The carrots from my root cellar taste
rubbery; the potatoes have grown long, dangling sprouts. Why
am I left? I pull my hand through my unruly beard—Bevy says
it is a habit—and find gray spirals wrapped in my fingers. My
hair should have run out long ago, but the replacements still
come. What good has it done me to know that the Maker
numbers the very hairs of my head?

If only I had known that my conversation with Franey in
late February would be our last. If only. I would have lingered.
I would have held on to her words, thinking of another question. Something that might bring a smile. But I did not know.
I thought only of Peter, taken with such suddenness as he
sought to break a new horse. Trampled inside his own fence.
I did not hear him yell until it was too late. No one ever said
where young Levi was that day. Or why he did not get help.
Now Franey too, gone at fifty-one. Such a young one. Anoth-

er saint. Gone. I can no longer walk over to watch her scratch in the dirt.

No one called me to give aid. Why did Levi not summon his sister Veronica? I cannot make it out, unless he thought Franey merely fatigued and grief-stricken from the loss of Peter. Yet Levi admits—he will not look me in the eye—that Franey and Aaron were both afflicted with much vomiting and diarrhea. Aaron has youth and pulled himself through, but Franey lost the battle in a matter of two nights. I was just down the lane, only a stone's throw away. Bevy says Levi used poor judgment. I say, he is eighteen; he should have known better.

When I was a lad, I did not know things could go awry either. I thought myself the master of my destiny. I only needed to work hard enough to get Father's approval. Then I could read Aunt Barbli's books. I only needed to join the church to get my Anna. Life seemed simple, without complication. Now all is mystery and incomprehension. My neighbors stayed true to the end. Why did it fall to them to be stricken at a young age? Here I have gone on past seventy. I see no new light. I look out on the fields, still brown with winter; I see no signs of the growing season to come. My flesh is old with dark spots, withered. I am next to worthless.

In late February Franey was out digging in her flower beds, moving leaves around. That was about a month after Peter's death. I went over for a short visit when we had a warm spell. Franey seemed shrunken, even smaller than before.

"You know that we will have more cold weather," I chided.

She straightened from her half-bent position, looking pale and stark. "I search for any sign of green," she said. "I thought there might be a jonquil poking up along this side of the house where they get protection from the wind." She came toward me, stepping gingerly on the soft, mushy earth. "I know winter has not had its final say. But the thawing gives hope. Perhaps the next hard freeze will change its mind and soften."

I barely knew Franey was ill. Now she is gone. Most of her twelve grandchildren will never know her, never see her get down on her knees and let them leapfrog over her. She did everything she could for me. I would have gladly said words for her. Why did Levi not call? Bevy tires of my questions. Poor Veronica, newly married, is nearly beside herself; she knew nothing of her mother's condition. Why is it that my hands were of no use to those who stayed by me? *"Ich aber ging vor dir über, und sahe dich in deinem Blut liegen, Peter Troyer, und sprach zu dir, da du, Franey Troyer, in deinem Blut lagest: Du Söllst leben. Ja, Peter und Franey. Du Söllst leben!"* I am no stranger to what cannot be explained, but I say to both of them: you should have lived.

My brother's death—my brother in the flesh—stirs me only a little. For over forty years I wished Yost dead. How like him to die on the same day that I knew grief for Franey. It is loathsome to desire a brother's death, but I thought I might restore my name if he were gone. Now he has been called to give account. I find no pleasure. He left, like Eliza, not knowing the truth. He lived his life thinking me a villain. I could not change his mind.

I did not attend any of the funerals, but Jacob has again cut off his moustache and returned to the Amish. He went in my stead to Peter's and again to Franey's funeral. Jacob reminds me of Anna, the way he carefully plans his work every day. He always expects a better yield with the next crop. He went to Yost's funeral as well, but made no mention of what Henry Stutzman had to say. I saw no reason to ask. I do not want to spend my entire day in the outhouse. Jacob did say that Yost's boys—the cousins he never played with—wrangle openly over Yost's barn. It brings no satisfaction. I wonder if my demise will be long and drawn out, like Yost's. Jacob heard that Yost had not stirred from his bed for weeks, that he became cantankerous, a burden for his wife, with bed sores oozing their pus. I should feel pity, but I do not. All I know is that Franey and Peter should be alive, not me. They still had fires to tend.

Some days I give feeble thought to approaching Bishop John M. He did not shrink from conversation when we chanced to meet years ago and talked of lamps with Peter. I wonder what Jacob would think if I knocked on John M.'s door. I know of no other church man who might be open. If I go, I risk hearing, "No." If I do not go, I take my chances on the mercies of God.

I go to Anna's grave with more frequency again. On my first trip this spring I thought I would not make it to the top. Winter had quite taken my breath away. All is still quiet there, but the ground is too wet and cold to lie prone. I hear nothing but the lonesome wind. Countless times I have told Anna about Peter and Franey. I know she weeps. On the day of Franey's funeral Jacob suggested that his oldest boy, Solomon, could stay here with me. I protested, but I was glad for his company. We climbed the hill together and sat under the thorny locust. Solomon drew his knees to his chin and looked across my valley. He pitched small pebbles over the edge of the hill. We watched all manner of conveyances come and go from the Troyers' homestead. We heard the mournful hymns. Jacob said that all of Franey's children were there; her brother who lives in Wayne County came also.

I wish that Veronica would fetch her new husband and live next door with her brothers. Oh, how I wish. But it is not for me to say. I helped build that cabin, but I have no say about my neighbors. All these years I have waited to clear my name. Now I am afraid to make attempt. How much easier to have the sod above me, not below. To throw off these legs of mine. To mount up with wings as an eagle. I would welcome the flight, but it is not for me to say.

11.

J O H N M .

May 1858

The locusts have started their buzzing already, a sure sign of a hot summer to come. I wake with their high-pitched ringing; I go to sleep with their shrill buzzing. They sing the loudest in the clump of elms I planted some thirty years ago, now grown large as a canopy. How an insect can be that shrill and remain hidden from sight is a major accomplishment. When they start dropping, we will have locust soup three times a day.

Our church, the stained and blessed church of God, gives forth a steady ring also. So readily it giveth light; just as easily it causeth a man to stumble in the shadows. The Evil One's power to cause me to question my walk, frightens. I am not allowed to doubt—I do not want to doubt—but I would not survive without Andrew. The Lord has sent this friend to keep me in the faith. There are those who do not approve of Andrew Miller over at Oak Grove in Wayne County, just as they do not support me here at Walnut Creek. When the snoopers ask, I have not always been forthcoming about my association with him. But I have not lost my mind to doubt. I have not lost my Christian spirit. Andrew is much younger, only in his early thirties. He could be my son; yet we talk as friends. He has replaced my dear brother, Joseph, who has passed on. It is not easy for Andrew or me to be at odds with others in the Amish church. We tire of the charge: "You allow too much looseness." A manuscript circulates among our people, written by a bishop back in Lancaster County: "Follow the *Ordnung* . . . keep to the old ways." These church disputes upset my innards. I suspect we did not take proper care with the sausages last winter. Katharina shows no problem with indigestion, but the heavy grease disturbs my stomach.

Andrew tells how the hounds were after George Keim at Oak Grove when he preached a different understanding of the Fall. Such pettiness, to spend time arguing over whether it was Eve or the serpent who lied first. It is true that George did not help himself by disregarding Matthew 18 and refusing to come to the meeting. But I say, let the brethren at Oak Grove decide their own affairs. There is no need for us in Holmes County to withdraw ourselves in fellowship from a bishop in Wayne County. The ban, the ban, the ban. That is all I hear. It is used as a weapon. I fear I may be the next object of its pruning.

I may soon be in even deeper trouble when word gets around about Reuben Hershberger. The locusts' noise will seem a pleasant hum by comparison. Katharina claims she does not sleep; her face has turned a darkish yellow with bags under her eyes. Some will voice doubts; others may take stronger action. But my conscience is clear. The look on Reuben's face was enough.

My Samuel troubles me more than Reuben. I named him after Isaac's father, Samuel, but he seems to want no part in the church. There are those who point and say, "See." And John K. is only nineteen, but I fear he will follow after Samuel. He accepted my advice about the middle initial, but that is the only place he listens. "Use John K.," I said. "Holmes County has a John Yoder along every creek. There is already a John J. Take Katharina's *K* for a middle initial or expect confusion wherever you go." He looked as if he had no intention of establishing a name among us Amish. I could see it in his eyes. I heard it in his words. Those words that cut me to shreds: ". . . a dead trunk, full of hypocrites. You and your Amish are like monkeys, thinking yourselves safe while grabbing onto a decaying branch." That is how the young see: truth, with eyes half open. It did not sit lightly to hear him say that my meat and drink appear as a bag of worms. This spring, he could have said, our church buzzes like the locusts.

With my first five I took too much pride; they followed easily, neither looking to the left nor the right. Katharina reminds me that Elias dabbled for some years. Nevertheless, I took credit in my mind, thinking my children could not go wrong because of my example and Katharina's. Now with my last two boys twisting and turning, I am not as eager to take responsibility. Katharina asks, "How do you expect your offspring to heed every word when you are restless in the saddle?" I scratch my beard. I have been careful not to express my discontent to my children, but perhaps they understand what I have not said.

Whatever my sons choose, I will not turn my back on them. Some would have us ban all those who leave the Amish church. I could never do that. I cannot see what shunning accomplishes other than ill will and hard feelings. Samuel is my son. I taught him how to get more distance when spitting watermelon seeds. John K. is my son. I made wooden stilts for him to pretend that he was taller than I and could walk faster. I would rather have my tender ones join the Mennonites—I can only say this to Andrew—and find nourishment, than to languish unfed with us. Why some find sustenance among us and others wither, I cannot explain. I know this though: every man who truly listens knows where to find water. I now think like Joseph; I am not so certain that water from one stream is safer to drink than from another. How his heresy left me shaken years ago.

Reuben came seeking water two months ago. A heavy rain pounded on the tin roof of my tool shed when he showed up. It was too warm for winter, too cold for spring. Mud had taken over our habitation, so that even the horses had difficulty pulling the wagon through deep ruts in our driveway. Reuben hitched his horse at the far end and came by foot; I chanced to look outside and saw him take great care, wiping mud from his boots. He turned his ankle first one way, then the other, scraping mud wherever he could find solid footing that was not full of its own ooze.

I made haste to open the door. I do not know why he came in the rain, except that it had rained every day for a week. He may have grown weary of waiting for a let-up. I persuaded him to bring his boots inside the shed and to hang his sopping hat on a nail. He looked like a drenched rat caught in a cistern. He glanced around, taking stock of my scythes and shovels. I tried to put him at ease, bringing wooden stools for us to sit on, apologizing that I am careless about putting away my tools. I went on at length about my displeasure when I misplaced a handsaw last winter. I talked too much; he made little response. He did not even comment on my augers.

Part of me was surprised to see him; another part seemed almost to expect him. When he had left Peter Troyer's that day when we last met—he says it has been five years—he looked back from the end of Peter's driveway. In the same instant, I turned back from Peter's barn and looked again at Reuben. I was embarrassed to be caught staring, yet he had turned in my direction as well. We stood thus not more than a second or two. He with his new lamp; I with my riding jacket. Then he turned again, rather abruptly, and strode toward his house. I have often thought of that shared backward glance, as though there are people we prepare to meet again.

When I finally gave him time to speak in my tool shed, he stumbled for words. His eyes stayed intent on his gray socks. "I wonder, have wondered for some time . . . ." He wiped raindrops from his forehead, his hair still dripping wet. He could not have been wetter had he come without a hat. "If you could see fit,"—he cleared his throat—"to reinstate me in the church." He paused again, glancing up sideways at me as if to see if I intended to throw him out immediately. I said nothing, but my insides churned. The sausages. I have heard many a confession before; I did not want to flinch. He went on, chin dropped to his chest again. "I was a member in good standing at one time, almost fifty years ago." He looked up and then down quickly. "Perhaps you have heard the story." He looked like he could not go on. I wanted to put him out of his misery. "My brother's baby, a girl of seven months, was murdered in their cabin. And I—." This time he paused so long—his jaws tightened—I considered finishing the sentence for him. "My brother and I were never friends."

He pressed his hand against his hair, spreading the wetness, forcing the excess down his ears. He wiped his forehead with his sleeve.

"Yes, I have heard the tale," I said. "What happened?" Of course I knew the story.

"No one came forth; no one acknowledged owning the hands that committed the awful deed. But someone had to be blamed. Someone had to bear the brunt of Yost's anger. I was the one." He pulled a red bandana from his pocket and wiped endlessly. "My good wife vouched that I had been home all night when the deed was done, but I was the one condemned to death. One hand of flesh pounded to a pulp by my brother; the other hand nailed by the church. I defended myself; I argued. That was my mistake. One of my mistakes. For my defiance, for my refusal to admit something I did not do, I was put out of the church." He looked at me. "You know, surely, I have been banned ever since."

I nodded my head and cleared my throat. He averted his gaze, looked at my shovels absently as if he were not finished. "I might as well have been guilty." He spoke softly. "I have been made to feel guilty." He looked around the shed like a cornered rat. "That day at Peter's, you did not walk away. Franey and Peter always spoke well of you. That is why I am here."

I shivered and got up to throw another log in the cast-iron stove. All the moisture of Reuben's wet clothes put a chill in the air. I paused, watching the flames of the half-burned logs surround the fresh length of sycamore. A cold blue light stayed buried within. There I stood at the center, at odds with many in the church. An object of suspicion. One who also argued. This request would only add fuel, more evidence for those ready to convict.

I turned back to Reuben. "Did you do it? Did you snatch the life of that child?"

"No, I did not," he burst out. Then he said more slowly, as if he had learned to guard his words: "I did not kill Marie Hershberger." We looked at each other, his eyes with their dark brown color softening to green. His face, old and wet; his eyebrows, rowdy and undisciplined. I believed him. The logs popped and hissed inside tight, black walls.

"And do you believe," I asked, "do you believe in God?" Reuben nodded, his right hand at his mouth to stop the tremble. How frightened he looked. A child's fear trapped in an old man's body. As if I could hurt him. I hastened on, rattling the next question I would need to ask again later. "Do you also believe that Jesus Christ is the Son of God who has come into the world to save repentant sinners?"

"Yes," he said, clearing his throat. "Yes, I do."

Panic rose within me. What would Andrew say? What would Katharina think? "This is a serious matter; I do not need to tell you that. I will need to speak with my fellow ministers. My inclination . . . ." I paused to wet my lips and felt the dry wiriness of my beard. Why could I not give immediate assurance? The shed felt close about me. Why had I added that log? I got up to open the outside door a crack. Perhaps I should keep my inclination to myself. Reuben's head bent again. I could see his legs shake; his body trembled. No one should have to suffer like that. "My inclination is to reinstate you. But I cannot do that on my authority alone. I must consult with others at Walnut Creek."

Reuben lowered his wet head into his hands; his shoulders shook. I placed my hands on his shoulders until he could quiet himself. I have never known how to comfort those who grieve.

"I am old," he said, when he could compose himself. "Many a day I despaired of ever hearing those words. Many a night passed when I despised myself. I thought my leprosy was for life." He looked up at me, his face lined with deep cracks. I could see that he trusted me, the way my sons used to believe my words.

"I cannot promise you, Reuben. You understand? I must ask the others, Johannes and Fritz; they must agree that this is the right step." I despised my not being able to say with certainty. "I am not able to do this on my own. I am but a vessel." Fear took hold of his face again. I wanted to say yes. I could not imagine ever coming back to tell him no. "I will speak on your behalf," I said, gripping his shoulder with my hand. He said nothing, and I added with a shake, "I believe you, Reuben."

Then he hugged his arms to his chest, and I realized that he wept silently. I did not know what to do; I was afraid that his distress and the inclement weather would take their toll. I did not want him to collapse in my tool shed. I wanted him to leave. I sat again; I fiddled; I waited. I thought of holding him to me, but I could not. I am ashamed. I could not.

He fumbled inside his pants pocket, searching for his handkerchief. He forgot he had replaced it inside his jacket. I had not even offered that he remove his wet jacket. He blew his nose weakly, as if the effort were too much. Then he wiped his nose slowly back and forth. His legs still trembled. "No one, no one but Anna, ever said that to me."

I grabbed his hand in both of mine and held tight until he quieted. My knees touched his pant leg. I pinched my eyes tight shut. "Draw yourself together," I said. Johannes would not be a problem to convince. Fritz, I was less certain about.

"There is something else," Reuben said. I straightened my back; my knees and feet jerked away. I had been too quick; I had responded too warmly. This was a man the church had shunned for almost fifty years. I should have exercised more caution, not wanted to overturn judgment in a day.

"I would like to be baptized again," Reuben said. He lifted his head. His white and gray and black eyebrows twisted every-which-way above his sorrowful eyes.

I sighed that it had not been worse. Then all the complications rushed forward. "You were baptized once in the Amish faith, right?"

"Yes," he said. "Long enough ago that it hardly counts."

"One baptism is enough." I did not like my reprimand, my strict tone of authority.

"I know. That is what the church says. But baptism would be like starting anew for me. Will you ask?" His eyes still looked glassy.

"I can ask, but that would be highly irregular. I do not think
. . . ." I do not like to be pushed farther than I am willing to
go. How often have I been told that I deviate when it is not
wise?

"Ask, please, for an old man. I seek no harm. For anyone."

I wondered whether I had been tricked by Reuben, taken
advantage of. "I will ask, but it is unnecessary. The rebaptism.
I will ask about reinstatement. I cannot say how others will
respond—it is useless to try to guess—but you have lived your
life with one foot in a steel trap. I will present your name to
the other ministers and offer your case." I sighed, thinking of
the cumbersome steps ahead. "If they give permission, we
will need to take the matter to the entire congregation." My
mind planned as I talked. "We can do that this spring at the
next preparatory service. To see if there is objection."

Reuben shuddered as if the dampness had seeped inside his
body. "Please ask."

"I never know what to expect with the members." My position has always been that we cannot deny baptism to one
who comes in sincerity and with lowliness of heart. But
Reuben would not have known that. "There are already six
young candidates who have asked to be received when spring
is here." I paused. "My advice to you, Reuben, is to put fear
from your mind and heart. Rejoice in the goodness of our Lord
who accepts us and wants to forgive us all our ways."

Reuben stood, his feet searching for solidness, as if my
words had baptized him and the rain had supplied the water.
He made no effort toward the door, and I feared he had yet
another request. "I wish Anna could know," he said. "I do not
deserve what she could not have." I thought he was going to
cry again, but instead he half-whispered, "She went to the
grave, outside the church by choice, because Yost outlived
her." He spoke so quietly that I could not be certain of every

word. "She kept me from death. Anna is the one. Without her I would have ended up a drunken, pitiful sot."

He tottered, shifting his feet. "If I am reinstated, I will not take another drop. There have been times since Anna's passing, and again since Franey and Peter departed, that I have wavered in my determination. But now, if I am rebaptized, I will give no more allegiance to the jug. Please ask. Anna will be glad."

I shook his hand in both of mine, felt his chapped fingers, torn and rough at the knuckles. "You are a good man, Reuben." I stepped toward him and we embraced. He is a large man, but I held him as a fragile woman. I thought of my father and how I had been robbed of knowing him. I had been too eager to leave home. He never had time enough. "None of us knows ought of the afterlife," I said as Reuben and I drew apart, "but it is possible that Anna knows of your request. Knows and approves."

Reuben smiled weakly but shook his head. "When it stops raining on her grave, I will tell her."

Before he left I was the one who remembered one more thing. "You do not—. How shall I say this? If you were to be baptized again, do you have a preference between a stream or a house?" His brow wrinkled with puzzlement, and I explained, "I thought your son, Jacob, might have told you. The place of baptism has been an issue for some in the Amish church. The stream represents a change."

He doubled his hand into a fist and held it to his mouth as one seeking to stifle a cough. What came out sounded more like a hog's snort. "No, it does not matter. Where or how." His face broke into a jagged-toothed smile. "Baptize me in an oaken bucket. In a horse's trough. In a rainstorm. It will not matter."

"You have it right, Reuben. How we fly at gnats and stumble over camels. Oh, that more of us could see the light." I could not say whether I was prepared to be banned over another baptism.

Reuben put his boots on again, so slowly I thought I would need to give him help. I do not know if he laughed or cried on his ride home, but he had reason for both.

For me, I went to my bed and wept. Katharina came and I laid my head in her lap, wanting to be consoled like a child. I would still be letting her smooth the hairs on my head if she would give the time. I told her all that had transpired.

She said little, but I gave her little opportunity. I went over everything. "It is right; it is the only right thing to do," I said, seeking to convince myself.

Not until later that night did we speak of it again. "I am glad for Reuben and sad for you," Katharina said, pulling back the covers on our bed. "It is the right thing to do, but it will add fire to those who criticize."

"Those are not the people I listen to," I said, snapping a reply. "It is the Reubens who speak to my soul. What is the church for?" I demanded of her, spreading my long arms wide. "The church loses its reason for being when it cannot respond to a genuine entreaty. Reuben is but a poor traveler along life's way." That is what I want to believe.

Katharina questioned why I have to stick my neck out when it is already weak from battering. I scolded. She is too concerned about what others think. We rehearsed all the arguments. She was right that Reuben's request would supply more ammunition; I was right about what is the right thing to do. We ended up consoling each other.

Katharina's fears, thus far, have been unfounded. Johannes and Fritz raised few reservations. "Irregular," is all Fritz said, one eyebrow raised higher than the other. The news will spread farther sooner or later. At our preparatory service only a few questions about Reuben surfaced, and none were pursued seriously. No one cared to linger. Most people know little of this story from the past and show a readiness to receive Reuben. If there were detractors among us looking to find fault, they could make a case against me for presenting Reuben as like unto a saint. And Anna too. I am not quick to make heroes of human beings, but I spoke of how God saw fit to raise up martyrs among us who have endured unjust suffering.

As it turned out, Reuben and the six young ones were baptized last Sunday—it stayed gray all day—in chilly stream water. No one complained about the temperature, the location, the locusts, or any of the recipients. My boots kept me warm. I heard again a persistent cardinal with its clicking noise. Reuben wobbled noticeably as he shook hands with each of the brethren after he was received as a member. None of us can fathom what this must mean to him, to have been barred from fellowship and now to be counted as one of us. I could not shut the door on rebaptism. I could not. His son Jacob was in attendance also. He expressed satisfaction numerous times; so much so that I felt embarrassed. I am blessed to have been a part of this righting of wrongs. If there are those of a different mind, I trust they will bring their grudges to me, not seek to make life difficult for Reuben.

Our present calm reminds me of what happens before a storm. Those moments when the trees hold perilously still, their leaves upturned. Katharina goes about looking grim, as if she too knows we have not heard the last. If Henry Stutzman turns his zeal against me, I do not fear for myself, but I believe it will go hard for Katharina.

"Do you expect pestilence?" I ask. "Bigger and bigger locusts?"

"It is not a laughing matter," she says. She is right, of course.

My enemies could seek to entrap me on many issues. I should not call my brother-in-law my enemy. It is all right to have honest disagreements in the church. If I want Henry to allow me differences, then I must be at peace with him and his stubborn ways. Katharina expects a miracle, but I do not see how we Amish can ever be of one mind. Even here at Walnut Creek Fritz strongly opposes giving our new deacon, Noah Troyer, any opportunity to preach. Fritz points to his Bible—one eyebrow raised—rubs his chest, and says a deacon should stay with the usual: distribute alms, mediate disputes, read a chapter of Scripture on occasion. I maintain that it is better to give a deacon opportunity to preach now and then, so he is not completely unprepared in an emergency. I dare not say it, but I believe Fritz only seeks to preserve his own preaching time.

I will never forget the smile on Peter Troyer's face when his son was selected as deacon. Peter kept his thoughts to himself like most of those from the Old Country, but he smiled broadly when Noah was chosen. Some people charged him with showing too much pride, as if it were better to stay subdued, even to grovel, when virtue is recognized. And Franey, how I miss her. A small body but a strong spirit. Hers was one face I could count on not to be distracted or asleep on Sunday morning. Her funeral left me at a loss; her death seemed entirely unnecessary. All I could think to say was: "His eye is on the sparrow." I said those words to comfort me, as well as her children. "His eye is on the sparrow." What more do any of us need to know?

When will we learn that our hassles distract us from the spiritual upbuilding of each member? When will we yearn to protect ourselves from *that* drift? I may be a rebel like Andrew and in need of watching. My son John K. may be right that we cling to a decayed branch. But I take comfort in my new brother Reuben. I have helped an old man find peace. That is why we labor, for those who truly find rest in the body of our Lord.

12.

$\mathcal{P}$ OLLY

June 1859

*H*ow will they ever make do? We just had word; those poor folks back in Somerset County had a killing frost on June 4th. Frost on the fourth of June! All their potato plants, shriveled; the corn and beans were up too. I never, ever, thought such a thing could happen. Seven, no, eight years ago, we had a heavy frost in May. But that was May. This is June, and still they had a killer. The rye, wheat, fruit trees, all lost. All of nature *verhuddled*.

How will my Leah and her Jack manage? And Molly, Andrew's forlorn widow. I do not even know this Molly, but for six years she has tended their seven children by herself. Grandchildren I never set eye on. The last one born sickly, only two months after Andrew's grave was piled high. Dead at 36, my poor Andrew. He had a head to prosper, but a jag of lightning struck him. Paul says I moan and groan too much. I say, those who have not suffered do not understand. I do not look at the stump of his hand. I have thought of returning to give this Molly aid, but she might turn out to be another Maggie and think I pinched the baby. I would like to take a peek at Leah too. But the wagon ride. Mercy. And Jack might think me a nuisance.

Paul says they can still plant buckwheat back East; there is enough growing time for that. I did not know Somerset County could go backward so fast. We lived on buckwheat when I was a youngster, but now we expect variation. Christina Kauffman thinks that many more from Somerset will migrate to a new settlement in Iowa. She says they do not stop in Ohio; they do not stop in Indiana. They go to this Iowa and call it the Promised Land. I do not like the sound of it, but Paul says Iowa is not nearly as far away as Oregon. I will ask Obadiah if that is true.

I wonder if I am meant to outlive all my children; only two left and neither close at hand. I could pay John a visit—people are always back and forth between here and Elkhart County—but even that ride is too long. My extra weight causes problems for my hip. My right one sometimes gets stuck and refuses to move with the rest of me. If I stop for a minute the hip catches hold and slips into place. I hear that one of John's eight has married; I wonder how he took to that. He always said with such assurance, "None of mine will wander off to Oregon."

I want to make sixty-six coverlets by the time I am seventy. Three score and ten. Only two more years. If the Lord giveth breath. One coverlet for each book in the Bible. I was right about the sheep even though John would not listen. My coverlets sell almost as fast as I can make them. I have three, no, four on hand. I do not know half of those who come to buy. Or where they get the word. I would work longer at my coverlets, but I do not want to steal from tomorrow. My eyes give concern. The Psalmist allotted seventy years as the life of a man. I suppose that goes for women too. I like the sound of it: three score and ten. With a little bounce near the end. It reminds me of, *"Ains, tsway, drei, Hicker, hocker, hei."*

Paul and Judith and I carry on with our regular duties. Their boys are all set up, so Paul does not need to look grim about that. I have not been to Obadiah's farm yet, but Paul says we will all go this summer. It is near to Farmerstown, where some people now mine coal by digging tunnels. I have the yarn balls ready to take to Obadiah's boys. Paul did not like it when I gathered walnuts last fall and set them on the back porch to dry. He claimed they would attract rodents. I used my leftover scraps of yarn to cover the walnuts. Then Paul had to mutter about the boys not wanting to hit red and yellow balls with their sticks. "Too bright. They should all be dark colors. Brown. These will get dirty." He does not approve of anything I do. I but wanted to use up all the scraps.

I have to ask Judith to thread my needle. Imagine, a camel with a hump getting through that eye! One day I could not find my purple threads anywhere. At first I said nothing to Judith. I told myself to wait and see. I was right. The next day all three purples stood behind my sewing basket—"*Ains, tsway, drei*"—where they should have been all along. Then my greens were missing. I do not know what prompts Judith. I have wondered if it may be Paul who meddles. Whoever does it tires of their trickery, and everything turns up. I have learned to be very wary.

Paul has nothing good to say about his cousin John M. When Paul brought home the tale that John M. had baptized Reuben, I knew that Paul had gotten things mixed up again. Now whenever John M.'s name is mentioned, Paul's eyes get thin and narrow, as if he tries to press out any thought of the man. I remind Paul that Reuben saved our Judith, but Paul does not listen. His lips squeeze tight. Paul says this is just like John M., keeping things stirred up. I do not want to argue, for then Paul works himself into a dither, and my sheep do not get fed as they ought.

As for Reuben, I do not know what to think. It is a blessing that Yost is not here. What a ruckus he would raise. Perhaps

Reuben deserved another chance. I do not know. I am not a minister. I am certain John M. would not meddle with a man's soul all by himself. No one saw Reuben take Marie in his hands. I never said that he did. I try not to think on it because I cannot sleep when I dwell too long. Then when I complain about my fitful night, Judith tells me not to doze so much in the daytime. I may sit in the rocker all afternoon, but I only take short naps.

I do not like it when Paul questions me as to where I was at the time. Especially not when we are eating. His stumpy hand sits there looking at me. I only saw a dark face—eyes— at the window and had to say something when Yost's eyes demanded an answer. The jury—those twelve good men—they were the ones who made inquiry. They had the most to say. One time when Paul was being persistent, I saw Judith give his bad hand a bump. Sometimes I cannot finish my supper. What if I made a blunder? I was too young to wait and see as I do now when my threads are missing.

Paul says that soon they will not shun anyone over there at Walnut Creek. I do not know what to think. John M.'s eyes were very kindly that day at the reunion. Paul says that this Elizabeth's death is a sure sign of punishment from God. I did not think John M. had an Elizabeth, but Judith and Christina both say it is true. John M.'s oldest. She was set to be a teacher at the new school they are starting. Judith says everyone is mum. Christina shakes her head. Paul's lips get very tight, and he scowls when he makes reference to sudden death. Then he stops when Judith bumps him with her foot under the table. Does he not remember that I have lost six? In spite of Elizabeth's death, Christina says the others plan to continue with their school. They say too many children are being attracted elsewhere. They meet on the Sundays when there is no church service and call theirs a Sunday, no, a Sabbath school.

I do not know what to think. They say this Elizabeth could read the German extra well. I do not believe that John M. could be Evil; not the way he showed interest in his mother's funeral. John J. has warned about the dangers of what he calls the American Sunday School Union. He says the words Sunday and School are only thrown in to mislead. We should be on our guard because they have too much organization.

I often wonder what my Christian would think of his relatives. The Yoder ones. How they turned out. John J., John M., even Isaac's children. His Zachariah, one of his younger ones, is said to be an exceedingly handy one: a farmer and woodworker as was his father, but also a blacksmith. He fashions bear traps and makes nails out of scraps of iron. The Lord has never tapped his shoulder—two of his brothers have been called—even though he has been named on numerous occasions. And Isaac's daughter, the one who married that immigrant boy, Hans Hooley, has now died, along with her babe, while giving birth. Mercy. I do not like to recall those times of womanly travail. Paul says I fret too much. He does not understand. All his boys know prosperity. It is only his teeth that keep him humble. He has but a few left, and Judith has to cook the dried beef until it is a thick broth.

I cannot get down on my knees to help her with the weeding. I can only stand a brief while to stir the stew so it does not stick. But I have my sheep. *"Ains, tsway, drei."* And two more years to reach number sixty-six. I must be on my guard though, lest I stumble. None of us can be sure until we reach the blessed gates. No, not one. Not even Paul. Brother John J. warns that old people sometimes get rich in material goods and poor in heavenly riches. That is frightening that I could slip and find myself outside, looking in the window. Mercy.

PART V

September 1860 — March 1861

1.

JONAS

September 1860

*N*othing has been natural this year. I have asked for a sign and received more than I know what to do with. Too many things have gone out of their way to be upside down. The swallows returned in late February—a false warming—then had nowhere to go when the rest of us wore our winter coats for all of April. Snow and ice. Then a summer of rain, rain, rain. The swallows nested in my barn rafters but could not find rest. They swooped at the cows with their long, pointed wings, causing them to stomp in agitation and hold back their milk.

Mary has commented about peculiar goings-on in the garden. The pea plants yellowed when they should have been white with blossom; the young leaves of our tomatoes turned black long before any fruit appeared. For years we thought tomatoes were poisonous, and we had nothing to do with them. Perhaps we were right. Some of our neighbors blame the rain. One dreary day after another. Rot, rot, rot.

Even Stephen has turned glum. He is finally gone from home—I did not think he would ever marry—leaving Mary and me to our rickety selves. What a change has come over him. How I detested his loud ways, but now it agitates me sorely when he sits with his head in his hands. His wife is sickly ever since their baby girl was born last year. Such glumness. From Stephen.

One day last June I was hoeing in the cornfield even though the ground was too wet. I had not much more than finished my noontime meal when the sky became dark. The early darkness reminded me of the blackness from the sixth to the ninth hour when Jesus was crucified. I made haste to the house. Whatever was coming, I did not want to be caught in an open field. Mary and I watched the hood of gray plunge down around us. We lit a candle; then we lit a second one. I remembered Shem and his warning of the Book of Revelation's prediction.

Mary sat at the table. I crouched near the window, sitting on the lid that covers the bucket of blue dye. I thought the end was near. The train's black smoke. At last it began to rain, a terrible downpour. Such deafening thunder demanding that I speak. Then the sky reversed itself and lightened for a brief while until the normal shades of evening were drawn. I could not sleep that night. I was given more time. During that sleepless night I vowed to obey.

Yet when we next had services, I shook hands with Brother Henry as was our custom. I said nothing. I am ashamed to admit: I found fault with him. I disliked the way he clutched the Bible to his chest as if it were his very own. He scowled more than usual as he preached. He frowned at the end of every sentence. "The Lord is gracious and slow to anger," he said. Then he scowled. "Hearken to the Lord's voice." He scowled again. I carry the burden of the silent fool. I am still the *schmutzfink*.

For the last three days I cannot always find my breath. When I cut cornstalks, I whack with my knife as usual and tie stalks together in a bunch. This is light work compared with other tasks. But when I make the whacks, I feel a dull pain in my chest, not severe, only faint. If I rest, the pain departs. This may only be my imagination—it does not always happen—but something of the same disturbance occurs when I walk to the house from choring. That is but a short walk, not rough, not steep, but sometimes I sit on the back porch to catch my breath before going into the house.

I wait for a sign, but then I ignore what comes. I am no good at following directions. I am like Mother when she lay at her death; half of my body is paralyzed and will not move with the urging of my other half. Last March I sought out Levi Speicher. We conversed—he implored me—but nothing more has happened. Even with Levi's shocked look, his waving the mallet, his repeated, "Tarry not," my feet have not budged. I have seen oxen with burdensome yokes about their necks and wondered how they plod on. I go through the motions every day. I fear that I may wait too long. I tarry in spite of the blackened leaves, the darkened sky.

• • •

I finally said it. Last night I whispered to Mary, "I wore the jacket. I wore the hunting jacket. I was outside—. The window."

She tried to calm me, thinking I spoke of my recent illness. She pressed her cool hand on my clammy forehead, "Shall I call the doctor? Shall I? Do you want the neighbor lad to fetch Levi's Frederick?" She squinted. "Shall I? Speak, Jonas!"

She asked and asked again, but it hurt frightfully to talk. The heaviness. Someone had carried a large field stone and placed it on my chest. All I could manage was, "Too far, Frederick. Get Henry."

"Henry who?" she asked, and I closed my eyes. My best work horse placed his hoof atop the stone and pushed down. "Simon's Henry? Henry Baechler down at Mt. Hope? Say who." She placed an extra cover on my legs. "I cannot think what Henry to bring healing."

I opened my eyes again. She is not a woman given to excess emotion like some, but the creases in her face were deep; the worry, heavy. "Henry," I said. Then, more weakly, "Stutzman."

"Henry, the bishop?"

I tried to answer a simple yes; I sounded like a sick bullfrog. My left arm ached more heavily than the molar that had burdened me until the day I jerked it out. Then I had to jerk out the tooth beside the hole. Then the next one. When the bleeding finally stopped, most of the pain was gone. Last night I tried to nod my head, but Mary was gone from my side. I had not intended to send her out into the night. I was all alone, my breathing labored. I could not get air. I would suffocate in my own house. The walls tilted around me. I vomited against the wall. I did not mean to stumble. My body, cold and clammy, then hot and sweating. My weakness. I lay on my stomach, my face buried in the pillow. I rolled weakly onto my back seeking air.

• • •

I watched the sky lighten this morning. I am still here. Henry has been here also. That is done. I do not know what will happen next, but after fifty years I have had my say. The pain may come again tonight, trodding with boots, but I have spoken.

I stood at death's door. Even this side of the entrance I felt the heat of vicious flames. When Shem's barn burned down, I remember the singed flesh of horses and mares. Last night I was about to make entry; my soul was all but claimed until something yanked me back. I do not know where I stand, but I have had my say. I poured out my filth and found a portion of the soul satisfaction that Shem preached. The cleansing from within. Not that I am content; not that I feel at peace. All those years I nodded understanding at Shem's words, then put a flap about my ears and sealed my lips.

The bishop's sleepshirt stuck out, disheveled beneath his outer shirt. He reached his hand to me. "Good morning, Jonas," he said. Whether for lack of strength or desire, I could not return the favor. His hand remained extended, as if frozen. Four fingers pointed at me. His thumb stood straight up, matching the clump of his hair that stood up stiffly. He put his hand on my shoulder. His fingers felt stiff and cool, chilled by an early, westerly wind.

"Mary says you asked for me," Henry continued. "I am sorry to see you in this weakened state." He began repeating the twenty-third Psalm and I closed my eyes. "Leadeth me. Restoreth my soul." For a few minutes I walked on safe, familiar ground; a door had opened. "Yea, though I walk . . . valley . . . shadow of death . . . fear no evil . . . thou preparest a table . . . ."

My mouth felt sour; I tried to wet the cave of my mouth. My tongue ran along the gap of missing teeth. I trifled with escape again. Perhaps there was no reason for alarm. My heart had raced before when I prodded Sam on returning from Ohio, certain that I would find Mary and the boys consumed. Even Shem's sermons had often quickened the beating of my heart. This too would pass.

"Is there something you wish to say, Jonas?" Henry came forward into my line of vision.

I closed my eyes. "No. I suppose. Yes." My voice quaked. I could not say it. Shem and Father were dead, but the words would not come.

Time passed. I do not know how much. Mary asked if I wanted broth; I shook my head and closed my eyes. Henry blew his nose. The trumpet sounded. "Shall we summon the children?"

"No." My answer came quickly. I looked at Henry. For once he was not scowling. Neither was he smiling. My time was up. I concentrated on his freckles. "I was the one—. Who did it." I closed my eyes and blurted, "I did the foul deed. I wore the hunting jacket. But I did not mean to." I tried to shake my head. "An accident."

The room was still. My weak hand rested on my chest. I heard Mary say, "He spoke this nonsense during the night. He repeats 'outside the window,' 'wore the jacket.' He makes no sense. His mind has left him."

I smelled Henry's breath; I knew he bent over me. I forced my eyes open. He was close enough that I could have counted the freckles, but they blurred before me. "What is it, Jonas? What is it that troubles? Speak more clearly." His tuft of hair stuck straight up.

"I killed the baby," I said. "My hands stuffed the baby between the upper and lower beds. I only meant to quiet her whimpers." I tried to take a deep breath but could not. The end was near; my body shook. I closed my eyes. "Her fussing roused her sisters. I did not mean to snuff the breath." I saw rats running among piles of shelled corn.

My head felt afire; no one made reply. I heard Mary walk to the chair in the corner of the room, the same chair where she sits to put on her stockings, bends down, makes adjustments with her hands, one leg propped across the other knee. I heard her sobs and knew that she muffled her face in her hands. Her wails started with the high notes and came down the steps. High and then low. My own eyes were dry and tight shut.

Henry's voice trembled. "Are you talking—," then he whispered, "about the case in Somerset County? Many years ago? Yost's girl?"

"Yes. I was the one."

Henry groaned. He sounded like a wounded animal, trapped with Mary's wail in the corner.

"It happened before I could think," I said. "I am *schmutzig* through and through." I tried to lift a hand to show Henry but gave it up.

"The death for which Reuben Hershberger was banned these many years." Henry said it as if he read a death certificate. He waited as if he needed to give me opportunity to correct him. I made no effort. I wanted death. Henry's long sigh hung in the room, crawled inside my chest, and made my skin prickly. I tried to open my eyes. I saw him rub his hair on the back of his head. Then he rubbed some more. I heard someone walk out of the room. What beautiful black hair Mary had long ago.

"Someone needs to tell Reuben," Henry said.

"Tell him—," I said, "tell him I despise myself. Lower than the worms." The horse came again and jounced on my chest. I clutched at the bedding. I did not want to ever rise. "No excuse. Changes nothing. Say I am sorry."

Henry came closer and took the measure of my weak, mortal condition. He scowled. He said he would bear the news. I shoved weakly at the extra coverlet, heavy on my legs. If left to die alone, I could not complain. The pains would claim me. The fire would come. It mattered not. Better to die with the rats.

"No hope for me," I said. "Too late."

"I cannot say," Henry said. "I have not dealt with such hardness. Why did you not—?" He backed away as if he feared contamination.

"Wretched. Creature to be despised."

Henry laid his fingertips on me. "Be still."

"Could you plead for me?" My fingers twitched; I could not reach his hand. "I did not mean—," I said. "I hid in the straw."

Henry shook his head slowly; I remember the same grimness in Shem. "Scripture tells us there is mercy for all. But this—." He stopped a long time. He stood with his arms crossed in front, his hands tucked in his armpits, his thumbs up in the air. "I will need to take your case to the church." He scowled. "There must be a righting of wrongs. I do not know what will be required. I do not know." He looked out the window where full sunlight had come. "You have done well to come before the Lord. But your tardiness—." He blew out his cheeks and shook his head as if he could not fathom the enormity. "You may have waited too long . . . for there to be mercy."

Henry said more, but I could not give attention. My chest ached. My arm ached. I wanted him to leave. I wanted death. Alone. I would remove my foul smell from Mary. I would save Henry from needing to find a suitable punishment.

Now at the close of day I still hang, dangling from the rope of my own making. Death has chosen not to bear me away. I linger. I am tired unto exhaustion; I do not want Henry to bring legions. While I slept someone brought broth to a table beside my bed. I smelled onions, but I had not strength to stir. When I woke again, the bowl was gone. I do not mind. I heard steps tiptoeing away.

2.

ℛ E U B E N

September 1860

Yes, it is true; I was about to try my hand at smear cheese yesterday, but I was interrupted by a knock at the door. I heard no sound in the driveway, so intent was I on reviewing the steps as Bevy had directed. When the churning was done, I had taken the time to spread fresh butter on bread. That is the way Anna and I always did; we sat down together for the first taste. The butter came out a deep yellow, as it does when the cows have been feeding on enough grass. I had water boiling over the fire ready to add to the buttermilk. It is good I was not in the midst of stirring to separate the whey and cheese. For that matter, it is good that I had not started to work the plunger up and down. Once that is begun, there is no stopping.

I do not mean to go on endlessly about cheese. That is not uppermost on my mind. But one day last spring I had mentioned to Bevy that I missed the smear cheese Anna made, missed the taste spread on bread and atop cooked potatoes. I had never given attention to Anna's method; I only knew that she began with fresh buttermilk. Bevy's face looked beaten. "Why Father! Why did you not say something? All these years since Mother is gone!" She is right; it has now been eight years since Anna departed. Bevy gave me a goodly portion of cheese from her supply, but she made sure I was there to watch the next time she made more.

I have often wondered in what form an angel might appear, whether trailing dusty white robes or perhaps making entrance out of the early morning mist. But this knock came early in the afternoon from my front porch. No heavenly host, no exceeding brightness to speak of. When I opened the door, Henry Stutzman stood there.

I have known of Henry for many years, known who he is. That he was made a minister and then a bishop, that he is a brother-in-law to John M. But we have not had exchange since I am untouchable. Have been. It stuck in my memory that Peter Troyer had mentioned Henry as siding strongly with the old ways. Two years ago when I was reinstated and baptized again, I half expected him to come to my door, castigating me for causing dissension. But he never came, and as time passed I thought myself safe from his examination. Until yesterday.

Immediately he took my fear away by reaching out his hand. I took heart and invited him in, explaining that it was my first try with the cheese. He had no interest in my endeavor, and I can thank him for not wasting any time. He seemed uncomfortable, fidgety, but not angry. It seemed as if he had rehearsed that we would sit at the kitchen table. He rested both his arms on the table with his hands clasped tightly, as if he were going to lead in prayer.

"Reuben," he said, "there has been a dreadful mistake. You have been its principal victim." He wiped a hand across his forehead and down his face, flattening his nose and smoothing his beard. "I, like many others, accepted the judgment concerning you. When I first heard of you, it was with your label attached: child murderer. I knew no other way. And since I had no reason not to believe the title, I paid no heed as to the truth of it."

These words came with such speed. No warning sound on the driveway, no long-winded introduction. I scarce could believe what I was hearing. "A mistake." Yet there sat Henry Stutzman across from me at my table, saying words that only Anna had expected. "Victim." My Anna. I dared not move.

Henry shifted his body away from me and slung his right arm over the back of his chair. He looked out the window; then he looked down at the floor as if he were telling a story that concerned someone else. "I was summoned during the night to Jonas Zug's house. As you may know, it is some distance to his part of Wayne County, but I rode at once from Farmerstown because I was told he was deathly ill. He has recently joined our church. A member." I thought Henry shuddered slightly, but it may have been my imagination. "He and Mary come when the roads are passable." Henry turned back to me, his arms on the table again. "I found Jonas in bed, faced with severe pains in the chest. As it turned out, his heart gave him serious discomfort in more ways than one."

At that, Henry looked at me as if he expected a response. I could but look him in the eye, waiting as I had done for years. I could not move; my back felt cramped in a vise.

"Reuben, the reason Jonas called me to his side was to make confession. He is the one who killed your brother's baby." Henry paused again as if he expected me to blurt something. "You were falsely accused all these years for something you did not do. Jonas has now said he is sorry." Henry shook his head. Then he shook his head again. "I am sorry too. I do not think the church can ever be sorry enough."

I leaned forward, folding my arms on the table in front of me, my forehead resting on my arms. I knew again how a small child cries over a hurt that seems to have no end. The mother seeks to give comfort, but there is no way to make the stinging stop. I did not hear Henry move, but I felt his hand touch my shoulder. Then both his hands rested on my shoulders.

"If only," I said from my muffled cave. Then I gave it up. There was no need to explain what might have been different. My nose dripped and I fumbled for my handkerchief. I did not want to lift my old man's face with its redness to look at Henry. I wadded my handkerchief, dabbing at my eyes. I tried to find composure. I have cried more times since, and the cheese stays unfinished.

Henry sat down again and said, "You were falsely accused," as if that were news to me.

I squeezed my handkerchief, stuffed tight in my fist. I wanted to pound the table. I wanted to call to Father, force him to turn to me on his one good leg. After a long while I blew my nose. "If only I could shake hands with my brother. If only Yost were here."

"Yes. I wish too that Yost knew the truth. Would to God that we all had known. That the many had not jumped at straws and arrived at false conclusions."

I sat back in my chair, numb. I did not know how to feel; I still do not know. Dazed. I heard words that I thought would never be forthcoming. I heard them from Henry Stutzman. Anna had said to wait, but I had not believed. Henry went on at length regarding Jonas. I could not make myself listen. I do not care about Jonas. Has there not been punishment enough? Why should I think on him? I do not know why he did it. I do not know what could have possessed him, striking with silent fangs. But how will it benefit anyone for him to suffer as I have suffered? It helps me not a whit.

Anna always said this unfairness would work itself out. "New light, Reuben." How did she know? After Henry left I went up the hill to tell her she was right. She did not seem at all surprised. I sat a long time. I thought on Bevy and Jacob. I thought on how their lives had followed vastly different paths than would have been the case, had I not been wrongly accused. I thought on Franey and Peter, on their many kindnesses. And Veronica's healing hands. When I returned to my house, the pot above the fire was empty and badly charred.

Before Henry left yesterday we stood on the porch. He looked out from where I look every day. My valley, where the morning mist rises and the sun breaks through. He pulled his jacket tight as if it suddenly had turned cold. "Sobering," he said, "a sobering day for many of us. But I am glad for you." He hesitated; then he stretched out his hand again and said, "Goodbye, my brother." I shook his hand, but I did not offer to help him with his horse. I only wanted him to depart before my heaving began again. I watched his back in a blur until I no longer heard his horse's hooves.

All of that was yesterday. No one has come today to tell me a different story. Henry arrived with such suddenness; I wonder if it may have been a dream. I wish I had thought to ask him to go tell Jacob; I cannot pretend that I am young and can ride my horse that far. If only I had told Bevy about my plans to try the cheese-making, she would come to check on the result. Perhaps Anna will get Bevy's attention. And John M. Who will tell him?

After all these years it is hard to make adjustment and believe. I am still Reuben, but my tarnished plate has been wiped clean in a moment. I look at my hand and remember Henry's grasp, hear his words, "Goodbye, my brother." I am almost for certain that it happened.

3.
P O L L Y
September 1860

*M*y heart pounds with the news. Mercy, mercy! I am too old for such blows. Paul came back from selling grain in Berlin and brought word. His cheeks puffed big; then his top lip puffed out. Jonas Zug has confessed to Bishop Henry that it was he who smothered baby Marie. Jonas Zug! Paul waves his hands every-which-way at the idea of killing an innocent child. Judith says it is ten times worse to have let another suffer unjustly. Fifty years; merciful heavens! There will be no sleep tonight. To think, I nearly married one who had the heart of a murderer. And the hands! Yost and Eliza spared me, even when I was not grateful. What would Christian say? I had to go lie down. And to think, I had been fretting over the whereabouts of the brown and green coverlet with the gold fringe. It no longer matters who has hidden it.

Yes, I gave Jonas the cold shoulder when he pressed his case with me. But I do not want Paul to ask questions. To think that I may have played a part in Reuben's suffering! Mercy! I did not mean to treat anyone unfairly. That must have been Jonas' face at the window. When Yost lowered his eyes to mine, all I could think was that I had seen a likeness.

I was sore afraid; I had watched Yost break many a chicken's neck with his bare hands. And the way he made light of Eliza's cares and laughed full-bellied at her worries, I did not want to come up against him.

Eliza had given warning as to our Berkey blood being related to Jonas'. Then when Yost imitated a child who was loopy in the head, it was not difficult to lose interest. Yet I cannot blame Jonas if he felt surprise at my turning away. I had admired his singing voice; it gave me the shivers when he hit those high notes. I imagined him one day singing for me. He was certain with every note, but slippery with his feet. And his eyes—. They had a way of creeping up, like a cat's.

Just last week, out of nowhere, I had thought of Jonas when I helped Judith cut up apples for apple butter. I had thirty-six quarters of apple; then I lost count. Three sections of apple for each disciple. Then in the midst I saw Jonas walking, first with his hands in his pockets, then fiddling with his suspender. Judith asked what it was.

"What is what?" I asked. I never know what to make of her questions. She exaggerates almost as much as Paul. Sometimes she says I lick the butter knife.

"What gives? You are so vacant." Judith bustled about, bringing more water. She likes to show how fast she can go, just like Eliza did. "Your knife has been at rest for five minutes."

I commenced cutting more apples. It is a blessing I did not tell her that I had heard Jonas' voice singing. I would not have known how to explain who he was, unless Judith knows of Abraham Zug. I know she knows Marie was my niece, but I do not think she knows more. I have seven living nieces on the Berkey side; one niece for each word in the first verse of the Bible: *"Am Anfang schüf Gott Himmel und Erde."* I may have told Judith long ago that I met this Jonas fellow when I lived with Eliza and Yost. I may have even said that we were cousins.

Now I cannot steady my needle. To think that my mind strayed to one who carried such Evil. How could he have kept secret all these years? Why did he not spare us all and spill his deed? We did not mean to make poor judgments. I thought Reuben's stubbornness had gone far beyond that of a mule. Instead, it was Jonas! Now I remember that after Reuben healed Judith, he said, "We all have our sorrows." I did not know. Oh, I have been a part!

I was but a young girl. I did not know bad things could happen. Here I am, old and tattered, near to 70 and still afflicted by deeds done in my youth. I did not mean harm. We were torn with grief; no one knew where to look. We needed to cast our eyes somewhere. First, one person remembered one thing against Reuben; then another, and another. It seemed the only road to take. But I did not intend to make my bed with Evil. How easily we cast stones when we know not the particulars.

How I wish Leah were here, although I do not know if I could tell her all. Even Yost's Susanna might give me comfort. My little lap baby. How she clung to me when little. Her family will be all the buzz for weeks to come. If Brother John J. thinks I should speak with Reuben, I will go. Paul says I make the wagon tilt when I climb aboard, but I will ask him to take me. I will say my sorrow to Reuben, but Paul can wait outside. He does not need to listen.

They say Jonas' life hangs in the balance. I do not want to ever set eyes on him. Whatever will befall him if his time is not up? Poor Bishop Henry, needing to bring correction after all these years of obstinacy. Such hardness of heart. I cannot bear to think of all the judgment necessary to right these wrongs. Mercy, mercy, mercy on us all.

4.

JONAS

November 1860

*J*have come home to receive my due. Father, of course, is no longer able to see from afar, and that is just as well. I know he would not welcome me nor kill a fatted calf. I have squandered my life in concealment; now I am known by all who hear of me without any cloak to cover my head.

Two months ago I stood at death's door, knowing I would spend eternity in torment because of my unconfessed sin. My poor soul found voice and Bishop Henry listened to my dreadful deed. I did not expect to make recovery—I could not get air to breathe—thinking it only a matter of time until I would needs give account at the Great Judgment Seat. But alas, here I am. Once my soul claimed release from its burden, my body also found its rest, and the stone was lifted from my chest. I have little strength; Simeon comes to chore and empties the chamber pot. Each day I am able to walk a bit farther. First to the kitchen, then outside the door, then to the beech tree. I do not like the cold, outside air, but I force myself to bundle up and shuffle around. The wind howls when I step outside, but I have also heard it many a night and day from my pallet.

I am at home but have no place at the table. Brother Henry

enforces the rules and regulations, as is to be expected. Some of my children are among that number who have had to put me out. When I left Oak Grove the second time, I prevailed upon Jeremiah and Adam, even Elizabeth and her family, to flee with Mary and me to the Farmerstown group. That way, in addition to the sound teaching, Mary and I were assured of a ride for the long distance with one of our youngsters. We benefited from the preaching of Bishop Henry and his two sons, Abraham and Moses. But now my children must all turn their backs. I am an old man; I have confessed my sin. When will there be pardon? I am not certain I desire to regain strength in my legs.

I have tried to give explanation, but nothing satisfies. Mary has been instructed not to engage in unnecessary talk. She blinks her eyes fast and asks, "Jonas, why did you not think? Could you not see the future? Even if you were young." I hold up my hands for her to stop, but she pays no attention. "Could you not have given thought before those hands found their dastardly deed? Could you not have spoken after you were bloodied?"

What am I to say? That I regret my foolhardiness? Yes, of course. I moved with too much swiftness. Then for fifty years with aching slowness. From one crime to the next: first, a babe; then, a grown man with two small children. Now, all of my family. There is no justification; it changes nothing to say I did not mean for any of it to happen. I convinced myself that I was no more *schmutzig* than anyone else.

Mary does not want to hear about Polly. I was young, twenty-two, when it happened, but I was feeling old in my unmarried state. It was not easy for me around the girls; I was not handy with the words or looks. I preferred to hang back at the edge of the crowd. But my feet itched to leave Father's cabin, to get away from hearing Mother heap praise on Abra-

ham. The only acceptable escape was to find a girl. Every suitable girl had been plucked. I found myself dwelling on girls of
sixteen and seventeen, thinking to get the jump on some
younger lad. When Polly Berkey came from the Brothers Valley settlement, my eagerness overran itself. She was the one I
had waited for. I tried to hold myself back, so she would not
think me a diseased leftover. I lived and breathed for Polly; I
fell asleep seeing her face, thinking to reach under her garments. I was a young man with a fever. Mary does not want
to hear that.

I say instead, "I am old; I am no longer welcome on this
earth."

"You have said that too many times." She blinks fast. "You
are at the end of the table because of your own doing. Blam-
ing others does not become you." She gets up and leaves mush
on her plate.

"I too have suffered," I say to her disappearing back. "It has
not been easy living with Evil; fear has been my meat and
potatoes."

I do not want pity. I want to have done with fear. I feared
Polly. I could not immediately cast her from my thinking. I
feared Yost and his dark cabin. I had intruded where my feet
were not meant to trod. I imagined Yost ripping clumps of hair
from my head. Within a few days I saw his mercilessness toward his brother. My eye began to twitch.

Without planning it thus, my hiding became natural. Deception fit more easily than revelation. Time passed: a month,
the summer's fieldwork, harvest. No one had looked my way.
Mother did not notice; all she could think of was how well
Abraham fared and how poorly I managed. Father thought me
downcast from living in his cabin. There were times when I
could not stomach food, when emotion overcame my eyes. I
watched them put Reuben out of church. I had nothing to do

with that; I merely stood to the side and let others do what they deemed necessary. I felt a dreadful guilt, but when I looked around, I found others unclean also. I took the easy way; that is all I can say.

I found me a woman; how I loved the black, black hair. The little ones came for Mary and me. I did not deserve them. I could not hold them, for my hands shook. Mary looked perplexed at first and said, "Are you of no use? Can you not soothe Adam's fretfulness?" I knew there could be no tenderness in me.

Often I wearied of my burden and thought to shed its weight. But I did not know where to lay me down. Not with Father, for he had become feeble. Not with Abraham, for he considered me worthless. These are all excuses, to be sure. Nor could I confess to Shem; I had my family to raise. I waited for Father to die; then I moved to Ohio, locating on the fringe. I could never rid myself of my shadow. When I was a lad, I tried to jump over my dark blotch on the ground. My shadow landed with me. I jumped and jumped, forward, back, sideways, but when I landed, my shadow always crouched at my heels.

I had thought several times to present myself to Levi Speicher, but he was in and out of the Amish church. This past spring I heard that he had removed himself again on his own accord. I thought it easier to approach someone who knew the tumult of belonging and not belonging. Thus it was that in March—barely eight months ago—I rode to his place. It was a chill morning with frost on the fields. I have still not told Mary. I found Levi in his barn making new stalls, wider but with less depth, for his cattle. I must have looked sick in the head for he asked almost immediately, *"Was gibt?"*

I gulped; this suddenness was not as I had planned. I thought we would study his soil, ready for plowing, then reminisce; perhaps we would discuss changes from wooden plows to ones with metal points. Instead he skipped the preliminaries and waited with his, *"Was gibt?"*

I turned away from the barn, as if the narrow tracks of wagon wheels and the ground softening from an early thaw interested me. "Nothing much," I said. "Life moves along, seemly good." My throat felt tight, as if coated with a sticky sap.

He stared at me, a mallet in his hand. "What ails you, Jonas? You look diseased."

I found myself caught in the act of coming forth. I did not know where to turn. I hesitated. "My father was one of the jurors," I said. Levi looked perplexed. "The Hershberger baby, smothered in Somerset County while the adults were out sugaring. Fifty years ago."

"Yes, I remember," said Levi. "All of us know the story of Reuben Hershberger."

"An inquest was held. You were one of the twelve, as was my father." I sat down on a stack of hay; I did not want him to see the shake in my legs.

"Yes, that is right." Levi rubbed his forehead with the heel of his hand. "We did not know where to cast an eye. Not at first. The next day, maybe later, it became clear. Reuben. What of it?"

I sat there, shaking my head from side to side as if I heard the slow beat of church music. The mournfulness, the solemnness. I waited for Levi to ask the next question, but he idly hit his mallet into the palm of his other hand. I could not retreat.

"It was not Reuben," I said. I looked out the barn door again. I imagined the muck-muck sound that a person makes, trudging through mud. "It was I. I put the baby between the mattresses."

Levi listened like a mute statue—like unto the one in front of the courthouse where I will need to go. His eyes looked to leap out of his head. His mallet did not move. I cowered, telling Levi that when Polly had not shown up at the singing, I knew her sister and brother-in-law sought to keep her from me. I was determined to see her that night. I would not allow her to slip away, unless that was her desire. I had peeked at the window. I had hoped to catch her going outside to the privy. I knew Yost and Eliza might tend to the sugaring that night, and I thought Polly would stay inside to watch the children.

Levi looked at me as at a stranger. Then he tossed the mallet wildly. I told the rest as quickly as I could. How I had watched Yost leave the house. How I had expected Eliza to follow. When Eliza and Polly came out together, I knew I had been tricked again. I sat with my back turned to Levi. He kicked at piles of hay like a young boy, as if he did not care that he would have to retrieve what he scattered. Dust flew everywhere.

"You did it, did you not?" he said. He was at my face like a mad dog. "All the time we lived as brothers, in Mifflin at Uncle Jakie's, at your father's, all the time you kept silent. You have made a fool of me."

I crouched back against the wall. He picked up the carpenter's mallet again and swung it in the air. I hurried to finish. "I entered the cabin without any notion as to what I thought to gain. Whether to do mischief—throw water on their fire— or snoop; perhaps find a slate and write a message to Polly. If I had a plan, it has long since departed. The cabin was dark save for the flickering firelight. As I snuck around, the baby began to fret. Mother always said I was clumsy. I should have turned and walked out the door. Let the baby wail. I am no good with the little ones, but I tried to quiet that baby. 'Hush,' I hissed; I shook the cradle."

Levi looked at me as if he wanted to lunge. We are much too old to wrestle. I continued as if I owed him a full report.

"Another child began to stir. Then the other one opened her eyes briefly, stared directly at me, and closed in sleep again. I had been seen!"

"Why? Why did you not think?"

I raised my hands in emptiness. I scarce remember, except that the unexpected intervened. That is the way it has always been for me. I told Levi about the screeching sound at the window. He sneered. "You know how timid I am with wild animals," I said. "I did not want to meet a catamount. I did not want to meet Yost."

Levi groaned. He yelled my name again and again. My father's name.

I feared that Levi's woman would hear the commotion and come snooping. I flung my arms helter-skelter as words rushed out. "I dashed my way out. Banged into a chair. Gave no thought. Not until I escaped the cabin. A ways from the sugar camp I remembered the baby. I could not believe it. I wrapped my arms around a large tree. Then I ran. I used poor judgment a second time. Feared to risk my life—."

"You feared for your life," Levi hissed at me. "*Your* life," he yelled. "Did you not care about anyone else?" Levi pounded his mallet into a post; he pounded at random. I feared he might destroy his barn. Because of me. "How could you do this?"

I said nothing more. All the things I have said inwardly, "I suffered too," sounded terrible. I despised myself. I did not want to say that I had not intended for Reuben to bear the blame, that I merely laid low and let others work their ill.

"Be quiet! I do not want to hear more," Levi yelled as if I were still speaking. "You played the possum. You! You need to tell this to others, not to me. Go to your bishop; fall before God Almighty!"

I begged of Levi not to speak about this with anyone. Having told one, I still was not prepared for the world's judgment.

Levi pleaded, "Jonas, please! Tarry not. You are an old man. What am I to do with this dreadful news? Stay quiet? You are not ready to meet your Maker." He roared with all the fury I could have expected from Abraham. "Reuben could die today!"

I am ashamed to say, my feet still did not budge. Instead I fretted that Levi might go to Henry Stutzman on his own.

Now I wait; I sit at the far end of the table, away from Mary. I sit outside with my three youngest who have left the Amish church of their own accord. I cannot say prayers for myself.

I have gone to Bishop Henry twice—when Simeon gives me a ride—pleading and begging to be restored. Each time it is to no avail. The first time I stayed on the wagon to talk; Henry would not invite me in. He says my deeds are too awful, too loathsome. He says restoration for such serious crimes asks too much. I do not know what more to say. I do not deserve forgiveness. But the heaviness, the stone pressed down, could come again in the night. I am old and troubled. Standing on shaking feet. Outside.

• • •

Mary blinks her eyes rapidly and warns me not to build up expectation. She is right; I am still unworthy. But my hope builds that I might be restored. I appeared before a judge of the state of Ohio. As Bishop Henry instructed, I presented a full statement of my Evil deeds. Murder—what a foul word— is considered a misdeed against the state. All of me shrank from making my case known. My bowels ran loose. But I knew I would make no headway with Brother Henry until I had carried out my responsibilities to the state.

I told my story to the judge in the courthouse—the Common Pleas Court in the town of Wooster—accompanied by

Henry and his two minister sons. The building stands like a throne, huge and built to excess. When I first saw the steps to the main door, I said to Henry, "I cannot ascend; I have not breath for steps like that." My lips must have turned a purplish-blue, for Henry instructed his sons to make a chair with their arms. That is how I made passage inside, my arms around their necks, my bottom wobbling and jostling on their arms. They insisted I was not heavy and it may be true; Mary says I look like a skeleton with skin clinging.

Once inside there were more steps. We bounced up in the same precarious manner to a second floor where the judge presided. We waited so long that Moses said we might need to return the next day. I could not imagine going through that rigamarole a second time. Finally we gained admittance to the judge's chamber, and I presented my sad case. When Henry and his boys returned me to my home that night, I was fully exhausted and went directly to my pallet in the corner. I did not want any of Mary's cold chicken. I wanted to be alone, curled on my side with my knees drawn to my stomach, my head resting on my crisscrossed arms. I let the others tell Mary of the proceedings; I did not care to listen.

As best I can understand, the judge seemed at a loss when presented with a case that took place fifty years ago in a neighboring state. I could not catch the drift of all his words, whether from my failing ear, or because he mumbled fancy words. From what Henry says, I believe the judge has all but washed his hands. Henry would not say directly, but I believe that is the gist.

For one thing, this Judge Hemphler—what a frightful figure he makes in his black robe—points out that since the murder occurred in Pennsylvania, that is where the trial should take place. Those of us connected in any way, myself, Reuben, Polly, even Levi Speicher, would have to journey to Somerset

County to give testimony. The judge knows in what manner I was transported to his chamber. He knows we are—all of us— old. All over seventy except for Polly. And she must be near. All the other principals, the parents of the child, the other jurors, are dead and gone. I could never withstand a trip of that magnitude.

Another item brought much surprise to Brother Henry. The judge informed him that a minister is not allowed to testify in court about what has been confessed to him as a spiritual advisor. It does not matter that the confession comes from a member of his church. Someone who has been a member. With all of this in mind—I believe this is what happened—the judge dismissed the case against me. Henry acted mum; he said he needs to give these developments more time. What else can there be to consider? My verdict sits again in his lap. And the church's. I do not know how long Henry means to let me agonize over the gravity of my sin. Day piles on day, but I cannot complain. My jaws stretch tight; my whole body aches from the strain. Henry said that he wants to see if I can walk as one in newness of life, as one who is truly sorry. How long must I be tested? My children will not come except for Simeon. I have not seen my grandchildren in months. I would not dare touch them if they did come.

Bishop Henry has not asked that I go to Reuben, but when I recover from my expedition to the courthouse, I will ask Simeon to take me. Going to Reuben could be no worse than shaking before that judge. It will be easier than appearing before Yost. Reuben knows I am sorry; Henry has told him. Reuben knows I have been put out. I must rest now and wait for more strength. The Lord has not hid His face from me entirely. There is faint hope. But I am old and troubled. My steps are short. A shuffle at best. Old and troubled and hindered with the bad ear.

5.

JOHN M.

November 1860

*L*ife moves with its normal twists and turns, until one day, of a sudden, the whole world tilts and sits on its side for awhile. Everyone looks different. Some people take on heavier frowns; others look like they lost weight. No one is exactly the same. That is the way it has been ever since Jonas Zug came forth. All of us are affected; we are all human and subject to grave error. Some now say that I was right to have reinstated Reuben, but I do not feel wise. Vindicated, perhaps, but no more right than when I responded to Reuben's heartfelt needs. Katharina is greatly relieved that those who found fault now stand with their mouths tied shut with a cord. Given our human frailty, it could have turned out otherwise.

Each year I care less about acceptance. I would rather be true to what I believe than be considered safe or saintly by the Henry Stutzmans of this world. And yet, because of Katharina, I cannot lean too far on that side of the fence. I do not want to be seen as a dissenter; I but want the respect due a brother. The fence I straddle is coated with ice. I could slip to one side or the other in a matter of seconds.

My critics say I do not preach the unity which following the *Ordnung* brings. But I attribute our spiritual decline to a preoccupation with items that are less than essential. Too many leave the church because they see us wrangling over trivialities: embellishments on our buildings and carriages, battles over whether to have a family portrait made.

I do not speak idly about ice. I am one who would rather postpone the onset of winter, but we have had an early storm that lasted three days. Ice coated the bare trees, the wooden pails, the barren fields. When the sun came out, everything glistened like a large gift, wrapped up and sparkling. I slipped and fell twice, making my way on gingery steps to the barn. I am fortunate I did not break anything. I would not let any of the womenfolk help with the milking; I reminded them that I do not set bones. We stood outside, my wife and my unmarried daughters, and we marveled at the beauty. It was splendid. Barbara held her hand to her eyes and said, "The brightness hurts," as we murmured our agreement.

"We have lived in darkness for too long," I said. I pulled Katharina to me; we wrapped an arm around a grown daughter, one on each side of us. Barbara and Katie. We watched the fields shimmer and held each other tight.

I thought on Elizabeth, my firstborn. How she squirmed as a babe; I did not know which way to hold her. Barbara and Katie remind me of Elizabeth every day. Dipping candles. Sewing dresses for others' children. The choice I made for them all. Elizabeth would have made a fine teacher. I heard her despondency, but I did not fully listen. Her wound sits far deeper than Rebecca's sudden passing. After each death I resolve to hold more loosely. Yet I cling to those who are left. I may have kept my daughters from the fullness of life. I did what I thought right—what I know is right—but I may have been wrong.

Everyone who judges is judged in the end. As soon as I say the church should confess its wrong for shunning Reuben, I expose my own walk for inspection. Who watches the watchmen on the walls of Zion? No one asks about Elizabeth. I should acknowledge to Henry that he did well by going to Reuben immediately with news of Jonas' transgression. But I know myself too well: I will not seek out Henry. There are too many other matters ahead of us on which we sit at opposite ends. He still wants to practice shunning as it has always been done. Andrew and I question the method of application. From talking with Reuben, I know that Anna followed instruction and never allowed him satisfaction. I would rather err on the side of lax discipline, even as my critics charge, than be responsible for unjust punishment.

Now we hear that Jonas Zug has taken a weaker turn again. Ever since he went to the courthouse, his body has not made recovery; he remains frail and confined to his pallet. I have thought to make a visit, but Henry might think I meddle. I do not know Jonas personally. His sister Franey is one mark in his favor; his brother Abraham, one strike against. I could transport Jonas to Reuben's house if he had the strength to go. If he survives the winter—if we all survive the long winter—I will make offer.

There is no end to this circle; no place where one person bears all the fault and another shoulders no blame. This Jonas, the silent deceiver. Despicable. Eliza and Yost. Did they invite their own grief? They may have been devious. Or oblivious. We will never know. And Polly Hostetler, what of her? I have not spoken with John J.; his own grief for his lost little ones consumes him. I wonder if he considers Polly innocent. I remember how she described for me in great detail my mother's funeral years ago. Now there are rumors that she added to the suspicion cast unfairly on Reuben. Rumors. Speculation. The ongoing parade of participants. Pointing or pointed at. The twelve jurors. The church. All of us seeking to blame and escape blame, to punish and go free. We are all in this somewhere.

Jonas will rest his heart, and I will rest my warts this winter. The bottoms of my feet hurt uncommonly much. Warts. That is all it is. A nuisance. Katharina does not like it when I take off my socks and pick at the hard lumps on the soles of my feet. She says I leave dead skin everywhere: on the floor, in the bed. Yet she soaks her feet and wants me to scrape tough skin off the tops of her toes. She tells me to straighten my back when I preach, that I have more slump in my shoulders. She may be right. I still tower above, but I do not feel as tall as I once did.

My friend Andrew Miller—why must he crack his knuckles?—deals with one unpleasantness after another at Oak Grove. Those steeped in tradition point to his congregation and mine as the dangerous fringe, perpetuating changes that George Keim also advocated. Andrew is young and inexperienced, but he has courage. The courage to lead. I would trust my family to his spiritual care. I will try to do for him what I could not do for Elizabeth: listen.

The rift grows between the rigid shunners and the less severe ones. One day the gulf will be too wide to be bridged. I do not see any other way. I do not know when or where the break will come, but it is like the pull on a suspender that stretches farther and farther, until one day it snaps outright from the tension. I may need to prepare Andrew: the only *beschluss* may be separation. If not in my time, then in his.

Andrew and I look tame compared with these progressive, new Mennonites. The General Conference, they call themselves. Most of them are immigrants, newly come from Europe: the Schmitts, Roths, Hertzlers. I have never seen the like.

They make my views look almost tolerable. They talk of missionary practice, and they openly support participation in education. Even holding office in local government is not a problem for them. Some of them go so far as to believe ministers should be paid a salary. Yes, a salary. It is good that they stay to themselves.

As if our church dissension and the upheaval from Jonas is not enough, it now looks as though our nation may be entering a period of great tribulation. Warfare bangs at our door because of slavery, matching North against South. If war breaks out I fear that many of our young men will not hesitate to join the fight. The church has been distracted with store-bought suspenders while neglecting to teach the things of the Spirit. Our posture of defenselessness, for one. I am heartened that Elias' boys seem to understand.

I believe there is yet work for me to do. My feet give aggravation, but I am not that old of a man. Even if we must endure five months of snow, it cannot stay cold forever. After ice comes melting. After dark comes light.

6.

$\mathcal{P}$ OLLY

December 1860

All I can think today is thankfulness—mercy—that I do not need to return to Pennsylvania. I have grandchildren there that I have never seen, but I do not want some judge to change his mind and say, "Polly Hostetler, go to the land of your birth." There has been talk for weeks that those of us left over from the Marie Hershberger case might need to return to the scene. How my knees buckled at the thought of a trial! My varicose veins, my hip with the bad catch, all made protest. Not even seeing Leah again could compensate for the damage from the journey.

Besides, my memory serves me poorly. Both Judith and Paul say I get things mixed up. I would fear to say with certainty what happened and at what hour. Paul's questions confuse me enough that I cannot sleep. What would I do in front of a judge? Mercy me! Judith offers a cup of hot water before bed, but that does not calm my nerves. I can only thank the judge for putting an end to these wild speculations about having another hearing. Brother John J. preaches with great force against the dangers of any of our number serving on a jury. If twelve men—just like the disciples—could be wrong concerning an infant, surely there is none among us so puffed up as to make a judgment under oath against another.

My mind swoops the way the bats darted about madly last summer. I could not count them all. One flew down the chimney and gave Paul a good chase before he knocked it silly with a broom. Why can we not forgive? Forgive and have done with it. Paul says Jonas' deeds can never be forgotten. Should never be. I do not ever want to see Jonas, but I believe we must receive him again into the fold. We do not make anything better by letting him stand outside.

Reuben had the most to forgive, yet his reach extends wide enough for all. I have not heard it said that he speaks ought against Jonas, or even murmurs against me, as well he might. We could all afford a little more lovingkindness these days. Paul could offer a kind word about John M.; our cousin cannot be as dangerous as once thought. Now all Paul talks of is a great war; he swings his stump of a hand like a sword. It cannot be right for one man to hold another as slave, but surely a way can be found to settle these differences without resorting to the battlefield.

These are not easy times for any of the Lord's men. Brother John J.'s children stick to the faith, but this year he lost three youngsters to death's winnowing. One in March and two in June. Those last two, a day apart, almost like my Marie and Barbara. Judith says another of old Bishop Isaac Joder's daughters has passed away. This one in her forties and old enough to know better. She had left Somerset and moved with her husband all the way to that Iowa land. Judith says not to criticize. Many from the Glades settlement have transplanted to Iowa because of problems with bundling and whatnot. Now this woman leaves four grown daughters and a poor, lonesome man in that terrible wilderness. Mercy.

I fear we all are too much taken with improvements and modern ways. Judith says that Esther Esch has what is called a cookstove, a whole cabinet on which to cook. She puts wood in the bottom of an iron box and lights the fire. The whole surface above—where the pans and skillets sit—gets hot. Judith blows softly through her round lips, "Think of the ease," she says. For once I agree with Paul. A cookstove might cause less reliance on God because of its convenience. Better for us to be old women at the fireplace than to learn the newfangled ways.

I took stock recently and counted eight yards of tow linen, six yards of white flannel, four yards of linsey, two yards of blue linsey, three bags of wool, and six skeins of yarn, each a different color: brown, green, red, gold, and two shades of blue. I am still partial to blue. Right now I have eight sheep: one for each child I birthed. When I sell two more coverlets, I will ask about buying a dinner bell. Paul refused to take a coverlet to Reuben, so I will ask Obadiah to purchase a bell from Reuben come spring. After the others have gone to bed tonight, I will count my coins again and make sure about the money. People say that Reuben is handy with anything fashioned from iron: augers, bits, lamps, even dinner bells. It would be a token to buy from one who has not known much kindness. A small way to make amends.

We will have a dinner bell next summer in the front yard. Or right outside the kitchen door. I will ask Judith where she thinks the best place would be. We could ring the bell each night to chase the bats away. A bell to remind us all how little we know.

7.

ℛ E U B E N

March 1861

I am still Reuben Hershberger. I have not been this world's most noble saint, but neither is my name linked with the Evil One any longer. My ordeal is over, but my life lingers on. I do not know how much longer I can manage by myself. I still like to roast a fat rabbit or squirrel, even a pigeon, over the fire. I have cords hanging from pegs above the fireplace so that I only need to fasten the meat to the cord and let it swing. Jacob brought me a wild turkey once.

Bevy has given me a mirror; she said she wants me to keep track of myself. I do not think she means it as a plaything, but I watch the way the light reflects on my ceiling beams. It works in the same manner as when I hold up one of my lamps. If this mirror can be counted on, I am surprised to see how much of my mother shows. The shape of my nose and lips are hers, but the forehead is my father's. Yost and I used to laugh at our likenesses, kneeling over the edge of the river. But those were shimmery, rippling images. I wonder if Yost's eyebrows grew as long as mine. It is no wonder that my great-grandchildren try to grab at the unruly hairs.

The spading goes slowly. Each year I turn over a little less. It does not take much space for my needs. Some potatoes, that is the main thing. Bevy will give me seeds and starts of whatever I want. It does not take much to fill me: a few beans, some carrots. She had to add an extra hook to make my pants fit tighter. I may let go of corn and squash this year. Bevy will bring me of her extras. I do not know what happened to Anna's canna bulbs; I cannot find them anywhere.

This has been a winter of rest such as I do not remember. I cannot think what I have done but milk Bossy and feed Sanders. Jacob insists that I keep my own horse, and I am glad. I know I could not ride him; my legs are too stiff to swing up. I have not gone up the hill yet this spring; a layer of snow lingers at the top and my muscles are weak. I catch my breath when I shuffle to the barn. Part of me thinks: what if I collapse en route? Another part says: what would be the harm? One place of repose serves as well as another. I go to Anna oftentimes in my mind; I have told her all that has transpired. I believe John M. is right that she knows all. I see the smile in the creases of her mouth. She nods and says, "All is well."

Daniel has lived on his parents' home place since Franey and Peter are gone. He tells me some of what has happened since Bishop Henry came knocking. Daniel had married a girl from Bishop Henry's district, so they still travel to Farmerstown when she is able. He is paunchy for a young man, but he has a gentle spirit like Veronica's and never seems vexed, not even with that obstinate horse of his father's. How I miss Franey. I think of her especially in springtime when I see small green shoots coming up on the side of their house—that cabin I helped build—that is most protected. Daniel's wife is not well and I fear for him. Veronica has called me to assist, but to no avail. I tried to comfort her afterwards; healing does

not always come. We dare not think we understand. Daniel
has the five little ones to look to—the oldest is twelve—as well
as tend to his wife who spends much time abed. Veronica does
all their washing of clothes, but the burden falls to him.

When Daniel came to borrow my hand adze for hollowing
new water troughs, he spoke at length of the proceedings with
his uncle. I had hoped that Jonas might come to my house so
that we could have conversation. Perhaps it is too much to expect. I believe I could shake his hand, now that some months
have passed. Anna never said ought about the particulars.
How little we know. It would be harder for me to grasp Yost's
hand. I do not know if I could see my way clear there. Daniel
says Jonas' strength is still faint, but there is talk of reinstatement. He has been treated as apostate long enough, with punishment and humiliation abounding. Daniel says there are
some who murmur that Jonas' sin is too heinous to ever know
forgiveness. Yost's son, Nicholas—the one who got the barn—
is among the vocal ones. I wager he has never transgressed.

If Jonas is reinstated I know how the proceedings will go.
All the usual will take place. I remember well when John M.
took my hand in the stream; my Jacob stood beside me and
helped steady me. The story of the Prodigal Son will be read,
the one who wasted all his father's goods. There are other passages as well. Matthew 18, with its instruction to discipline
and cast out. The story of the lost sheep will be recounted.
Someone will read from the Psalms about chastisement and
penitence.

I do not know how Jonas looks—Daniel says he is thin and
has lost all his hair—but he will be called forward to kneel at
Bishop Henry's feet. He will hear the usual questions put to
the erring one. He will need to acknowledge that his chastening has been laid on him justly. John M. made a point that
such did not apply to me. Jonas will need to promise to guard

himself henceforth against sin and to adjust his daily walk. When he says that he believes the All-High God has heard his prayer and forgiven his past sins, Bishop Henry will put his hands on Jonas to help him arise. Perhaps he will have a son to lean on also. When John M. placed on me the Kiss of Peace, he said, "This is the gate of the Lord." He also said that other verse that Anna always repeated, even when I was despondent and threw our best hickory nuts in the fire: "Thou hast delivered my soul from death, and mine eyes from tears, and my foot from slipping."

Daniel tells me that I have suffered far more than his uncle. I scoff. Little is gained by making comparisons. Who is to say? What do any of us know? I remind Daniel that he has his own burden, a sickly wife, while I was given Anna. I tell him again how his mother Franey brought me a warm custard when others considered me Evil. One day this winter when Veronica tended to his family, Daniel came to my door, lugging his parents' big family Bible. He acted secretive-like, but he smiled and scratched his belly. Inside the back cover he showed me a drawing, very old, of two birds with their beaks almost touching. The red and blue have faded, and there is a small tear along the bottom edge. He knew nothing of the drawing's origins, but he said he believed it must have brought his mother happiness to look upon. I agreed, for it is a beauty.

I do not have much to show for my life that will last: some usefulness in fashioning iron, a scattering of people healed of their infirmities. Jacob has done far more good with his politics; he is determined that Trail will have its own post office soon. I hope to be acceptable when I stand before the Great Throne. That day cannot come soon enough. I would gladly give up my puny garden to greet Anna in the sky. But until then I will be content to tend the soil I have been given. Perhaps I will try cabbages this summer.

ᴀUTHOR'S NOTE

*T*he kernel of this mysterious story (a seven-month-old infant killed by an unknown person) has been passed down orally among the Amish since its occurrence in 1810. A brief account, including a description of the resolution of this terrible act some fifty years later, can be read in various Amish and Mennonite publications, such as the 1912 book, *Descendants of Jacob Hochstetler,* edited by Harvey Hostetler (Elgin, Il: Brethren Publishing House).

In writing this novel I took care to present accurately historical developments in the United States from 1810-1861, as well as the religious beliefs and social patterns of Amish families in Pennsylvania and Ohio during these years. As I developed specific characters and their families in the novel, I often relied on the information found in Hugh F. Gingerich and Rachel W. Kreider's *Amish and Amish Mennonite Genealogies* (Gordonville, PA: Pequea Publishers, 1986); however, I did not limit myself to historical lineage. Family charts for the main characters in the novel and a glossary of German and Pennsylvania Dutch words used follow this note.

Alongside my concerns for authenticity, I exercised the writerly license of creating fiction: I changed the names of the main people involved. Characters, situations, and ramifications came to life on paper as I imagined answers to the question: "How could this have happened?" At the same time, I hope that the characters and their motivations ring true to the world we know.

Hershberger Generations
(Characters named in novel)

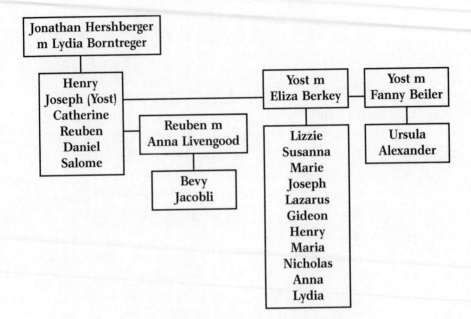

Jonathan Hershberger
m Lydia Borntreger

Henry
Joseph (Yost)
Catherine
Reuben
Daniel
Salome

Reuben m
Anna Livengood

Bevy
Jacobli

Yost m
Eliza Berkey

Yost m
Fanny Beiler

Lizzie
Susanna
Marie
Joseph
Lazarus
Gideon
Henry
Maria
Nicholas
Anna
Lydia

Ursula
Alexander

The children of Isaac Joder

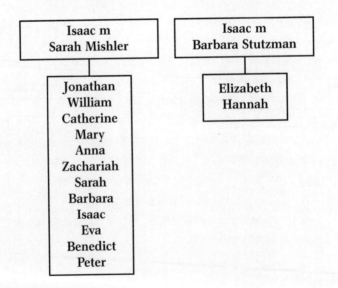

Isaac m
Sarah Mishler

Isaac m
Barbara Stutzman

Jonathan
William
Catherine
Mary
Anna
Zachariah
Sarah
Barbara
Isaac
Eva
Benedict
Peter

Elizabeth
Hannah

Zug Generations

(Characters named in novel)

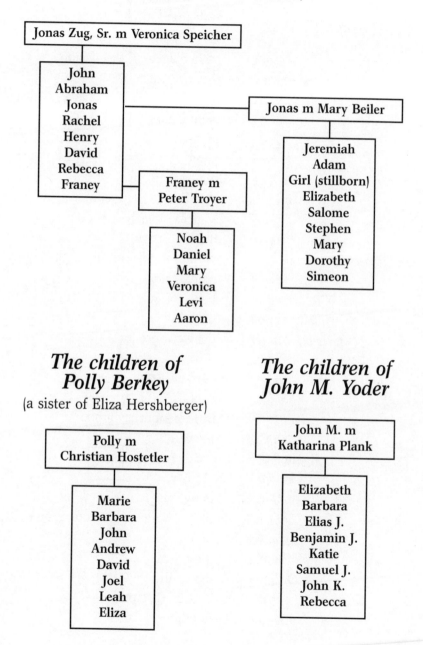

Jonas Zug, Sr. m Veronica Speicher

John
Abraham
Jonas
Rachel
Henry
David
Rebecca
Franey

Jonas m Mary Beiler

Jeremiah
Adam
Girl (stillborn)
Elizabeth
Salome
Stephen
Mary
Dorothy
Simeon

Franey m
Peter Troyer

Noah
Daniel
Mary
Veronica
Levi
Aaron

The children of Polly Berkey

(a sister of Eliza Hershberger)

Polly m
Christian Hostetler

Marie
Barbara
John
Andrew
David
Joel
Leah
Eliza

The children of John M. Yoder

John M. m
Katharina Plank

Elizabeth
Barbara
Elias J.
Benjamin J.
Katie
Samuel J.
John K.
Rebecca

GLOSSARY
of German and Pennsylvania Dutch Words

Abrath	advice against, dissuasion
Ausbund	title of songbook
bels kapp	headdress
beschluss	conclusion
bitte	please
bobbel	baby
brauching	to effect healing
bruckle	cold bread soup, sometimes served with berries
danke	thanks
Dieners Versammlungen	annual ministers' meeting
dumbkopf	blockhead
Es tut mir leid.	I am sorry.
Gelassenheit	humility
Geliebte Mutter	beloved mother
gnuddla	turds
Gott allein	God alone
halduch	cape
haubchen	little bonnet or hood
himmel	heaven
hinkle dreck	chicken droppings
klutzich	clumsy
knix-knux	naughty
"Loblied"	title of song: "Hymn of Praise"
Meidung	ban
mutze	long dress coat
Ordnung	discipline
Ordnungs-Gemeinde	church discipline
rivvels	noodles

ruhig	quiet
Satz	rising
schmutzfink	filthy creature
schmutzig	dirty
schnell	quick
sei ruhig	be quiet
strubbles	disheveled, usually refers to hair
Übel	evil
ungeschickt	without knowledge
Unpartheyishes Gesangbuch	title of songbook
"Unser Vater—"	Our Father—
"Vergib uns—"	Forgive us—
verhuddled	rattled, confused
Vorsinger	song leader
wahnsinnig	insane
Was gibt?	What gives?/What's up?
zerbrechlich	fragile

Pennsylvania Dutch Rhymes

Es kisselt und kasselt	It is sleeting and snowing
Und du der stadt hier.	All around the town.
Vas bringen sie mit?	What do they bring along?
Ein haus voll kinder	A house full of children,
Ein stahl voll rinder	A stall full of heifers,
Ein eissinger buck	An iron bull/ram,
Ein bixie geladen	A loaded gun,
Ein drumme geschlagen	A drum beating.
Beduss, beduss, beduss	[nonsense rhythmic sounds]

A Rhyme about Two Women

De oldt hockt huls	The old one cuts wood,
De yoong layst shpay.	The young one gathers up the splinters.
De oldt huckt im fire-eck	The old hag sits by the chimney
Oon grotzt era bay.	And scratches her legs.

A Counting Rhyme

Ains, tsway, drei,	One, two, three,
Hicker, hocker, hie.	[nonsense rhythmic sounds]
Tsucker oof'm brei,	Sugar on the puddings,
Sols oof'm shpeck.	Salt on the "speck,"
Hawna, gay weck	Rooster go away,
Do shtinksht nuch hinkel-dreck.	For you smell of chicken dirt.

The Lord's Prayer

Unser Vater in dem Himmel.	Our Father in Heaven
Dein Name werde geheiligt.	Hallowed be thy name.
Dein Reich Komme.	Thy kingdom come
Dein Wille geschehe auf Erden	Thy will be done on earth as it
wie im Himmel.	is in heaven.
Unser täglich Brot	Give us this day our daily bread,
gib uns heute	
Und vergib uns	And forgive us our debts
unsere Schulden	
wie wir unsern Schuldigern	as we forgive our debtors.
vergeben.	
Und führe uns nicht in	And lead us not into temptation.
Versuchung.	
Sondern erlöse uns	But deliver us from evil.
von dem Übel.	
Denn dein ist das Reich	For thine is the kingdom
und die Kraft	and the power
und die herrlichkeit	and the glory
in Ewigkeit.	forever.
Amen.	Amen.

ABOUT THE AUTHOR

Evie Yoder Miller grew up in the rural community of Kalona, Iowa.

Through the years she has had short stories, essays, and poems published by a variety of small presses. Her Ph.D. is from Ohio University.

Currently she teaches writing and fiction writing at the University of Wisconsin-Whitewater.